Adulation

— A NOVEL —

Adulation

— A NOVEL —

ELISA LORELLO

amazonpublishing

Text copyright © 2012 Elisa Lorello
All rights reserved.
Printed in the United States of America.
No part of this book may be reproduced, or stored in a retrieval system, or transmitted in any form or by any means, electronic, mechanical, photocopying, recording, or otherwise, without express written permission of the publisher.

Published by Amazon Publishing
P.O. Box 400818
Las Vegas, NV 89140

ISBN-13: 9781612184241
ISBN-10: 1612184243

For Fenny

PART ONE

Danny Masters

October 11, 2010

O F ALL THE THINGS DANNY MASTERS WAS told he should be afraid of—terrorists and *E. coli* and Toyotas yet to be recalled and the so-called homosexual agenda—nothing frightened him as much as the blank screen. The first page of a new script always made his stomach churn, and the voice of insecurity started in on the psychological warfare: *Those previous successes? Flukes. Save your pennies, brother, 'cause you're about to fuck up big time...*

Today was no different. The cursor on the blank screen didn't so much blink as *wink* at Danny, who was certain it was mocking him.

"Stop that," he said.

The cursor continued to blink. Or wink.

When he got an idea—a spark of ingenuity, a snippet from a song, a burst of inspiration—he was off and running. It was *waiting* for it that drove him berserk. Because that was just the thing: He *couldn't* wait for it. He couldn't force it, had no idea when inspiration would show up at his doorstep (or usually, in his case, in his shower). Besides, ideas were floating in and out of his mind all the time. He'd be driving and hear bits and pieces of conversation between characters in his head, a baritone voice delivering a monologue, a father and son arguing. But when it came time to sit down and actually *write* it, it went into hiding, scattering like cockroaches when the lights went on.

The cursor blinked.

"Go fuck yourself," said Danny. He wasn't sure whether he was talking to the cursor or that voice of insecurity in his head. Probably both.

Today was Danny Masters's birthday. Forty-five.

The cursor blinked forty-five times. He counted them.

Forty-five wasn't so bad. He was fifteen years sober, for one thing. He still had a thick mane of ash-brown hair (with very little gray), still had his memory, and still could run two miles without keeling over. He could do everything in his forties that he'd done in his twenties; it just hurt the next morning.

Hundreds, possibly thousands, of birthday wishes and gifts had bombarded him today. The e-mails, cards, flowers, and packages crowded his in-box as well as a corner of his office. As he'd been doing the last few years, he planned to give some of the flowers to his daughter, Ella, or his assistant, Dez, and donate the rest to a local hospital or nursing home. He would then open the gifts with Ella, who still, at the age of fourteen, liked the act of unwrapping presents even more than she liked the presents themselves. She loved the disguise of the box, the pristine ribbons tied in a bow, the promise of something good inside. That his fans would take the time and care to spend money on him—buying him books, rare movie posters, bottles of champagne (which he also gave away), artwork (those that consisted of portraits of him always creeped him out), gift certificates to restaurants, bookstores, Amazon.com, and so on—never ceased to astound him. Paul Wolf, his friend and the director of Danny's film *Exposed*, had given him one of the typewriters Robert Redford used in *All the President's Men*.

And yet Danny felt horribly alone.

His office was in a renovated hotel acquired by the Kingsmen Studio Corporation in Los Angeles. Shortly after selling his first screenplay, he'd been issued the space: a receiving and waiting room where his assistant worked, and his own office—complete with a full bathroom, walk-in closet, sturdy walnut desk, picture window with a view of the east lot to his left, a TV projection screen on the cream-colored wall to his right, and a black leather couch flanked by two knee-height bookcases opposite his desk. His Emmy awards for *Winters in Hyannis* were strategically placed to draw the eye upon entering. The entire space resembled a bachelor pad, and many people seemed deflated when they entered it. Someone with Danny's success and talent surely had earned enough street cred to warrant an office in the grown-ups' executive building, with carpet so soft one could fall asleep on it, kitchenettes and minibars, and private movie theaters. He probably stayed for sentimental reasons more than any other. It certainly wasn't an ugly space, and it contained lots of light and comfort.

At the very least, the office was simply the place where he typed as well as conducted the business part of his career. There was a difference between *typing* and *writing*.

The writing happened when he took walks around the studio lot, or used the shower, or sat in the stands during a Dodgers game.

Danny took a sip of some kind of latte (he never paid attention to the flavors) from the sturdy paper Starbucks cup and made a squinching face; its contents had cooled considerably. Not surprising, since it'd been sitting there for at least an hour. However, that one sip seemed to give him the jolt he needed; he was ready to put something, anything, on the page.

. He started with a setting:

```
INT. PUBLIC RADIO STATION — MORNING
```

With *Exposed* about to premiere and already getting Oscar buzz, the doctoring of two best-selling book adaptations finished, and the legal complications involved in getting out of optioning the Harold Grey memoir after discovering that Grey had fabricated most of it, Danny was ready for something a little lighter. It was time to get back into television, he'd decided.

He'd been kicking around the idea of doing something more comical for a while. He was good at writing political thrillers and courtroom dramas—all the critics and his fans told him so—but he was in the mood to look at the brighter side of life. He'd gotten the idea to do a show about a public radio station program called *The Seven Year Itch* (he wanted to call the show that as well, figuring the Marilyn Monroe film of the same name had been forgotten by the ADD generation) in which the hosts were a married couple who, as they gave out comical relationship advice, behind the scenes revealed the absurdities of their own relationship. And yet, of course, in their end, it was the absurdities that made said relationship work.

Using the names Jack and Diane temporarily (the John Mellencamp song had just played on the radio), he read what he'd just written, reciting the dialogue and hearing *Winters in Hyannis* stars Robbie Marsh's and Gabby Hanson's voices in his head as he did:

```
INT. PUBLIC RADIO STATION STUDIO - MORNING
JACK (average-looking, 30-something) sits at a radio
console drinking from a mug that says COFFEE BEATS SEX
on it.

DIANE (Jack's wife, also 30-something, pretty, although she
puts effort into her looks) enters in a huff, pulling off her
winter outerwear on the way to her seat.

                    DIANE
          Sorry I'm late. Where's Barry?


                    JACK
          He's in the john, and why are you late?


                    DIANE
          I told you I was going to the eye doctor today.


                    JACK
          Yes, you did. What for?
```

                         DIANE

For a consultation.

                         JACK

Who goes to the eye doctor for consultations?

                         DIANE

I'm thinking of getting my eyes lasered.

                         JACK

You wanna get your eyes lasered?

                         DIANE

Yes.

                         JACK

Does this involve a military contract?

                         DIANE

It's a medical procedure, idiot. It's called LASIK
surgery. A way to permanently fix your eyes so that
you no longer have to wear glasses or contacts.

                         JACK

What's so bad about glasses or contacts?

                         DIANE

Wouldn't it be neat to always have clear vision?

JACK

It'd be neat to shoot lasers out of my eyes rather
than have someone else shoot them at me.

Oh, man. He could actually smell the stink emanating from the screen, but he knew he had to push on. He tried to outshout his inner critics by assuring them that it was just a rough draft, that he would revise and all would be right in the world again. And it was premiere week for *Exposed*, he reminded them, which amounted to an avalanche of television appearances, guest blog posts, interviews, photo ops, and anything else the studio wanted him to do. To his knowledge, he was the only screenwriter who carried as much camera time as someone like Robbie Marsh or any other big-time screen star. Reporter after reporter, male and female alike, described him as "handsome," "charismatic," and "charming." As far as he was concerned, he was just a white guy from Long Island with eyes both the shape and color of almonds, long lashes, a complexion that was part tan from the California sun and part gray from twenty-plus years of smoking, high cheekbones and a square chin, and straight hair that seemed to behave only when cut into a tapered, wispy, neo-Beatle mop top that he constantly brushed back with his hands. (His agent had hired a stylist who'd tried to give him other looks: the flat-top buzz cut made him look like a militant Muppet, and any strand that fell past the middle of his neck screamed midlife crisis.)

Charlene Dumont often used the same descriptive words as the reporters, although he never knew what she saw in him. She, after all, was stunning: long, luxurious locks of bottled auburn hair, eyes the color of the beach waters of Pulau Redang in the South China Sea in Malaysia (their lashes actually touched when they kissed), a five-foot-seven-inch body (she was just a half inch taller than he, albeit ten years younger) that was meticulously sculpted thanks to two hours of Pilates five days a week, and a speaking voice that could arouse him during a recitation of the Patriot Act. She did drama. She did comedy. She did TV and movies and Shakespeare in the Park. She could even dance and sing a little bit. If she ever picked up a pen, he'd kill himself.

Charlene's celebrity attracted the gawkers and papa-*rat*-zi, as Danny called them—her stardom was blinding compared to his, and he knew it was possible that that also kept them at odds. Danny's fans were in love with his writing; Charlene's fans were in love with *her.* Of this much he was certain.

And it was that adulation that kept him doing the interviews and the promotion, kept him in the spotlight, even when it meant having to report how many years he'd been sober, or having to answer the question regarding the possibility of wedding bells for him and Charlene in the near future, or whether the latest split was for good, or if Charlene was ever going to star in a Danny Masters show or film, or what he thought of Charlene's latest movie, guest appearance, fashion magazine spread, etcetera— rather than what he should be talking about: the *writing.* Adulation was worth having to suffer through strobe lights and camera flashes and microscopes, right-wing evisceration of his political views and editorializing, left-wing evisceration for not getting more directly involved in "the cause," and the occasional mentally unbalanced fanatic who somehow managed to find out where he lived or what kind of car he drove. Looking over his shoulder whenever he walked along a public street had become habit. And that was the double-edged sword of fame. One minute he sought out the attention; the next minute he avoided it. If only he could negotiate the whens and wheres of the spotlight on *his* terms. If only he could negotiate public and private.

As long as they all stayed away from Ella, then they could have him. That was the deal he'd made with himself and Frannie.

The cursor had begun mocking Danny yet again when his iPhone rang to the Gershwin tune of "How Long Has This Been Going On." His pulse quickened when he saw Charlene Dumont's photo (a sultry black-and-white tease from a *Harper's BAZAAR* shoot) accompany the ringtone. A Pavlovian response.

He picked up the phone and touched the screen. "You know what I miss?" he said without even bothering to say hello.

"What do you miss?" said Charlene in a way that indicated she knew this indulgent ritual all too well.

"Landlines. I miss big, fat, ugly telephones with rotary dials and cords that could cut off the circulation in your finger if you wrapped them too tightly and ring so loud they would make you jump in your seat."

"So get a vintage phone from the props department at the studio."

"Yeah, but then I wouldn't get to see your lovely face on my phone when you called."

"This is your problem, Danny. Choices. You either have too many or none at all."

Danny took another sip of cold coffee, made the same squinching face as before, and moved from his desk chair to the leather couch in his office. He leaned back and propped his feet on the coffee table. "To what do I owe the pleasure of this call?" he asked.

"Your birthday, of course. And I finally got to see *Exposed*."

His stomach completed a somersault. "What did you think?"

"Please, honey. Did you really think for one second that I would find it anything less than brilliant?"

Actually, he did.

"Maybe you're a little biased," he said.

"You're gonna get the Oscar this year. You know that, don't you?"

He cringed. "Don't! Every time someone says that, I look for the lightning bolt that's going to strike and kill me. I'm thinking about wearing rubber-soled shoes from now on."

"Geezus, you're more superstitious than a baseball player who wears the same socks without washing them throughout the entire playoffs because he thinks the team'll lose if he does."

"So, what, you think I shouldn't shower until the Oscar nominations come out?"

"Seriously, Danny," said Charlene. "The film was terrific. The performances were out of this world. You and Paul and everyone did an amazing job."

Danny couldn't contain his smile. "Thanks. I'm glad you liked it." He paused for a beat. "Did it make you fall in love with me again?"

Charlene's sigh gave him the answer he was hoping for.

"So how 'bout dinner tonight?" he asked. "Consider it your birthday gift to me. I'll even pay."

"I'm still in New York. Doing a benefit show tonight."

He should've known this, he realized. And he knew she was irked that he didn't.

"I'll fly out and meet you."

She sighed again, this one sounding more like she was tired, possibly of him. "Don't. I'm on a break from rehearsal, and I just wanted to tell you that I saw the film and loved it. It's some of your best work. And wish you a happy birthday." She paused for a beat. "Loving you is never the problem, Danny. You know that."

He let the silence linger for a moment, not because he wanted to but because he needed a moment to compose himself. "Well, it was very sweet of you to call. Thanks." The words came out stilted. "I've gotta get back to work. I'm starting a new pilot. The TV show I was telling you about."

"You breaking out into your usual cold sweat?"

"Feels even worse than usual because of all the excitement for *Exposed*. Between that and *Winters*, the goalposts got twice as high and moved back forty yards."

"You'll get over it. You always do," she reminded him. "And let me know if there's a part in it for me."

He held out the phone and looked at it, as if Charlene could see the look on his face and know it was really meant for her, remembering when he used to do the same thing with a landline and thinking the gesture had more dramatic effect back then. "Are you kidding?" he asked. "Seriously, are you?"

"Oh, Danny," she said, and he could almost see her batting her eyelashes, giving him the coy look that he could never resist.

"Don't do this to me, Char. You know I'd write you a part in an instant if you asked. You also know I have no plans to be upstaged by you anymore."

"So our sweet moment is over?"

"You started it."

"You know that whole wearing-rubber-soled-shoes-to-protect-you-from-a-lightning-strike is a myth, right?"

"You auditioning to be the next Mr. Wizard too?"

"OK, I gotta go," said Charlene, her voice lacking affection. "Congratulations again. And happy birthday."

"Bye, Charlene." He clicked off the phone and tossed it on the couch, missing big, clunky telephone handles that made a satisfying *slam*.

He wanted a cigarette. He also, to his surprise, found himself wanting a drink. Those impulses had, for the most part, faded over the years. Rather, he had learned to live with them to the point that he hardly noticed them. But every now and again, that particular thirst would demand to be quenched, and he'd learned to be mindful of it, to talk himself through it until it passed. To quench it with a call to Ella or Paul, or smoke a cigarette instead, or walk around the studio lot. Anything but the bottle.

As if reading his mind at that moment, Ella called; his iPhone played some obnoxious song by some pop star that she had insisted upon as her designated ringtone.

"I'm so sorry I can't be there to celebrate with you, Daddy," said Ella. He loved that she still called him "Daddy" from time to time.

"Not as sorry as I am," he replied. Every year he spent his birthday with her, but this time she was on an overnight field trip at a marching band competition in Dallas.

"It's a big one too. Forty-five, right?"

"That's not so big."

"Just don't go start Botoxing or anything like that." He could almost see her rolling her eyes in disgust.

"Guys Botox?"

"Well, aren't you at that age where men start going off the deep end?"

"Who told you that?"

Ella didn't answer.

"How's Dallas?" he asked.

"Haven't seen any of it. We've been practicing nonstop."

"Well, good luck with your competition tonight, darlin'. I'm sure you'll nail it."

"If we can get the horns in sync, yeah. What are you gonna do for your birthday?"

"Probably watch a movie."

"Don't guilt me, Dad," said Ella in a voice that sounded exactly like her mother.

"What makes you think I'm guilting you?" he replied, a touch annoyed, probably more at Frannie than Ella.

"Just 'cause I'm not there doesn't mean you should sit in a dark room by yourself. You have friends. Go out to dinner with them. Go see a Laker game, or whatever sport is playing right now."

"Maybe I will," he said, almost believing it.

"Where's Charlene?" she asked.

"Charlene's in New York," he said, deflated.

"Oh."

"I miss you, El."

"Me too. I'll see you soon, Dad."

Danny returned to his desk and downed the last of his cold coffee. He sat in front of his laptop, read the few lines of dialogue he'd written, and deleted all of them. Once again, the cursor winked at him coyly, in that same seductive, manipulative way as Charlene, like the sirens luring Odysseus and his fellow travelers to their doom. By the end of the day, sandwiched between phone-tagging his agent and back-to-back interviews to promote *Exposed*, he'd completed the equivalent of two good minutes of a one-hour show.

———

It was almost midnight when Danny pulled into the driveway of his home, a five-bedroom, six-bath new colonial that was slumming it by most celebrity standards, and spotted an unfamiliar car in the space where Charlene usually parked. The only light in the house visible from the outside came from the living room. It was set on a timer programmed to come on at eight p.m. Clenching his fists, he wished for a weapon—pepper spray, a Taser, something—as he made his way up the brick path and toward the door, suddenly grateful for Ella's physical distance from the house.

He turned the key and slowly opened the door.

"Hello?" he called, his voice cracking on the second syllable.

Silence.

He crept from the foyer to the living room and into the kitchen, turning on lights along the way and wondering whether to start opening closet doors. The likelihood of there being an intruder was remote, he reasoned with himself—Danny lived just outside of LA in a gated community with other wealthy Hollywood personnel and roaming neighborhood rent-a-cops—not to mention he had a state-of-the-art security system, although it was presently turned off (had he forgotten to set the alarm when he'd left for the office this morning?). But no neighborhood was foolproof.

"I know someone's in here," he called out, attempting to assert his voice in a more menacing way, as if that would somehow scare off the perp. He was about to extract one of the knives from the wooden block on the kitchen counter when the intercom clicked on.

"Upstairs."

Charlene.

Danny breathed a sigh of relief followed by a huff as he left the kitchen and set the alarm before bounding up the stairs, two at a time. He found her in his bedroom, leaning back on her elbows near the edge of the bed, wearing nothing but his Armani tuxedo shirt (the undone bow tie hanging lifelessly around her neck) and red stilettos. Her hair was pushed to one side and draped over her shoulder in big curls, her legs teasingly crossed. She had *posed* for him. Typical. Clichéd, even. Scripted. But damn, it got him every time.

The blood rushed from his head, straight down south.

He folded his arms and cocked his head slightly to one side. "I thought you had a benefit tonight."

"I left early. Blew off the press and everything. Convenient thing, this time difference."

Danny unbuttoned his shirt and took a few steps toward her. "That was very sweet of you."

"I knew you'd be sulking by yourself with Ella out of town."

"How did you know Ella was out of town?"

Charlene frowned. "I listen to you when you talk, you know."

Danny took another step forward, his shirt completely off and his belt unbuckled. "You scared the shit out of me, you know. Try coming home after a long day and finding a strange car in your driveway."

"But then you wouldn't have been surprised." Charlene propped herself onto her knees and pulled Danny by the arm, and he flopped on the bed beside her. He was momentarily disappointed that she broke her pose until she proceeded to coo "Happy Birthday" to him in his ear, Marilyn Monroe–style, her voice soft and sexy.

This, he thought. It was as good as any drug, any pill, any drink. And he knew this was why they kept getting back together, why he could never bring himself to break up with her completely. She was intoxicating. She was addictive. And the mere thought of having to get over another addiction, one more bad habit, exhausted and saddened him.

He could barely wait for her to finish singing before he ravished her, and she kindly responded.

Sunny Smith

October 11, 2010

T ODAY WAS GOING TO BE JUST ANOTHER DAY, when it should've been something special. Of course, at some point I could count on a chocolate cake bought by my coworkers from the bakery two doors down from Whitford's, the one with the overly sweet buttercream frosting and roses, and a Shoebox card signed by whoever had been scheduled to work in the store the last two days. And I was scheduled to leave early because my parents and Tim were treating me to dinner at Bobby Flay's restaurant in Manhattan. But by the time I was out of Starbucks and on the way to work, I knew it wasn't going to happen. My throat was on fire, my head was stuffed like a pillow, and I wanted to go back to bed.

Forty.

When the hell did it happen? I remembered my mom being forty. Sort of. And it seemed like only yesterday that my brother, Tim, had turned forty, despite its being two years ago.

It wasn't so bad, really. I mean, aside from the gray hair and the frown lines and the kangaroo pouch that seemed to appear overnight (and even those things weren't so bad), I didn't *feel* much different from when I had turned thirty.

But wasn't I supposed to be married—or rather, have *stayed* married—by now? Wasn't I supposed to be living in a colonial-style house and driving a minivan and taking my kids to oboe lessons and cheerleading practice and hitting up my friends to buy boxes of Girl Scout cookies? Wasn't I supposed to be a published author by now?

Wasn't I supposed to be more than a stockroom manager?

Yes, I was. Yes to all of it.

I ignored the voice of Judi Dench as Armande in *Chocolat* as she advised me, "Don't worry so much about 'supposed to...'" She wasn't missing out on the chance to see Bobby Flay, much less taste his food.

Just as I was pulling into my usual spot behind Whitford's Books and Café, the Check Engine light appeared on my dashboard, and I groaned. My best friend, Theodora, had dubbed my 2002 yellow Volkswagen Beetle "the Old Banana," although "the Lemon" was a more appropriate moniker. I'd been so adamant about owning a Beetle that I'd failed to research *Consumer Reports*. Had I done so I would've found out that 2001 through 2004 models were nothing more than cute little shitboxes—or, as Tim called them, balloons on wheels. You'd think *it* was turning forty today.

I grabbed the Starbucks tray and my messenger bag and headed for the back door in the alley. Jingling my ring of fat industrial keys until I found the right one, I opened the heavy back door (unable to smell the musty odors of metal and cardboard—one more sign that I was getting sick) and cut through the stockroom to the front of the store. Brightly lit and full of warmth (sunlight permeated the floor-to-ceiling picture windows during the day), the earthy, autumn tones of orange and yellow and terra cotta seemed to make the books feel just as welcome as the customers. Honey-colored bookcases were an aesthetic improvement on the mock cherrywood cases of big-box bookstores, each section labeled in umber, lowercase Helvetica font on burnt orange signage. The industrial carpets (the color of brownies, yet emitting a chemical smell) had been vacuumed and recently shampooed. The café followed the color scheme of the store, albeit amped up in brightness and intensity. Square tables and chairs, boxy couches and ottomans, Plexiglas counters—the place looked like a Mondrian painting if you squinted at it.

Half of Huntington Village was already open, and passersby were already stopping to browse at the best sellers displayed in the picture windows. I'd wished there were room to place some of the café tables there instead, or even outside. Over the years, this part of town had become so populated and active that I called it mini-Manhattan. Outside was thick, noisy, congested with cars. Inside was tidy, quiet, devoid of customers. I loved when the store was like this—so peaceful—and a part of me wished there were a way we could preserve it as our own private playground yet somehow still stay in business. Of course, the thought that followed was *Then go work in the library, stupid,* and I pushed it aside to greet Angela, our manager.

"Hey, Sunny. You just get here?" she said.

"Yep. Did a Starbucks run. Here," I said, handing her the towering cup from the tray. "The pumpkin caramel latte is back. Venti. Molto venti. If it was any more venti it wouldn't fit through the door."

She practically bowed down to me in reverence. "You. Are. A life saver," she said before eagerly taking a sip and making swooning noises afterward. She then crossed the sales floor to the café (which was going through its own opening ritual), took one of their coffee cups, and dumped the contents of her latte into it. An employee sporting a Starbucks logo in Whitford's was as frowned upon as mentioning the A-word—Amazon.

I headed back to my stockroom, disappointed that Angela didn't remember to wish me a happy birthday (then again, I doubted she'd remember her own birthday, much less her name, before her first cup of coffee). But when I got there, I found my work station decorated with streamers, wrapping paper, and a Photoshopped snapshot of my ex-husband, Teddy, and me taped to my computer screen, with Teddy's head replaced by that of Danny Masters, the celebrity screenwriter on whom I was rockin' a massive crush (yes, that sounded way too junior high for someone who'd just turned forty). He looked determined rather than carefree, youthfully mischievous, but not gleeful. The caption in a cartoon bubble pointing to his mouth (a perfect balance of upper and lower lip without being too puckered or feminine) offered to do lewd things to me for my birthday. I couldn't help but laugh, wondering how I had missed the display on the way in.

Georgie.

Underneath that, a Post-it note was also stuck to my screen. *MUST TALK* was scrawled in Georgie's handwriting with thick black Sharpie, with block caps and underlined

twice. Something to do with Marcus, his beau, I guessed.
I removed the photo and stuck it in my messenger bag,
and then transferred the Post-it to my to-do list.

When I returned to the floor fifteen minutes later,
Angela had just unlocked the front doors and the first
customers sauntered in, one of them carrying a crumpled
Whitford's canvas tote bag and a tall thermos.

"Hey, Ange, when does Georgie get in? I need to kill
him," I said in a tone incongruent with my threat.

She laughed. "After work, OK? We've got a children's
book writing workshop with Emma Walton Hamilton this
afternoon, and he's going to be stressed. I take it you saw
your workstation?"

"I saw the photo."

"All Georgie's idea."

"I figured that."

Angela grinned. "Well, happy birthday, Sunny."

"Thanks."

"So how does forty feel?"

Ah, see? I was right; the coffee had kicked in.

I shrugged. "Like I've got cotton in my head. But I
suspect that's this damn cold I'm coming down with."

"I thought you looked a little run-down. Why didn't
you call in sick?"

"Didn't feel so bad when I woke up."

"Sucks to be sick on your birthday," she said. I nodded in agreement. "Still, you look good. I mean, you look
younger than forty."

I did a quick inspection of my Whitford's "uniform"
in the reflection of the picture window behind the cash
wrap, only this time I took notice of something I'd never

seen before. Sure, the oversized hoodie, straight-legged jeans, and Reebok sneakers were the same. My hair was in its usual ponytail, and I wore no makeup—also the norm for me. But what Angela was complimenting as youthfulness was, in fact, immaturity. At least as far as appearance went.

"Thanks," I said again, this time stifling a sneeze.

Ever since e-readers became popular, Whitford's customer traffic had decreased exponentially. In addition to the café to recapture the clientele, Whitford's debuted its own e-reader (poorly named the "Trinket") during Labor Day weekend, just in time for Christmas. We'd recently removed several rows of shelving and display stands to make room for the new booth (which, ironically, we called "the Pen") that housed display models and on-site technical support. Although the product rivaled the Kindle and its competition technologically speaking, the fact that it entered the market so late in the game was setback enough for the critics.

I loved Whitford's and didn't want to see them go the way of Blockbuster and Tower Records—extinct, thanks to technological progress and all things Apple—which was where they seemed to be headed. Whitford's had never dominated the market, nor had they been simultaneously praised and scorned for being so large and masterful, like their rivals Barnes & Noble and Borders had. Rather, it was a relatively small, family-owned chain that operated like an independent store—half the size of the big-box stores (although still quite spacious), aimed at keeping inventory small and customer relations cozy while connecting to the local economy through community outreach (Georgie's job). "Books, not bottom lines, are our passion" was their slogan. I'd been working for them since high school, when I'd begun as a part-time sales associate. They'd been just as loyal and loving to me as I was to them. Having worked my way up to a full-time stock manager, I now received a fixed, yearly salary, decent benefits, and, with the exception of the Christmas season and the Trinket debut, worked predominantly weekday shifts and no evenings. The pay, of course, was crappy, but better than most retail jobs. Besides, working in the stockroom gave me the pleasure of being around books all day without having to deal with the people who read them. Best of all, I left work at work, came home by dinnertime, and had oodles of time to write—at least, that had been the plan.

I'd been working in the stockroom for almost two hours, my only company being the eighties new-wave station on the radio, when Georgie entered looking like a Michael Kors spokesmodel. Since the summer ended, he'd been going to the tanning salon despite my telling him how fake it looked, and had grown his dark brown hair out to look less Jim Parsons and more Matt Damon.

Georgie, Theodora (whom we called Theo for short), and I had been best friends for twenty years, since they both came to Whitford's as seasonal help during college. I could hardly remember how I had lived life without either one of them. Whereas Theo was always my counselor and confidante, sister extraordinaire (to say nothing of the fact that as a chiropractor she gave the best treatments), Georgie was my kindred spirit. We tried to avoid the girl-with-gay-best-friend (or gay-guy-with-girl-best-friend) clichés, and woe to anyone who dared to even whisper the words "Will and Grace" to us—they incurred the wrath of a glare with all the force of a tsunami. And yet sometimes we had no choice but to surrender to the stereotypes: Georgie was way better at shopping than I was, and I was way more into sports, for starters. We were probably all evenly matched in the kitchen, although Theo was the best baker and I kicked ass when it came to stir-frying. Georgie, on the other hand, made killer drinks.

He set a shirt box covered with Smurfs wrapping paper on my workstation and threw his arms around me, swinging me back and forth, before I had a chance to warn him of my contagions. Ah, Georgie. He gave the best hugs regardless of the occasion.

"Happy birthday, my sweet Sunrise!"

"Thanks," I said, my voice muffled in his chest—Georgie also had a good four inches on me. "You probably shouldn't have done that, though. I'm pretty sure I've got Theo's cold. In her defense, she gave me fair warning that she was sick. But how could I resist an opportunity to split a pitcher of mudslides, followed by several rounds of drunken Wii Bowling?"

"Serves you right," he scolded. "So? How does the ol' four-oh feel?"

"Feels like the ol' three-nine."

"Well, you know what they say: Forty is the new twenty."

"I thought forty was the new *thirty*."

"Between Botox, Reebok EasyTones, and the Dr. Oz show, there's no reason why you can't be as smokin' as you were in college."

"Really? Because between my hair and my heels, I was six feet tall in college. Plus I wore genie pants. That is not something to aspire to."

Georgie let out a cackle that always brought a smile to my face. "So what are you wearing for Bobby Flay tonight, Sunny Delight?"

I swallowed and winced as I met a thousand needles in my throat. "I'm canceling tonight. I can't sustain a night in the city feeling like this."

He looked at me, incredulous. "Are you serious? No. There is no way I am letting you sit alone on your birthday and feel sorry for yourself."

"Who said anything about feeling sorry for myself?"

He folded his arms and gave me a look that defied me to prove him wrong.

"I'm going home and watching DVDs in bed with a bowl of chicken soup. If Bobby Flay doesn't get to see me, then no one else does."

"Sunrise Smith, you are going *out* for your birthday. You think Danny Masters is going to be sitting in bed with a bowl of chicken soup tonight?"

How had it slipped my mind that today was Danny Masters's birthday too? Both of our names were marked on my calendar. Even the photo that Georgie had taped to my workstation didn't tip me off. I tried to picture what Danny Masters might be doing tonight: a star-studded party; dinner at some trendy restaurant that sold sushi for a hundred bucks a pop; or perhaps somewhere special with just him and his daughter. Was he on again or off again with Charlene Dumont? If they were on again, then they were probably in Palm Springs, or Mexico, or the south of France, or perhaps even the Hamptons, or *somewhere* that mattered. And if they were in bed, then surely there was no soup involved.

"Danny Masters probably doesn't have a wall of mucus preparing to line his nose and throat," I said.

Georgie made a face. "TMI, dearie. C'mon! We'll go dancing!"

The thought alone made me woozy. "On a Monday? Please, Georgie—I feel like total crap."

"Well then, that settles it. Theo and I are going to come over and take care of you. We can watch John Hughes movies."

"We always watch John Hughes movies. Let's do Cary Grant movies instead," I suggested, considering that was what I'd been planning. "Wanna sleep over? You haven't done that in ages. Oh, and what's up with the Must Talk? Everything OK with Marcus?"

"Everything's fine. Open your present," he said.

I picked up the gift and tore the paper gently to preserve as much of it as possible. "Good choice of paper. It's going into my collection." The paper revealed a box from Nordstrom. Opening the box, I lifted the gold tissue paper to find an exquisite, finely woven sweater.

"From Theo and Marcus too. It's a Stella McCartney. Next year, you get Jimmy Choos to match, I promise. Once I hit the lottery, sky's the limit."

"Holy shit, it's gorgeous," I remarked.

"'Bout time you started dressing to impress."

"I love it, Georgie. Thank you. And thank Marcus for me too. I'll call Theo during break. She can't meet us for lunch."

"You didn't see what's under the tissue paper," he said.

I tentatively lifted the thin, crackly paper to find an envelope with Whitford's letterhead on it, from which I extracted three tickets to the premiere of *Exposed* at the Cannon Film Festival, followed by a panel discussion with Sharon Blake, Shane Sands, Paul Wolf, and...*Danny Masters*. I dropped my jaw and looked at Georgie, who looked as if he was ready to shriek like a fifteen-year-old girl at a boy band concert. No doubt I was wearing the same look.

"Wha...how...how did you get these?" I stammered.

"It was pure luck, let me tell you. I managed to get 'em online mere seconds after they went on sale. And they sold out in like five minutes. You do know that the other tickets are for me and Theo, of course. Poor Marcus has to work. And you can have Danny; I'm all for Shane."

"Marcus is OK with that?"

"He's got his own crushes."

I stared as if I were holding the last Golden Ticket to the Wonka factory. "I don't know what to say...thank you doesn't even begin to cover it." And then it hit me: "My God, Danny Masters is going to be in the same room as me. OK, so it's a big room, with a stage, and he won't even know I'm there. But still." Then I squealed and hugged Georgie. "I can't believe you did this for me! All of you!"

Georgie's bright blue eyes sparkled and he smiled widely after our hug. "You're welcome," he said. "And we're coming over tonight to watch your stupid Gen-X movies with you even though you're totally germafied. We'll do the Must Talk then."

He was lying about the movies being stupid. I knew he loved them even more than I did.

Georgie, Theo, and I sat in my bed, huddled under the thick comforter, separated by pillows, and snitching popcorn from two enormous bowls I usually reserved for Super Bowl parties (I was relegated to "the germafied bowl"). I had wanted to do a marathon of *To Catch a Thief, Charade,* and *The Philadelphia Story,* but Georgie and Theo won the coin toss, as did John Hughes, and we were in the middle of *Sixteen Candles,* to be followed by *Ferris Bueller's Day Off* and *Pretty in Pink.* We rarely made it to the end of the second movie when we planned these marathons, but still insisted on lining up all three. The night table beside me was littered with Kleenex, Nyquil, Tylenol, Ricola lozenges, a digital thermometer—everything but a prescription pad. Along with a classic princess phone (restored and painted baby pink, and working), a stack of novels occupied the other table, the top one half-read, the others waiting in anticipation. One of the perks of working at Whitford's was the 30 percent discount. There was something about the smell of crisp pages, the weight of the cover in my hands, the bending of the spine that just couldn't be duplicated by any technological marvel. I liked counting the pages to see how far I'd come or how much farther I had to go. I liked to keep one page between my fingers, as if it couldn't wait to be turned. Sometimes I even liked to make notes in the margins.

Not even halfway into the movie, we had gotten caught up in one of our favorite games—recasting movies of any generation with members of the Brat Pack. *The Great Escape, Harry Potter, Star Wars*, you name it. The epic or serial films were especially adaptable to this game. Theo was put in the position to settle the argument about who would make a better Edward in *Twilight*—Rob Lowe or Emilio Estevez. I was adamant that it had to be Rob, while Georgie was gangbusters for Emilio. Runner-up, of course, would be relegated to Jacob. "I don't really care," said Theo, "but Andrew McCarthy is so Mike Newton."

Just as the school dance scene began in *Sixteen Candles*, I asked Georgie about the Must Talk note yet again.

He took a deep breath. "OK. Don't kill me, but I have news about Teddy."

I felt a thud in the pit of my stomach at the mere mention of my ex-husband's name. Feigning bravery, I sat up and popped a lozenge into my mouth. "Go ahead."

"You know my cousin Eric is Facebook friends with Teddy, right? They have connections through work or something."

Already I didn't like where this was going.

"Yeah?" I said.

"Well, Eric told me that Teddy announced he's getting a divorce and changed his relationship status to single."

I jerked so forcefully that I tipped the popcorn bowl over. "A *divorce*?" Georgie nodded his head slowly. My mouth hung open, jaw momentarily frozen, before I followed with, "When did this happen?"

"You mean, when did he make the announcement, or when did I find out?"

I didn't bother to clarify.

Considering one of the reasons why Teddy and I split up was because he cheated on me, this news shouldn't have surprised me. But it did. Floored me, in fact. Teddy had been so hell-bent on being a dad—and not just any ol' dad, but Father of the Year. That included a stable marriage—or, as he called it, "a solid family unit." He and Ramona had lasted way longer than we had, and they had two children.

How was I supposed to feel about this? I wondered. Considering he'd left me for Ramona, was this some kind of karma? Had the gods finally delivered on my jilted heart's desire for their marriage vows to be sealed in the Temple of Doom? It sucked that my own relationship status had remained unchanged all this time, but I suspected that even if I had been blissfully remarried by now, the news still would have thrown me for just as much of a loop.

Georgie hesitated while Spandau Ballet's "True" blared in the background of Molly Ringwald's own love life problems.

"There's more."

I groaned. "Oh, for fuck's sake, what else?"

"He mentioned you in the comment thread."

My eyes reduced to slits, and Georgie handed me a pillow in self-defense; clearly he could tell I wanted to hit something, and he didn't want it to be the messenger. I clutched and squeezed the pillow while I said through clenched teeth, "What did he say?"

"I don't know, but Eric said the word *spinster* was in there."

Theo nervously eyed all the breakables in the room.

No. Teddy knew the rules. He was not to use my name, post photos, etcetera, in public ever again.

"Theo wasn't sure if I should tell you," said Georgie, "but I thought you were better off hearing it from me than some loser."

I darted my eyes to Theo. "You knew about this?"

"For consultation purposes," she clarified in an effort to stave off my death glare.

My eyes darted back to Georgie. "I would've been better off hearing it from Teddy—no, scratch that. I shouldn't be hearing it at all."

"He was probably drunk when he posted it," said Theo.

"Like the last time?" I asked, raising my voice.

I stared at the TV without actually watching it while my memory bank reopened the Teddy account. We had met during my junior year of college at a party following a basketball game. He was a year older than me and quite good-looking. Blond hair, blue eyes, tall, preppy... think the guy that was in *The Karate Kid* and *Back to School* and all those eighties movies—you know, the one who always played the tool. That right there should've tipped me off. He wasn't really my type, but I assumed the alcohol was the reason for our hitting it off.

Although we flirted all night and even made out a little bit, nothing came of it. Not until almost five years later, shortly after I broke up with another guy. Teddy came into Whitford's to purchase a bunch of Dr. Seuss books for his niece. Something about that touched me. I was still working on the floor and behind the cash wrap in those days, and the moment we saw each other, sparks flew—literally. One of the overhead lightbulbs popped, and thankfully no one was hurt. But Teddy and I knew better. Actually, I was surprised that he remembered me—we'd both been kinda soused that night—but he told me on our first official date that he'd never forgotten me and had kicked himself for not getting my number.

On paper he was perfect: smart, handsome, athletic, family-oriented, religious, you name it. He didn't mind sitting through chick flicks and was more than happy to hold my purse while I tried on clothes. He'd buy me little teddy bears on anniversaries and slipped notes in my lunch bags when I wasn't looking. He was the only boyfriend to whom I'd ever showed my novel manuscripts, and he encouraged me to find an agent, fully supporting my plan to work at Whitford's until we had children—then I'd quit and be a writer and a mom. Or rather, a mom and a writer. He very much wanted me to be a mom.

We dated for a year, got engaged, and lived together for another six months before the wedding and actually tried to get pregnant before the I dos, much to my parents' chagrin (despite their touting of the sexual revolution and the fact that my brother had been a prenuptial conception). In hindsight, I think they must have had some kind of intuition about our inevitable demise.

"Is this really what you want?" Mom had asked.

"Of course it's what I want," I had replied, annoyed. "Why would you say that?"

"I know you want *Teddy*," she'd said. "I just question what you want more—to be a mother or not to be without Teddy."

I'd dismissed her and brushed the conversation off as absurd. But looking back on it, I saw what she saw. I had become *impatient* to find someone with whom to spend my life. Someone to and with whom I'd dedicate my novels and live blissfully in the 'burbs until the kids went off to college, and then we'd buy a camper and take a cross-country trip. I'd had a string of boyfriends, none of whom lasted for more than eight months, and could rattle off their names the way Will Hunting named all his imaginary brothers in *Good Will Hunting* (Marky, Ricky, Danny, Terry, Mikey, Davey...). But none of them felt "right" to me, or like—dare I say it—"the One." I'd never been a comparison shopper, and I didn't always know what I was looking for, but once I found it, the search was over. In the case of a mate, there always seemed to be some missing puzzle piece, although I never knew what it was. All I knew was that I hadn't found it. And by the time Teddy came along, I had decided that it would reveal itself within the course of our marriage. Perhaps it would be our child, I told myself. Besides, how would I ever find anyone better than Teddy? He even put the seat down, for chrissakes.

A year after we got married and my menstrual cycle became more erratic (prompting a number of false alarms), we started seeing the specialists. And about six months after that it was finally confirmed that I had an ovulation problem (and we couldn't afford in vitro fertilization), Teddy insisted that he was put on this earth to be a father—a biological father, that is. Adoption was not part of his plan, nor were surrogates or stepchildren.

Then came Ramona and, shortly afterward, what I've since called "the Humiliation."

Thing is, before Teddy, I'd never given the idea of having children much thought. I wasn't opposed to it, but rather than forming my life plan around it, having children was more like a contingency plan. With Teddy, however, it had become the whole plan. But for some reason, finding out I couldn't have children had somehow rendered all the other life possibilities pointless. In the way I had lived all my life knowing the Twin Towers were always relatively nearby, with no sense of urgency to visit them, when they were suddenly gone the heap of regret was as massive as the rubble left in their wake.

And in the blink of an eye, I was forty and watching twenty-five-year-old movies with a single girl and a gay guy in my bed. Georgie seemed to have been reading my mind all this time (and, bless him, wasn't the least bit offended). He yanked me back into the present moment with a forceful "*Fuck him*, Sunrise. Rather, he can go fuck himself. Any man who doesn't stick by you no matter what never deserved you in the first place. And it's not too late—you can still adopt. Angelina Jolie hasn't taken all the orphaned babies in the world. You're strong enough to be a single mom."

"It's not that," I started.

"Then what's wrong?"

Tears came to my eyes. "I just…what's happened to me, Georgie?"

I made a honking noise as I blew my nose and went to the bathroom to apply a Breathe Right strip. When I returned Georgie and Theo both looked at me, then at each other.

"*That's it,*" said Georgie, fed up. He picked up the remote, aimed it at the television like a pistol, and clicked it off, not even bothering to stop the DVD player. He then hastily gathered the spilled popcorn, dumped it back into the bowl, and moved it to the floor next to the bed.

"We need a pad and pen," he said. I pointed to the drawer of the night table next to Theo. She opened it and pulled out a legal pad, along with a purple ballpoint pen, and handed both to him. "This is great," he said, scribbling the words "40 FOR 40" at the top of the page in block caps and underlining it twice. "We're gonna make a list of forty things you want, and you're gonna spend the next forty weeks crossing everything off the list."

Theo squealed. "Ooooh, that is a *fabulous* idea!"

"Are you kidding me?" I said.

"I have never been more serious in my life," said Georgie.

"Shouldn't we watch *Ferris Bueller* first?"

"Screw *Ferris Bueller*—this is 2010! *Carpe diem* and all that shit."

"What are we supposed to write?" I asked.

"I don't know. Be like the song and reach up for the sunrise. Live up to your name."

I scoffed and rolled my eyes. Both Georgie and Theo knew how much I hated the name bestowed upon me by my ex-hippie parents.

"Fine. Change name," he said as he wrote the words in block caps. "What else?"

I looked at him, dumbfounded.

"Oh, come *on*." He seemed to be genuinely annoyed. "You mean to tell me that you're so out of touch with yourself you can't even think of one thing that you'd like to do or have or be? Whatever happened to getting published? What about buying a house? I mean, geez, Sunny—how could we have let you stray so far?"

"Georgie, those things take *years* to happen, not forty weeks. And some of them never happen. For one thing, I can barely save enough for an IRA—forget about buying a house! And you know that finding a literary agent is about as difficult as getting a part in a movie or a play."

He ignored my objections. "Never stopped you before. Now, what's number two on the list? Just call 'em out as they come to you—they don't have to be in any particular order of importance."

I let out a loud sigh, and they went ahead without me. "Publish novels," said Theo as Georgie wrote. "And don't bother with the lame-ass excuse about getting an agent, 'cause you know you can self-publish."

"You know, I don't even know if that's such a priority anymore," I said. "Getting published, I mean."

He eyed me for a second, knowing I was full of shit, before returning to the pad. "We'll edit later. What's next?"

I shrugged. Georgie flinched with delight as the next idea came to him. "Ooh, I know." He giggled as he scrawled the next item, blocking the pad with his forearm so I couldn't see it. That giggle was the sound of mischief.

"What?" I asked. "What are you writing?"

He turned the pad to Theo, who let out an even more sinister laugh as she read it, before revealing it to me: SLEEP WITH DANNY MASTERS.

I rolled my eyes again. "Man, you do dream big. How 'bout I just meet him and shake his hand? Hell, I'll settle for holding the door of his taxicab open for him."

"Please, Sunny—you think he takes a *cab*?" said Georgie.

"Whatever. How 'bout we just go out for coffee?"

"Nope," said Theo. "You wanna jump his bones and you know it."

"I also wanna jump Rob Lowe's bones, the guy from *White Collar*'s, and all of Duran Duran's—not all at once, of course. That doesn't mean I believe it would or could ever happen. Not to mention that they're all married."

"Or gay," Georgie added. "And why not?"

"Which one is gay?"

Georgie waved a hand in impatience. "Whatever. Of all the celebrities in the world—"

"—and who says I have to sleep with a celebrity?"

"—I'd say Danny Masters is the one you have the best chance to be with."

"Who lives on the other side of the country..."

"So? Get on a plane," said Theo.

"And doesn't know I exist."

"You'll have to work on that without becoming Creepy Stalker Woman," said Georgie.

"Why do you think I have the best chance to be with him?" I asked, despite my having made a mental list of answers many times over.

"For starters, you're both writers—and I don't care what you say; I hold your stuff up to his any day of the week and twice on Sunday. You're both from New York, and the part of New York that counts. You share the same birthday, and you're only five years apart in age," said

Theo. She sounded like a fictional TV lawyer during opening arguments.

"Danny Masters also happens to be a recovering alcoholic, a self-described control freak, divorced with a child, and hopelessly in love with Charlene Dumont."

"Who might very well be nothing more than a rather convincing drag queen," said Georgie. "Besides, you're basing this characterization on, what, the Internet? 'Cause that's always right." His voice was laced with sarcasm.

"I am not going to sleep with Danny Masters within the next forty weeks."

"Well, I ain't crossin' it off, so you'll just have to."

"You know, I don't wanna be some fangirl," I said. "I respect Danny Masters. I respect his writing and I admire his career."

"And you find him attractive," Theo pointed out.

"I find lots of men attractive."

"There's nothing wrong with you admitting that you like a guy," she pressed.

"There's a big difference between liking a guy and having a crush on someone you've only seen on TV or in a magazine or whatever. The first behavior is real. The second is juvenile."

I knew whom I was really trying to convince.

"Thing is, Sunny. I don't think it's just a crush for you. Call me crazy, but I think you genuinely like this guy. I don't think he's superhuman, and I think if he met you, he'd genuinely like you too."

Damn Theo and her sharing of my brain.

I persisted. "This is someone who has rubbed elbows with everyone from Robert Redford to Paul McCartney to Barack Obama. He's made something of his life. He travels the world. He probably spends in a week what I make in a year." I sneezed before continuing. "And as you so aptly pointed out, anything I've learned about him via the Internet and the corporate media is highly suspect. So how can I make any kind of assessment as to whether this is someone I'd actually like to date or could be compatible with?"

"Sunny, if Danny Masters ever got a look at you, I'm sure he'd want to get to know you, provided you're wearing the sweater we just bought you and not dressed for work," said Georgie. "Besides, at one time he was just another fucked-up Long Islander like you and me."

I shook my head rapidly, as if trying to shake off the wish for it to be so. "It's never gonna happen."

"Why?" they both asked.

"Under what circumstances would we be anywhere near each other?"

Georgie waved his hand in front of my eyes. "Hello? Tickets to the premiere? Q and A afterward?"

"Yeah, right. Like he's going to see me in the audience. I'm going to have some aura glowing that makes me stand out from hundreds of people. And he's going to immediately forget about Charlene Dumont or whoever else he happens to be fucking at the moment."

"You know, someone with a name as perky as yours shouldn't be so pessimistic. Besides, you're getting a makeover." He tapped on the pad with the pen. "On the list. I say we schedule it before the premiere. In fact, let's make a weekend of it in the city. We'll book a room, get makeovers, go shopping, the whole nine yards. Hell, if Danny

Masters doesn't notice you, at least a hundred other guys will. Either way, you can't lose."

"So you're saying no one will notice me if I don't have a makeover?"

Georgie rolled his eyes. "Wasn't it by your design to go unnoticed, Sunny? Your solitary confinement is over. Get your ass back in gear. It's time."

He had a point.

Danny Masters

HER PARTING WORDS TO HIM WERE SIMPLY, "Call me."

Charlene left just after eight a.m. to fly back to New York to resume her film obligations, and Danny decided to go to the office early rather than linger in the cavernous house by himself. They hadn't talked much during her brief visit; rather, they mostly had sex until they fell asleep, exhausted.

"What does that mean?" he had asked three years ago, the first time she had spent the night and left with those same parting words.

"What do you mean, what does that mean? It means *call me*. On the phone."

"Yeah, but do you expect me to call you at a certain time of the day or a certain day of the week? Is this a courtesy call? An about-last-night call? Am I calling as a friend or as your lover? I need these things spelled out for me."

Charlene had given Danny a patronizing look. "Why do these things always have to be so complicated?" It was a question that seemed not to be directed at him, but rhetorical in nature. "It means that I had a wonderful time last night, that I like the sound of your voice to keep me company when we can't be in the same room together, and if you feel so inclined, you can pick up your phone and talk so that I can hear it. And since when are friends and lovers an either-or? Why can't you be representing yourself as both when you call me?"

"I just want to make sure I know where I stand," he had responded. "Guys are afraid of fucking up, you know."

"No, *you're* afraid of fucking up." They'd been on two dates, and already she knew him so well.

"So be it. You know," he said after a quick beat, "you can call me too. You don't have to wait around for me."

"First of all, I don't wait around for any man. Second, I don't chase men, and I don't make the first call. It's just a little personal insurance for my peace of mind."

"It's a power play," said Danny.

He'd watched Charlene study him intently at that moment. "Do you write such fantastic arguments because of your need to instigate one yourself?"

He had often wondered this same thing. But he also knew that with Charlene Dumont he was going to be constantly battling for power, and he had already wished it wasn't the case. And it wasn't even that he wanted power over her—no, he just wanted to be on the same level.

So when Charlene left him with those very same words this morning, those two words that defined their relationship as nothing more than a never-ending game of "chicken," he felt weary. And they were as unclear to him this morning as they were the very first time she'd said them to him.

When Danny got to the office, Dez was already at her desk sorting his mail, wearing her phone headset and

talking. The image always conjured a switchboard opera-
tor from the fifties and sixties—and yet the twenty-eight-
year-old always sported the trendiest fashions to go with
a neon-pink, pageboy hairstyle. A jealous ex-girlfriend of
his had once accused Danny of sleeping with Dez, and
when he denied the notion as absurd because he was pretty
sure she was a lesbian (or perhaps bisexual), the ex then
accused him of wanting to. He had laughed in response,
but wondered if perhaps his body language was revealing
some unconscious desire.

"What are you doing here so early?" he asked.

She gave him an exasperated look. "You've got a schedule of interviews a mile long, not to mention the meeting
you have with Ken Congdon about the new show." Her
words always shot out of her mouth rapid-fire.

"Yeah, I know. I'm way behind on it. It's been kinda
hard to concentrate on writing what with all the premiere
week nonsense."

"You got calls from Paul, Joannie from Kingsmen
casting, Steven Spielberg wants you to rescue a script for
a project he's slated to direct, and there's a charity dinner
that you agreed to attend but for which you haven't sent
in your seating chart yet."

Danny frowned. "There's a seating chart?"

"You bought the table, remember?"

He moved on. "That was all since you got in this
morning?"

"The charity thing and Spielberg were voice mails
from last night. Plus more birthday messages."

He opened the door to his office and headed for his
desk, passing the already-wilting bouquets of flowers and

opening his laptop as he sat down. "Get Spielberg back first. We'll deal with the rest after that."

Dez followed him inside. "How was your birthday celebration last night?"

He avoided eye contact with her and pretended to be occupied with papers on his desk. "I just went home was all."

"Charlene left this morning?"

He looked up and found her patiently waiting for an answer, seemingly unfazed by his baffled expression. "How—what—did she call you before I got here?"

"I can smell her perfume on you."

Danny inspected himself, as if the scent was visible. "Oh." His brow furrowed. "It's a clean shirt, though. And I showered."

"I don't know what to tell you. So was this just birthday sex, or are you two official again?"

Although Dez rarely, if ever, shared any hint of her own love life (not that he would have the first clue how to advise her if she had asked for it), she never hesitated to offer her unsolicited two cents when it came to his.

Rather than tell her to mind her own business, he raised his eyes above the laptop and peered at her.

"OK, so I'll get Spielberg on the phone," she said, and went back to her desk.

Danny returned calls. He read e-mails. He did three back-to-back phone interviews. He tried to work on the pilot script, staring at the screen and tapping on the keyboard without actually typing, but just couldn't find the motivation for the characters. They had to have a reason for existing, a purpose besides the obvious. They had to *want* something. Who gave a crap about a couple of married radio talk show hosts? At the moment, he didn't. Maybe this wasn't the right angle for a show. Maybe political thrillers and courtroom dramas were all he was good at. And what did *he* want? He stared out the window and waited for an answer, but none came.

———

At around two thirty Danny left his office and drove to a bistro where Ken Congdon, his executive producer for *Winters in Hyannis*, was already seated at a table on the patio and talking on his BlackBerry. He approached the table and extended his hand to Ken, who stood up and shook it heartily. "Good to see you," said Ken. "Happy birthday."

"Thanks."

"What are you, fifty, sixty years old now?"

"Feels like it some days."

"I was feeling fine until AARP started sending me junk mail."

Seconds after the server took their drink orders (an aspiring actor, Danny could tell—after so many years in LA, he could spot them as if they wore an insignia), Ken brought up *Exposed*.

"I saw the advanced screening the other day. That is one fucking great movie, Danny. I think it's your best."

"Thanks, Ken. Paul and the cast really get the credit."

"They're only as good as the material they have to work with. Start writing your acceptance speeches now."

The drinks arrived, and Danny was equal parts grateful and disappointed that the server didn't mix them up.

"Let's talk about the new show," said Ken, perusing the appetizer menu.

Danny took a sip of his Diet Coke and fidgeted with the lemon wedge that had been perched on top of the glass. "Yeah, about that. I'm having a little trouble with the angle."

"What have you got so far?"

He could feel his face turn hot. "About thirty minutes of shit."

Ken didn't even bat an eye. "What's the premise?"

"That's just it. Right now there isn't any. All I've got is this married couple who are radio talk show hosts, and no obstacle other than themselves."

The server came back to take their food orders.

"Can I make a suggestion?" asked Ken.

Danny nodded and gestured a signal of permission to proceed.

"You're writing about a public radio station, aren't you? So make it about the ups and downs of running a public radio station in a corporate, partisan world."

"In other words, *Winters in Hyannis* meets NPR? I don't want to repeat myself, Ken. Worse still, I don't want to be accused of repeating myself by the critics."

"David Kelley's had what—four, five shows about law firms?"

"And not one of them recycled."

"And how is this a repeat if it's set in a radio station?"

"It's political," argued Danny.

"Look, anything you do in television from now on is going to be compared to *Winters*, just like everything you do in film from now on is going to be compared to *Exposed*."

Danny shuddered. "Every time someone tells me that I need a Xanax."

"*Winters in Hyannis* is your *Pet Sounds*, Danny," said Ken. "Embrace it. Have you heard what Brian Wilson has been up to?"

"You're not talking about the baseball player, right?"

Ken gave Danny a look that proved he knew Danny was joking, but refused to indulge. "He did an album of Gershwin covers."

"Really?" Danny, a fan of both the former Beach Boy and George Gershwin, was surprised he hadn't heard about this sooner.

"You know what it really was?" said Ken. "Gershwin meets *Pet Sounds*. And it was fucking awesome just the same. You know why?"

"Because *Pet Sounds* is fucking brilliant and people can't get enough of it. Including Brian Wilson. There's a reason why he called it *Pet Sounds*." Danny finished his Diet Coke and felt unsatisfied. "But I really wanted to do something lighter this time, Ken. Something with comedy and romance rather than the political stuff."

"You're good at the political stuff. Politics is conflict and argument, and that's your forte. Comedy and romance? Really? Too fluffy for you."

"Romance has plenty of conflict and argument."

"Yours does, maybe."

Shit.

After talk about timelines, casting, and budget projections for the new show, Ken held up a hand to catch the server's attention and asked for the check. He then took out his wallet and credit card.

"Look, you're obviously way too swamped with the premiere to think about all this. Forget the show for now. Think about it, write a pilot, and come see me when it's done."

"Sure thing, Ken."

———

Back at the office, Danny called Ella and left a message on her voice mail. "Hey, El. It's your decrepit old dad. I was just checking to see if you were back from Dallas yet and free for dinner. I'm on a plane to New York tomorrow. Um…" He hesitated for a second, wanting to say more, but at a loss for words. Perhaps he'd used his day's allotment in the script. "Anyway, give me a call, darlin'. Love you."

Ten minutes later his iPhone rang. The obnoxious pop song.

"El?" he asked, as if doubtful.

"You called?" said Ella, followed by what sounded like gum popping.

"Yes, I did, from my office phone. Didn't you listen to the message?"

"Why should I listen to the message when I'm talking to you now?"

"So that I don't have to repeat myself."

"What's so bad about repeating yourself?"

"I don't like the sound of my voice."

She huffed. "Is it really that hard to be you?" Danny couldn't help but laugh; she was teasing him with one of his favorite phrases.

"Hey, I don't go to therapy for nuthin'," he replied.

"Ugh," she said. "I hate when you tell me things like that."

These days it was hard for Danny to tell when he was going to get his sweet little girl who called him Daddy and when he was going to get the teenager whose father was an embarrassment to her. "It's hardly news to you," he said.

"Yes, but I don't need to be *reminded* of it." She huffed again. "So why'd you call?"

Danny couldn't tell if she was genuinely annoyed with him. "Well, I'm flying out to New York for the *Exposed* premiere tomorrow, so I was wondering if you'd like to have dinner with me tonight."

"I can't."

He felt a wave of disappointment crash over him. "You're still in Dallas?"

"No, I got back a couple of hours ago."

"Then how come?"

"Um…"

Danny instantly recognized her hesitation.

"Oh, don't tell me."

"Tell you what?" He could tell Ella was stalling.

"What's his name, El?"

She paused before speaking, as if contemplating the consequences of divulging the information.

"You know Johnny Timber from the band Avalon Gone?"

Of course he knew Avalon Gone. He still owned their albums on vinyl.

"Yesss…" he said cautiously, not liking where this was going.

"His son Richie goes to my school."

Ella was enrolled in a private school attended by many children of celebrities ranging from rock stars to politicians.

Danny's stomach did a somersault.

"Does Johnny Timber do drugs?"

"How should I know?" asked Ella.

"Does Richie do drugs?"

"Dad!" *Now* she was genuinely annoyed.

"How long has this been going on?"

"He officially asked me out after marching band practice a couple of weeks ago."

Something about this amused him. "Johnny Timber's son is in the marching band?"

"He's the best drummer we have. I'm tellin' ya, Dad. The kid's a natural."

This sounded like something a parent would say. Yet another side to Ella—the one who was maturing into a young adult right before his eyes.

"So, what, are you two going steady or something?"

She laughed. "Going steady? Please. How *American Graffiti* can you get?"

That his fourteen-year-old daughter just referenced *American Graffiti*—or rather, something symbolic of its time, made his heart swell with pride.

"Well?" he asked.

"We just go to the mall or the movies and stuff," she said. "And we're chaperoned at home. Don't worry, Dad. I'm not gonna get knocked up or anything."

Danny bowed his head, put his free hand to his eyes and covered them. "Keep up talk like that and you're going to prolong my therapy, you know."

"Sorry," she said.

He couldn't tell if she was apologizing for getting a boyfriend, growing up, or rejecting his dinner invitation. Nevertheless, he felt bad for all three reasons.

"It's OK, El. I miss you, though."

"Yeah, I miss you too. How's the writing going?"

"It's going well," he lied. "See you soon?"

"We'll Skype while you're in New York."

He nodded in resignation. "Sure."

"Are you going to see Charlene while you're there?"

Ella was eleven when Danny and Charlene started dating, and at first she had been charmed by Charlene's poise and beauty (and who could blame her?) but conflicted because she didn't want to betray her loyalty to her mother. She'd also gone through a jealous streak, accusing him of wanting to be with Charlene more than her, which crushed him—that Ella could think he put *anyone* above her! Lately, however, rather than being resentful of his time spent away from her, she seemed indifferent to it. He almost wished she'd yell at him again, call and ask why he didn't see her enough. Frannie had assured him that this was female adolescence. Teenage girls hated their parents.

("I thought they hated their mothers and attached to their fathers," Danny had said in response.

"They do hate their mothers," said Frannie. "They think their fathers are stupid.")

"I don't know," he answered. "Maybe if we can get our schedules to match. I'll barely have a moment to breathe what with the premiere and all the nonsense that goes with it."

"I'm really proud of you, Dad."

Danny choked up for a moment. The president of the United States—hell, God himself—could have said the same thing and it wouldn't have meant as much as it did coming from Ella.

"Thanks, hon. I'm really proud of you too."

"For what?" she asked, snapping her gum again.

"Do I need a reason?"

She didn't answer, and he could almost see her shrugging.

"Well, have a good time with what's-his-name," said Danny.

"Richie," said Ella.

Derelict, he thought. *Future recovering addict. Fucking* drummer.

"Yes, Richie."

He said good-bye, put the phone on the desk, and turned his attention back to his laptop. The damn cursor was mocking him yet again.

CHAPTER
FOUR
Sunny Smith

T HE 40 FOR 40 LIST SAT ATOP THE STACK OF
books the following morning, looming over me like
some to-do list from hell. I perused its contents with a
sense of hopelessness, its impossible expectations showing no particular order of importance:

Change name
Self-publish novels
Sleep with Danny Masters
Exercise
Redecorate each room in
apt. for $40 apiece
De-clutter
Organize closets
Get makeover
Get a spa treatment
Travel somewhere that
requires getting on a
plane
Go on 10 dates (same person
or separate)
Start a new novel

Submit short stories to
magazines
See a Broadway show
Attend a concert
Buy flowers once a week
Save $10 per week
Join a Meetup
Go to a sporting event
Sign up for tennis lessons
Go out to dinner with
parents on day not marked
by special occasion
Attend tree-lighting at
Rockefeller Center
See Radio City Christmas
Spectacular without heckling

Read 40 books

Download music recorded in this century

Up fruits and veggies servings per day

Try one new recipe per week

Keep a plant alive

Get a pet

Move someplace that allows pets

Get rid of all Suave products

Volunteer somewhere

Take up painting

Attend a writers' conference

Host a dinner party with more than Georgie, Marcus, and Theo as guests

Finish a New York Times crossword puzzle

Sell the Old Banana

Go out to the movies twice a month, or rent one new movie once a week

Wear lipstick every day

Theo had gone home sometime before one a.m., while Georgie had fallen asleep beside me. I called in sick to work and buried myself under the covers. A congested cough had taken over my sore throat and runny nose. Georgie, who was in the bathroom while I was on the phone to Whitford's, emerged with a jar of VapoRub for me. "I'm going home to die," he informed me, his eyes red and watery. "I've got your cold, darling."

I moaned. "I'm sorry," I said, my voice weak and scratchy.

He waved his hand as if to bat away my apology. "I'll send Marcus over later with his kick-ass home remedy. One dose and not only will you be comatose for ten hours, but you'll also wake up the next day ready to leap tall buildings in a single bound."

Georgie wasn't kidding. Not only was I able to return to work the next day, but I also caught up on the previous day's work, plus prepared the agenda for the team that would take my place for Friday (as part of my birthday surprise, Georgie had already prearranged the schedule with Angela so we'd both have Friday off).

We worked until five o'clock on Thursday, picked up Theo on the way to the Long Island Rail Road station in Huntington during rush hour, and arrived in Manhattan before eight o'clock. While most commuters passed the time either antisocially entranced in their electronic gadgetry or sleeping, the three of us chattered nonstop. I hadn't been to the city in almost a year and was giddy with anticipation.

Georgie, who was sure that the Mayan prophecy was correct and we were all going to eat it in 2012, had no qualms about maxing out his credit card for the ritzy Dream Hotel in Midtown, and as soon as we checked in and dropped our luggage, we immediately went out to eat. Despite Manhattan being the city that never sleeps, we decided to make it an early night. Even though Marcus's secret herbal remedy had cured us, Theo insisted that the two sickies share one of the beds in our double room to save her immune system, and we acquiesced with no complaints.

I woke up wide-eyed at six o'clock the next morning, knowing all too well that this was the day I was going to get a glimpse of Danny Masters in the flesh. It was one thing to see him on TV talking to Diane Sawyer or Charlie Rose; it was something else to see him in three-dimensional form, breathing the same air. A reminder that he was as human as the rest of us. Would he be able to see me in the audience? Would he know I was there? Would he care?

No, I decided. No, he would not. But I wanted to look good for him anyway.

After breakfast we all went to our salon appointments at the hotel spa, Theo and Georgie already dressed to kill. Theo especially was runway ready, sporting a baby pink V-neck cashmere sweater, black leggings, and boots that only accentuated her tall, sleek frame. Her mane of jet-black corkscrew tendrils fell flawlessly just below her shoulders (enhancing her violet eyes). It wasn't that Theo was drop-dead gorgeous by media standards; it's that she knew how to dress as if she were. But Theo could wear a muumuu and I'd think she was the most beautiful woman in the world. Her laugh and disposition made her so. I've often thought Sunny would've been a more suitable name for her than for me.

"Wow. I didn't know there was a dress code for makeovers," I said.

They exchanged glances. "So do you think now's a good time to tell her?" said Georgie to Theo.

"Tell me what?"

Theo wore a guilty expression. "We only booked an appointment for you."

I was slow on the uptake. "Why?"

"Because we don't need makeovers; you do," said Georgie, and before I could verbally express my hurt, he gently touched my arm. "Look, Sunrise. You know we love you to pieces, and we weren't doing it to be mean. But you pretty much said so yourself the other night that you're in a rut, and this is the first step to get you out of it."

"We'll be with you the whole time," said Theo, as if I were a child at a dentist's appointment.

"That'll be fun," I said sarcastically.

"Oh, ye of little faith," said Georgie. "I think it's going to be tons of fun."

His words weren't completely out of his mouth when I was introduced to Luciano, the stylist assigned to me. He greeted me with a kiss on each cheek, as if we were old friends meeting for our weekly lunch. His complexion was dark and velvety, and he wore his hair in a short style of thin, tight dreadlocks. One could see that underneath the tight, black T-shirt were quarter-bouncing abs—in fact, he could easily quit his job in favor of a modeling gig.

"Call me Luc," he said, and started running his fingers through my hair after I removed my ponytail and released my hair in a couple of quick shakes. "Spectacular. I've got clients that would make deals with the devil for hair like yours." His voice was bold and bassy, with a mix of dialects.

"Thanks," I said, not expecting the compliment.

"It's perfect. I mean, *perfect*. Not too thick, not too thin. Not too straight, not too stringy. Could be a little more hydrated, but we'll fix that with product. What do you use at home?"

"Just shampoo and conditioner," I said, embarrassed to reveal the brand name.

"She buys *over the counter*," Georgie tattled, saying the last part just above a whisper and holding a hand up against his mouth to block others from reading his lips. Both he and Theo had followed us to Luc's station rather than wait in reception. They weren't kidding when they said they'd be with me the whole time.

Luc made a face. "Seriously?" I tried to smile apologetically at him in the mirror. "Well. That ends now. And we have *got* to cover all this gray," he said before adding, "and *what* is with the ponytail?"

"I work in a stockroom."

Luc opened his mouth in exaggerated shock. "*What?* A hot chick like you?"

"I'll bet you say that to all the women who sit in your chair."

"Beautiful, if you saw some of the women who sat in my chair, you'd call me the Miracle Worker. *You* are not an ugly woman. You've just got a style that is doing nothing for you. It matches your job, not your personality."

"*Thank you!*" Georgie said emphatically, sitting in the stylist's chair next to me and throwing up his hands. "I've been telling her that for God knows how long." I shot him a look; he was so loving this. So was Theo, who was grinning like the Cheshire Cat.

"So what brings you here today?" asked Luc.

"Well, I just turned forty, and I'm treating myself to a new look."

"Good for you."

"Plus we're going to the premiere of *Exposed* tonight, and the cast is going to be there, along with Paul Wolf and Danny Masters," added Theo.

"Paul Wolf I've heard of, but who's Danny Masters?"

Once again the thought of a mere glimpse of Danny Masters made my spine tingle. "He wrote the screenplay," I said. "He also wrote *Winters in Hyannis*, the TV show," I tacked on.

Luc seemed unimpressed, and I doubted whether he'd even heard of *Winters in Hyannis*, much less seen it. Rather than recite the entire Danny Masters catalogue, as I would normally do, I offered a different piece of information.

"Shane Sands will also be there," I said.

He perked up. "Well then, we've got to get you gorgeous for Shane tonight. What are you wearing?"

Before I could tell him about the Stella McCartney sweater Georgie, Marcus, and Theo bought me, they described it on my behalf. "We're going shopping for the rest after this," said Theo.

"Make sure you accessorize properly," said Luc. "Sex is in the details. Now," he said, running his fingers through my hair yet again. "Let's get to work. Do you trust me?"

I took a deep breath. "Go for it."

Luc met my eyes in the mirror solemnly. "Good. 'Cause if you don't trust me, there's no point in moving forward."

Luc disappeared behind a wall and emerged ten minutes later carrying two small plastic mixing bowls, each holding a long-stemmed flat brush and full of goop, and a box of foil sheets. He divided my hair into sections with the end of a tail comb and clipped each off to the side. He then began partitioning the top section into finely threaded slices with the stick end of the brush, and methodically laid each on a sheet of foil, slathering it with the goop-saturated brush before folding the foil over it. The ritual continued with the other sections. When he finished, my head was covered with shingles of foils, and that was only the first step. All the while he grilled me with questions.

"So where do you live?" he asked.

"Out on the Island. Huntington Village."

"You married? Divorced? Dating?"

I decided to keep my answers curt: "No to the first, yes to the second, and no to the third."

"How long you been divorced?"

I counted backward in my head. "Seven years." Luc whistled, the kind you do when someone has just told you something shocking or impressive, like "Americans consume one-point-two billion pounds of potato chips each year." Something about that whistle unnerved me. Did it signify disbelief? That seven years was a long time to be divorced? That I was pathetic? Did he somehow know that I could count on one hand how many dates I'd been on in those seven years and come up a few fingers short?

"When was the last time you were on a date?"

Yes, apparently he did.

"Um…" I couldn't even venture a guess.

"Sunny's in a bit of a dating drought," said Georgie. "That's why we're here."

"Isn't there a bottle of peroxide or something you could pour on his head?" I asked.

Luc smiled. "Peroxide is so eighties. So what do you do for fun?"

Again I needed a moment to consider my options, especially since the first thing that came to mind was an image of me in the Whitford's stockroom, and although

I liked my job, I wouldn't call it fun. "I watch movies, I read a lot. And I write too. Or at least I used to."

"What do you write?"

"Novels."

"That's cool. Have you published any?"

"Not really," I replied, feeling foolish.

"Sunny is a great writer," said Theo. "She'll be published by the year's end, mark my words."

This time Theo received the wrath of my glare, although how intimidating could it be when I had enough foil on my head to get better reception on someone's radio?

"Don't give me that look," said Theo. "Hello, Forty for Forty?"

Damn my friends.

"What are they about?" asked Luc, seeming to ignore Theo.

"They're mysteries," I said, "all set on Long Island. One for each decade, starting with the fifties."

"I can dig that. I'm not much of a reader, but I'd probably read something like a mystery if it wasn't all Sherlock Holmes and Agatha Christie and that old stuff."

"That old stuff is so good, though," I protested. "But mine are more modern with a commercial appeal."

It had been so long since I'd talked about my novels that I felt tears coming to my eyes; I missed them.

After the second process of color application, Luc escorted me to a row of hair dryers, where I sat on the cushioned chair as he lowered the dome over me like the Cone of Silence, adjusted the setting and timer, and left again, only to return moments later with a delicate china plate containing a blueberry scone and a matching cup of espresso for me. Nice. Theo and Georgie thumbed through hairstyle books, occasionally turning a page toward me and pointing to a model, as if they were reading a picture book to me, and dog-ear-flapping pages of cuts they deemed appropriate.

The shampoo was a welcome change following the drone of the dryer, which felt more like being in a sensory deprivation tank. A young assistant dressed in black and wearing an apron washed out the color with a tea-tree-extract shampoo followed by a peppermint conditioner that actually gave me chills, it was so invigorating, and a scalp massage that nearly prompted me to ask her out for dinner afterward. She then directed me back to Luc, who double-checked his color work and complimented himself several times. He then went to work on the haircut, his scissors as fine a tool as a sculptor's chisel or a chef's knife. He continued to ask more questions, and I couldn't seem to get beyond a two-word answer.

"Sorry," I finally said.

"For what?"

"It's not a very interesting life."

"I'm not the one you should be apologizing to, gorgeous."

The hollow crater that my life had become was widening, as if I were seeing it on a screen, and the camera was zooming farther out to show what it really looked like. The giddy anticipation I'd taken with me on the train last night and awakened with this morning had washed down the drain along with the shampoo.

Luc spun the chair around so that I couldn't see my reflection and began to blow-dry and style my hair. After some last-minute touches—smoothing out pieces with a texturizing product, checking for evenness, a random snip here and there—my friends' eyes went wide and their mouths opened in surprise and admiration.

"You. Look. *Hot,* Sunny," said Georgie.

"Doesn't she, though?" said Luc.

"You really do," added Theo. "You look ten years younger too."

Luc beamed proudly. But for some reason I couldn't bring myself to accept it as anything more than them fulfilling their obligation as my friends to buck me up. After all, one little haircut wasn't going to change the facts that Luc had put front and center: that I was divorced, alone, unpublished, dead-ended, and forty.

Luc turned out to be not only my hairstylist but also my makeup artist. He complimented me on my bone structure (he'd complimented Theo on her bone structure too, so I was hoping for something more original—like nice lips or something) and recommended I try a mix of earthy and neutral colors. He worked in silence this time, applying hues of plums and maples and golds, each brushstroke and pencil line against my skin feeling delicate and soft.

When he was finished, he spun the chair back around, and I met my reflection.

Wow.

Holy shit.

My hair had been transformed from a dull, gray-ash brown to a warm, caramel hue with shimmery highlights. He'd taken off four inches ("Good-bye, ponytail," he said with enthusiasm) and shaped my tresses into a layered pixie with long bangs and wispy pieces framing my face. Between the absence of gray and the hiding of forehead frown lines, I was looking back in time at a younger, wiser version of myself. Moreover, the precision of each line and shade and highlight and contour was such that you noticed my features, not the makeup. My cheekbones were visible, accentuated with just a touch of bronze in the blush. My eyes looked stunning, awake, and radiant. My nose looked almost dainty, as shapely as noses can be. My lips looked round and full and inviting.

I hadn't looked this good on my wedding day.

"You weren't kidding when you said you were the Miracle Worker." I rose from the chair and hugged him after I finished gawking at myself in the mirror. Somehow my reflection managed to make me forget every bad feeling I'd had only moments ago.

"Thanks, beautiful. You made it easy," he said.

I turned to Georgie and Theo and struck a pose. "What do you think?"

"I think you need a photo shoot in Central Park," said Georgie.

"Excellent idea," said Luc.

I walked out of the salon with chic bags of shampoo and conditioner, texturizer, two tubes of lipstick, and a makeup primer, totaling somewhere around $250.

We went clothes and shoe shopping next, grabbing hot pretzels along the way. Georgie and Theo could've easily quit their jobs and opened a personal shopper business in Manhattan. They handed me garment after garment in the fitting room, threatening to steal my original clothes, leave me in the fitting room, and not come back if I peeked at a price tag. They also made me try on every pair of Jimmy Choos, but I just couldn't justify the price. I did, however, splurge on a pair of taupe, butter-soft suede Nine West boots, versatile and sexy and comfortable all at the same time, and a pair of purple, faux-alligator-skin, three-inch pumps on clearance. I could start saving money after my birthday festivities, I decided.

By the time we returned to the hotel to change and freshen up, my wardrobe had increased by a pair of designer jeans, a "date dress," a low-cut blouse with a floral print, a flowing cashmere cardigan, a Nine West handbag to go with the shoes, matching costume turquoise earrings and necklace, and the sexiest bra and boy shorts I had ever seen. Good God, I was going to be paying off this credit card bill until my fiftieth birthday.

"You *have* to wear them to the premiere tonight," said Theo in regard to the lingerie. "Trust me—everyone is going to take one look at you and know you are going to get laid tonight without even knowing why."

I laughed. "That is ridiculous, Theo! It's also a lot of pressure."

"And this is why you're still single."

Thing is, she wasn't exactly wrong—I mean, once the entire outfit was put together, underwear and accessories included, I couldn't help but feel sexy. And yet I also couldn't help but feel as if I'd lost all my armor, as if I were about to go out wearing the bra and boy shorts and nothing else.

And to think the day wasn't even close to over yet.

We ate at the hotel's restaurant around four o'clock, but by then I was so excited I could barely pick at anything more than a salad. We speculated on what each star would be wearing, strategized where to sit, and formulated plans in case we were separated at any time. Afterward we walked to the Directors Guild Theater at least an hour early in order to ensure that we had good seats. To our surprise, hardly anyone else had had the same idea (we'd figured the place would be swarming with Shane Sands fans, all obnoxious teenagers); it seemed that the theater had had the same anticipation and set up a velvet rope barrier that extended a quarter of the way down the block. The main entrance doors were locked.

Not even twenty minutes into the wait, I turned to Georgie and Theo.

"I need a bathroom."

"You went before we left," said Theo.

"I know, but the wait is making me nervous."

"Fine," said Georgie. "Text us if you get lost."

I turned to Theo. "You coming?"

She shook her head.

It wasn't too cold outside, but I shoved my hands into my pockets and hunched my shoulders nonetheless. I marched in my new boots down the sidewalk in quick strides (you can't help but feel as if you're constantly in a rush in Manhattan, even when you're not) and turned the corner. A man stood a couple of feet away in front of a door, taking a drag from a cigarette. The glare of the sun caused me to squint. At the split second that I crossed his path, a flash of recognition registered. I took in a breath, only to catch the smoke he'd just exhaled, and I spit it out in coughs.

And there he was. Danny Masters.

Danny Masters

H AD IT BEEN HAPPENING TO ONE OF HIS characters, he would've scripted it as a comedy of errors.

His flight had been delayed for mechanical problems and was turbulent.

He barely made it to *The Daily Show* in time, which left Dez, who was traveling with him, to take his luggage to the Plaza Hotel for him.

The next morning, thanks to a scheduling snafu, he had to cancel his appearance on the *Today* show in order to appear on *Good Morning America*, and poor Dez got an earful from some producer's assistant.

His satellite feed for *Ellen* got bumped from first to second slot.

Between all that he had back-to-back interview spots on radio shows (one on which a caller blasted him for his assertion that fan fiction was intellectual property theft and written by hacks), entertainment TV show spots, photo op after photo op with the cast and Paul Wolf, and two bites of a Big Mac that nearly made him hurl before he finally made it to the Directors Guild Theater. (Dez was late bringing a change of shirt and tie and his shaving kit.)

He desperately wanted a moment to himself. And he wanted—no, *needed*—a cigarette.

Finally he turned to Paul and the event coordinators frantically shuffling around him.

"Guys, if I don't have a smoke in the next ten seconds, I'm gonna have to go shopping for a gun."

A stagehand pointed him to a backstage exit that put him on Fifty-Sixth Street. He stepped outside, pulled a Camel from a half-empty pack tucked in the inner pocket of his sport jacket, and lit up. The weather was mild for October, yet the air was still crisp and breezy, and he pulled his jacket closed by grabbing the lapels and folding his arms as he flicked ashes onto the sidewalk. The sun seemed poised for setting, as if waiting for some director to call, "Action," although it was still bright enough to wish he was wearing shades.

He took a long drag from the cigarette and felt the absence of a drink in his hand. Funny that after fifteen years of sobriety, the physical ritual still left a nagging impression on him—the way he balanced the cigarette between his fingers in the same hand that held a thick, sturdy scotch glass or a bottle of beer. He loved that pose, actually. To him, that little bit of body language was the essence of cool. It made him feel five inches taller, ten times better looking, and fifty times more like a rock star.

The absence of it, however, only reminded him what he really was: a recovering alcoholic writer. Not that that was a bad thing. Just…ordinary. And sobering.

He'd taken another long drag and exhaled just as a woman turned the corner and walked right into the line of smoke. She halted her hurried pace and coughed.

He took her in, head to toe, in one fleeting look. And she took his breath away in an instant, without warning or reason.

"So sorry about that," said Danny.

"Oh, that's OK," she said as her eyes registered recognition of him. It caught her off guard, he could tell. Her eyes widened a little and she tried to harness a smile. "I was, um…I'm just looking for a restroom."

She was perhaps an inch or two shorter than he, her hair the color of light-brown sugar, with highlights. Her skin—soft and smooth, polished like a gemstone—was slightly olive-toned. Her eyes were round, irises the color of azure, lashes long and thick and dark. She seemed youthful despite the hint of crow's feet, but tired underneath what had to be a professional makeup job. He'd seen enough photo shoots to recognize one. Or perhaps she was a makeup artist by trade.

Nevertheless, she had appeared, just like that.

Danny dropped the half-smoked cigarette and stamped it out with his foot.

"That's the back door to the theater," he said, pointing to the entrance behind him. "Do you want to see if I can let you in?"

"Oh. No, thanks. I'm sure there's one at the deli down the street or something." Her voice sounded slightly raspy.

He extended his hand. "I'm Danny."

"Yes, hi," she said shyly, hesitating before taking his hand. "Sorry, I've just gotten over a cold. I wouldn't want to pass it on to you."

"That's OK," he said, taking her hand anyway and shaking lightly as his heart pounded. Something made him want to keep holding it. It was recently manicured, but the skin on her fingertips was dry, and this time he guessed she performed some kind of manual labor for a living, perhaps as a cook.

She seemed to let go with just as much reluctance as he, despite her concern about being contagious. "I'm here for the premiere tonight," she said.

He grinned and turned slightly to avoid the beam of falling sunlight bouncing off the skyscraper across the street. "That's great. I hope you like it."

"I'm sure I will." She looked at the flattened cigarette butt on the ground. "I didn't know you still smoked," she said, and before he could respond, she followed with, "That was rude. I'm sorry."

Danny was amused rather than offended. "Not at all," he said. "I'm down to just one or two a day, usually in stressful situations," he lied.

"Have you had a stressful day?"

He looked at his watch. "This is the first break I've had all day. I flew in from LA yesterday and haven't had a moment to myself since."

"Me neither, come to think of it. My friends and I came in yesterday, and we've been practically glued at the hip until now."

"From where?"

"Excuse me?"

"Where are you from?"

"Oh. Long Island," she said, slapping her palm to the side of her head, as if to knock some sense into it. The gesture delighted him.

"Of course," he said. "Long Islander. Should've recognized you were a compatriot by your accent." He looked at the cigarette butt on the ground for a second before fixing his gaze back to her, trying to think of something to say to keep her there just a little bit longer. "You smoke?" he asked. *What a fucking stupid question.*

"Me? No."

He studied her features, mentally tracing each contour as if trying to memorize them, resisting the urge to invite her for a cup of coffee, blow off the film premiere and the Q&A and go somewhere and talk for hours. He pulled his jacket closed and leaned forward.

"What's your name?" he asked.

For a split second, she wore a bemused expression; then, just as she opened her mouth, a guy in a black leather jacket and black pants approached them from the opposite direction, talking loudly on his phone in a heavy Brooklyn accent, and stopped when he saw Danny, barely pausing for breath.

"Holy shit, Joey. Danny Fuckin' Masters is standin' right in front of me. You know who that is? Hey Danny, *Glengarry Glen Ross* is my favorite movie."

"Thanks, I didn't write that one," said Danny.

"No? Well, you shoulda."

At that moment, Danny and the woman exchanged complicit glances before he turned back to the goon.

"I couldn't agree more," he said, unable to contain the smile cajoled not by him, but her.

"Anyway, I only know who you are 'cause of Charlene Dumont. Hey Danny, you're bangin' my girl, know what I'm sayin'?" said the goon, making a lewd motion with his fist and laughing. Meanwhile Danny mourned the prematurely crushed cigarette.

"Well, there's a Gershwin song for you."

Danny's attention shot back to the woman, who'd uttered the crack barely loud enough for him to hear it, and he burst out laughing. She put her hand to her mouth and stifled a giggle of her own when she realized he'd heard her.

"I'm tellin' ya," the goon continued obliviously, "she is smokin' hot."

"Yes, she is," Danny said, deadpan, his eyes locked into a gaze with the woman's. *Dammit, what is her name...*

"Hold on, Joey. Hey Danny, let me get a pic wit-chuh. I ain't never gotten my picktch taken with no director before. Here, sweetheart," said the goon, practically tossing his phone to the woman, his buddy Joey still presumably on the line, "take a picktch."

The woman flinched and caught the phone. Danny begrudgingly let the elusive Joey's friend lean in and extend his arm around him in one fell swoop. He looked at her behind the phone, yearning to pose with her instead, wondering if he should make the request to do so.

"I think I got it," she said.

"Thanks. Now, if you'll excuse me, my break's over, and I gotta get back inside," he said to the goon.

But before Danny could ask her to stay for just one more minute, the goon said, "Wait, we gotta do it again. You weren't lookin' right."

Just as he did so, the woman said, "It was nice to meet you," and she hurried away.

"Hang on," Danny called out, but she'd already turned the corner. He wanted to follow her, but just as the goon extended the phone out for another picture of them, the door opened and Paul Wolf called to Danny.

"We need you," he said.

"OK," he said to Paul. And then, to the goon, "Thanks, but I really gotta go now." He was impatient, even irked, as he opened the door and ducked back into the theater, hearing the goon shouting, "Hey, you ain't fuckin' Al Pacino, ya know. Show some respect. Can you believe this guy, Joey?"

Danny pushed his hair back, rubbed his eyes, and exhaled a deep, forceful breath as Paul greeted him backstage a second time. "That was a quick smoke."

Danny seemed surprised. "Was it?" He checked his watch to find that not more than five minutes had passed.

"Yeah, you OK? Doesn't look like it helped much."

As Paul said the words, Danny felt the pang in his lungs for more nicotine. Wistfully he looked back at the door and wished to be on the other side of it.

"No," he said. "It didn't."

CHAPTER
SIX

Sunny Smith

"**Y**OU *WHAT?*" SAID GEORGIE AND THEO IN unison when I returned to the line, which had sprouted like a beanstalk in the short time I'd left it.

"Shhh," I said. "I don't want the world to know."

"Seriously? He was just standing there, taking a smoke break," Georgie said more like a statement than a question.

"I didn't know he still smoked," said Theo.

"What did he say to you?" asked Georgie.

"I honestly don't remember," I replied. That wasn't entirely true; I remembered being startled to see him standing there, a previously two-dimensional image come to life. I remembered him not shaking my hand so much as *holding* it, his hand warm, not too big or overpowering. I remembered him asking me what my name was and my mind going blank. I remembered the way he looked at me, right when the Tony Soprano wannabe said "smokin' hot." I remembered his eyes: red, weary, trying to avoid the sun. I remembered feeling like we'd just exchanged a key to each other's hearts, unlocking them for mere seconds and getting a sneak peek. I saw loneliness in those mere seconds. I saw wanting. I saw a friend and—what was the word he used?—a *compatriot*, someone who came from the same place as me.

OK, so I remembered plenty.

"It was, like, two minutes ago!" said Georgie, exasperated.

"It happened pretty fast."

"What did you say to him?" asked Theo.

I'd always imagined what I would actually say if or when I finally came face to face with Danny Masters: *You're my favorite writer of all time? I studied your writing style the way art students study the Impressionists? Hey, I'm divorced too?*

I mean, what could anyone possibly say to Danny Masters that he hadn't already heard?

"Something really stupid about him smoking," I replied, mentally kicking myself. Come to think of it, pretty much everything I said warranted a mental ass-kicking with a steel shoe.

"That's it?" asked Georgie.

"Some guy came over and monopolized the conversation, so I left."

Georgie's mouth dropped open. "Are you *crazy?*" he practically shouted.

"Clearly I had nothing of value to say." Another lie. I wanted to tell him *everything* at that moment, wanted to tell him my whole life story and ask him about his, wanted to share my deepest secrets. But every time I opened my mouth, it all went into hiding. I had grown up having never been at a loss for words. Not until Teddy humiliated me and I'd lost the ability to speak up for myself. Even my writing had become stunted since then, for I had become an unreliable narrator. Having gotten married with the wool pulled over my eyes, and having spent the last ten years of my life shut away in a stockroom, how could I trust that what I'd seen and felt at that moment with Danny was real?

Besides, if I told Georgie that Danny Masters had asked me for my name and I'd not given it to him because of a momentary spaz-out, he very well might have disowned me.

"Um, hel-lo? Your name? Marital status? Phone number? E-mail address?"

"Then he would've thought I was some creepy stalker fan. Look, I was nothing more than a passerby during a smoke break, that's all," I said, rationalizing this for me more than for my friends. "I'm sure that if he had to describe me to a sketch artist, he'd have no clue."

"Given the way you look?" said Georgie. "I highly doubt it."

"I'm siding with Georgie on this one," said Theo. "You look so smokin' right now. There's no way any guy wouldn't notice you."

The compliment made me uncomfortable. The last thing I'd wanted was to be noticed. And once I washed all that makeup off and took off the fancy clothes, what would be left to see? What was underneath?

"What did he look like?" asked Georgie.

"He looked..."

We couldn't have been standing on that sidewalk for more than a few minutes. However, I had recorded every detail as if I'd studied him in a museum for an hour. He looked shorter in person (such a clichéd thing to say), just a few inches taller than me, which I liked. (Teddy was over six feet tall, and I'd had to strain my neck to kiss him.) He was wearing his hair longer than usual these days, and I suspected it was because he'd been too busy to have it cut rather than setting some fashion precedent. Not a trace of gray (although for some reason I had never previously considered that Danny Masters colored his hair, but when living in a youth-obsessed town, not coloring his hair would be unusual behavior, I guessed). But Danny Masters would look good with gray hair. He looked handsome, but rugged and rumpled, like the stereotypical writer, wearing jeans and Doc Martens and a wrinkled button-down shirt with mismatched sports jacket, and five o'clock shadow.

And yet that's not what I saw when I recalled those few minutes with him. He'd mentioned the hectic day, not having had a moment to himself, smoking under stress, and suddenly I realized that I hadn't just met a celebrity, despite the media and society telling me that's what he was. He was someone else—someone much more familiar to me, yet invisible to the world.

"Tired," I replied.

"God, Sunny, I can't believe it," said Theo. "You just met Danny Masters."

"Who met Danny Masters?" said someone in the line.

"She did," said Georgie and Theo in stereo, pointing to me. I wanted to bop their heads together like the Three Stooges.

"When?"

"Just now, around the corner."

Three people left the line to go look for him, and I found myself calling after them, trying to explain that it wasn't like he was just hanging out around the corner, waiting to be seen. They returned just as quickly and reported back. "He wasn't there. Are you sure it was him?" As if I'd made it up.

The theater doors finally opened around five forty-five and we entered, handing over our tickets and making a beeline for the front rows. It would be awkward to view the film when sitting so close to the screen, but Georgie and Theo both wanted a glimpse of Shane Sands and insisted that I be in viewing range of Danny Masters, in case he noticed me.

"Right. 'Cause he's gonna stop in midsentence, point to me, and say, 'Dude, I know that girl.'"

If only!

"Stranger things have happened," said Georgie.

We wound up smack in the middle of the second row, so close that someone onstage would be able to get a whiff of Georgie's cologne or be distracted by Theo's salmon-pink cashmere scarf. I caught myself leaning forward and craning my neck in the direction of the side exit, trying to get a glimpse of anyone who might be lurking there, watching the audience amble in, chattering and texting and taking pictures with their smartphones. I knew who I was looking for, hoping to see, but no one was there.

Finally the moderator, a film professor at NYU, took the stage and introduced the film and its stars—Shane Sands, Sharon Blake, director Paul Wolf, and, of course, screenwriter Danny Masters, who had changed into a new shirt (albeit just as wrinkled) and sports jacket. The five o'clock shadow was gone. They all waved to the audience, and I desperately tried to telepathically get his attention. Georgie, as if he had picked up on my brain waves, took matters into his own hands by putting his fingers between his lips and letting out a whistle that nearly blew out my eardrum. I elbowed him in the arm and he yelped. "Ow! You made me bite my finger."

"You made me go deaf," I retorted.

Worse still, it didn't seem to have worked.

The stars left the stage, the lights dimmed, drawing shushes from the audience, and for the next two-and-a-half hours I was swept away into Danny Masters's world, where I was happy to be.

CHAPTER
SEVEN
Danny Masters

DANNY MASTERS LOVED THE SOUND OF applause. Long ago, when he was a child, he had played the wizard in his school production of *The Wizard of Oz*—the perfect part for him, as it turned out, because he was the only one who didn't have to sing. If only he'd had some kind of musical ability. He would have become a rock star, a guy with tight pants and long hair and a guitar, with women hiding under the bed in his hotel room, flinging their underwear onstage, wanting a piece of him.

But short guys from Long Island, with the exception of Billy Joel, didn't become rock stars. In particular, short, half-Jewish guys weren't guitar virtuosos, had no intonation, and ran the music industry from the other side of the recording studio. At least that's what Danny's father had told him when he asked his father to buy him an instrument—any instrument—for his eleventh birthday. More specifically, any instrument that could get him girls.

But when he stood on that elementary school stage, wearing a grown-up's sports jacket and a shiny black top hat, Danny had looked out at the crowd and seen a mosaic of faces of parents and aunts and uncles and teachers looking back at him, all smiling, their eyes reflecting pride and satisfaction and accomplishment. The vibrations of applause and cheers had entered his ears and circulated throughout his entire body, pulsing like a heartbeat. It was as if each clap chanted a message: *You matter.*

Oh, yes. He needed this. He was going to need this elixir for the rest of his life. It was the only way he could escape the abyss of obscurity in which he lived.

As it turned out, he had no more acting ability than he had musical ability, something that had become clear as he got into high school and was relegated to the stage crew rather than callbacks. Not that that was so bad—he was happy to be a team player, and he loved his theater friends ("show geeks," they were called by the jocks and cheerleaders). And he was at least able to savor the applause knowing that somehow he had been a part of the thing that had compelled it.

By the time he got to high school and took a creative writing class in lieu of art (his drawing was even worse than his singing), Danny's teacher saw the flair he had for dialogue, and she insisted he try his hand at writing a play.

So he did.

Using the Shakespeare plays in his English textbook as a guide for formatting, Danny wrote a one-hour, three-act play about a debate between two presidential candidates from opposing parties who just so happened to be father and son. He showed the script to his teacher (who chaired the drama committee), who showed it to the drama committee, who then showed it to the drama club, who produced the play that semester. And when his creative writing teacher called him out to the stage, he crept out and was almost knocked over by the applause. The cast took turns patting him on the back and shoulder and tousling his hair. His mother's eyes glistened with proud tears. Even his father's absence seemed inconsequential in the cloud of the clapping, the adulation, all for his accomplishment, his words. For *him.*

Seeing his name on the cover of a program was one of the proudest moments of Danny's life. He cut out the graphic on the program (a drawing completed by one of the art students) and pasted it, along with "A Play by Daniel Gold" onto a Playbill from the Neil Simon play on Broadway he'd attended during Christmas break. He then framed and hung it on the wall beside his bed—right where he could see it—as if it were hanging in a dressing room or an office, accompanied by Tony awards and perhaps even an Oscar someday.

He wrote a two-hour, four-act play the following semester, and they produced that as well.

Acting felt like work. But writing, although also work, felt right. He later realized that he'd had this gift all along, but assumed it was a normal relationship with language that everyone possessed. Words seemed to piece together in his brain like squares of fabric on a quilt. And he could arrange them any way he wanted. Words, like musical notes, had rhythm and texture and intonation, and it was an intonation he could hear and feel. They had octaves and volumes and pitches. They had shades and colors and intensity.

And, he eventually found out, they could make women swoon.

A monologue or a speech could produce the same effect as a guitar solo if delivered correctly by the right speaker, he'd learned. Jack and Bobby Kennedy knew that. So did Martin Luther King Jr. and Laurence Olivier. And sometimes the silence was just as important, if not more, than the words. William Goldman taught him that in *Butch Cassidy and the Sundance Kid*.

By the time Danny graduated high school the drama club had performed four of his plays, including one about the Watergate break-in/Nixon cover-up that he'd written for his American Government class project, and the most popular being his contribution to the Senior Follies: a courtroom farce in which the teachers were on trial and the jury was the senior class. He had a flair for humor too, he discovered much to his delight. He'd studied the Marx Brothers and Neil Simon and Buck Henry with the same determination and focus as he studied Tennessee Williams and Arthur Miller and William Shakespeare. This same creative writing teacher (whom he publicly thanked when he got his first Emmy Award for *Winters in Hyannis*) helped him compile a portfolio and send it out to colleges with strong visual and performing arts programs. Even his father seemed proud when Danny received a scholarship to NYU. Or perhaps it was relief that he wouldn't have to foot the bill himself.

But neither attention nor applause came as frequently to the writer as it did to the performer, he'd learned. Writing was a lonely, solitary act, and although Danny eventually got used to this notion, he had never found it entirely satisfying. However, when he'd tried collaborating with other playwrights or screenwriters in college, they almost always wound up walking away exasperated by his need to control the process. And although breaking up with a writing partner was never as bad as breaking up with a girlfriend (although one time they were one and the same), he always hated himself afterward for being so difficult yet so unwilling to change.

It was surreal how taking the stage in the present moment could make Danny relive all that—the pats on the back, the tears in his mother's eyes, the satiation—except that since then the ante had been raised. The audience, men and women alike, stood and hooted and whistled and cheered. It was for all of them—him and Paul and Shane and Sharon—collectively, he knew. But it felt very, very personal. He strode toward the director's chair on the far left of the stage and hoisted himself up, picked up the minute microphone clipped to the canvas on the back of the chair, and attached it to the lapel of his sports jacket.

He scanned the crowd. The lights in the theater had gone up, so he could see the audience clearly in the first five rows or so. Despite his beginnings as an actor, he'd come to loathe public speaking and had picked up the trick of finding a fixed point on the right, left, and back walls of a room so that he could give the appearance of looking at the people without having to actually make eye contact, unless someone was asking a direct question.

He knew what he was looking for. Rather, *whom* he was looking for. Ever since the encounter outside the theater, before the goon interrupted them, he'd been thinking about her, even as he changed and shaved and groomed himself and closed his eyes, dozing off for a good twenty minutes during the film.

And then he found her.

She was sitting in the second row, in his direct line of vision. It was her eyes that caught his attention—big and round and glistening, although not with tears. And she wasn't starstruck either. He'd seen enough starstruck eyes to know the look—something between a deer caught in the headlights and a sophomore high on weed. A doped-up deer. No, she was looking at him not with adulation or adoration or even infatuation. It was something else, something he couldn't put his finger on. Whatever it was, he believed it to be genuine.

If only he'd gotten her name, goddammit. If only he could go up to her right now and ask her for it. And really, he could, couldn't he? After all, he was Danny Fucking Masters, wasn't he?

"So," Ryland Quinn, the moderator, began, "first of all, I have to say on a personal note to Danny Masters: as an NYU graduate, it's a pleasure to be sitting here onstage with one of the rock stars of the NYU alumni."

Funny that he should use those words.

More applause.

"Well, it's a pleasure to be here. And thanks to all of you for coming," Danny said, gesturing to the audience. "I'm really glad you liked the film." The audience cheered and applauded again.

"Since a film starts with a script, I thought we'd start with you, Danny. I think we all know the Valerie Plame case inspired you to write this story, although it's completely fictional, and yet it seems so real."

"Well, thank you." Forget fixed points. Danny looked straight at the girl (no, she wasn't a girl—she was a *woman*, mid-thirties, he guessed). "It's the Valerie Plame story that seems like the fiction, doesn't it," he said, to which the audience broke into laughter, followed by scattered applause.

"Yes, it certainly does," said the moderator. "So why then did you want to write this?"

"Of all the things to come out of that real case, it seemed like no one felt satisfied in terms of accountability. I mean, really, a guy named Scooter going to jail and taking one for the team, although honorable in its own way, was really more pathetic than anything else in terms of justice. The nice thing about writing is that you have absolute power."

He wrung his hands like the evil villains in spy shows, to which the audience laughed again, as did his fellow guests sitting next to him.

"I decided to create a world in which not only was the covert agent's identity exposed, but also the operations she was in charge of—some of which were not all kosher—the unscrupulous reporter's anonymous source, the source behind the source, and the top dog. I wanted this one act to bring down an entire administration. If anything, I was probably following in the footsteps of William Goldman's treatment of *All The President's Men*. Only there is no human hero or heroine here. Not to be cornball, but truth, justice, and the American way are the heroes and heroines of this story."

The audience applauded.

Ryland Quinn moved on to Paul Wolf, followed by Shane Sands and Sharon Blake, and Danny had to consciously steer his attention away from the woman (irrationally believing that she'd disappear if he did) to look at his co-panelists and nod, or laugh, or pay attention lest the conversation be turned to him again. And from the corner of his eye, he saw her seeming to try to do the same. She was sitting between a man and a woman—the friends she'd mentioned, he presumed—and occasionally whispered something to either one. The man in particular was good-looking and well-groomed, wearing a suede jacket and brightly colored pressed shirt. What if he was more than her friend?

With each question Danny was growing weary and bored, and each one directed toward him was more superficial than the last. Things got worse when the microphones were turned over to the audience: questions about specific lines or scenes devolved to comparisons to *Winters in Hyannis*, rumors about alleged tensions between Danny and actors cast in his previous work, was it true he was tapped to write a screenplay based on Bill Clinton's autobiography, etcetera. This was supposed to have been a serious event, attended by film buffs and aspiring screenwriters and readers of more than *People* magazine. Danny kept hoping the woman from the sidewalk would ask a question—any question, even a superficial one—so that he could, if nothing else, ask what her name was. But she kept her hand and head down. Suddenly this world he lived in—one with flashing lights and cheering fans, of dizzying heights of success and impossible goalposts to clear, where Charlene fit in so well and he, at best, was just hanging out with the cool kids—was meaningless to him. He wanted to be back on that sidewalk outside the theater with her, where his feet were firmly planted in the ground. He wanted no interruptions, no distractions, no expectations. He just wanted to know who she was.

"This question is for Danny."

Danny couldn't see the speaker way in the back of the theater.

"I just wanted to know if Charlene Dumont is here, waiting for you backstage, and if you two are on again," she asked.

And then he saw red: No matter how well he wrote, no matter how much critical acclaim he received or how much money he made, in the end the spotlight went to Charlene. Danny could hear the goon's voice ringing in his ear: *Hey Danny, you're bangin' my girl, know what I'm sayin'?* And behind that was the voice of his father, telling him he was nobody, a loser.

"I guess you'll just have to find out on the Internet," he replied, trying to come off as charming rather than snippy.

"Why don't *you* tell us?" she asked in a syrupy, flirtatious voice. Next to Danny, Paul covered his mic and muttered, "Oh, come on, lady." Danny looked at Paul, who seemed to be mirroring the disgust he felt, and then looked out into the direction of the voice.

"Look, my love life isn't a matter of national security. That movie you all just watched? I *wrote* it, OK? I wrote the fucking thing. I've won Tony and Emmy awards. I'm not some...*wannabe*...who does nothing but sits behind a computer screen living vicariously through other people's lives and trolls around discussion threads. I'm damn good at what I do, and I made something of my life. And while

I may not be saving the whales, I deserve a little more respect. You people need to get a life. Really."

Oh, shit.

Where did those words come from? He couldn't remember thinking them, couldn't figure out from what storage facility his brain had retrieved them, but nevertheless, they'd fallen out and settled over the audience like germs from a sneeze. Worse still, he saw the look on *her* face— she was horrified. No, *horrified* wasn't the word. She was offended. Wounded. Pissed.

And before he had a chance to retract them, the moderator brought the discussion to a close. Once again the audience applauded, although it was somewhat more muted than earlier. Polite rather than elated. The vibration was more like a distant echo, and his gut felt completely hollowed out.

Although under a close watch by security, attendees were permitted to approach Shane, Sharon, Paul, and Danny to get autographs and take photos. Despite his having spoken such harsh words, his fans approached him with enthusiasm, gratitude, and praise. Danny kept looking past each person whose hand he shook to the next one, hoping to see her, saying thank you robotically and forcing the corners of his mouth up in a smile. The lack of sleep, the craving for nicotine, the anxiety of his blunder, and the push of the crowd made him feel woozy. Just as Paul gave security a nod and grabbed Danny by the arm to pull him backstage, Danny turned and found himself face to face with *her*. He felt a jolt.

"Hi!" he exclaimed.

My God, she's beautiful, he thought. Not because of her hair and makeup and outfit. Nor was she beautiful like Charlene—Charlene looked as if she'd been sculpted from marble. No, underneath the makeup a softness shone about her, the epitome of what used to be known as the "Ivory Girl" look from the seventies soap commercial.

Danny looked at her with such intent to know her, and it strangely felt like home.

He took her hand and was about to ask for her name, but before he made a sound, she spoke first.

"Mr. Masters, I have been proudly working at a bookstore for twenty years. I've also written four novels. And although I have never been published, I am no *wannabe.* You, sir, are a jackass and a failure."

She then let go of Danny's hand, turned and walked away.

A camera flash went off.

He blinked several times. Paul then pulled his arm away from the lingering fans and took him backstage.

CHAPTER
EIGHT
Sunny Smith

How could I have been so stupid? *HE WAS holding my hand,* for chrissakes. Not shaking it, but *holding* it, just like he did outside the theater. Or at least that was how it felt in that moment, right before I lost my sanity.

"I can-not be-lieve you," said Georgie to me as we stepped out of the theater and into an entirely different Manhattan, the one that glowed and sparkled and vibrated in the dark, and the car horns and chatter were more like music than noise pollution. If only I could enjoy it. "You called your favorite writer a *jackass.*"

"I can't believe *him,*" said Theo, trying to keep up with our hurried pace. "Insulting his audience like that."

"He didn't mean *her* specifically," said Georgie to Theo, turning his thumb to me. And then, to me, he asked, "Why'd you take it so personally?"

"Because he did mean me. He meant you too. He meant people like us who have worked a job their whole lives with crappy hours and menial pay, who didn't go on to graduate school or be something lofty like a hotshot lawyer or president of the United States. He meant people who weren't fortunate enough to get the breaks he did."

"He meant people who have nine cats and watch TMZ until their eyes glaze over and play Angry Birds for eight hours while they're at work," argued Georgie. "He meant people who watch *Winters in Hyannis* thirty-five million times to the point of knowing whether the coffee cups are really filled."

"I can recite whole episodes," I pointed out.

"You're different, Sunny," said Theo. "You're a writer studying the craft and style of another writer."

"Nice try."

"Fine," said Georgie, disingenuously acquiescing. "He meant *you*. Did you have to call him a jackass, though?"

"And a failure," added Theo.

"He's lucky I didn't call him an asshole," I said.

"No, *you're* lucky you didn't call him an asshole," said Georgie.

"Why?" I asked.

"Because hopefully you can still salvage this."

We stopped at the street corner, and I looked at Georgie incredulously. "What makes you think there's anything to salvage? What makes you think he gives a shit about what some loser stockroom manager says to him?"

"And what makes you think she's ever going to see him again?" said Theo.

"I'm just saying," said Georgie as we crossed the street, seemingly pushed along by the crowd, "that he obviously put his foot in his mouth. It was that airhead who asked the Charlene Dumont question. You could tell it pissed him off. He was directing it at *her*."

"So does that make me an airhead too?" I said.

Georgie put his hands up and made a noise of exasperation. "Will you just forget that? It's not what he meant, and you know it."

"For a so-called brilliant writer, he sure exhibited a poor choice of words," said Theo.

We wound up at the Carnegie Deli, split a slice of cheesecake the size of one of my new boots, and said very little. I could barely swallow the first bite, my insides were so tightly bound in knots.

"So what'd you think of the movie?" Theo piped up.

It suddenly occurred to me that we'd spent the entire walk talking about the drama after the film rather than the film itself.

I sighed. "It was terrific, of course. The writing was terrific. The cast was terrific. The directing was terrific. Everything about it was terrific."

For the first time ever, it pained me to feel such awe for Danny Masters's writing. It pained me to offer him praise, when I felt as if he'd just physically slapped me in the face.

"I swear he was looking right at you during the entire Q and A," said Georgie to me.

"How would you know?" said Theo. "You were gawking at Shane Sands the whole time."

"I pay attention, Miss Theodora," he said, pointing at her with his fork.

"He was not looking right at me," I said, although secretly I had been preoccupied throughout most of the Q&A with that very observation. "It just seemed that way. He was looking at someone else—the woman sitting in front of us, for instance—or perhaps someone else a few rows back. Maybe he had family there or something. Whoever it was, it wasn't me."

"And why wouldn't he be looking at you?" asked Georgie.

"I'm sure there are far more interesting people to look at than me."

Georgie sat up straight. "Oh. My. God," he said, raising his voice and drawing looks from the other patrons packed into the tables crammed together. He self-consciously slouched in his chair and lowered his voice. "Sunrise, have you looked in a mirror at all today? You are *fucking gorgeous*," he said, enunciating both words with a beat between them. "Between the hair and the makeup and the outfit and the shoes…hell, get me drunk and *I* would sleep with you tonight."

"So would I," confessed Theo, laughing.

"Doesn't matter. Stand me next to Charlene Dumont and—"

"Oh, who gives a rat's ass about Charlene Dumont?" interrupted Georgie.

"Um, I think *Danny Masters* does," I said. "And as far as my looks go, I'm sure that had it been any other day of the week and not one where I blew over six hundred clams on getting all dolled up, he wouldn't have even seen me, much less talked to me. Just blown his smoke in my face and taken another drag."

"So what did you make of his answer to the airhead?" asked Theo. "I mean, do you think his defensiveness is a sign that they're *not* together anymore or that they are?"

"Not," said Georgie emphatically. "Big-time N-O-T."

"I don't know," I said, feeling deflated and sucker-punched, but the person who'd sucker-punched me was me. I was envious of Charlene Dumont for having had the fortune to know Danny Masters at all. For a moment, maybe—just maybe—he really had liked me. But I'd ruined it.

"You know, this is exactly what he was talking about. Here we are sitting and eating cheesecake and speculating about his love life rather than talking about the film. I mean, there's so much substance we could talk about, from character to theme to acting to directing to writing to the subject matter itself. But no, we're talking about Danny Masters and Charlene Dumont just like every other catty gossip who's got nothing better to do."

Georgie looked at me and huffed. "Fine, Sunny. From now on, Charlene Dumont is on the banned topics list. We'll talk about politics, we'll talk about religion, we'll talk about gay marriage, and we won't talk about the envy of drag queens everywhere. Then we can all kill ourselves."

"What is it with you and your drag queen conspiracy?" asked Theo.

"I say we add Danny Masters to that list," I added, "and take him off my Forty for Forty list."

"Not a chance," said Georgie, his fork aimed at me this time. "He stays. He may have been a jackass tonight, but you'll get the last laugh."

"By sleeping with a jackass?" I said. Theo burst out laughing again, covering her mouth full of cheesecake.

"I have to side with Sunny on this," said Theo. "He's a great writer and all, but I think he's a little too high and mighty for his own good. He was talking *at* the audience tonight, not *to* them."

"That's because he'd done like a gazillion interviews in three days and has probably been asked the same five questions each time," I remarked. *Shit shit shit, stop defending him!*

"Whatever," said Theo. "Truth be told, I think you can do much better than him."

"I think so too," I lied.

I looked at Georgie, hoping he would see right through me and call me out on my lie, but he didn't.

"Put Shane Sands on the list," Theo suggested.

"No way," said Georgie, a hint of jealousy in his voice. "The list stays as it is."

"Whatever," I said, echoing Theo.

The last bite of cheesecake waited to be claimed, but none of us did. I stared at it, momentarily lost in a thought that I dared not speak. Thing is, when he'd taken my hand, it hit me at that moment: This was a guy I could date. Moreover, this was a guy with whom I could just *be.*

How awful was that? To think that of a guy I'd only met for five minutes, who lived in another universe, and then call him a *failure* to his face?

Georgie, Theo, and I took the train back to Huntington the next morning, the three of us sleeping all the way. When I got back to my apartment, I took a shower—it was a shame to lose the fabulous hairstyle. Worse still, because Luc had turned the chair away from the mirror when he was working his magic, and because I'd been so busy ogling myself afterward, I'd forgotten to ask him to show me how to style it myself. It was too short to put in a ponytail now, so I blew it dry and tried to push it all back with a hairbrush. The result was a windblown fluff. I imagined Luc looking at me, disappointed (hell, probably *insulted*), like watching someone graffiti all over your oil painting.

Having been on an Internet fast for the last forty-eight hours, I turned on my laptop and logged in first to my e-mail in-box, which was clogged with notifications from Facebook by people who tagged me in a video, its tagline "jackass."

"What the...?" I started as I clicked on the video that showed me, my face obscured, calling Danny Masters a jackass and a failure.

Oh. My. God.

My cell phone rang.

"Are you seeing what I'm seeing?" I asked Georgie without even saying hello or needing to check the caller ID.

"Where in Zeus's name did it come from?" he asked.

"How would I know? And how does everyone know it's me? You can't even see me. Hell, *I* wouldn't have known it was me."

"You have a very distinct way of saying *jackass*," said Georgie. "You put a lot of emphasis on the *jack* and then slightly linger on the *ass*, and you have that hardcore Long Island accent that separates the sound of *jack* from the sound of *ass*."

"You're a fucking linguist now?"

"I rest my case."

"My accent is not hardcore."

"Besides, you posted your last status update from the theater, remember? And who else do they know who works at a bookstore and is a Danny Masters fan? They put two and two together."

I groaned.

My phone beeped, alerting me to Theo. I let it go to voice mail.

"Is there any way to take it down?" I asked.

"Take what down?"

"The video."

"Why?"

"What do you mean, *why?*"

"You're famous, Sunny Delight! Look how many hits it's gotten already. Just think what would happen if you came forward; you'll probably get your own reality show in a few months, and you'd better include me."

"Are you kidding me? I am not coming forward!"

"Why not?"

"Look, it's bad enough I told the man whose writing I worship—"

"Yeah, right...it's the *writing* you worship," he interrupted.

"I called him a jackass."

"And a failure," he reminded me. As if I needed reminding.

"I'm not going to take a bow for it now."

"What, you're just gonna deny it?"

"I sure as hell ain't gonna confirm it," I said. "And what's with the sudden change in you? Last night you were pissed at me for it."

"That's before I knew there was footage. Besides, now that you've got his attention—"

"Assuming he knows it's out there…"

"—the two of you can go on *Oprah* and work it out before her show goes off the air."

I huffed. "Good Lord, you are delusional, Georgie. Really. You've got to stop watching so much Bravo."

My landline rang next; the caller ID displayed my brother Tim's number. I ignored him too.

"I'll bet they're all talking about it on Masterminds," he said. Masterminds was the unofficial website for Danny Masters fans.

"What if Whitford's finds out that it was me?" I asked. "They're so cautious about their corporate image, and rightfully so."

I could almost see him rolling his eyes. "You work in the stockroom, for chrissakes—who's gonna be offended, the books?"

I sighed loudly. "I gotta go, Georgie. Talk to you later." Without waiting for him to say good-bye, I disconnected, and then called back my brother first. He picked up on the second ring.

"Hi, Sunny."

"Hey, Tim. Is this about the video?"

"What the hell, Sunny?"

"How'd you know it was me?" I asked.

"Who else says the word *jackass* like that? Hey, did you cut your hair?"

I habitually reached for my ponytail, only to grab at air. Tears suddenly brimmed in mourning for the loss. I rubbed my eyes and hung my head as I sank into the love seat in my living room. "I honestly don't know what came over me, Tim. He made this stupid remark, and for some reason I took it personally."

"Maybe you could get the video pulled down."

"I don't know who took it. Besides, making a big deal of it is precisely what makes it a big deal." I sounded like Theo.

"Anyway, I think it's cool that my sister is a celebrity now. Just think: If you'd been drunk and spit in his face, you probably would've been invited on *Jersey Shore*."

"Thanks for the support," I snapped.

"I'm totally supporting you!" he said before I hung up on him. Finally, after returning Theo's call and repeating my conversation with Georgie, I turned off my cell phone, disconnected my landline, and went back to my laptop. I logged in to Masterminds. In addition to a bio, trivia, links to news, interviews, articles, and any blog posts about him, the site also included a fan forum for all discussions Danny. I regularly participated in some of these discussions under the name "Sunnyside." There I found a rousing discussion going on about the video, as I'd both expected and feared. I scrolled down past the first few posts:

I was *there*. He called his fans wannabes, and insinuated that he was better than the rest of us. It was a stupid thing to say, but I don't think it was such a big deal that he should be called a jackass and a failure for it. I mean, he was right, in a way. The man's got how many Emmys? Not to mention that he's probably going to get the Oscar for Exposed (which was amazing, btw). Yeah, I don't think he's a failure. She was probably the failure. She was probably everything he described.

I was there, too. It was more than a stupid thing to say. It was downright rude and offensive, and he totally deserved what he got.

She's a bitch and a loser. She got offended because Danny Masters was probably right.

Any time you think you're above anyone, you're nothing but a pompous douchebag. Does Danny realize that many of his fans are bright, hardworking people? Or does he even care about us peons who paid for his Mercedes and his house and his kid's future college education?

I love his writing, but he was totally wrong to make such a comment. And maybe she was stooping to his level by calling him a jackass and a failure, but at least she didn't pander to him like the rest of us would. Admit it, half the people on this board think he walks on water and is above reproach, and he's not. He's an alcoholic. Sure, he may be sober, but it doesn't change the mentality.

She's a wannabe like the rest of us are. At least I admit it.

I worked my way back about two pages before feeling sick to my stomach. It was Teddy and the Humiliation all over again: people who didn't know a thing about me personally having something to say at my expense. However, they seemed to be just as hard on Danny, if not harder.

Just as I was about to log off, a new comment appeared:

Hi. I'm Danny Masters. You may not believe that, but it's true. Based on the conversation taking place here, you're obviously all aware of an incident that occurred during the premiere of Exposed last night. I had made a crack that disparaged folks by referring to them as wannabes, and one attendee let me know in person that she was offended by the remark.

I hope this apology travels as fast as that video clip did. I also hope you'll go see the movie if you haven't yet. I don't think one innocent misstep should discount any of the hard work the cast, crew, director, and I put into the making of this film.

Thanks for your time.

My insides fluttered and twisted in knots as I read the comment two more times. The alleged Danny Masters who posted this apology didn't seem to be the guy who'd smiled at me outside the theater, who'd looked *at* me rather than past me. Who'd held my hand rather than shaken it. Where was the apology, exactly? And to whom was he apologizing? Me? The inquirer at whom he had lashed out at? Maybe some publicist typed this. And if that was the case, then I'd let him know that it wasn't a "misstep" (and it sure as hell wasn't "innocent") or a mere faux pas that should've been said only behind closed doors. Danny Masters had done damage.

CHAPTER
NINE
Danny Masters

T HROUGHOUT THE TWENTY-PLUS YEARS HE'D lived in Los Angeles, Danny's body had never fully adjusted to Pacific Standard Time. The ringtone of his iPhone beside his bed jarred him awake—he'd flown home almost immediately after the disastrous Q&A. What's more, he'd blown off Charlene. He knew the sex probably would've made him forget about everything: the smoke break, the woman, the goon, the film, the Q&A, the foot in his mouth, the hurt in her eyes. The two word-darts she'd shot into his chest. *Jackass* he could take. He'd been called that and worse by his father, the critics, and just about every ex-girlfriend. But *failure!* Only his father had ever called him that, at least to his face. That dart contained poison, and it spread to every part of his body. Not even sex with Charlene could provide enough antidote.

He squinted at the phone's screen to read the number and touched the Talk button.

"What," he mumbled in a groggy voice.

"What the hell did you do now?" asked Jackson Dobbs, Danny's longtime publicist.

Danny groaned. "Don't tell me it's on some fucking blog already," he said, more awake now and trying to sit up in bed. He was still in his clothes from yesterday, minus the sports jacket.

"Worse," said Jackson. "It's on fucking YouTube. Not the remark you made—although I heard about that from Paul—but the bitch who called you a jackass is."

"She's not a bitch," snapped Danny. "Besides, this time it was deserved. And don't you dare spin this to make her look like the villain, you hear me?"

"Fine, fine," said Jackson. "Geezus. Anyway, it's already got something like two thousand hits."

"Overnight? Holy cow, doesn't anybody sleep? And I didn't see a phone in her hands when she made the comment."

"Looks like it was taken by someone standing behind her."

"Fucking great," muttered Danny, rubbing his eyes with his free hand. "Well, there's nothing I can do about it."

"We can trace it and get the lawyers to do a C and D on the grounds of character defamation."

Danny laughed more out of ire than humor. "We are not going to send out a cease and desist letter for what I am assuming isn't more than ten seconds of video. It's not intellectual property, it's not a sex tape, and two thousand hits is far from viral. Just let it have its day in the sun, and it'll go away."

"Fine," said Jackson.

Danny slid to the edge of the bed, put his feet on the floor, and hunched forward, rubbing his eyes again and pushing his hair back. He'd had better morning afters when he was drinking.

"You said it's on YouTube?" he asked.

"Yep."

"OK. I'll go check it out, and then I'll post an apology on Twitter." Robbie Marsh, a tweeting fiend, had persuaded Danny to jump on the Twitter bandwagon nine months ago. But Danny found Twitter to be boring and had stopped using it.

"That's probably a good way to go, although apologies sometimes seem disingenuous. And maybe Twitter's not the best place to do it."

"What, you want me to hold a press conference?" Danny said sarcastically.

"There's a lot of chatter taking place on Masterminds—"

"No."

"I think it'd be good if you posted something there," said Jackson.

"Even though I have no official affiliation with the site? Won't that mislead people?"

"Who cares? You have no official affiliation with the site."

"Yeah, but I don't want anyone thinking *I* actually hang out there."

"Look Danny, you just insulted all the fans who went to your premiere. You wanna insult the rest of 'em too?"

Danny inhaled and exhaled forcefully, as if taking a long drag from a cigarette, and God, how he could use one right now.

"Fine. I'll post something there."

"Good," said Jackson. "Now for the good news: *Exposed* is projected to break all box office records for a Danny Masters-scripted film premiere, not to mention blow away the competition for the weekend."

"That's great." He couldn't have sounded less interested.

"You've got one more Q and A to do tonight at the Palace Theatre, and then you're pretty much done with the publicity tour."

"OK, Jackson. I gotta get my ass in gear. I'll talk to you later."

"You're welcome."

"I'm sorry, man," said Danny, "it's just been a rough week with everything. I just wanna get to work on the next thing, you know?"

"Go look at the YouTube video and Masterminds first."

They exchanged good-byes, and Danny tossed the phone on the bed, went to his laptop, and typed the URL address for YouTube in the search field. On the homepage, he typed: "danny," "masters," and "jackass."

How telling.

He hit Enter, and the results took him to the frozen image of his stunned expression. He played the shaky, fuzzy video, lasting all of about twenty seconds. He watched himself smile, his head bobbing up and down, saying "thank you" repeatedly to fans' exclamations about and praise for the film. Based on their behavior, one wouldn't know that he'd offended anyone. And then he watched himself see *her*—his eyes, even on the murky video, were so revealing, the way they flickered for a split second. The way he leaned in a little bit, as if to pull her to him. Happy to see her. It was all there for the world to see. Could *she* see it? He wondered. He had so hoped he would be able to see her face, but from the angle of the camera, all he could see was most of her hair and not quite a profile. Even with the volume maxed out, he could just barely hear the words: *Mr. Masters, I have been proudly working at a bookstore for twenty years. I've also written four novels. And although I have never been published, I am no wannabe. You, sir, are a jackass and a failure.*

A wave of nausea overtook him.

He went back to the bed, picked up his phone, and dialed Jackson, who picked up on the first ring.

"You watched it?"

"Yeah," said Danny. "And it's up to five thousand hits now."

"It might go up to ten by the end of the day. And I'm sure the blogs are posting about it as we speak."

"It was a stupid remark," said Danny. "I don't even know how or why I said it or where it came from."

"Well, you'll have a chance to fix it. Go on Masterminds—trust me, that'll put it to bed."

Danny put the phone down again and returned to his laptop. He went to the Masterminds website, where a full-scale blowout was taking place. A link to the video was posted, followed by a slew of comments either defending him ("I was *there*," one fan wrote) or calling him a lot worse than a jackass. Anger replaced the hunger that had settled in the pit of his stomach. With the exception of two or three, none of these people had been there. None of them had a right to comment on things they knew nothing about. And weren't these people proving his point? Didn't they have anything better to do?

As far as he was concerned, he only owed one person an apology. And suddenly he was even more pissed off that she hadn't given him the chance to give it to her in person.

Danny hastily typed a message, proofread it for errors, and submitted it to the Masterminds forum. He then went to the bathroom, dry heaved, and practically crawled back to bed, curling himself in a fetal position. *Failure.*

Within sixty seconds of Danny's posted apology, five replies had appeared, all of them thanking him for his response, for taking the time to visit the site, for his wonderful writing, and for making their day. Sitting at the desk in his bedroom a couple of hours later, he read each reply, thinking that perhaps Jackson had been right after all. Until the next one appeared:

With all due respect, Mr. Masters, people love your writing because it contains substance, content that is provocative in thought and discourse. They're not "wannabes," they're human beings. You mentioned an apology, but nowhere in your post did the words "I'm sorry" appear. Are you apologizing for speaking your thoughts out loud or are you apologizing for saying something that was unequivocally *wrong*? Is your apology for those people or one woman who spoke out? You call your insult "an innocent misstep." It was far from it. You said it with such conviction. If you are sincere in your intentions, then you owe your fans more than an ambiguous mea culpa.

Anger swelled inside Danny as he read the comment, its author identified as "Sunnyside," condemning and criticizing him for no other reason than because she (he assumed the commenter was a "she") could so anonymously play judge and jury without consequence.

He proceeded to type:

Sunnyside, unless you live in my head, you have absolutely no right to speculate on my intentions or scrutinize my word choices. I didn't have to come here to make penance. In fact, I would've been happy just going on with my life and letting the whole thing blow over. But it's people like you who need to be appeased, who think you're entitled to an explanation from me. I am not your servant, not your property, not your public access channel. I am not a role model, not a preacher, not a politician. I am a *writer*. I owe you nothing, but now you owe *me* an apology.

There. Take that. He shouldn't have taken the bait, and he knew it. But he hit Send anyway and abandoned his laptop in search of some coffee in the kitchen. However, as if some magical rope had tethered him to his laptop, he returned to see if Sunnyside had deigned to reply. And sure enough, in addition to the now dozen or so replies, both to his original post and now this second post, was this:

For what reason do I owe you an apology? My tone was not hostile. I called you no names, and I made no assumptions. I carefully read what you wrote—read it several times, in fact—and never found a specific, direct apology. You may think I'm in no position to make assumptions, but I know for a fact that although your fan took it personally, she was also offended on behalf of the others to whom the remark was directed, whether they were in the audience or not.

Perhaps you're correct. Perhaps I don't have that right. But you went on to say: "I would've been happy just going on with my life and letting the whole thing blow over." How can one read that and not feel as if your apology was disingenuous? And what does "people like you" mean? How can you possibly know anything about me?

"Fuck!" Danny exclaimed when he finished reading, and furiously pounded his fingers on the keyboard.

Public figures have one-sided relationships. An audience not only gets to watch my shows or plays or movies, but also gets to read about me on Wikipedia, IMDb, and God knows where else, or see me on Letterman or Colbert. They occasionally get a piece of me in 140 characters or less. They're getting more words from me right here on this forum, and at no extra charge. When I meet my admirers, I don't get to ask them about their life stories, where they went for dinner last night, how many children they have, what their last project was at work, etc. Many of them don't tell me, and frankly I don't need to know. I don't appreciate the voyeuristic aspect of celebrity-ism. I don't think any one person should be or feel entitled to have access to any other person's life just because they entertain people for a living. Hell, even the president of the United States can't take a vacation with his wife and kids without the 24-hr-news vultures scrutinizing what kind of ice cream he bought and what he looks like in his swimming trunks. "People like you" referred to those who offer unsolicited advice. And while I'll concede that I don't know anything about you, I'll also charge that half of what you think you know about me is false.

He clicked Send and waited, staring at the screen, practically willing a reply from Sunnyside, when his phone rang.

"What the fuck are you doing, man?" asked Jackson. "I'm on this forum and I'm watching this train wreck in real time."

"I'm doing what you told me to do," said Danny.

"I told you to post an apology. I didn't tell you to get into a war of words with one of these nutcases."

Suddenly, inexplicably, Danny felt protective. "She's not a nutcase."

"You're making this ten times worse—you know that, don't you? You're turning a five-dollar parking ticket into a five-year sentence. What's more, if you keep replying to her and no one else, you're going to alienate the rest of your fan base. And what makes you think she's a she?"

"You're right," said Danny.

"Just delete all that shit, get off the goddamned Internet, and do something else."

"And let it just hang there?"

"Let what hang there? Seriously, Danny, are you on crack?"

Danny waited a few seconds before refreshing the web page. Nothing.

"OK," he said. "I'm done."

"Let it go, man."

Danny went downstairs with his phone and onto the patio to smoke a cigarette. He made calls to Dez, Ken Congdon, Gabby Hanson, and others who had left messages congratulating him on the opening night success of *Exposed*. Strange, that premiere suddenly felt like aeons ago. He reentered the house and made himself a BLT on rye, but couldn't swallow more than a few bites. He then called Ella, but got her voice mail. He called Frannie's house and got her voice mail as well.

His iPad sat on the kitchen counter. He used it to check Masterminds. No reply from Sunnyside.

"I gotta get outta here," Danny said to no one as he grabbed his keys from the counter and took off for a drive on the Pacific Coast Highway, blasting a playlist of classic rock music and skipping all the songs by Avalon Gone.

Ninety minutes later he returned to the house and checked Masterminds again. Still nothing.

He silenced his phone and tried to take a nap, but dammit, he couldn't escape the voice in his head—the *female* voice—demanding he return to the Masterminds page. He wanted a reply. Expected it. Once again he refreshed the page and scrolled through what had to be at least fifty replies since his post, if not more, until he found the one he was looking for:

We all have a choice in how much of our lives we want made public. The world of Facebook and forums and phones that take photographs often makes that difficult, but we can choose not to be on Facebook, not to post on a public forum, not to appear on Letterman.

I can tell you which films won the Best Screenplay Oscar for the last five years, Adapted and Original, and I can give you the names of those well-deserving scribes for at least three out of the ten. Of those three, I couldn't tell you what they look like, couldn't pick them out of a lineup, wouldn't know them if they bumped into me on the street. Ditto for my favorite TV shows, books, and songs (if they weren't written by the singer/band who recorded them). I know what Nora Ephron looks like. I know what David E. Kelley looks like. You, sir, I see everywhere. The covers of magazines. The metaphorical "Page Six" of gossip-trash rags and TV shows. Strutting down the red carpet. I know of no other screenwriter or director who goes on prime-time television, public and corporately owned radio, and the top periodicals in the country to promote his/her films (they usually leave it up to the actors to do that).

I am no more a fan of voyeurism than you are, but celebrity- ism is self-inflicted. It can be avoided to some degree. Look at Paul Newman or Robert Redford. But you can't have it both ways. You can't walk into a room saying "Look at me!" and then complain that everyone is looking at you. You can just walk into a room.

Some of your fans' stories are astounding. Some of them became historians and even politicians because they were inspired by Winters in Hyannis. Some of them became lawyers because you created characters that were blissfully in love with the law. Some of them entered schools to be writers and directors and actors and filmmakers and television producers because of a play or a film or an episode that you wrote. Some of them got sober because if you could do it, then so could they. Not everyone wants a piece of you. They just want you to say hello to them and shake their hand, and then they'll be on their way. For some, that's enough.

He read slowly, and this time, when he saw the words "You, sir," it hit him: My God, could Sunnyside be *her*? For some reason he'd believed she didn't spend her time on such forums. For some reason he saw her sitting in coffee shops on days off with a book in one hand and a latte in the other, a pair of horn-rimmed, retro fifties-style glasses perched on the tip of her nose. He pictured her poised, yet laid back, laughing easily and not taking herself too seriously. Although she had taken *this* seriously. She had taken it personally. And perhaps he was so pissed off at this commenter because she'd been right all along. Was he remorseful for having made the wannabe remark or was he remorseful for having offended *her*? Yes, it had been a stupid thing for him to say. He knew that. Yes, he was wrong. But he'd made way bigger mistakes than this, and he'd been atoning for them ever since.

There was only one person who deserved his eternal remorse, but no amount of it would ever make up for the trauma he'd inflicted upon her fifteen years ago, the night he'd quit drinking for good.

But he'd keep trying, because it was all he could do.

Or was this part of his atonement—that he'd have to apologize for *everything* for the rest of his life?

Sunnyside was *her*—every fiber of his being inexplicably knew it.

He called Robbie Marsh.

"Is there a way to get someone to contact me via the Internet without a thousand other people contacting me as well?" asked Danny.

"Excuse me?" said Robbie.

"I want someone's e-mail address, someone on a public forum, and I can't ask her for it without giving her my own or asking her to post hers publicly. So I was wondering if there was a way I could do it without actually doing it, or something."

"Why are you asking me?" asked Robbie.

"I thought you were the computer genius," said Danny.

"I have a mild Twitter addiction and I play a few online video games, but that's about it."

"A 'mild addiction' is the equivalent of 'a touch of pregnancy,'" said Danny.

"Sorry, dude," said Robbie. He paused for a beat before continuing. "Why don't you use the direct message function?"

"The what?"

"This is about the video thing and Masterminds, right? I was on it earlier."

"You know about Masterminds?" asked Danny.

"I post something there every now and then. They're mostly a cool bunch of people. Anyway, right under the username of whoever posts a comment, there's a link that says 'Message.' That means you can send a message and she'll receive a private e-mail rather than it being posted publicly. Course you have to be an official member of the site to send and receive direct messages."

Danny felt like someone had just punked him. "For fuck's sake, why didn't you tell me that before?" he yelled.

"What am I, psychic? How did I know you didn't want all that stuff on there? Although, dude, you should really delete those posts before it starts trending on Twitter. On the other hand, I think it's starting to work in your favor. Friend of mine told me the theaters are packed for *Exposed*."

"Yeah," said Danny, not listening to him. "Thanks, Robbie. I'll talk to you later." He put the phone down, set up a new e-mail account, officially subscribed to Masterminds as D. Masters, and sent a direct message to Sunnyside:

If you're the woman from the street outside the theater, the one who called me a jackass—then I want to get to know you. Not just to make amends, but because I think you're someone worth knowing. Even if you're not her, then that's OK too. And had I known I could, I would've made this all private. Not the apology, *but everything that followed. Tell me *your* story, starting with your name.*

Best, Danny.

And that was that.

For the first time in over twenty-four hours, he felt relief. And suddenly he was hungry. He was ready to go to the LA premiere, ready to deal with the press, ready to take on the world.

He only hoped she would be there when he got back.

And sure enough, when he got home and checked his e-mails, she was waiting for him: Message from Sunnyside.

Danny's heart stopped for a nanosecond before speeding up. He read her reply:

My name is Sunny. But you don't want to get to know me. I'm not who you think I am.

He stared at the words at first, seeing them more than reading them. But what did they mean?

He stood up and looked around the empty room, brushing his hair back with his hands as he did so. After turning out the light, he went to the bed, fully clothed once again, sat up and leaned against his pillow, and stared into darkness, silent.

Jackass. Failure.

Sunny Smith

"**I** CANNOT BELIEVE YOU ARE HAVING AN online argument with Danny Masters," said Theo as we bit into cheeseburgers at the pub equidistant from Whitford's and her chiropractic practice. Two days had passed since Danny had thrown down the gauntlet in a direct message, and I had responded with *You don't want to get to know me—I'm not who you think I am,* unsubscribed from Masterminds, and not returned since.

When I had first received the notification—Direct Message from Danny Masters—my heart leaped into my throat. Me—he was messaging *me*! But his invitation terrified me. What little confidence or hope I had acquired that day in the city had washed off with the makeup. Every time I looked in the mirror and saw my reflection— flawless face and runway-ready hair and trendy outfit long gone—I grew more convinced that Danny had become temporarily infatuated with someone who didn't exist, and now all he wanted was what he couldn't have. He wanted me to like him again, nothing more. And although he'd revealed his humanity for a split second in and outside the theater, it had been overshadowed by ego and arrogance, I'd decided.

Moreover, I didn't tell Theo or Georgie about the direct message. They would yell at me, tell me I'd just made a huge mistake, make me message him back and tell him I was hacked. I didn't want to hear it.

"It was just that one day," I said in reference to our online volleys. "And for all I know, I was having an argument with a guy who directs porn movies."

Theo laughed, dipped one of her fries in barbecue sauce, and popped it in her mouth. "You know what I think? I think you're afraid to admit to yourself that you really truly believe that this is the guy you are meant to be with."

"Really truly?" I asked. She ignored my mockery of her adverb indulgence and cocked her eyebrow at me. "Georgie's got you drinking the Kool-Aid now, huh," I said.

"Well, maybe Georgie's right this time. I can actually see you two together. Why can't he be the one for you? I mean, how do you know it wasn't destiny bringing the two of you together?"

"In fantasy land, maybe. Anyway, this whole thing has gotten out of hand. I'm off Masterminds for good and am going back to normal life."

"Well, isn't *that* fun," she said as she dipped another fry. "You need some excitement and adventure, Sunny. Get out into the world: go whitewater rafting, hike the Appalachian Trail, backpack across Europe—anything to get you out of that dank stockroom."

"Hey, I like my job," I said in defense.

"I mean, my God, you're *forty*!"

"You make it sound like a death sentence."

"That's a *good* thing. You're forty and single and childless."

Her pep talk was depressing me more by the second.

"So are you," I pointed out.

"Precisely. We've got no one to answer to," she said, "but at least I've got a career and I go out on dates."

"I've got a *job*, Theo."

"Which you can leave at any time."

"It's not like I've got stockpiles of money in a vault somewhere. I just about make ends meet."

"Then make a plan."

"I already have that Forty for Forty list."

"And how's it coming along?" she asked.

I shrugged. "It's only been what, a week?"

She looked at me, exasperated. "So? Pick one thing, the one you want to do the most. Like writing. You used to *love* to write. The words couldn't get on the page fast enough. And you couldn't wait to show us your novels when they were finished. What happened to that love? I can't believe it just vanished one day."

Her words conjured memories of the days when I got so lost in the worlds I'd created, when Theo and Georgie and I would sit in a triangle on the floor, legs crossed, taking turns reading the pages out loud. Even Teddy used to be so supportive. Suddenly I was filled with longing for those pages and those places. They felt like lost children to me.

I pushed my plate away, my appetite gone. "I don't know, Theo. I guess I stopped finding things to write about."

She looked at me skeptically. "So then publish the ones you've already written. What about all those independent author, e-book success stories you told me about?"

"Do you know how many e-books are listed on Amazon now?" I said, cowering at the thought. "At least a million."

"You know what your problem is? You have an excuse for everything. Stop making excuses and just do it! Write a book, take a trip, go to LA and find Danny Masters—you can do and have anything you want. You've squandered your life away, all because Teddy cheated on you and told the world about it on TV."

I looked at her with daggers in my eyes.

"Thank you for reminding me," I said, my voice cold. "And thank you for making it sound so casual."

She took my hand. "Of course it was a shitty thing. But how much longer are you going to let it victimize you? It's been way too long already. It's bad enough he cheated on you and didn't stand by you when you found out you couldn't have children. But why should you throw your life away just because Teddy was a tool?"

Tears slid down my cheeks. "I guess I've grown fond of my cage," I said quietly.

"Door's unlocked, Sunny. You can walk out any time you want."

Whoa. Somehow knowing that was even scarier than the cage itself.

After lunch and outside the pub, Theo and I hugged each other before we walked back to our respective workplaces in opposite directions. Thank goodness I had work to keep me busy. October 15 through November 15 was the stock manager's shitstorm, when double the number of pallets came in, all in preparation for Christmas. The goal wasn't so much trying to get everything out onto the floor as it was trying to figure out where to put it in the stockroom before it was scheduled to go out. Over the years I had developed a "sort-and-store" method, in which

I strategically rearranged the metal stacks in order to place the specialty shipment within easy reach.

I was already knee-deep in the process when I reentered the store and headed back to the stockroom. I passed the conference room and saw Georgie with two men: one of them was Phil Taylor, our former store manager, now in charge of the district. The other man looked unfamiliar. Georgie's face displayed a wounded, worrisome expression.

I returned to the front of the store and went behind the cash wrap, where Angela was sorting through customer holds. "What's going on in the conference room?" I asked in almost a whisper, despite there being no customers or sales associates within the vicinity.

"Georgie's under review again," she replied in the same hushed tone. "Syosset is outselling him almost by twice as much. Hell, I think even Bridgehampton is doing better than he is."

In addition to organizing and planning events in the store, Georgie's job also consisted of community outreach. That included selling books to school districts, organizing community book fairs and reading programs, and planning and organizing events that benefited not only the local community but also the Whitford's bottom line (not their passion—my ass!). Georgie hated this part of his job and did it poorly; thus, at the end of every sales quarter his head went on the chopping block, only to be spared until the next time. I had my theories about why he was never fired. For one thing, he was great when it came to booking events at the store. He managed to get A-list authors, best sellers and celebrities alike. Some events were so successful we had lines out the door and around the corner. And that was the part of his job he really loved. Georgie was great when it came to events planning—I'd often told him that he should be in public relations. And although he could schmooze with the best of them, he wasn't a salesman. At least not when it came to direct selling. If the customer came to him, he could get them to buy half the store and some of the fixtures too. But he hated going out into the community and finding schools and groups to work with him. He called that part of the job "whoring himself out" and found it to be the unfortunate trade-off to getting to meet a reality star or a celebrity chef, not to mention the health insurance that came with his salary.

"Who's the guy with Phil?" I asked.

"That's Joshua Hamilton, the new regional manager," said Angela.

"What happened to Cory?"

"She got promoted to VP of Something in corporate. It was in the newsletter."

I was surprised to have either missed or forgotten that detail, given that I devoutly read the company newsletter each month. Georgie always made fun of me, insisting I was the only one who read it at all. "I think they're keeping it going just for you," he had teased.

"Anyway, this new guy was some big shot from Borders, and now he's the interim regional manager," said Angela. "Although I guess that's not saying much considering Borders is in trouble."

"You think it's his fault?" I joked, looking toward the back of the store, as if I could see the conference room from where I was standing. Angela laughed. "What's he like?" I asked. "Nice? Mean? Wishy-washy?"

"Cute, actually," said Angela.

"Cute as in Robbie Marsh cute?"

"Older. Salt-and-pepper hair. And a slightly receding hairline. But still cute."

"Hmm," I said, and headed back toward the stockroom, checking my sweatshirt for barbecue sauce stains and finding none, when the conference room door opened and I smacked right into the new guy. A noise came out of me sounding like "Oomph!" as I looked up at him, startled. He held my arms to steady me.

"You OK?" he asked, his voice sounding full and robust, like someone who did voiceovers for a living.

I looked up at him. Definitely not Robbie Marsh cute. His hair was indeed receding, forming almost a widow's peak. His skin was very light, his face round, his eyes blue and framed by crow's feet when he smiled. He wore wire-framed glasses and was dressed in gray flannel slacks and a black dress shirt. Nice-looking, but not impossibly gorgeous. Definitely forty-something.

"Uh-huh," I said, nodding my head, trying to make myself say something more intelligent and feeling self-conscious in my usual work attire. My hair fell lifelessly around my makeup-free face. So much for the makeover.

The new guy looked at me as if I'd been dressed to the nines, however. He extended his hand. "I'm Josh," he said. "You must be Sunny, the stock manager I've heard such good things about."

I shook his hand. "Nice to meet you." His handshake was firm yet friendly. Not at all like—no, no, *no*, I was not going there…

"Hey, Sunny," said Phil. "How are things?"

"Things are good," I replied. "How 'bout with you?"

"All good. I heard you just had a birthday. The big four-oh."

I nodded. "Yep."

"Happy birthday," said Josh, who, I noticed from the corner of my eye, had not stopped smiling. Throughout my tenure at Whitford's, I'd met all types of managers, ranging from dictators to cheerleaders. Within seconds I pegged Joshua Hamilton to be a cheerleader.

"Josh is our new regional," said Phil. "I'm giving him a tour of the stores. I'd like to take him back to the stockroom, if that's OK with you—show him how Whitford's best stock manager does things."

My stomach started twisting into knots. "Oh, sure. C'mon back." I led the way, trying to get Georgie's attention as I passed by the offices adjoining the conference room, but he was already on the phone. Poor thing. He looked like he'd just been yelled at by his sixth-grade teacher for not doing his homework.

"Sorry for not giving you the heads-up," whispered Phil as we lagged behind. "Josh likes snap inspections." Maybe he was a dictator after all, I thought. I rapid-fire entered the four-digit code into the keypad and held the door to the stockroom open for them to enter. I'd swept and straightened up before I left last night, but given that I was still in the midst of the sort-and-store, no one could tell.

"Well, here's home," I said.

"That's great," said Josh to Phil, as if I wasn't standing in front of them. "She treats this place like it's home. That's the kind of attitude I like."

Total cheerleader.

"Oh, I'm a Whitford's gal all the way," I said. "I think I'm the oldest employee here. I mean, I've been working at this particular store the longest." My face started to get hot.

"Fantastic," said Josh. He looked around the stockroom, seemingly impressed. "How are you handling the craziness?"

"OK. Setting up the Trinket center was a hell I've never experienced before, but we've got a great team here."

He laughed. "I can't even imagine. What do you think of the Trinket?"

I nervously looked at Phil, who seemed to be waiting for the shoe to drop. "I think it's great. Put it on my Christmas list."

"You own a Kindle, don't you," said Josh. My face flushed again, and I was sure this time it turned the same shade as my peeling nail polish. He smiled in amusement, the way my brother Tim used to look when he teased me relentlessly. "That's OK. Me too. I own every e-reader on the market. The Trinket's good; you should get one."

"I would've bought it had it come out first."

"I believe you," he said. "So how's your staff?"

"My team? They're terrific. I trained them all myself."

"Sunny is just as great at employee training," interjected Phil. "Human Resources would love her."

"Do you have enough help?" asked Josh.

"I think so. A store of this size, I only need one associate during the regular year, two right now, but of course you already know that. I'd love to have two year-round, but I know the deal." Personnel and payroll were contingent upon hours. Hours were contingent upon volume. Volume was contingent upon business. Business was down.

"Excellent. Is there anything you need?"

I definitely had the feeling I was being tested. "You know what we could use? Some more hand trucks to bring in the shipment. Ours keep mysteriously disappearing," I said. "And those Dumpsters in the alleyways need to be better lit at night. We don't do too many nighttime garbage runs, but a lot of our neighboring stores do, and many of them are college-age girls. Although I guess that's more of a town issue."

Funny how I could speak up so easily when it came to work. I'd become an important person at Whitford's—an indispensable, go-to manager. Why had I not applied that initiative to the rest of my life, especially following my divorce? Theo was right—I was squandering my life away.

"I'll look into it." He paused for a beat. "Well, we've taken up enough of your time, Sunny. Keep up the good work. Pleasure to meet you," Josh said as he extended his hand again. I shook it, and almost laughed when he winked at me. Please. Both men turned and headed back to the floor, and I turned back to my workstation, exhaling forcefully, as if I'd been holding my breath the whole time. Suddenly I heard my name and whisked around to find Josh standing in front of me again.

"You free for dinner tonight?" he asked. "I live in New Jersey and am staying on the island overnight."

He was asking me out on a date? I was standing there in jeans with dirt stains on them, an oversized sweatshirt with a faded New York Jets logo on it, and no makeup, and he was asking me out on a date?

"I guess so," I said shyly, my stomach fluttering. "I hope you'll let me go home and change first."

"Of course. How about we meet in front of the store around seven o'clock?"

"OK."

"Great. See you then." He turned and headed for the floor again.

Holy crap. My stomach started fluttering as I tried to concentrate on my work, to no avail. I kept seeing that smile and those crow's feet behind the wire-rim glasses. *Joshua Hamilton*. I silently repeated the name. Holy shit, my new *boss* asked me out on a date! Sans makeup, sans Stella McCartney sweater, sans sexy lingerie underneath. He saw me in my natural habitat and liked me anyway.

This thing with Danny Masters—whatever it was—had to end. I was forty, for chrissakes—way too old to act like a teenage girl with pinups on her wall and pictures in her wallet and hearts doodled all over her notebook. I was too old for idols and infatuations. I needed a life. I needed a man. A *real* man, and not the dream of one. Joshua Hamilton fit the bill.

No no no—he was my *boss*!

Fifteen minutes later Georgie appeared at my workstation looking tense.

"So, did you pass inspection?" he asked.

"The new guy just asked me out on a date."

He stood frozen in place. "*What?*"

"The new guy. Josh. He just asked me out to dinner."

"And you said *yes?*"

"Of course I said yes. Why shouldn't I?"

"Never shit where you eat, Sunny. No, wait—that's not the right expression, is it? Never fuck where you work. No, that's not it either..."

"Are you telling me not to date our boss's boss's boss?"

"*Yes.*"

I frowned. "It's not like he works directly in the store."

"Doesn't this company have a policy against employees dating each other?"

"I thought that was just within the same store."

"You're playing with fire," he warned. I couldn't remember the last time I'd seen or heard him act so seriously. "This can only end up bad for you."

"My God, Georgie, it's one dinner! And maybe it's not a date. I mean, look at me—do I look datable?"

"Please. Honey. It's a date."

"I'm not going to sleep with him."

"You'd better not. In fact, don't get all dolled up. You can wear makeup, but no date skirt. In fact, no skirt at all. Dress corporate. And definitely no heels."

"Geez, why don't I wear a burka while I'm at it?"

"That would work too."

"What's wrong with you? I thought you'd be thrilled that I was going out with someone that didn't involve submitting an online profile and a photo of me holding a cat. Besides, it's on the Forty for Forty list."

"I'm thrilled with your getting back into the dating world, but not with your choice," said Georgie. "Trust me—Joshua Hamilton is a charlatan."

"And this is based on one twenty-minute meeting in which he chewed you out?"

I felt awful the second after the words came out, especially when I saw the look on his face, as if I'd just garroted him.

"Whatever, Sunny," he said as he put up a hand to block anything else I might want to say, and turned to leave the stockroom.

I grabbed his arm. "Wait a minute, Georgie. I'm sorry. That was really mean." He didn't make eye contact with me until I asked, "So what happened?"

He rolled his eyes. "Same ol', same ol'. I'm not being aggressive enough, my quotas are too low, I'm on probation... They do this every quarter, and it's a bluff every time—you know why? 'Cause I bring in the big bang when it comes to the in-store events. That's where everything evens out."

"Yeah, but the thing is, they can't afford to break even anymore."

"In this economic climate, they're lucky to have open doors. Not to mention that the Kindle is kicking everyone's e-reading ass."

"You'd better be careful, Georgie. The next time they might really fire you."

"Please," he said, rolling his eyes yet again. "Let them. I fucking hate this job."

"You say that constantly and do nothing about it. Why don't you quit once and for all?"

"You're not the only one who's idling in neutral, Sunny. But at least Marcus and I have a plan."

What kind of plan? I wanted to ask. This was the first I'd heard of it. But I was so wounded that I went on the defensive instead. "I have a plan."

"No, Sunny, you have a list." He looked at his watch. "I'd better get back to work. Mr. Wonderful and his ass-kisser are still in the building. Call me when you get back from your date tonight. And it had better be before midnight."

Georgie left the stockroom, where I stood, all alone, suddenly feeling swallowed whole by its contents.

CHAPTER

ELEVEN

Danny Masters

DESPITE THE MINOR BACKLASH FROM THE
YouTube video, *Exposed* continued to top the box
office sales and generate Oscar buzz for Danny, Paul
Wolf, and its cast.

But Danny didn't care.

After hearing from Sunny, he'd compulsively checked
his iPhone and MacBook for notifications that she had
changed her mind. Each day he logged on to Masterminds
and skimmed through the pages of discussion threads,
looking for her (the conversations had moved away from
the jackass video and ahead to reviews of *Exposed* and
complaints about why Danny hadn't bothered to personally respond to any of *their* comments). When she didn't
appear, he then spent hours reading *every* comment
and contribution Sunnyside had ever offered, trying to
get to know her that way. From what he could tell, she
was witty, yet there seemed to be a quiet honesty about
her. Unlike some of the other females on Masterminds,
she didn't comment on his appearance or his love life,
didn't quote lines from his shows and films as part of
puns and jokes. Instead she talked about the *writing*. She
pointed out intricacies of character. She quoted only to

note a turn of phrase, a rhythm of delivery. And she was a good writer.

Each day Danny metaphorically opened the door or looked out the window and found no one there.

Little by little, disappointment gave way to anger.

Who did she think she was? Who did she think he thought she was?

On impulse, he wrote and sent her another message asking just that, only to get a rejection notice: *The recipient must be a registered member of Masterminds.*

Already she'd bailed out?

He punched his fist on the desk, slammed down the screen of his MacBook, and stood up.

"Fuck her," he said.

Dez opened the door and peeked her head in. "Fuck who?"

Danny looked at her, startled. He didn't realize he'd uttered the expletive so loud.

"You and Charlene having another row?" she asked.

He shook his head. "It's nothing," he said as he stormed passed her. "I need a smoke."

Danny entered the office of Rajesh Patel, known around Hollywood as the Guru to the Stars. Author of the best-selling books known as the Chakra Series (starting with *Root Red* and ending with *White Light*), Dr. Raj did everything from chakra balancing to feng shui blueprints to guided meditation to good ol' Freudian analysis. In some cases, he even made house calls—rumor had it that Brad and Angelina had helicoptered him to an undisclosed Caribbean island so he could teach relaxation techniques to one of their children who was experiencing separation anxiety.

Normally Danny wouldn't be caught dead going to someone who practiced what he described as "crackpot psychology," but Raj was so damn likable. They'd met in the hall outside a parent-teacher conference at Ella's school (Raj's son was a student there, although Raj had since withdrawn him in favor of home schooling) and the two surprisingly hit it off. When Raj had suggested that Danny visit him for a complimentary chakra-balancing session, Danny heard himself saying yes—and not even the "let's do lunch" sort of yes. And when he accused Raj of having secret powers of hypnosis or sending subliminal messages, Raj laughed out loud and said, "How did you know about my secret powers? I'm thinking of having a superhero created in my image."

"You know I think you're a total quack and a brilliant capitalist," Danny had said to Raj at their first meeting.

"That's OK," said Raj. "I have no ego."

Yes. Danny liked him. And Raj liked Danny too.

Raj's office was a magnificent sanctuary of fountains, wind chimes, candles, and exotic plants—something for each of the feng shui elements—encased by loft-style, floor-to-ceiling windows overlooking Los Angeles (he had a similar setup in Manhattan). Fluffy velvet and silk throw pillows of all sizes were strewn about ("What is this, a harem?" Danny had asked the first time he saw it), with butter-smooth Italian leather couches and chairs condu-cive to falling asleep, which Danny had done on more than one occasion. And although Raj insisted a nap was as good as any therapy, Danny would complain that if a nap was going to cost him eight hundred dollars an hour, then he might as well get a hooker to join him.

Raj embraced his friend, followed by placing his hands together in front of his chest and bowing to him. "*Namaste*, Daniel. So good to see you today." It'd been a lifetime since anyone but his mother and his teachers had called him Daniel. The name felt unfamiliar to him, but Raj said it with such ease and fondness.

Danny returned the bow. "Good to see you too." He sat at the edge of one of the couches and kicked off his shoes, something Raj had encouraged on his first visit. "How the hell are you?"

"I'm doing very well. And how are you?" asked Raj, whose accent was more Californian than Indian, although he spoke slowly, almost like Mr. Rogers used to, and politely, hardly ever using profanity.

Danny shook his head in tired exasperation. "It's been a helluva week, man."

"I saw your film. It was well written and well executed."

"Thanks," said Danny. "I'm glad you liked it."

"So tell me about your helluva week."

Danny paused, trying to find a good starting place. "Well, of course it's been interview after interview after interview. Advanced screenings at film festivals in various parts of the country, critics' and corporate screenings, premieres at opposite ends of the country, the works. I've hardly seen my daughter at all this past month, and I miss her like crazy."

"And how is the beautiful Ella?"

Danny appreciated the adjective but frowned when giving the answer. "Dating a drummer." He pressed on without giving Raj a chance to inquire further. "I had an interesting encounter at the premiere in New York City that turned into a bit of a fiasco."

"What happened?" Raj's facial expression was more one of amusement than inquisition; it was the face he wore for just about any topic of discussion.

"It started when I met this woman."

"I doubt that, but continue."

"Now you see, when you say things like that, it's impossible for me to continue because I want to know where it did start."

"We'll get to that. Please continue."

Danny obeyed. "I was at the Directors Guild Theater on the afternoon of the premiere and stepped out for a smoke break, and there she appeared. I can't even begin to describe her—I want to say *ordinary*, but that makes her sound plain, and she was anything but. I don't know, maybe *real* is the right word? Even though I could tell she'd gotten made up for the occasion. But I mean, she's nothing like Charlene."

"Charlene's not real?"

Man, was *that* a loaded question.

"Funny, I'm wondering how Charlene would respond to that question if you asked *her*. Charlene's become a product of her environment. She's a brand. And I think some days she has trouble distinguishing the person from the brand. Hell, some days *I* have trouble distinguishing the person from the brand."

"Are *you* a brand, Daniel?"

He let the weight of the words sink in for a moment. "Of course I'm a brand. I became a brand the minute I let them change my name."

Danny Masters had always hated his last name. Still, after all these years. He hated how cornball it was, how it made him sound more like a weatherman for Fox News than an award-winning writer for television, film, and stage. But fresh out of college, following the overnight success of his first play, he'd been billed as a phenom at age twenty-two and he'd landed an agent who'd started introducing him around Hollywood as "The Master." When Danny had applied for his Writers Guild card, he learned that there were two other Daniel Golds. His agent pressured him to officially register himself as Danny Masters because it was catchier, more memorable. As easy on the ears and the mouth as Danny himself was on the eyes. "Besides," his agent had said, "you're no ordinary writer. You are going to be a *star.*"

He hated to admit it, but his agent had been right. However, he'd been Danny Masters for almost twenty-five years, and it still hadn't grown on him. He wished he'd had the courage to do what John Mellencamp did after growing out of his record company-fabricated "John Cougar" image. "Mellencamp" was far less rock and roll than "Gold" was Hollywood glitterati, and yet Mellencamp still sold a helluva lot of records. The Internet Movie Database and Wikipedia sites had already outed him as Daniel Gold, but it didn't seem to affect him much. To Charlene and his adoring fans, he remained Danny Masters. To Ella, who went by Gold (as Frannie had when they were married), he was "Dad" or "Daddy" on a regular basis up until her thirteenth birthday, and that was the only name that sounded like music to him.

But maybe he had so willingly agreed to the name change for other reasons too. His father, Artie Gold, had never been one to proudly point to his son onstage and brag that he was his pop, never went on the record to claim that he had taught Danny everything he knew, and never attended any of Danny's premieres. And Danny wished Artie Gold had been the kind of intrusive father who wanted a piece of his son's spotlight, who wanted something, anything to do with his son.

As far as Danny Masters was concerned, he was as related to Artie Gold as he was to Raj or anyone else.

Danny said none of this out loud, however, and hastily continued his story. "Anyway, I talked to this woman for maybe five minutes tops—and I know what I'm about to say is like a bad soap opera line, but I swear I felt this connection to her."

"It may be a bad soap opera line in that the words to describe it have become banal, but the experience is as real and authentic as can be."

"You would think that, you quack."

Raj chuckled softly, acknowledging his friend's teasing. "So tell me about this connection."

Danny's memory conjured the woman he believed to be Sunny, and his body reacted: his heartbeat sped up, his spine tingled, and his blood rushed. But it wasn't the frantic feeling that came when he thought about or saw Charlene. There was no adrenaline rush, no instant erection, no ravenous craving. Thinking of Sunny stirred a deep longing, however.

"It felt like being ten years old and lying in the grass with your dog," said Danny. The image came to him at that moment. To his surprise he felt tears come to his eyes.

Raj sat still, legs crossed, almost statue-like, and allowed himself to absorb the words.

"That's quite an analogy."

Danny pinched the space between his brows and the bridge of his nose to hold the tears at bay. Not that he had never cried in front of Raj. And despite his crackpot psychology, Danny liked that Raj never made him feel like a fool. He couldn't say the same about past guidance counselors, school psychologists, and even the shrink he was court-ordered to see following the Incident.

But he didn't want to be so vulnerable right now. Maybe because he was just too damn tired. He'd not been sleeping well.

"Leave it to me to fuck it up, though," he said.

"What happened?"

"She was at the premiere. During the Q and A, I said something really stupid, something about my fans being wannabes—I swear it was like some ventriloquist guy sitting behind me, working my mouth with a string—and she took exceptional offense to it."

"How do you know this?"

"Because she came up to me after the Q and A and told me so. Then she called me a jackass and a failure and walked away."

"A jackass *and* a failure?"

"That's not even the best part," he said. "The best part is that someone standing behind her recorded the moment for posterity on his goddamned smartphone and posted it on goddamned YouTube. It's got about twenty-five thousand hits now. Maybe more. Which isn't much in the Kardashian scheme of things, but still."

"That's quite a cosmic response to one blunder, don't you think?" said Raj.

"Fuck yeah," said Danny, taking out a cigarette. He knew he couldn't smoke in the building, but liked that Raj let him hold the cigarette or act as if he were smoking it. "What gives?"

"Is it possible that you've subconsciously sabotaged a relationship with your soul mate?"

Danny dropped his chin to his neck and folded his arms. "Come on, you know I don't believe in soul mates any more than I believe in Santa Claus and the Tooth Fairy."

"There's no Tooth Fairy?"

"And why would I deprive myself of such happiness?" he asked, already knowing the answer. He'd been over these reasons with Raj and all the shrinks before him. His fears of inadequacy, of being a fraud, of being incapable of letting anyone in enough to see the real him lest they run in horror. Of not deserving to be fully pardoned for his sins. For his crime.

"What's the woman's name?" asked Raj.

Danny shrugged sadly. "I never got her name."

Raj raised his eyebrows. "Now that is interesting."

Danny looked at him with feigned disgust. "You would think so."

"You won't even allow yourself to know her name, much less spend the rest of your life with her."

"Look, some goon came over and started in with all the fan nonsense before I could get her name. How is that my fault?"

"Your subconscious invited it."

Danny looked at Raj skeptically. "Sure." He paused for another few beats, putting the cigarette in his mouth and taking it out again when he realized he couldn't take a drag. "It gets better. I tried to make an apology on this fan forum, and got into a battle of words with one of the participants."

"Just one?"

Danny nodded. "Goes by the name of Sunnyside. A lot of people have been trying to get in on the conversation, but I only responded to the one."

"Why is that?" asked Raj.

Danny paused again, as if about to take a leap.

"Because I'm pretty sure it's her."

Raj looked amused.

"I know it's crazy, but there you go," Danny added, knowing full well Raj didn't think it crazy at all.

"People misrepresent themselves all the time on the Internet," said Raj.

Danny looked at him, confused. It didn't seem to be the logical response to his last statement. And yet he wasn't sure what he was about to counter with would make much sense either. "They misrepresent themselves in person too."

"How so?" asked Raj.

"She was sweet as pie outside the theater. Shy, unobtrusive, funny. Then she calls me a jackass and a failure. I mean sure, I deserved to be called a jackass, but a *failure*? What the fuck? Then when I try to apologize, she laces into me even more. Then when I finally message her privately—and had I known you could direct-message people, I would've," Danny rambled, "she leaves me this message that says, 'You don't want to get to know me.' I mean, what the fuck is up with that, Raj?"

Raj's eye contact with Danny was unwavering, making Danny increasingly uncomfortable as he fidgeted in his seat, craving his cigarette.

"What do you want, Daniel?" asked Raj.

Danny stared out one of the windows and into the smoggy skyline.

"It was my birthday a few weeks ago."

"Happy birthday."

He nodded in acknowledgment. "Charlene flew out from New York just to be with me, then flew back the next morning."

"Did you see her while you were in New York?"

He shook his head. "Couldn't get our schedules to mesh," he lied, and stared out again. "The birthday sex was incredible."

Raj didn't respond.

"I'm forty-five now," said Danny seconds after Raj's nonresponse became unbearable yet again.

"What does forty-five mean to you?"

He shrugged. "It's a number." He wasn't sure if he really believed that; he just didn't know what else to say. He wasn't even sure what the question meant, but didn't want to ask.

"Did you set an intention for your birthday?" asked Raj.

Danny shrugged again. "What's the point?" He put the cigarette in his mouth again, then took it out just as quickly and tapped it nervously on his thigh.

"The point is to make your life the way you want it to be. Setting the intention alerts the Universal Life Source, who gladly responds to your thought vibration."

"Do you know how silly that sounds, even coming from *you*? Especially since I know you believe it."

Raj chuckled again. "Mock all you want, Daniel. The more you resist, the more you reveal."

"I've had a pretty remarkable life, don't you think? I've got more money than God, I've got a Tony and three Emmys, and if the critics are correct, I'm gonna score a hat trick with an Oscar, although I probably jinxed it just now by saying that. I'm fucking every man's dream girl, and I've got the greatest daughter that I totally don't deserve. Far from being a failure. So why would I sabotage meeting one random woman one random day on one random street?"

"Because you decided a long time ago that you don't get to have it all. But the little girl lived, Daniel."

A wave of nausea washed over Danny.

"So did you," said Raj. "But you're not really *living.* You're cluttering up your cosmos with another interview, another appearance, another photo op. You're writing another script, another plot, another scene. You're taking another trip, dropping another grand, but you're not seeing the treasure within, the one that has no dollar sign attached and is more dazzling than the greatest diamond on earth. Danny Masters is an apparition."

Danny was floored.

He stared past Raj, who sat still, unfazed by the silence.

Without announcement or any kind of gesture of hug or handshake, Danny stood up and walked out, got into his car, and drove for at least an hour without any distraction of radio or phone or even the characters who constantly chattered in his mind. He hadn't even smoked the cigarette he'd been so preoccupied with in Raj's office; in fact, he'd forgotten where he put it.

Finally he pulled off to a scenic overlook and killed the ignition after closing the top of the convertible. He sat motionless and stared at the ocean, a palette of beauty out of his reach.

Raj's words haunted him.

The little girl lived, Daniel.

Danny Masters is an apparition.

He wept alone behind tinted windows, the pain squeezing his heart so tightly he believed it was capable of killing him.

CHAPTER

TWELVE

Sunny Smith

I PUT TOGETHER AN OUTFIT FROM THE CLOTHES I had purchased in the city and tried to recreate some semblance of the fab hairstyle Luc had given me, this time with a lot of texturizer and moderate success. I only hoped that Josh wouldn't try to run his fingers through my hair; he'd have to clean them with a Wet Wipe afterward.

He was talking to Angela at the cash wrap when I entered the store at five minutes before seven, and he seemed pleased to see me. In fact, his eyes widened and a smile came over his face—not the managerial cheerleader smile, but something more genuine, not unlike the way Danny Masters had looked at me. But Danny's was more like contentment, like listening to a satisfying piece of music. Or had I made that up? Perhaps I was remembering the moment as I wanted it to be and not as it had really happened.

Josh held every door open for me and drove us to Nocello's in Northport in a red Subaru. Normally I didn't ride in the same car with my date, but I had a vial of pepper spray, not to mention that I could threaten a mega harassment suit against him if he messed with me. But something told me I could trust Joshua Hamilton, despite Georgie's warnings to the contrary.

I hadn't been to Nocello's since Teddy and I attended a wedding reception there; the place had gotten a makeover both in decor and menu. Josh put on his managerial façade, called the server "guy," and ordered a glass of chardonnay for himself and a cosmo for me after asking what I wanted.

We engaged in polite small talk until the server took our orders, and then Josh unloaded the big guns, practically demanding my life's story. I gave it to him in truncated clips, stopping at my divorce.

"I'm divorced too," he said.

"I'm sorry to hear that," I replied.

"Why didn't it work out for you?"

"I can't have children," I said, washing my self-blame down with a forceful sip of my cosmo. "At least, that's where the trouble started. After that, well...let's just say my husband really wanted to be a father."

"And this upsets you because..." said Josh.

I looked at him, stupefied.

"Look, having kids is way overrated. They suck the life force out of you every minute they're not asleep. I mean, sure, sometimes in a good way, but..."

I went from stupefied to horrified—suddenly Georgie's warnings were going off like foghorns in my head.

"Don't get me wrong—I love mine," he backpedaled. "I'm just saying that everyone tells you it's this beautiful thing and you should love every minute of it, but it's not and you don't, not all the time."

He noticed my expression and frowned. "Oh, don't tell me I blew it just because of that. Look, I'm being honest. And I love my kids—really, I do. But parenthood is manual labor. You've got to know that."

"I appreciate your honesty," I said, deadpan.

"It makes you more attractive to me," he said as he sipped the last of his wine.

"What does?" I asked, perking up.

"Your not having kids."

"Oh," was all I could answer.

"If it was so important to you, then why didn't you adopt?"

"My husband didn't want to," I explained. "And I didn't want to be a single parent."

"That's not so bad. Being a single parent, I mean."

One minute this guy was telling me parenthood sucks, and the next minute he was telling me it's not so bad? What, was he running for office?

"You really think so?"

"I do. Society puts all these pressures on what a family is supposed to look like, and it's all some *Leave It to Beaver* myth. None of it—the father and mother, the tidy house—is true. All of it is idealized, and single parenthood and divorce are villainized."

"I believe that."

"Trust me, had my wife and I stayed married, we would've done far worse damage to our kids than our divorce did. I actually think I'm a better father now than I was before."

I nodded, unsure of what to say next, and found myself wondering what would've happened to Teddy and me when our kids had grown up and moved away. I was envisioning us as two strangers in an empty house with nothing to say to each other when Josh interrupted my thoughts.

"You couldn't have wanted them that badly," he said. "I know several single women, and even a single guy, come to think of it, who went through hell and high water to have a child, be it through adoption or in vitro or hiring a surrogate."

I felt as if he'd just pushed me against a wall. "Just because I didn't want to raise a child alone doesn't mean I didn't want one."

Josh looked at me not only unpersuaded, but also as if I was trying to pull a fast one over him. "Sunny," he said.

"This is a great first date," I said.

He was either indifferent or naive to my sarcasm. "I guess it's a matter of what you really want most and what you're willing to give up in order to get it. But I say you're no worse off for having come this far without a child. If anything, you'll live longer. I don't doubt for a minute that you would be a terrific mom. Anyone who runs a stockroom the way you do would be sure to run a household with the same love and adoration. But face it: It wasn't your path. If you really wanted a kid—I mean *really wanted* one—by God, Sunny, nothing would have stopped you."

Something about the way he said those last words got to me, as if he was privy to information I'd not disclosed. I liked the idea of being tenacious, and I had been at one time, or so I thought. But when was the last time I had *really wanted* something?

I was a great mapmaker. In high school I'd organized treasure hunts to raise money for the school literary magazine and the yearbook in lieu of tired bake sales, and the place became a labyrinth for me to sketch out intricate plot points and riddles, a jigsaw puzzle one piece at a time. And along the way the scavengers found Wacky Whippers and rubber bracelets and Rubik's Cubes, the ultimate prize being a coveted Sony Walkman complete with cassette player *and* AM/FM radio. But when it came to mapping out my own life, I'd painted in broad strokes: go to college, get married, have a family, and become the female Stephen King in terms of monumental publishing success. The milestones felt so inevitable that the details of how they would actually come about hadn't occurred to me.

It struck me that I hadn't wanted children as much as I had wanted Teddy, and I couldn't have the latter unless I wanted the former. It further occurred to me that I hadn't wanted Teddy as much as I'd wanted whatever it was that I was looking for in a relationship and could never quite find.

"How could you possibly know that?" I asked Josh, hoping my tone masked longing with skepticism. "You just met me."

You don't want to know me. I'm not who you think I am. I could see the words in my mind's eye.

"You're right," said Josh. "I don't know you. But I'd like to."

"Thanks," I said, hyper-aware of the awkward silence where I was supposed to answer, "I'd like to get to know you too." But at that moment I wasn't sure what I wanted.

I decided to go for broke, lay it all out on the table. After all, I had nothing to lose at this point. Besides, Theo was right. It was time to stop letting what Teddy did control my life.

"My husband cheated on me," I blurted.

"That sucks," said Josh.

I took a sip of my drink. "That's not the best part, though. The best part is that he informed me about it by way of a candid interview on TV."

A look of horror registered across his face, and I couldn't tell if I'd pushed the envelope too far or if he was empathizing with me.

It was my turn to backpedal. "I'm exaggerating. He was drunk in a bar, and the local news happened to be there. But still. It doesn't get much better than that."

His expression softened, and he seemed to want to reach across the table and take my hand, uncertain of where the first date boundary lines were drawn.

"You didn't deserve that, Sunny."

He said it so earnestly, with such compassion that it brought tears to my eyes. I switched to a glass of water and took a sip in an effort to quickly compose myself, lest a tear slip out and down my cheek.

We finished our meal, and although we both passed on dessert, we continued to sit at the table and talk.

"So what do you think, Sunny? I know I came off a bit rough, but I'm a really decent guy if you give me a chance."

The moment seemed to present itself. "About that…" I started.

"Uh-oh," said Josh. "You're not attracted to me?"

"No," I said. "I mean, yes, I think you're good-looking and nice and all that."

Oh, good Lord…

"It's just that…" I searched for tact, then decided to just have out with it. "Well, you're my *boss*. And I'm hesitant to get involved with someone in the company. I've never done it before, and I'm concerned. Especially given the imbalance of power."

"Excuse me?"

"You're a regional manager and I'm a stock manager. Major, major conflict of interest, not to mention that ultimately I have to answer to you."

Josh seemed to consider this as if the thought had never occurred to him. "Well, if it makes you that uncomfortable, OK. But I'm not worried about it."

"Why not?"

"First tell me why you are. Tell me your concerns." He said this in a very professional tone.

"For one, I'm worried about what others in the company will say. I am totally, completely devoted to Whitford's," I said, mentally admonishing myself for the double adverb: *totally completely?* "Like, sports fan loyal. I know the names of everyone in corporate, right down to the janitors. I wear the baseball cap with the logo at the company picnic."

"I'm not planning to make an announcement in the newsletter."

"I *read* the newsletter," I added. "Every month. And what happens if one of us loses interest or breaks it off, regardless of why?"

"I wouldn't fire you or anything, if that's what you're worried about. And how often does a regional manager show up at the store—once every other month? Every three months? It's not like we're going to see each other every day. Look, these things aren't a problem unless someone makes it a problem. Keep your work life at work and your home life at home, and everything's OK."

"Yes, but you have to evaluate my job performance."

"Actually, that's Angela and Phil's job."

"Which brings me back to my original point," I said.

"Sunny, you're not having an affair with the president of the company, you're not sleeping with the director to get a better part in the movie, and you're not sexually harassing anyone. I like you, and I'd like to start seeing you."

"You live in New Jersey," I pointed out.

"Thank you for reminding me."

"I don't do long-distance dating."

He laughed again. "That's long-distance dating to you? Let me tell you about my cousin. Met his wife on the Internet in a chat room. She lived in Indonesia. After three months of what turned out to be ridiculously expensive phone calls and a bunch of e-mails, he went over there to meet her in person. Another three months after that, she packed her bags and moved to Connecticut to marry him. They just celebrated their ten-year anniversary."

"Yeah, but it takes just as long to get over the George Washington Bridge as it does to get to Indonesia."

He nodded his head in concession. "Good point. So I'll take full responsibility for the traveling. I'll come to you."

"That hardly seems fair."

"Sunny, throw me a bone here!"

Despite his blasé attitude toward parenthood and his Tony Robbins-type managerial style, Joshua Hamilton was witty and smart. I surmised that we had enough things in common to hold a conversation and share a pleasant afternoon, and enough differences to teach each other a thing or two.

"There's no pressure, really," said Josh. "I think you're an attractive, intelligent, funny woman, and I'd love to spend some time with you. That's all. No strings attached. You don't even have to give me an answer tonight. Tonight I say thank you for the enjoyable evening and for keeping me company so that I wouldn't have to spend another night eating takeout in my hotel room."

"I had an enjoyable evening too," I replied, not sure whether I meant it.

We were quiet in the car during the ride back to Whitford's. By the time we got to the parking lot and he pulled up next to the Old Banana, I had decided not to see Joshua Hamilton socially again. There were too many potential complications. In fact, I regretted the entire evening, already dreading the next time he'd be making an unannounced store visit and inspecting my stockroom yet again.

He kept the car idling as I fumbled in my purse for my keys, and after I found and jingled them, he leaned over, gently took hold of my chin with his thumb and forefinger, and kissed me gingerly on the lips, lingering there only for a second. "Good night, Sunny," he practically whispered, his eyes soft and lit by the glow of the streetlamp.

And just like that, I changed my mind.

CHAPTER

THIRTEEN

Danny Masters

DANNY HAD SWORN EARLY ON THAT HE WAS not going to be like his father, that he would drink only to have a good time with his friends and know when enough was enough.

The problem was that even when he knew he'd had more than enough, he didn't want to stop.

In college he was serious and studious and wrote every day. His only other commitment was to meet girls, and he did so by showing up at poetry slams and Psychology 101 experiments and auditions for his plays. He drank on the weekends and was happy when he drank, not angry. He was everyone's buddy, the charmer, ol' Schmooze Boy. He made no one in his presence feel less than or invisible. And Danny was god-awful funny when he was drunk. Not stupid-funny, like crushing beer cans against his forehead, but witty, a storyteller. He made up stories on the spot, usually about his father, making him out to be a buffoon. And every time one of those stories ended with his audience erupting in laughter, he'd think *Take that, you fucker.*

When he drank until he passed out and awoke the next morning (or afternoon) hung over, he nursed himself not for the purpose of getting well as much as to ready himself for the next weekend. By the time he finished college, he could no longer wait for the weekend.

Danny's only power over Artie Gold came at the hands of his writing and his drinking. Every antagonist he created, be he politician or prosecutor, in the end fell from glory, crushed not by physical violence but by words, either sweeping oratory or verbal assaults. Danny gave each protagonist the voice he never had, the one his father had always managed to take from him and his mother had never encouraged him to use. A guidance counselor in the eighth grade—one of the nice ones and not the idiots—had suggested that he write dialogue as a way of channeling the anger that was starting to show up in fights Danny instigated on school grounds and in classrooms, or in the form of burns from cigarette butts he put out on his forearms just to get someone's attention. He'd never told his creative writing teacher in high school, the one who'd first noticed his flair for dialogue, that that was why he was so good at it. That he'd been scripting every confrontation he'd dreamed of for years.

Artie didn't hit Danny or his mother. He wasn't abusive in that sense. But he was a bully. He belittled Danny for the sole purpose of raising himself up. Political dramas came easily to Danny because they were chock-full of rhetoric, opportunities for speech-making and proselytizing by polar opposites wanting to take each other down rather than come to a mutual understanding or respect. He had read *Tyranny of the Majority* in college and decided that he'd take tyranny down by the stroke of a pen. Danny would verbally beat the shit out of a bully in three acts.

The underdog would always win. Justice would be done. The silenced would always be spoken for. And when writing couldn't give him that voice, the bottle did.

When he'd graduated college and his senior thesis had been produced Off Broadway, attracting attention from the critics and his soon-to-be agent, Danny's weekend drinking benders had spilled over into weekdays. Yet they weren't so much benders as the kind of drinking his father would do, the kind that had a schedule or routine and didn't end in icy stoicism or passing out as much as a lonely stupor. When his next play, *Madness*, was produced on Broadway and optioned as a movie, Danny Masters was catapulted into stardom, leaving behind Daniel Gold, phenom playwright. Reporters wanted to talk to him. Photographers wanted to take his picture. Image consultants wanted to take him shopping. Women wanted to take him to bed without him needing to get drunk first. The attention both exhilarated and terrified him, for he wondered when they were going to find out that he was just a stupid, white, half-Jewish kid from Long Island who wasn't supposed to amount to anything. His star was going to burn out any day now, that's what his father said the night Danny won the Tony award for *Madness*. When the film adaptation (starring a then-teenage Robbie Marsh) topped the box office the summer he turned twenty-six, Danny paid off his school loans as well as his parents' house. When his father found out, he pushed Danny against the living room wall—the only time he'd ever used physical force. Danny then moved out to Los Angeles and set up permanent residence there.

With every accomplishment, Danny could hear Artie Gold's menacing, slurred voice (even in sobriety): *Your star's gonna burn out, you punk, and you'll wind up the same nobody you were before.* Every positive review, every award, every meeting with Mike Nichols or Steven Spielberg or Harvey Weinstein delayed that burnout for one more day and scared the crap out of him. Only applause and adulation appeased him, blocked out the impending doom. And when there was no applause, when there was no one to adore him, there was the bottle. Danny drank for the liquid confidence. He drank to keep up the applause. He drank to keep up the façade of being Danny Masters.

He'd been to therapy in an attempt to understand why his father hated him so much, why he stayed with his mother if she and Danny were the burdens he claimed them to be. He even once confronted Artie about it, screamed at the top of his lungs: *What did I ever do to you, you miserable fuck?*

"You were born," Artie said, matter-of-factly. "I didn't want a wife. I didn't want a kid. I wanted my life to be my own."

"Why didn't you tell me I was an accident?" he later cried to his mother.

She looked at him with such sorrow in her eyes. "Because you weren't an accident. Not to me."

"Then why didn't you leave him?"

"Because I thought one day he'd realize that he needed me, and you too, and that we were worth the sacrifices he believed he made."

Danny first met Frannie Reichman at a spa in LA—she was an aesthetician. By the time she'd finished applying his mud mask, he had asked her out for dinner and a movie. They both detested the ridiculousness of their rhyming names, but detested the formality of Daniel and Francine even more. When they married a year after *Madness* was nominated for a Golden Globe award, he thought his drinking days were over. After all, he had someone who loved him now, just as he was (or so he thought—"just as he was" at the time was "not drinking"). And for the first year, he was fine. He drank socially and in excess only at a wedding or two. But when his first TV series was picked up by one of the major networks, Artie Gold's voice came back to haunt him again, and this time from the grave—he'd died on July fifth the year before, his liver no longer able to function. Moreover, the stakes had gone up—instead of weekend box office numbers, Danny had to maintain household share points and battle against *Friends* and *ER* and the ever-growing number of cable channels and choices. He became hostile toward Frannie when she didn't validate him enough (and of course she could never validate him enough). He lashed out at his writing staff when they didn't fact-check their research closely enough and viewers voiced their complaints following that week's episode. And he got into a public war of words with a critic who accused Danny of being a one-trick pony. *Your star's gonna burn out, you punk...*

———

He never even saw her.

Danny was in New York days after the 1995 Emmys, his thirtieth birthday creeping up. His show had been nominated for two awards, including Best Drama. Just days before, Frannie had announced that she was pregnant with their first child, and he was equal parts thrilled and terrified (when was he not?).

He lost.

For the first and only time, he'd not won an award. He had not expected to win (he never expected to), but the loss signaled the first dimming of the light. The sun was setting on Danny Masters and his dumb luck. The world was cluing in that he was nothing special.

He'd gone to a party and lost count of the number of flutes of champagne he'd downed while yukking it up with television's best and brightest. It was daybreak when he cajoled his New York agent into loaning him his car for a drive out to the Hamptons (or so he said), promising to return it later that evening, and in no time at all he was serpentining through the back streets of his old Bethpage neighborhood on Long Island. He knew them by heart. Hell, he could find his old house blindfolded, the one his mother sold shortly after his father died, before she moved to Florida (she passed away when Danny was thirty-five). And yet he couldn't remember the houses all looking so similar.

At first Danny thought he'd hit something in the middle of the road, a downed tree limb, perhaps, for he had no idea that he'd strayed so far off to the side of the road. He never saw the nine-year-old girl walking her golden retriever, almost as tall as she was, first thing in the morning before school. He never saw her flinging in the air like a rag doll upon impact, according to witnesses. The impact had knocked his wheel out of alignment, and the car careened over a mailbox and into a tree. He hit his head on the steering wheel hard, causing a gash at the very top of his forehead, the blood cascading down and making him woozy. Pressing the back of his tuxedo sleeve against the wound, he stumbled out and surveyed the damage.

"F-ff-fuck," he slurred.

He saw the dog first, a sight that not even the most realistic war film could make as gruesome. The dog's body was bloodied and contorted, and its eyes were open, each looking out the opposite direction.

"Oh f-f-fuck!" Danny moaned and covered his mouth before turning away and throwing up. It was then that he saw the girl out of the corner of his eye. Her body was also bloody and contorted, though perhaps not as grotesque.

"Oh fuck oh fuck oh fuck," Danny repeated, the panic level rising inside him like floodwaters. By then about a half dozen neighbors had come out of their houses, including one from his old house, and within minutes the street was barricaded and lit up by police cars, an ambulance, and a tow truck. For only a split second, Danny had considered making a run for it, but the lucid part of him knew that even if he were not surrounded by law enforcement, if the accident had taken place on some abandoned road, he would've called for help. He would've stayed. He had caused this, and he knew he needed to be accountable. No, the impulse to run had nothing to do with escaping punishment—it was to escape himself.

The cops restrained neighbors who wanted to beat the shit out of Danny (one of whom had emerged from his home with a shotgun), and they pulled him far off to the side and away from the EMTs who were working on the girl like a pit crew worked on a racecar, at lightning speed and oblivious to the chaos around them. An officer gave him a breathalyzer test and interrogated him on who he was, where he'd been, where he was going, etcetera, while an EMT applied first aid to the gash on his forehead. The officer handcuffed Danny and took him to the hospital, where he threw up again and felt an almost unbearable pounding in his head. Everyone—neighbors, cops, EMTs, medical staff—looked at him with judgment, disgust, fury, and he knew he deserved every look.

"Is she OK?" he'd kept asking, but no one would answer him.

When he'd been left alone in an emergency room cubicle, feeling woozy and nauseated and the pounding in his head decreasing to a throb thanks to whatever meds they'd given him, he closed his eyes and leaned forward, his blood-spattered wrist handcuffed to the bed rail, and was ready to offer God the deal of a lifetime.

I will do anything—anything—you want if you let that little girl live. I will spend the rest of my life in jail, will voluntarily enter the gates of hell when my time comes (he was going there anyway regardless, he knew). *Please, God, just let her live. Let her live let her live let her live…*

The second offer to God, should the girl not live, would be an eye for an eye, of course. First chance he could get, he would kill himself.

He was sitting there, waiting for a doctor or the police officer to return, planning his suicide when he remembered Frannie and her news just days earlier.

Somehow, at that moment, he *knew* that Frannie was going to have a girl even though she hadn't been far enough along for the sex to be determined. The clarity of that moment, that knowing, was startling.

She'd be better off without me was his first response, but the thought after that was the realization, again with stunning clarity, that he didn't want to live without her, and vice versa. No, he wanted to be there to see his daughter take her first steps, grow up, go to college, get married. And in the blink of an eye, the bargain needed to be renegotiated. He prayed more fervently than he'd ever prayed in his life for the girl he'd hit to live, because there was no way he could live with himself if she didn't (although he drank because he already couldn't live with himself)—he'd have to kill himself, and he wanted to live for his daughter. He wanted to fix it, to fix *everything*. And he believed—no, he *knew*—he could. He'd take care of both girls. He'd see to it that if he lived and stayed out of jail, he'd spend the rest of his life making sure they'd never suffer ever again, especially not at his hands. Hell, maybe he'd even make them proud of him one day.

The police officer reentered the room and told him that although the girl was in critical condition, the doctors believed she'd pull through. Danny wept as he was released from the hospital and taken to jail, charged with driving while intoxicated, for starters. He hadn't realized that he'd been saying *Thank you God, thank you God, thank you God* like a mantra until the officer driving the cruiser told him to shut the fuck up, that he didn't deserve God's benevolence. Danny nodded in agreement, his head throbbing too much to say anything else.

In addition to the DWI, Danny was charged with reckless endangerment of a minor and attempted manslaughter.

His agent had gotten him a lawyer notorious for defending delinquent celebrities who trashed hotel rooms, hit their spouses, unsuccessfully smuggled drugs or guns in their travel bags, or drove while under the influence. He had officially joined the ranks of "Celebrities Screwed by Success," as one headline put it. (Years later, when he had done a Google search of himself and the accident, he saw other headlines: "'Madness' Writer Hits Child, Gets Arrested for DWI"; "Hollywood Phenom in Drunk Driving Incident"; "Drunk Screenwriter Plows Into Pedestrian, Kills Dog.") The case was settled out of court; pleading to the DWI only (the other two charges had been dismissed), Danny agreed to do two months in jail, six months of community service, and enter an alcohol treatment facility (he'd already sworn to never consume another drop the moment he heard the girl was going to live, and hadn't since). His driver's license was revoked for a year.

Insisting that the girl's identity be kept anonymous, Danny's lawyer, at his request, asked the court to issue a gag order, and the court acquiesced. To avoid a civil suit, he paid the family two million dollars for pain and suffering (his last movie having grossed ten million dollars at the box office). Additionally—and this was neither a condition of the plea nor the settlement—he set up a college fund for the girl, and every year on her birthday he deposited the equivalent of her age in denominations of one thousand dollars. On the anniversary of the accident, he made donations to various charities—M.A.D.D. or S.A.D.D., animal shelters, children's hospitals, etcetera— also in denominations of a thousand dollars equal to the anniversary year, in the girl and her family's name.

However, he'd neither seen nor heard from them since, and he was forbidden to make contact with her.

Editorials at the time said that Danny Masters had dodged a bullet, that had he been African American or white trash or anyone other than an award-winning screenwriter, he'd be rotting in a cell right now, and he knew they were right. Even the judge had said, "God is giving you a second chance, although I can't for the life of me understand why you deserve it." Danny had agreed with that as well, and had asked himself and God the same question many times since. As the years passed, with the exception of the occasional mention by reporters during interviews, especially during premieres, or when he wrote a character with a drinking problem (bound by the gag order, they were only allowed to say that he'd pled guilty to DWI after crashing his car and hitting a pedestrian), the Incident—although to call it that was a gross understatement—seemed to have faded into people's memories as nothing more than a stupid, frat-boy stunt, like cow-tipping or indecent exposure. Hollywood, the world, and his fans had forgiven and forgotten. Even Frannie forgave him, saying years after she divorced him that it was the disease of alcoholism and not his intention that had caused the accident that morning. But Danny could never believe it.

Ella had never known more than what Google told her, and he never told her the story in full because he couldn't bear the thought of her disowning him. But Ella, having never known or seen him as anything but sober, couldn't fathom that the guy in the mug shot and her dad were one and the same.

More astounding, his success soared. Everything he wrote was gold, winning the praise of critics and fans and industry professionals. Deep down, he knew that at the end of the day, he'd have to keep writing at that level not just to win his daughter's love, or his fans', or Charlene's, or anyone else's, but to make sure he kept up his end of the bargain with God.

And yet it was never enough.

CHAPTER
FOURTEEN
Sunny Smith

"SO, HOW WAS IT?" ASKED GEORGIE WHEN I got home from my date with Josh and called him, as I'd promised.

"It was fine," I said.

"That's it?"

"Mmm-hmm," I answered. I'd decided that I would reveal details only if he asked for them point-blank.

"Are you going to see him again?"

I paused for a beat, knowing he wasn't going to like the answer. "Yes, I am."

Georgie's pause lasted even longer. "I hope you know what the hell you're doing, Sunrise, 'cause I sure don't."

I couldn't remember a time when Georgie had not supported me, and his defiance suddenly felt like a knife in my back.

"That's just fine, Georgie, 'cause it's none of your business," I snapped back.

"Look, I know you've been lonely and you're kicking yourself because of that Danny Masters disaster—"

"That's not it," I interrupted.

"And for some reason you're freaking out about some little video."

"Some little video?" I protested. "I want that godforsaken video to *go away*—I don't want to be reminded of it every five seconds."

"No one has said a word about it in the last two days. It's already run its course. I think everyone has somehow managed to move on with their lives. You want *you* to go away, have been trying for years to disappear, and I can't for the life of me understand why. Regardless of what you said to Danny Masters, you spoke your mind, and you've been so terrified to do that ever since Teddy. So Teddy got drunk and announced on TV—"

"In the middle of a live segment, I might add—" I interrupted.

"Of a stupid game—"

I interrupted him again. "It was a *Yankee playoff post-game show*—"

"Whatever—that he was dumping you because you couldn't have kids. Big fucking deal. It was fucking *News Twelve Long Island*, for chrissake—not CNN."

"Are you forgetting how many phones calls I got? How many my parents and brother got? Are you forgetting that he said my name as he announced that he was *cheating on me*?" I fumed.

I knew the scene as if I'd just replayed the tape yesterday: Teddy had been watching the game at the Main Event with his buddies—he'd been going out quite a bit with his "buddies," in fact—or so he'd told me. News Twelve was covering playoff fever around the island and just so happened to go to that particular sports bar. And Teddy, totally tanked, pulled the reporter's microphone to him and slurred on live TV, "I just wanna tell my wife

Sunny Smith so it reads: Sunny Smith that I'm leaving her for Ramona Brooks because she can have my babies."

The reporter finally decided that maybe Teddy didn't have anything relevant to say about Mariano Rivera's fierce pitching arm and regained control of the mic.

And so I learned about the end of my marriage at approximately the same time the rest of Long Island did.

"I do remember, only because you keep reminding me. I also remember you not taking the bastard for everything he had in the divorce. But it wasn't Oprah doing a show on infertile couples, and it wasn't the reason everyone was watching. Hell, it was a *sports segment*—the moment they finally had the decency to take the camera off Teddy, they went right back to their usual boring coverage, and everyone else went on with their lives."

"Almost everyone," I corrected.

"And whose fault is that? You could've moved on, but you chose to retreat into your shell like some frightened tortoise and never come out. And here we are, still talking about it. Get. Over. It!"

I found myself grateful we were having this conversation over the phone—how much harder would it have been in person? He was in my face as it was.

"Besides, it's not like you were the national spokeswoman for fertility. Valerie Plame getting outed as a CIA agent? Elizabeth Edwards having to hear from the *National Enquirer* that her husband was cheating on her while she had cancer? A college student killing himself because his roommate posted a video to the student body that outed him as gay? A teenager getting rocks thrown at his head for simply *being* gay? *That*'s some serious shit, Sunny. Your little fifteen minutes of fame wasn't even fifteen minutes. And *everyone* has forgotten it except you. You're the one that's stretched it out for the last seven years. You're the only one who carries it around like a crutch when you've walked just fine all along."

As every word he said sank in, I felt so ashamed and foolish I couldn't even speak. He waited a few seconds before firing the next round.

"You've been so fixated on this absurd notion that everyone is looking at you in judgment that you've never been able to see that Teddy exposed *himself* as the tool he is, not you. The people to whom you really matter love you no matter what. And the people who don't know you don't matter at all. How is it that you never learned that lesson?"

"*He* mattered to me, Georgie. He and the life we were supposed to have."

"And what about your life now? Shouldn't *that* matter? I gotta tell you, what's been truly heartbreaking to watch is that you never even put up a fight, even though your parents raised you to do otherwise. You decided playing it safe was playing it smart. You know what was so great about that video you abhor, and those Masterminds posts that came afterward? You stood up for an injustice—in the scheme of things, it wasn't a big one, but you stood up and spoke your mind nonetheless. And you did it to someone you *admired*, someone who let you down. You never even put Teddy in his place. We've all been waiting for you to *say something*, Sunrise. To *do* something. That Forty for Forty list was supposed to get you to come out and take your life back."

I took a long pause. "Georgie, what the hell happened in that meeting today?"

"Forget it."

"No! Why are you withholding things from me? Your plan, your distrust of Josh… We've always told each other everything."

I thought about the direct message from Danny Masters that I'd kept secret and wondered if Georgie could hear the hypocrisy in my voice.

"We're talking about *you*. You wanna get back out into the dating world, then great. But if it's with Joshua Hamilton, then you're making a huge mistake."

"Good night, Georgie," I snapped.

"Good night," he replied, his voice bitter.

After slamming down my princess phone and returning it to the night table, I picked up the 40 for 40 list and perused it once again.

I opened the drawer and pulled out a red Sharpie, emphatically crossed out SLEEP WITH DANNY MASTERS, and returned the list and the pen to the table before turning off the light.

Shit. Going to bed mad at your best friend sucked. As I lay there in the dark, staring at the ceiling and replaying my date, trying to commit every sensory detail to permanent memory and recalling Josh's good-night kiss several times over and in slow motion, I wondered if I did know what I was doing. To not have Georgie's support? Hell, he had even approved of Teddy when we'd first gotten together, before Teddy's inner tool came out.

The longer I waited for sleep, the farther back my memory took me.

The last seven years of my life scrolled slowly, dully past me. Endless days of routine, of complacency, of silence. Hours of wasted time, of words sitting in a drawer, hidden away. It almost felt like the movie *Groundhog Day*—every day was an opportunity for me to do it differently, to break out of the rut simply by opening my mouth. All this time I was afraid of being annihilated for being found out for who I was, be it a mystery writer or a history buff or someone who wanted children not for herself but for her husband.

I was afraid of having people find out that I was afraid. Vulnerable. Naive.

And Georgie was right—I had no grounds for such a phobia. I was a white, heterosexual, Catholic, middle-class, post women's lib, Generation X female who'd been raised by loving parents who never divorced and a brother who had looked after me when we were growing up. I was smart, creative, funny, and good at my job. I loved books and movies and where I came from. I didn't smoke, didn't do drugs, didn't have any kind of addiction or disease or disorder. I had a good memory—too good, maybe, or maybe it wasn't good at all in that it distorted images and events and sound bites. No one I loved had died a tragic death, and I had a place to live. And I had the best friends in the world who wanted me to be successful, to be happy.

I was forty years old, and I'd squandered so much time being afraid. Just like Theo said.

Perhaps that's why I loved Danny Masters's films and TV shows so much. His protagonists always got the last word, always stood up with the courage of their convictions, and in the end got rewarded rather than punished for it. They had their flaws and demons like all good characters; they struggled and got beaten down every now and then. But when the bully beat them down, they got up and beat back.

My own heroines possessed the tenacity that I was missing. They were charming and adaptable, owning every room they entered. Nothing was impossible to them, and they never met a challenge they didn't like. Obstacles were inviting. They relentlessly uncovered every clue, pursued every lead, deciphered every code, and dogged every suspect the way Columbo used to (although my characters did it with more spunk and less befuddlement). Unlike Danny Masters's characters, mine never expressed political or doctrinal opinions. But they did bring the guilty to justice. They were Wonder Woman without the sexy costume.

And yet, not a single one of my protagonists was a mother. Why had I never noticed that before?

Ironically, Teddy had taught me self-defense. How was it that when he struck the most crushing blow, I rolled over in concession without even putting up a fight? How did I let him convince me that it was my fault in the first place? Maybe that's what my mother had seen when she hypothesized that the idea of having children was more desirable to me than the idea of being without Teddy. Maybe she had somehow seen that I was going to let him walk all over me.

I want to get to know you, Sunny. The words echoed like an endless loop until I finally fell asleep, alternating between the voices of Danny Masters, Joshua Hamilton, and, to my surprise, my own.

Danny Masters

DANNY PULLED HIMSELF TOGETHER AND drove home. Ella was coming to stay with him for the weekend, and he could hardly wait. He was about to call Frannie to ask her if Ella could come a few days early when his iPhone played "How Long Has This Been Going On."

"Hey, Char." His voice sounded scratchy.

"Where are you?" she asked.

"I just got home."

"So did I."

His heart started to race. "For how long?"

"A week."

"What happened to filming?"

"Principle photography postponed due to a death in Bill's family."

"I'm sorry to hear that," he said.

"So?" said Charlene. "Your place or mine? I'm dying to put my hands on your body."

He rubbed his red eyes, feeling run down and weary. "Let's meet at your place," he said, and put the car into gear once again.

Charlene's town house in Malibu was super chic— bright, bold colors and patterns and fabrics designed and decorated by Nate Berkus; custom furniture and fixtures; a single woman's place, neither child- nor pet-friendly. It had been photographed for some magazine spread recently, named one of the top ten places that make your own house look like a hovel, or something to that effect, thought Danny. As he looked around, he saw that Charlene's home was as corporately sponsored as she was—product placement everywhere. Yes, indeed, Charlene Dumont was a brand.

She emerged at the doorway dressed in a faded T-shirt, Juicy sweatpants, and flip-flops (all various shades of pink), her hair balled up in a scrunchie and her makeup washed off. Still, she was breathtakingly beautiful. He slammed the door of his convertible and made his way up the walk.

"Damn, honey, you look like hell," she said.

"I've had a rough day."

"What's the matter?"

He didn't want to tell her about his conversation with Raj, or the storm it had stirred up, much less think about it.

"I'm having a hard time writing lately."

"It's all this Oscar talk," said Charlene. "It's messin' with your head. Not like you haven't had this problem before."

She wasn't wrong, he realized. But she didn't know everything else—the gaffe at the premiere, the exchanges with Sunny... Or maybe she did and that's why she was here. Charlene had a knack for showing up just when Danny needed to see her most. It was almost as if she read his brain waves, as if he had a direct telepathic line to her.

He was suddenly overcome with remorse. "Hey, I'm sorry I didn't see you in New York." He went to her and kissed her sensuously. She was wearing his favorite perfume, and he was convinced it was some kind of witch's love potion concocted solely to make him submit to her. He would lie down in traffic for her if she asked him to while standing close enough for him to get a whiff. Just as she was breaking away to go inside the house, he pulled her back to him and inhaled, hoping to become high as a kite.

"I missed you, baby," he said softly, nuzzling her and burying his head in her shoulder.

"Well, take me inside and show me how much."

The two of them entered the town house arm in arm, and no sooner had Charlene closed the door behind them than Danny pulled her T-shirt over her head and pinned her to the wall in the foyer, where he began kissing her neck. Charlene giggled (he knew her ticklish spot) and began to loosen his belt buckle, but Danny lightly slapped her hand away and made her take her own pants off first. She obliged, revealing a black lace thong. She slid away from the wall and out of the foyer to allow Danny to get an eyeful, and he would've rushed her like a linebacker had her tease not been so tantalizing. God, her *body...* Michelangelo couldn't have sculpted a better body out of marble. Even her toes were sexy, pedicured and painted purple like little grapes, and he wanted to nibble on each one.

Removing her matching lace bra and draping it over the banister, she proceeded up the stairs daintily, her back straight as if she was balancing a book on her head. Danny followed her up, undressing on the staircase as he took every two steps, giving her a head start so he could watch her.

"Where shall we go? To bed or to the bath?" Charlene asked.

"Bed," demanded Danny. "Bed bed bed bed bed." *Make me forget,* he thought.

She giggled again, and he could no longer wait. He scooped her up and carried her into her bedroom, dropping her on the bed before he pounced.

———

Danny woke up at night, alone in the bed, and already knew where to find Charlene without needing to call her name. He wandered out into the hallway and stairwell to retrieve his clothes, haphazardly dressed himself, and found her outside on the balcony. She wore a short terry robe and held a glass of chardonnay and a cigarette. When they'd first dated, Charlene had rid her place of alcohol so as not to tempt Danny, but recently she had restocked her wine rack without asking him if it would bother him. He fixed his gaze on the glass—the shape of a wineglass (especially when full of wine) appealed to him the same way her body did. The color of the claret or the pinot noir or the zinfandel was as inviting as one of her silk teddies or lace garters. If he could have just one more sip...

"Hey, sleepyhead," she said as he kissed her cheek. "You enjoy your nap?"

"What time is it?" he asked.

"Almost ten thirty."

He took a Virginia Slim from her pack (she smoked only after sex) and lit it, leaning against the railing and viewing the nighttime panorama before him, dotted and dappled with twinkle lights. "Wow," he said, blowing smoke rings into the air. "That's a postcard waiting to be made."

As he stared at the horizon, he could feel Charlene turning to face him. "Are you really OK, Danny?" she asked.

"I'm fine," he answered, not looking at her and blowing another smoke ring.

"You seemed desperate for something in there before."

His mind went back to the bedroom, wondering what in his lovemaking had evoked a sense of desperation. He thought he'd left Raj and flashbacks of the accident on the stairs, dumped them there along with his clothes.

He blew another smoke ring.

"I heard about the video. Couldn't have been fun hearing someone call you a failure," she said.

"I'm over it," he lied.

"Are you?"

Danny turned to face her. "What are we doing here, Char?"

She stood up and forcefully put out her cigarette in the ashtray on the balcony's ledge, refusing to give him an answer.

"Are we back together? Are we just using each other for sex? I have to know what you want, Char. I have to know what *I* want."

"I want to be uncomplicated," said Charlene. "Can't one thing in this life be uncomplicated? Can't *we* be uncomplicated?"

"How can not clarifying this relationship be uncomplicated?"

"It's too complicated to have to put a label on it, tie a schedule to it, and then make sure we're keeping that schedule. Isn't it enough that we enjoy each other's com-pany and each other's bodies without needing to commit to anything?"

They'd been having this argument for three years, only for the first two, she had wanted the commitment from him. She had once committed to a guest appearance on a TV show shot in Las Vegas for the sole purpose of luring Danny there with the hope that he'd impulsively whisk her off to some chapel to tie the knot. In fact, she *told* him of this plot one night when she'd gotten drunk following a rough day of filming. And while he did go to see her, he also let her know that under no circumstances were they even sneezing near a chapel. She even had a "Mrs. Masters" T-shirt made, the letters scripted in rhinestones across her chest, and she was so mad at him for not sticking to the plan that she used the T-shirt as a rag to clean her bathroom when she returned to LA.

In hindsight, Danny's refusal to commit had nothing to do with a lack of desire or love or even some fear of considering how it would affect a then-preteen Ella. No—simply put, his refusal to commit had been the only card he held in this relationship, the only hold he'd had on her. And yet, somehow the balance of power had shifted there too. He had no idea when the tables had turned, or how, or why. He wasn't sure when he became the one asking for more. Nevertheless, it had happened, and he couldn't help but wonder if Charlene's refusal to commit was for the same reason as his had been. He suspected she liked holding all the cards in this relationship now.

Maybe he just didn't want to be alone.

He and Frannie had a reasonable joint custody agreement, although in the last couple of years he had wanted Ella to live with him full time. And he knew Ella wasn't opposed to this idea, despite her keeping it from her mother so as not to hurt her feelings. But he knew that even if Frannie consented, his schedule of cross-country meetings and speaking engagements and location shoots and interviews and any other commitment he had couldn't possibly allow him to care for Ella the way she needed, and he didn't want her to be a nanny's girl like so many other celebrities' children.

But Ella was getting older. Perhaps things could be different now? Maybe that's what this sudden desire to settle down was all about. But who was he kidding? Charlene was not a suitable mate when it came to settling down.

After mulling over Charlene's question, Danny finally answered. "I need some stability."

"Maybe you just need a vacation," she suggested. "Or a week at a spa. You've been burning the candle at both ends for a long time. I mean, first there was *Winters*, then there was *Exposed*, not to mention all the other stuff that came in between. You've got to be just totally burned out by now."

"I need a good stiff drink," he said, letting out a sarcastic chuckle.

"You can't have a good stiff drink," she said without a trace of empathy in her voice, "so don't even joke about it."

He could feel the bile churning in him. How could he even *think* such a thing, much less rationalize it as a joke, after reliving the horror hours ago? He took another drag from the cigarette, exhaled, and looked back out at the horizon again, disgust joined by immense sadness.

"Don't you want to settle down?" he asked. "When do we get off the roller coaster?"

Charlene contemplated his question for a moment. "When nobody loves us anymore, I guess."

CHAPTER
SIXTEEN
Sunny Smith

DESPITE GEORGIE'S OBJECTIONS, I'D BEGUN dating Joshua Hamilton a week after our dinner at Nocello's. We disclosed our intentions to Angela and Phil, who, to my surprise, seemed to have no problem with it. (If anything, Angela seemed a little jealous.) Phil's one condition was that Josh had to schedule store visits on days I wasn't working, and Josh's superiors "strongly discouraged" him from talking about company business on personal time.

Georgie insisted that I was dating Josh solely for the sex, and I argued profusely against it (it wasn't *solely* for the sex). It was the kissing—damn, that man could kiss. I swear he got a master's degree in it. I couldn't help but think that his ex-wife must miss him a lot.

If only I could adequately explain Josh's kissing method: He started out gentle and soft, like he was putting his lips to a baby or a trophy, the way athletes do when they've won the championship. His lips were neither too dry nor too moist—ever—as if he let them steep over a steaming cup of tea before he went anywhere. They lingered over my lips for a moment, luring me in to their supple goodness, and then it was as if he pulled my bottom lip open with his top, and sort of blew into my mouth (twice as fantasmic when he did this trick with my earlobe). After that, he French kissed me with slightly more force, but not invasively. He constantly freshened his breath—if I didn't know any better, I'd swear he woke up already minty fresh—and had straight, white teeth.

Meanwhile, his hand was caressing some part of me, depending on what number date it was and how receptive I was—my forearm, my cheek, my neck, right by the carotid artery, or just around the curve of my right breast (he was left-handed)—but I was so stimulated by the kissing that the caressing almost felt like an extension of it.

His kisses were so sexy, so intoxicating that I lost myself, and I was the one going further, leaning into him more, moving his hand to my knee and pushing my skirt up.

Or maybe it was just me—I was horny as hell, not having had sex in years. And so I shamelessly gave in on our third date, inviting him into my apartment (lit only by the streetlamps outside shining through the windows), pulling out a handful of wrapped condoms from my clutch purse, and leading him into the bedroom with an extended arm.

"It was a symphony," I said to Theo on the phone after Josh left the next morning, me still blissed out in my bed. "A ballet. An aria. A—"

"I got it, Sunny," interrupted Theo. "He's fucking Fabio in the bedroom."

"You meant that as an adjective and not a verb, yes?"

"Yes," she said. "Kinda rushing it, aren't you? What about your six-date rule?"

"Did you hear what I said? It was 'Rhapsody in Blue.' Besides, do you know how long it's been for me? My vibrator and I were about to file jointly."

I could almost hear Theo wince. "I don't need to know these things."

I snorted. "Oh, please. You told me you named yours Ed."

"Whatever. So where is Mr. Wonderful? Don't tell me he hit and run."

"He brought me breakfast in bed," I said, turning to lie on my back and replaying the memory of Josh carrying in two plates of burned buttered toast and two mugs of coffee, one with the Whitford's logo on it, the other a faded *Hard Rock Café Boston* logo. You'd think he'd made bacon and eggs and served them on china plates with mimosas in champagne flutes, the way I described it. "Then he had to leave to get to a store in Stanford. Wanted to make it to the ferry in time."

"Mmm-hmm," said Theo skeptically.

A few days before Thanksgiving, we both had too much to drink, and I showed Josh the 40 for 40 list.

"This is fantastic, Sunny," he said in his managerial cheerleader voice as he perused the list (I had learned by our third date that everything with Joshua Hamilton was "fantastic"). "Hmm, you haven't checked too many of these off. No. No, that won't do at all. We're going to change that, starting tomorrow."

"What, you're going to whisk me away to Paris or something?"

"No, we're going to get you published."

"How?"

"You're going to self-publish—and it pains me to say this—to the Kindle. Because, let's face it, that's where the action is. But we'll get you on the Trinket too."

I felt woozy and tried to sit up straight. "I don't know if any of my stuff is publishable. The agents didn't seem to think it was."

"Do you know how much good writing agents turn down in a day, a week, a month? Surely you're aware of how much the publishing industry has changed in the last twenty-four months."

"I see evidence of it in the shipment every day."

"So you of all people know the shit that's been going on the shelves. Publishers and booksellers want *bankable* content, not quality."

I frowned. "Come on, Josh. That's not only cynical, it's a sweeping generalization."

"There's an author who self-published solely to e-book format last year. She had two series of fantasy novels. You know how many units she sold in one month? *Two hundred thousand.* Two hundred thousand smackers in one month. She was a millionaire before the quarter was even up."

"I don't write fantasy. I write historical fiction—mysteries set on Long Island in the twentieth century. One for each decade, starting with the fifties."

"Even better! You can market it as a series."

"Yes, but who wants to read anything about historical Long Island other than geeky Long Islanders like myself?"

"People in Dumbfuck, Nowhere, who think Long Island is a glamorous place to live. And I'll bet there are plenty of other geeky Long Islanders such as yourself."

"But—" I started.

"Sunny!" said Josh, probably louder than he intended, being tipsy. "Strike while the iron is hot and fucking publish your books! What have you got to lose?"

The argument with Georgie invaded my mind at that moment, and I tried to push it out. Neither of us had acknowledged it since it happened.

What *did* I have to lose?

There was a time when I took rejection rather well. I diligently, ritually sent stories to magazines and literary journals and wrote pithy query letters to agents. Occasionally an agent requested the first fifty pages, or even the entire manuscript, and I'd sent them, hoping for the best but accepting the outcome either way. I could've opened a mail center, I was so organized. The possibility of rejection had never deterred me from pursuing my goal.

The same mentality applied to my love relationships. And that wasn't to say that I didn't feel the sting, or question whether I was chasing nothing more than a moving cloud when the rejection letters (or breakups) came. As long as the rejection was a private affair, then I could handle it. But the Humiliation with Teddy had changed all of that. He had made a fool out of me in public, and if my inadequacies as a wife and procreator could be outed, then who was to say any inadequacies that someone decided I had as a writer wouldn't undergo the same outing and humiliation? Not that I thought myself a bad writer—I loved the stories I wrote—but I already knew that I could not, would not please everyone. That wasn't the problem. It was this age of exposure. I didn't want the adulation any more than I wanted the evisceration. Become intimately familiar with my writing, fine. But pay no attention to the woman behind the keyboard.

I'd made petty excuses because it was easier than admitting that I was terrified of being discovered. And I'd become obscure as a result.

What did I have to lose? My invisibility cloak. It had become my security blanket.

"Will you help me?" I asked Josh.

"I would be honored to help you," he replied.

It was the first time I'd been proactive in years, and I couldn't believe how good it felt. Like I'd just gotten a shot of B-12.

The very next day I gave Josh the first manuscript of what we decided to call the Long Island Mystery series, *Long Island Ducks*, and he read it from beginning to end within days, copyediting and making notes along the way. According to him, it didn't need much by way of revision, just clarification of a description here, tightening of a plot line there, making sure everything fit, no characters' names changed halfway through, no dead bodies suddenly showing up alive, that sort of thing.

"It's really good, Sun," he said. "And it's marketable. I don't know why you gave up on this."

"Guess I thought the boat had already sailed," I lied.

"The detail is remarkable. You really did your homework."

"I was a history major in college."

"Really?"

I nodded. "Spent my senior year doing an honors project that involved historical research of twentieth-century Long Island. That material became the settings and background and stories in my novels."

"That is totally fantastic, Sunny. Wow."

I smiled. "History is, after all, nothing more than storytelling."

"I never thought about it like that."

Neither had I, for a long time.

I started spending nights and weekends I wasn't with Josh formatting my Word files and studying the basics of book cover design on Photoshop. I planned to upload the book to Kindle Direct Publishing first, and price it for one dollar, under the name Sunrise M. Smith, a decision I'd made reluctantly.

The CHANGE NAME entry on the 40 for 40 list had started out as a joke, but I started to seriously consider it this time. My parents named me Sunrise Morning Smith because I was born precisely at sunrise. They had been enchanted with the idea of calling me Sunny Morning, no doubt hoping my disposition would match. The names Jackie, Janis, and Glory had all made the short list (I had come very close to being named Morning Glory, in fact). In retrospect, being named Jacqueline Smith probably would've been tough during the *Charlie's Angels* fad, although I would have rather endured that teasing than all the stupid weather metaphors.

My brother's full name is Timothy Leonard Smith, and my mother once confessed to me that his middle name was supposed to be "Leary," after that "Turn on, tune in, and drop out" guy who used to encourage people to do LSD in the sixties, but then they imagined him filling out job applications. This was my parents' role model. Him, and John, Paul, George, and Ringo. And Bobby Kennedy and Martin Luther King and Gloria Steinem, of course. My guess is that had they conceived a third child, they would've named it Jerry Garcia Smith, even if she'd been a girl.

My name never felt like me—I never felt "sunny." Not that I was clinically depressed or anything like that. But "sunny" was the last word I'd use to describe myself. I had taken Teddy's last name, Hanover, when we were married because I preferred the sound of Sunrise Hanover to Sunrise Smith. Sunrise Hanover sounded like a corporation dedicated to clean energy. But I'd gone back to my maiden name because of the Humiliation and not wanting a lasting reminder of my failed marriage. It was bad enough that I had joined the ranks of the divorce statistics, something I'd vowed not to do when I was a hopeful and idealistic teenager. Sunny Smith didn't sound as bad as Sunrise Smith (although the latter looked more sophisticated in print than the former), but really, how asinine was it to pair such an unusual first name with what is perhaps the most common surname of all time?

"I'm thinking of going with a pen name," I said to Josh. "Hell, I would settle for Morning Smith, although that sounds way dumber."

"No. You need to take full credit for this," he said.

"Fine. But no author photo," I insisted. "I draw the line."

"You should at least set up a Facebook fan page."

"Josh, I'm not interested in having fans. Readers don't need to know me in order to like what I write. They don't need my picture next to their bed to understand the plot, or know what my voice sounds like in order to hear the character's voice."

"But you do need them to buy your books and then tell their friends about them. Like it or not, we live in a viral, networked world now. And people enjoy having access to their idols. Can you imagine if the Beatles tweeted back in the day?"

"Let me tell you something," I said. "I saw John Mayer's Twitter feed and it took me just two days to realize that I didn't give a rat's ass what was on his mind every five seconds. In fact, I'm surprised it took me that long."

He laughed, but maintained his position. "But it's more than that, Sunny. Don't you have favorite writers who have inspired you? Wouldn't you love to be able to tell them what their writing has meant to you?"

"Of course," I said, feeling horrible as the word *failure* pounded against my brain.

"What's so bad about someone wanting that moment with you?" he asked.

I decided to start with Twitter and set up an account with the username @SunriseMSmith. It was, ironically, one more step into the world.

Josh and I spent Thanksgiving apart, but exchanged Christmas presents and went to Tim and his wife Carrie's Christmas party together.

"He's so *mature*," remarked my mother. "Way more mature than Teddy ever was."

Dad liked him too, and Tim was even more smitten with him than I was once he found out that Josh was part of a fantasy football league. They spent over an hour in the corner of Tim's living room comparing stats and teams and players, clinking beer bottles every few minutes and gesturing as if watching an actual game. Josh had even offered to teach me how the league worked—I'd always been baffled by how seriously people took it—but Tim guffawed and wished Josh luck.

We spent New Year's Eve at the Whitford's company party in Manhattan (Georgie had declined, opting to help Marcus cater a party in East Hampton instead). We had also agreed to wait till after the holidays for me to meet his children. For one thing, we both wanted to wait to see where our relationship was headed before getting his kids emotionally involved. For another thing, the holidays were such a busy time for Whitford's that we hardly had time for ourselves, much less anyone else. Georgie insisted that the real reason Josh was delaying my meeting his kids was because he was avoiding his responsibilities as a father, acting out his midlife crisis in full force. He also insinuated that perhaps Josh wasn't taking this relationship as seriously as I was.

"It's not like I'm some bimbo half his age," I argued. "And besides, we both proposed it."

"Right," he said. "Just like you and Teddy *both* wanted kids so badly." The word was so cutting with sarcasm I could actually feel the slit across my heart. The wall between us was getting higher and thicker each day— instead of taking his lunch breaks with Theo and me, Georgie was now brown-bagging his lunch and talking to Marcus on his phone in the break room. If the three of us went out (and it seemed that Georgie wouldn't go anywhere with me anymore without a third party present), all things Joshua Hamilton had moved to the top of the banned topics list, along with Danny Masters, the Kardashians, and pop stars under the age of twenty.

"Look, do you realize how much this is hurting me? How much I miss you?" I had said to him one night, in tears.

"And you think this is a picnic for me?" he'd choked back.

"I just don't understand why you don't like him."

"He doesn't like *me*."

"You don't know each other."

"And I'm perfectly happy to keep it that way," he said. "Listen, Sunrise. I know he's, like, Mr. Sex God—guys like him have to be—"

"What do you mean, guys like him?"

"—and you were needing someone to cuddle up with besides me, but really, you could do so much better than him. Hell, you're better off trying to get back in touch with Danny Masters."

"Georgie, if I didn't know any better, I'd swear you were jealous."

"I have a *partner*, Sunny. Notice I didn't say a lover or boyfriend. This isn't some bullshit stereotypical gay fling where I'm looking at the next guy while out with my own. Honest to God, sometimes I think you're no better than anyone else. Marcus and I are *in* this relationship."

"I'm *in* as well," I argued. "And so is Josh."

"Whatever."

"So this is how it's going to be from now on? You're not going to support me until I break up with this guy?"

"I *am* supporting you right now," he said. "You just can't see it."

———

Seeing the listing for *Long Island Ducks* on Amazon, and my name on the cover, was beyond exhilarating. I immediately took a screen shot and posted it on my Twitter and Facebook pages; the idea of an author fan page was suddenly tempting. When my first sale appeared on the Kindle Direct Publishing sales report, I erupted in tears of joy. By the end of the first week, fifteen units of *Long Island Ducks* had been purchased, and I was over the moon. Theo and even Georgie were beside themselves with excitement, as was Josh.

"I am so proud of you," he said to me one night in bed. "It's only going to get better from here."

"I hope so."

"Must be great to cross something big like that off your Forty for Forty list."

I nodded, feeling the warmth of the very thought of it, never mind having actually done so. "You have no idea. *I* had no idea. I never imagined taking charge of my life like this would feel so empowering, so contagious. I feel like my life is in motion again."

"That's fantastic, Sunny, it really is." He kissed me, and then a devilish look came across his face. "Now it's high time we talk about that other item on your list."

"What other item?"

"Sleep with Danny Masters."

Oh, for fuck's sake…

CHAPTER
SEVENTEEN
Danny Masters

FADE IN:

INT. PUBLIC RADIO STATION BUILDING - MORNING

JACK WOODWARD (35 years old, the stress of the job has taken a toll on his face) enters the building, a briefcase and paper coffee cup in each hand. Passersby greet him by name.

CUT TO:

INT. JACK'S OFFICE - MOMENTS LATER

JOSIE STARK (late 30s, attractive, professionally dressed) sits at Jack's desk. She is putting in eyedrops when Jack startles her.

                    JOSIE
     It's about time you got here.

                    JACK
     It's six a.m.

JOSIE

Legal has been circling the wagons since this thing
broke.

JACK

There was a line at Starbucks. Can you
believe that? Five thirty a.m. And there's a line.
You'd think they were handing out crack.

JOSIE

And that goes to the top of the list of things I don't
care about right now.
Jack sits on the other side of his desk. Looks disoriented to be on that side.

JACK

What's the problem, Josie?

JOSIE

You're kidding, right? We're getting calls from every
local news organization about the firing of Gordon
Ramos, not to mention far right-wing pundits calling
on Congress to cut off our funding yet again. One of
them referred to us as "elitist" seventeen times, and
that was all in one sentence.

JACK

Did he use it as a noun or a verb?

JOSIE

Will you take this seriously, please? We're losing sponsors, donors are withdrawing their pledges, and our affiliates are distancing themselves from us.

JACK

All because we fired one of our local reporters for making incendiary remarks?

JOSIE

Not just any local reporter, Jack. Gordon has been a news reporter with this station since you were in diapers. Not to mention that he's Latino.

JACK

We didn't fire him because he's Latino. We fired him because he referred to the Main Street Mosque as "a terrorist camp" and the Quran as "a book of satanic verses." I don't care how senior he is. You don't go saying that in a culture that is already grossly misinformed.

JOSIE

I'm not so sure he was wrong.

JACK

Please, *please* tell me you didn't just say that.

JOSIE

I didn't mean it like that.

JACK

'Cause I'll follow him right out that door, voluntarily and willingly.

JOSIE

That's not what I--I meant that he was voicing what people already secretly think and are too afraid to say. His words were taken out of context.

JACK

What the hell context preceded "terrorist camp" and "satanic verses"?

JOSIE

I'm just saying, the video was edited, and we got it out of context.

JACK

Is this all your way of saying you're re-hiring him?

JOSIE

I'm saying we may have acted too rashly without doing a full investigation.

JACK

Welcome to 21st century journalism, Boss.

Life slowed down once the *Exposed* premiere season ended. The interviews and promotion ceased, the phone calls and e-mails were reduced to their usual levels (which was still higher than those of the average person), and the YouTube video had become a thing of the past.

So had Sunny. Or at least Danny had decided to make her such since he still hadn't heard a word from her. Whatever the encounter outside the theater had been was just that—a pleasant exchange with a fan that, unfortunately, had turned ugly. And just as he didn't mean what he had said during the Q&A that evening, he told himself that she probably hadn't meant what she said either. *Just forget it*, he thought.

But he couldn't forget it. The words *jackass* and *failure* haunted him, especially when he sat at the computer to write. He'd erased everything he'd written for *The Seven Year Itch* pilot—including the show's title—and started over, taking Ken's suggestions about streamlining it more to the kinds of things he typically wrote. Throw out the comedy idea, as well as the cheesy romance angle, but keep the married couple and the public radio station in a more serious setting. He wasn't sold on the title *Working Together*, but decided to keep it until a better one came to him in the shower.

None did. Nor did the good dialogue, character motivations and revelations, or story ideas, for that matter.

Dez, Charlene, everyone told him it was a temporary slump, that he'd get his swing back in no time and to enjoy all the good ink *Exposed* was getting. The word *Oscar* was volleyed about not only for Danny, but also Paul, Shane, Sharon, and the film itself. The hype still made Danny nervous; he was convinced there was no better way to jinx a win than by prematurely calling it a shoo-in, but he reveled in the praise for it.

Danny spent Thanksgiving with Charlene and her family. Typically he spent the day with Ella, but this year she requested that he spend Christmas with her instead—namely by taking her to New York. When he asked Frannie about it, she gave him her permission. "It's the only thing she really wants. That and a new coat to wear in New York."

"Did she give any particular reason why?" he asked.

She shook her head. "I think she wants you all to herself this year."

He liked the idea of that.

Mr. and Mrs. Dumont were such a sharp contrast to Charlene's A-list lifestyle. They still lived in the Indiana house she grew up in (although Charlene had paid off their mortgage after signing her first multimillion-dollar movie contract); he was a retired police officer, she a nurse-turned-manager of a doctor's office, six months away from retiring. Danny almost regretted politely declining their invitation for him and Charlene to spend the weekend at the house. Charlene had two sisters, both married with children—suburban soccer moms who were still starstruck by Danny Masters as well as by their sister's stories about attending award show parties and being on the set with George Clooney and vacations on exotic islands. She was softer around the edges when she was with her family, as if she was finally out of camera range and could breathe a sigh of relief. And yet she clearly enjoyed regaling her sisters with her stories.

Her parents asked Danny about Ella and his work, praised him for *Exposed,* and apologized for comparing it to *Winters in Hyannis.* He was happy to indulge them, appreciative of their hospitality and home cooking. He especially enjoyed watching football with her dad and brothers-in-law. They asked Charlene if she was getting enough sunlight (Danny couldn't help but be amused by the question considering Charlene's home was in Malibu), eating properly, making time for herself, etcetera. Charlene answered each question dutifully, but with a little bit of an eye roll, until Danny admonished her in private.

"Stop being so condescending to them. They're treating you with love and respect. I would've killed to have my father take that kind of interest in me. You have no idea how lucky you are to have been raised in this family, and you're treating them like they're your fans."

"It wasn't always roses," she protested. "My father wasn't home a lot. My mother was always taking care of someone. Hell, the only time I ever got any attention was when *I* was sick."

"I find that hard to believe," he said.

"Don't tell me how to behave in front of my family," she snapped. "They're *my* family, not yours."

He could hardly wait for Christmas.

Danny and Ella did the touristy things in New York first—visiting the tree at Rockefeller Plaza and taking snapshots with Prometheus blurred in the background, yet visible in all its iconic stature; attending the cheesy holiday show at Radio City Music Hall (and geezus, when had the Rockettes gotten so *young?*); visiting FAO Schwartz and watching Ella turn seven again as she hugged stuffed animals as tall as she was. The two of them walked up and down Broadway, and Danny pointed out theaters he'd been to, including the one where *Madness* had been performed before it was adapted for the big screen, and a building where he'd shared a two-bedroom apartment with three other people—all actors—and no hot water.

Like so many native Long Islanders, Danny had spent his youth taking Manhattan for granted. It was a treasure chest he could open any time, knowing its contents were precious jewels but never taking the time to appraise them. He loved the New York of so many movies he'd seen—all those Woody Allen films, and Scorsese and De Palma, from romantic to dirty to scary to electric to mundane, even. He remembered being ten years old and loving the opening credits to *Miracle on 34th Street*, and young Danny was seeing the city from another time: cleaner, simpler, black-and-white not just in picture but in the abstract as well. That was the New York he wanted to live in. Why had he never created that in any of his works?

The day after Christmas, Ella asked if they could drive out to Long Island.

Danny's insides turned to stone. "Why do you want to go there?"

"I want to see where you came from," she said.

Ella was now old enough that he could tell her it wasn't the happiest of places for him, that it didn't

conjure good memories. But when she looked at him
with pleading eyes and begged, "For me?" (a gesture
he couldn't help but think was performed in deliberate
manipulation, and was manipulation ever not deliberate?), he knew he was whipped, and she probably knew
it too. Poor Richie.

They drove out to Bethpage, and Ella asked all kinds
of questions about who he used to play with and if he had
a dog and what his bedroom looked like and what colors
the walls in the house were and did he take the bus to
school—questions that Danny knew any forty-five-year-
old should be able to answer—but for the life of him,
he couldn't. He couldn't remember playmates, couldn't
remember posters on the wall or petunias in the backyard,
couldn't remember after-school activities or sneaking
out past curfew. He could remember the ashen face of
his father, sullen, bitter, an angry word always seeming
to hang from his lips in waiting, like an unlit cigarette.
He could remember the smell of the smoke, although he
thought perhaps that was more from his present than his
past (or maybe it was because he had been craving the
cigs so bad, curbing them while he was with Ella, who
demanded he keep it down to one a day and way out of
her presence, and by God, she'd better not smell it when
he was done). He could remember the face of his mother,
wrinkles framing her eyes and mouth and over her brows
and even around her chin. He remembered her eyes sunk
into her face, her bangs the color of her skin, her voice
mousy and rarely heard. He remembered wondering
why she looked older than all the other mothers, but he

couldn't remember what the other mothers looked like or when he'd seen them.

They drove down the street, *his* street, and Danny slowed to a stop when he approached the yellow cape, repainted and re-sided and smiling, adorned with flower-beds and dormant azalea bushes covered with Christmas lights that looked like they'd been dumped there in the daylight, and a carpet of grass that no doubt would be dazzling green come springtime, a plastic Santa Claus waving to the neighbors and passing cars. The mailbox at the edge of the driveway was wrapped in live pine garland, its little flag raised.

The house looked way happier than he ever had felt in it.

"It's cute," said Ella. "Way smaller than I pictured it."

"It does look small, now that you mention it," said Danny. "It had three bedrooms and two bathrooms. My parents' room was downstairs, and mine was upstairs. The other room was kind of like an office. I was never allowed in it."

"Mom says your parents weren't very happy because your father drank," said Ella before tacking on, "and that *you* weren't very happy either." She spoke with authority, expertise. Not a trace of trauma.

"Yes, that's true," he replied, wishing she would change the subject, the car still in park. "Unfortunately I inherited that from him."

"But you stopped drinking."

"Yes, I did."

"Because of the accident."

Please God, make her stop. And please don't let her ask me to take her to the scene.

"Why are you bringing all this up, El?" he protested with more annoyance in his voice than he intended. "You know I don't like to talk about this."

"I'm sorry, Dad," she said, sounding more mature and less like a remorseful child. "I guess I've just been wondering if that's what makes you so sad now."

Danny turned sharply to face her. "What makes you think I'm sad?"

"You've been this way ever since your movie came out. It's like you played your last baseball game because your knee went out and you're bummed about not being able to play anymore."

Ella rolled on before Danny could put together a response. "Everyone knows you're going to get the Oscar, but you're acting like it's the end of the world. You'll still write movies and TV shows and anything else you want to write. Write a novel or something," she suggested. "Or can you only write dialogue?"

He had looked pensively past her and at the house next door to his own, trying to make out the faces of neighbors past. "I'm not sure."

"Anyway," said Ella, "I just wanted to know where you came from."

He looked at his daughter, noticing how her hair fell softer and straighter than when she was younger, how her skin showed traces of blemishes, a breakout of acne thwarted by some magical skin care system that most teenagers couldn't afford, and wouldn't allow himself to look any further.

"Do you regret having me as a father?" he heard himself ask.

A look of shock overtook Ella's face. "*What?* Of course not! Are you nuts?"

"I mean," Danny backpedaled, "it can't be easy having a father who's so public, dating someone who's larger than life, seeking the spotlight..."

It was the first time he'd admitted that.

"And then there's the alcoholism thing and the scandal with the accident. I know you've gotten grief about that from your classmates."

"Please, half of my classmates' parents have been in rehab or got divorced over cheating on their spouses with hookers or their exes or their exes' brothers and sisters, or they've come out as gay on reality shows or something. Forgive me for saying this, Dad, but you're not nearly as fucked up as some of the parents of kids I go to school with."

He couldn't help but laugh. "Thanks, El."

"Have you ever thought about moving back here?"

"*Here?*" he asked, horrified.

"No, I mean Long Island in general."

"Oh. Not really," he lied. The idea of doing so had flashed across his mind's eye like a comet when he'd met Sunny that day outside the theater. "Why?"

"Because you seem more comfortable here. I mean, not right here in front of your old house, but in general. You seem more like yourself, although I've mostly seen you in LA. Weird, huh."

"That is weird," he replied, somehow knowing what she meant but not understanding how it showed or if anyone else had ever noticed it or why he'd never done anything about it.

"I think you should consider it," she offered.

"It's not really feasible for me to move back here," he said after a moment of consideration. "I'm not talking financially, just in terms of my work and where you and your mother are concerned. I could never be so far away from you."

"You travel all the time," Ella pointed out.

"That's different. I know I'll be back. And it doesn't mean I like to be away from you. If there was a way your mother and I could've stayed together, we would've."

"Not likely," she muttered in that teenage *whatever* tone, and it irked Danny, although he didn't press her to explain it. "Anyway, I really like it here."

"The city or Long Island?"

"Both."

"Wait till we get to the Hamptons. It's not as nice as it is in the summer, but the beaches are to die for. Definitely rivals the Pacific."

"You should at least get a house there," said Ella. "That would be so cool."

"I'll think about it," he said. "I'm really glad you asked me for this trip. It was just as much a gift for me as it was for you." He leaned over and pulled her to him.

"I'm glad too. Thank you for taking me here even though you didn't want to. And definitely think about it."

"I definitely will," he promised.

He'd done nothing but think about it since.

Sunny Smith

H E KNEW. MY BEAU KNEW ALL ALONG ABOUT me and Danny Masters, so to speak. Apparently the red Sharpie pen wasn't opaque enough. I silently cursed Georgie for putting SLEEP WITH DANNY MASTERS on the list. I cursed myself for forgetting it was there when I had shown Josh the list in my drunkenness. I cursed Josh for not mentioning it until this point, and I cursed myself once more for having shown Josh the list at all. Hell, why not curse the damn list while I was at it. Why he'd waited all this time to confront me about it, I had no idea. But it vexed me. More than that, it creeped me out a little.

"You can start with why you've got such a crush on him," said Josh.

I propped up my pillows and sat up in bed, trying to get comfortable. I couldn't remember the last time anyone, if ever, had asked me to explain it.

I took in a breath, exhaled, and opened my mouth to begin, but nothing came out. How stupid would it be if I told him that I believed Danny and I had chemistry? How stupid would it be to call him *Danny*, as if he were just another buddy? What were the odds that I could successfully change the subject? Spontaneously combust? Be kidnapped by aliens?

"Believe it or not, my ex-husband turned me on to him," I began. "Writing-wise, I mean."

Teddy had always loved cop shows, couldn't get enough of them, and was rather disappointed to find out that the network had replaced his beloved *Law & Order* with a midseason replacement, a new show, something about the Kennedys in Hyannis before the JFK and RFK assassinations. Or rather, a fictional family not unlike the Kennedys. The real family gave its approval because the writing was so good, and the network gave its approval because of the Kennedys' approval. (I had found all this out sometime after the second season.) I couldn't stand *Law & Order*, so I always read a book during that time or worked on whatever novel was in progress. We'd been married about six months, but we already had a routine.

Begrudgingly (and perhaps out of habit in that "same Bat Time, same Bat Channel" manner), Teddy sat through the pilot episode of *Winters in Hyannis*. And the following week he sat through the next episode. And the next. And the next. After six episodes, Teddy was hooked. "Hey, Sunny, you should watch this new show," he said. "I think you'd like it."

"What is it, *Law & Order: Who Gives a Shit?*"

He couldn't help but laugh. "No. It's this show about the Kennedys, only fictional—they're called the Winters. But you know it's the Kennedys. It's basically about these two brothers, Tom and Ben—JFK and RFK, respectively—and what they're like before they decide to run for president. Like, in their really young years, like college age."

These were the days before Hulu or YouTube, so I had to wait another week before I watched the show with Teddy, and I was confused as hell, having come in at the middle of the storyline. Poor Teddy had to explain something to me every five minutes, missing half the episode himself as a result. But I loved it. When I looked up the show online, I was surprised to find out that the guy who wrote *Madness* created it, and so far had written all the episodes too. Like most of the population, I loved *Madness*, thought it had been robbed at the Oscars, and had seen it enough times to recite the dialogue thanks to repetitive late-night and weekend showings on TNT and AMC.

Josh interjected. "So it's just his writing you're in love with."

"Well, I suppose that's how it started," I said, wondering how far I was going to let him in. "I hadn't seen any pictures or interviews of Danny Masters back then, and despite my watching the awards shows, I guess I never really paid attention to him."

Meanwhile, *Winters in Hyannis* had become a hit, and the critics loved it just as much as I did. And just like you start seeing the car you want to buy everywhere you go, suddenly Danny Masters was popping up—on talk shows, in *Entertainment Weekly*, *People* magazine, IMDb, you name it. (Who knew he had written so much, and how had I missed it all?) However, it was his appearance on *Inside the Actors Studio* (the first episode to showcase a screenwriter only) that clinched it for me. The way his eyes became glassy when James Lipton asked him about the creative writing teacher who recommended he write plays. The way he showed such loyalty to and compassion for his protagonists. His deadpan sense of humor, timing, and delivery in response to the really personal questions, knowing just when to take a sip of water. (He even did a spit-take). The way he opened his mouth as if to say one thing, and then surprised James Lipton with something else in an East Coast accent peppered with little bits of LA inflection. The way he seemed to be flirting with the audience.

And of course, the way he looked.

He reminded me somewhat of an absent-minded professor, dressed in faded blue jeans and a plain black, button-down cotton shirt and nubuck Oxfords. His hair was brown and thick, his skin slightly tanned, his eyes inviting. He wasn't movie-star gorgeous, but he was definitely attractive, charismatic, laid back, thoughtful, sensitive. Charming, even.

My type.

Of course, I loved that he was a native Long Islander, wondering how many degrees of separation there were between us—we were only five years apart—surely I must've known *someone* who went to school with him or worked at Baskin-Robbins with him after school or was friends with an ex-girlfriend or *something*. And yet I had never found the link. I also loved that he was a Beatles fan, an only child, that he called Joey Buttafuoco "the prototype of the asshole," and that the sound or noise he loved was his daughter's laughter.

Had I not been with Teddy, had Danny been just another regular Long Islander, had we met at a bar or through friends or had he come into Whitford's, I would've liked him, would've wanted to keep talking to him for as long as I could. I would've given him my phone number if the opportunity presented itself. And so many times I wished that had been the case, especially after Teddy and I split up. At times I found his inaccessibility to be almost painful, like being lactose intolerant yet loving cheesecake and living next door to Junior's in Brooklyn.

If only I'd known him before everyone else did. If only he'd known me.

Some days it was hard to tell whether his writing was the icing on the cake or the cake itself. I had become a Danny Masters connoisseur, getting my hands on anything and everything he'd ever written and watching it, reading it, studying it, stopping just short of rubbing it into my skin. The dialogue in my novels had improved tenfold following a stylistic observation and application of his use of cadence and rhythm. So did my storytelling. If he mentioned a certain book that he liked during an interview, I read it. I watched all his favorite movies. Pretty soon I noticed that when I wrote, I wrote not just with Georgie and Theo in mind, or Teddy; I wrote with *him* in mind as well. The greatest achievement wouldn't be hitting the *New York Times* best-seller list or having my books turned into movies starring George Clooney or Meryl Streep. No, it would be finding out that Danny Masters liked what I wrote. That it made him laugh, or kept him in suspense, or inspired his own writing in some way.

I suddenly became conscious that I was telling all of this to Josh—my brain ran an instant replay of my ramblings, and regret hit me like a wave.

I felt my face get hot. "I'm sorry," I said, wanting to disappear. "I shouldn't have gone on like that." I hoped he had tuned out at some point and turned his thoughts to sports or sales figures or something else. But his eyes were so intently focused on me, as if he'd hung on every word. Damn.

"What would you say to him if you ever met him?" he asked.

I took in a breath. "I've already met him."

"No kidding!" he said, a lilt in his voice. "When? Where? Don't tell me he came to the store one day."

"Georgie, Theo, and I went to the *Exposed* premiere in the city, and he was doing a Q and A with Paul Wolf, Shane Sands, and Sharon Blake."

"Holy shit! How'd you score tickets to that?"

"Georgie," I said sadly. "For my birthday."

Josh raised his eyebrows. "He really gets around, doesn't he?"

I pulled away and shot him an angry look. "What does that mean?"

He put up his arms in defense. "Whoa. Back off. I just meant he's very resourceful."

"You know, I don't get why you don't like him," I said. I had tried to broach the subject once before, but to no avail.

"I've got no problem with Georgie as a person. As an employee, he's not a team player."

"How can you say that? You don't work with him day in and day out. He works his ass off."

"And hates every minute of it."

"Says who?"

"Can we get off it, Sunny? You were telling me about meeting Danny Masters—which, by the way, I can't believe you didn't mention the night we went to see *Exposed*."

We saw it on our fifth date. I had to keep myself from crying through most of it.

I turned away from him in bed, regretting having brought it up. "It was no big deal," I said.

"Did you shake his hand?"

I shrugged.

"Did you talk to him?"

Shrug.

"Was Charlene Dumont there?"

"Not when I met him."

"Wait, was that the night some fan called him a jackass and a failure? Someone posted the video on Facebook."

My face began to burn and I pressed my lips together tightly as Josh picked up his Droid from the night table beside him, opened up YouTube, and searched for the twenty seconds I so wanted to banish from existence.

"Have you seen this? The look on his face is priceless..."

Before I could object or make a getaway, he had me by the arm and played the clip. I tried to talk through it, but he shushed me, and I watched the expression on his face change from amusement to recognition in the same time it took Danny Masters's face to morph from pleasant to bewildered upon that fateful utterance.

Josh turned to me, agog. "Holy shit, Sunny—that's *you!*"

My mind raced; should I play dumb? Flat out deny it? Come clean?

Shrug.

"Why didn't you tell me that was you? Shit, that's hilarious! Here I've been dating a viral star all this time and never knew it."

Elisa Lorello

"It wasn't exactly my finest hour. I wish the whole thing had never happened, and I sure as hell wish it hadn't been recorded for the world to see."

"So what did he say? I mean, I know he called someone a wannabe or something like that, but what were his exact words? I wanna hear it straight from the horse's mouth—what got you so riled up?"

I glowered at him, disgusted yet again. "You calling me a horse?"

"Aw, come on—lighten up, Sun! If you met him again tomorrow, what would you say to him?" he asked.

"Something stupid, probably," I replied.

"No, I'm serious. What would you say to him?"

"I really have no idea, Josh. I've never been good with hypothetical situations."

What a lie—writers relished hypothetical situations. Josh either bought it or let it slide without calling me on it.

"What would you *want* to say to him?" he asked.

Wait till you see me in a hoodie? Sing "I've Got a Crush on You" to me? Have amazing, fantasmic, run-the-train-off-the-rails sex with me?

I wanted to say I was sorry, of course.

"There's nothing I have to say that he would care to hear," I said, and then finally turned off the light and readjusted my pillows for sleep.

"Wow," said Josh quietly. I had no idea if he was angry, confused, or just plain hurt. I closed my eyes and silently willed myself to drift off to the world beyond my window, a world in which Danny Masters wasn't akin to a slice of cheesecake and I wasn't lactose intolerant. A world that, up until now, only existed in words. And I sighed in sadness, because the words, regardless of their loquaciousness, weren't enough. Not by a long shot.

PART TWO

Danny Masters

January 25, 2011

D ANNY MASTERS DIDN'T HAVE TO SET HIS
alarm for the crack of dawn that morning. He knew
that if he was nominated for an Academy Award for Best
Original Screenplay, Paul, Ken, Jackson, Dez, and a host
of others would call to congratulate him.

Besides, he wouldn't be able to sleep. He knew that
as well.

And sure enough, around 5:42 his iPhone rang beside
his bed.

It was official.

Charlene opened her eyes and said in a groggy voice,
"Congratulations, Danny. Welcome to the Emerald City,"
before rolling over and falling back to sleep. Danny got
out of bed so as not to wake her and took call after call,
thanking them for their well-wishes. He said little but
talked rapidly, feeling a mix of elation and awe.

He brushed back his hair with his fingers and stared
out the window.

The Emerald City. It was an appropriate metaphor, he
realized, in more ways than Charlene could've known in

her half consciousness. He flashed back to the scene when Dorothy and her companions (and which one was he this time—the Scarecrow? Cowardly Lion? Tin Man? Toto?) set their sights upon its magnificent skyline. "It's bigger and more beautiful than ever." It was. To reach this point of his career was like having the Holy Grail within one's reach. It was the ultimate achievement: acceptance not only by the public, but also by the industry, by his peers, by the *craft*.

But he wasn't there just yet. He had to run through that goddamned poppy field first. And that was the scary part. He would have to hold his breath for four more weeks; after all, what could be a more potent opiate, a better high than being nominated for an Academy Award? There was the potential of getting *too* high. And what happened when he finally reached the gate? Would he be turned away? Worse still, what if he were let in? What if he *won*?

He remembered Ella telling him, *You're acting like it's the end of the world.* She wasn't wrong. What was beyond the Emerald City?

"Enjoy this," Paul said to him. "Enjoy every minute of it. It's a thrill of a lifetime. A Disney ride."

"I'll try," said Danny.

That goddamned poppy field. He'd have to make a run for it. But shit, that sure was a pretty skyline.

CHAPTER

TWENTY

Sunny Smith

Oscar Night, 2011

TYPICALLY GEORGIE, THEO, AND I HOSTED an Oscar party, and last year Marcus made the most fabulous hors d'oeuvres. But I didn't feel much like sitting through the tension between Georgie and me, pretending it wasn't there, with poor Theo stuck in the middle. Nor did I want to feel all eyes on me as I watched Danny Masters stroll down the red carpet with Charlene Dumont, his eyes flickering as he smiled that charismatic smile of his, saying over and over again that it was an honor just to be nominated. I didn't want my friends telling me one more time how crazy I was for blowing him off and not coming forward about the whole jackass thing.

I hadn't intended to watch the Oscars this year, all indications showing that it was going to be *Exposed*'s night, including Danny's. He had already won the Golden Globe, the Critics' Choice, and the Writers Guild awards for Best Screenplay, while the film snagged various trophies in acting, directing, score, cinematography, everything but product placement, it seemed. Although not much of an Oscars fan, Josh wanted to watch because *Exposed* had been his favorite movie of the year. Plus, he admitted, he wanted to see Charlene Dumont with Danny on the red carpet because he had a little crush on her, having seen her in just about everything she'd done, including a couple of commercials before she hit the big time. Figured.

We sat cuddled on my couch together, watching the preshow prance along the red carpet as we ate Chinese food out of cartons and opened a bottle of wine. I was dressed up as if we were going out rather than staying in (Josh had said the best part of our first night sleeping together was that he finally got to see what was under that hoodie). I was visibly nervous and fidgety.

"What's up, Sun?" he asked. "You'd think *you* were nominated for an award."

"I'm just not used to watching this without my friends," I said. "It's a big change for me. I kinda miss them."

"Change is hard, but inevitable. Not worth it to waste so much energy on the little things, though."

"To me, the little things are worth everything."

"That's one way to look at it... Hey, there's Danny Masters and Charlene Dumont—holy shit, she's a goddess. Sorry, Sun. Hope that doesn't bother you."

"Yeah, I get it," I said, my eyes practically boring a hole into the television screen, trying to telepathically communicate with Danny: *I'm here...* He looked alluring: clad in a classic Armani tuxedo with a white silk tie, his hair slightly longer and wispier than when I had seen him back in September, sprayed back in total Hollywood slickness. He was stopped on the red carpet by someone in the entertainment media (who it was I had no idea, but wow, was she *young*) asking him whether he was nervous, whether he was expecting to win ("You know, it's an honor just to be nominated..."), who Charlene was wearing (a phrase I always found to be rather weird), whether she was proud of him, and on and on. Georgie would've known before she even told the little girl (seriously, she looked fresh out of high school) who she was wearing, but I didn't pay attention, too fixated on Danny and feeling the pounding in my chest—as if I were watching the two of them walk down the aisle rather than the red carpet.

I felt Josh's eyes on me. "Hey, you OK?" He tucked a lock of my hair behind my ear.

I sat up straight. "I'm fine," I said, knowing he knew I was lying. "Got your bingo cards all ready?" Theo had introduced us to Oscar Bingo a few years ago and the games got rousing, the stakes being a trove of baked goodies or, on one occasion, a bowl full of cash. Josh was amused as he scanned the two cards I'd printed out for him (we decided to do two apiece, and I'd report to Theo the following day), Sharpies in hand.

Sure enough, within seconds of the show's start, we each called out a Clooney sighting in the front row, and I watched Josh mark an obtrusive X on the card. I was happy to share this little ritual with him, but I was also missing Georgie and Theo fiercely. Besides, with every camera pan across the audience, my heart thumped upon sight of Danny, and like radar, Josh eyed me each time.

Time passed in excruciating slow motion. Josh started scrolling through his e-mail in-box on his phone and sending replies. The more bored he became, the more restless I became.

Ninety minutes into the show, January Miller, last year's Best Screenplay Oscar winner, stood statuesque and graceful in an amber-colored, glittery gown whose designer Georgie would be naming with his eyes closed. She read from the teleprompter with a voice as elegant as she looked. Danny's was the third name called. I sat on the edge of the couch, leaning forward, as if watching game seven of the World Series, bottom of the ninth, bases loaded, three and two count, two outs, Yankees down by one, Jeter at the plate. I brought my hands to my face, ready to shield my eyes in case of disappointment, forgetting Josh was next to me.

And the Oscar goes to...

Dear God, kill me now. One blow to the head. Make it quick and painless.

Danny Masters.

The audience cheered unanimously, a few standing up as they applauded while a camera closed in on Charlene smooching him (which seemed to snap him out of his daze). It followed him as he made his way to the stage, his path blocked by Paul Wolf and the *Exposed* cast with congratulatory hugs. I tried to study his face—was it one of expectation? Surprise? Humility? Arrogance? Did I detect a hint of sadness? Suppressed elation? It was hard to tell, for the picture had suddenly blurred.

I was crying.

I felt Josh's hand gently rub my back, and I closed my eyes and hung my head, my ears straining to hear Danny recite his acceptance speech—you could tell he'd memorized it—with lightning speed so as not to be drowned out by the orchestra. One by one, the names sped past me like moving cars—his manager, agent, high school teacher, Paul Wolf, the cast, the crew, his daughter Ella, and then I thought I heard…

Sunny.

I snapped up at attention.

Holy shit, did he…? Was that…? Did he just…?

The orchestra music drowned him out, and he was led offstage.

Josh's mischievous, amused look returned. "Sunny!" he said, shaking his head in astonishment. "We're gonna have to get you a publicist!"

Not even a minute afterward—the show hadn't even cut to commercial yet—my landline rang. I picked up the receiver of the Mickey Mouse phone on the end table next to the couch.

"Sunny, I can't believe it—Danny Masters just mentioned you by name at *the Oscars!*" said Theo amidst a room full of excited chatter.

Georgie took the phone from her next, although I wouldn't be surprised if Theo had to goad him into taking it. "Congratulations, honey," he said sarcastically. "The *E!* Channel is gonna be knocking at your door any minute now."

The roller coaster ride had begun, without my permission, yet again. A flood of text messages and Facebook notifications barraged me. I wished I could deny it, but how many Sunnys could Danny Masters (or anyone else, for that matter) encounter in one lifetime? Did such coincidences really exist? Dr. Raj Patel, the self-help mega best-seller, had recently done a PBS special entirely on the nature of coincidence and synchronicity. I found myself wondering what he would make of this.

Josh teased me like a group of elementary school kids on a playground: "*Sunny has a boyfriend, Sunny has a boyfriend*," he sang. "And it's not *me*!" he laughed.

"Don't you know what this means?" Theo asked the next day during lunch. She didn't wait for my reply. "It means he still thinks of you, Sunny! Danny Masters *likes* you! You have to get in touch with him. It can't be that hard. Call the studio, call a newspaper, hire a PI, something."

I looked at her incredulously. "I am not going to stalk Danny Masters. And don't you think every Sunny is calling him right now, not to mention a bunch of Thelmas, Agneses, Joans, and Carolines—and probably a few Toms, Dicks, and Harrys, come to think of it—who've suddenly changed their names to Sunny? And how do we even know *sunny* was a name? Maybe he was saying something like, 'It's sunny skies from now on.'"

Theo wore an expression that implied I was stupid. I probably would've given me that same look.

"Seriously, I have no idea what you're afraid of," she said. "What more do you need, a hit on the head?" I didn't answer her. "And when are you going to patch things up with Georgie? I'm sick of being your go-between."

"I'm really sorry about that, Theo. That was never my intention."

"I never told you this, but there was a time when I was jealous of you two. You've always had a closeness with Georgie that you never had with me."

I reached out to take her hand. "That's not true."

She opened her hand and welcomed mine. "I mean, I'm OK with it now. It's different, that's all. I was afraid you were going to use me to take his place, and maybe a little part of me would've liked that. But now I see how miserable you both are, and it makes me miserable too. I miss the three of us."

We both had tears in our eyes. Beautiful, smart, funny, unafraid-of-life Theo. How could she think for even one second that I didn't love her as much as I did Georgie? And how could I make her happy again?

"I do too," I said softly. "Like crazy."

Danny Masters

Oscar Night, 2011

T HE NIGHT HAD BEEN SURREAL.

Previous Oscar winners had told Danny it would be that way. His head would be in a fog the entire night, his stomach an endless pit of anxiety. If he won, some force other than his legs would transport him to the stage, make his lips move, wrap his hands around the golden idol as if it were an Atari joystick from the early eighties. He'd think the oddest things at the most inopportune moments, they'd said, like how phallic the statue was, or thank God he didn't have to be wearing a gown and six-inch heels, or holy shit, what was his mother's name.

Of course if he lost, he'd been warned to look gracious and accepting, for the camera would be capturing the expressions of the losers, and more often than not, viewers watched *those* faces rather than the winner's. They wanted to see some sign of resentment, outrage, injustice. So Danny had practiced his loser look in the mirror just as much as he'd practiced his acceptance speech.

The moment fellow screenwriter and last year's winner, January Miller, enunciated his name, the words leaping from her lips, he heard a collective yawp, followed by a whoosh, as if the world had gone into slow motion and the oxygen was sucked out of the room. Were it not for Charlene cupping his face and planting a juicy kiss on his mouth, he might have forgotten she was there. He didn't remember walking to the stage or stopping along the way to hug Paul Wolf and Sharon Blake and anyone else who happened to be in his path. He didn't remember saying the words of his acceptance speech, although he hoped he'd said them all and not forgotten anyone. (He did remember, halfway through, wondering if any of Charlene's lipstick was left on his mouth, and he wiped it profusely at one point.)

And he had not remembered when and why he decided to hold up the statue and say, *Sunny, I hope all is forgiven.*

He'd not considered the ramifications of saying such a thing. He'd not thought about the camera that would simultaneously be on Charlene, watching *her* every reaction—first the tears (and he was pretty sure she'd been practicing that just as much as he'd been practicing his speech), then a flash of confusion, uncertainty in her eyes, all in an instant, before remembering where she was and who was watching her. He'd not considered that the press's very first question would be, "Who is Sunny, and what needs to be forgiven?" He'd had no desire to put Sunny into the spotlight, to explain to the world before he did to Charlene or Ella or Frannie or anyone else who she was. Heck, *he* didn't know who she was or why, almost five months later, he still cared. Her last words, *I'm not who you think I am,* still rang in his ears like tinnitus.

In a stroke of good fortune, the mic had cut out and the music signaled he was done. Thus no one heard anything beyond "Sunny," and no one asked for an explanation when he was off stage and in the pressroom, camera flashes rapid-firing, creating strobe-light optical illusions before his eyes. He had dodged a bullet.

The parties following the ceremony also passed in a haze—more flashbulbs and camera phones, more on-the-spot interviews by waif-like girls with long hair and fake tans wearing close-cut gowns and updos with enough hair spray to catch fire if they stood too close to a flame, and lots of handshakes, pats on the back, toasts, and applause. He drank everything nonalcoholic that he could find, surprised that what he missed more than the taste of the champagne was holding the flute itself. In fact, he was surprised that he was barely craving a drink at all and hypothesized that winning an Academy Award, and all the adulation that came with it, was a better intoxicant. And he knew he would tell no one how good it all felt, how the night totally belonged to him. He would deny the soft, seemingly distant panging (although he could feel it in the back of his throat) that the one person he wanted to tell was Sunny. For the duration of the party, people wanted to be his friend, wish him well, get in on his next project. *That* was what he drank all night.

He and Charlene came back to Danny's house just before the sun came up, and she kicked off her platform stiletto shoes, followed by the dress (both made by the some Italian designer), which she had to practically peel off like a Fruit Roll-Up. Danny had undone his tie hours ago, and he had stepped out of his shoes the moment they entered the house. She pulled countless bobby pins out of her hair, her updo sprayed so tightly it remained in place even as she tried to shake it out, and he guessed more had fallen out as she took a shower and scrubbed off her makeup. Meanwhile Danny sat outside on his deck and watched the sunrise, smoked a cigarette, and then closed his eyes. He was jarred awake when Charlene, dressed in sweats, flip-flops, and a towel wrapped around her head like a turban, kicked his lounge chair and said, "Now you tell me who Sunny is, and so help you God if you've been doing her all this time."

Danny paused for a beat to absorb the shock. "You heard that?" he asked, and when she didn't move a muscle he blurted, "It's not what you think," thinking, *My God, how clichéd*, as he said the words. Not to mention stupid. Even Charlene seemed disappointed.

"Really?" she said, her tone laced with sarcasm. He couldn't tell if it referred to his word choice or to the excuse. Perhaps both. She sat beside him and snuffed out his cigarette for him, waiting for an explanation.

"She's the woman who called me a jackass at the thing back in October," he confessed. The sun had fully risen and shone brightly, forcing him to squint as he spoke.

"And what was so important that you had to tell her in front of the whole goddamned world? In front of *me?*"

His mind raced for an answer. "I honestly don't know; it was a spur-of-the-moment thing. I just wanted to say something nice, I guess."

"Oh, please."

"Char, what do you want from me? I've had no contact with her since it happened. Besides, you seem to be the only person who even heard it," he said, although he knew fans were probably transcribing the speech as he had spoken the words.

"What I don't understand is why you mentioned her at all. What do you care about what one ungrateful fan said five months ago?"

"Because I thought she might like to be acknowledged in a positive way this time." Danny considered lighting another cigarette, but changed his mind after his stomach growled. Meanwhile Charlene continued to glare at him.

"What, Char," he said. "Just say it."

"You've been different ever since that premiere. It's like you're constantly preoccupied."

"Do you know how much pressure I've been under, especially with the new show? I've scrapped three different versions of one pilot script already, the latest version isn't even finished, and the press is already comparing it to all my other stuff without having read a word of it. They're judging it based on rumor. Now I'm an Oscar winner. Which, by the way, I'd like to enjoy for one damn minute, if you don't mind. Can we do that, please? I mean, look at it."

He'd placed the statue next to him while he dozed off, and gripped it again, feeling its cool sheen against his clammy hand. Charlene, no stranger to awards herself with two Emmys and two Oscar nominations, succumbed to the statue's hypnotic powers momentarily, studying its contours and admiring its luster, prying Danny's fingers loose so she could hold it herself. It seemed to have rendered her breathless for a moment.

"You've done it all, Danny," she said to the statue, her voice sounding soft and distant. "I mean, what comes after *this*?"

"Welcome to my nightmare."

Sunny Smith

I N JUST THREE WEEKS SINCE THE OSCARS, despite my trying to keep a low profile where my books were concerned (I now had two on the market and was getting ready to upload the third in the series), all kinds of people I'd known (and I use that word generously) in high school or college were coming out of the woodwork to tell me that they'd found my books and read them and they were really good and was it true that Danny Masters meant me when he said "Sunny" at the end of his Oscar acceptance speech and how did I know him and if I did was it possible for me to get their script in his hands and, hey, that jackass thing was awesome and, whoa, what was I still doing working at the bookstore when I was now a famous author and was I going to adapt my own books into movies and could they be in them and how hard was it to publish a book and if I needed somewhere to invest my royalties they knew a guy… Many of them found me either via Facebook or the Twitter account I had set up.

My parents were thrilled with my success; lately they'd been calling every week and asking me how the books were doing.

"You know you can check yourself," I said. "The rankings are right there on Amazon."

"It's more fun hearing it directly from you," said my father. He and my mom recommended my books to everyone they ran into—grocery store cashiers, librarians, the mail carrier, their mechanic, even the folks in the Quaker group they'd recently joined. Yes, my parents were becoming Quakers. It seemed to suit them, actually.

"Does this mean we need to buy one of those i-reader-doohickey-thingies?" asked Mom.

"You can download the software and read it on your computer," I said.

"I'd prefer to have a good old-fashioned paper book, if it's OK with you," said Dad. "If we're going to kill trees, let's use 'em for books."

Truth be told, I enjoyed their attention. They ended every phone call with "I'm so proud of you," and although they'd always been supportive of me no matter what I did, they seemed to have finally realized my writing was more than a hobby. And yet, I realized that by letting my novels sit in a drawer for all those years, and not having written anything new since splitting with Teddy, it was no wonder that they'd thought it was just a phase. Besides, when I was married, had I not spouted on about becoming a mom? With so many contradictions, it was hard to take any commitment I made seriously.

The idea that strangers were reading—and judging—my writing terrified me. Fifteen reviews had already been posted, so far all of them favorable, and none written by my friends. And yet I also couldn't help but be excited. It had pained me to see those manuscripts stuck in a drawer all these years, the collateral damage of my self-imposed obscurity. I had forgotten the exhilarating feeling of seeing my name in print, despite my wishing for a different name. I had given birth to every one of my books. I hated the banality of the metaphor—authorhood was no match for motherhood—but it did bear a slight resemblance.

Meanwhile Josh had joined Masterminds and relayed the conversations taking place there; the regulars that I had once been friendly with had insisted that Sunnyside, the woman from the jackass incident, and now mysterio-Sunny from the Oscar speech were one and the same. And all were speculating as to my whereabouts while hoping for another appearance from Danny Masters. I was dumbfounded.

"There can't be a connection, can there?" I asked Georgie when he came into the stockroom to check on an order and I filled him in on my latest sales report. He'd been coming in a lot less frequently since I'd started dating Josh. "I mean, how can these buyers possibly know the Sunny that Danny Masters blurted is Sunnyside, who is Sunrise M. Smith? I would never put those two together. How do they even know *sunny* was a name and not some random comment that got cut off? How many even heard him say it?"

"It's that old Wella Balsam shampoo commercial, remember?" he said. "You tell two friends, and they tell two friends, and so on, and so on, and so on."

"Yeah, but who told whom?"

"Who cares? Just take the money and run."

Before the Oscars I was averaging sales of ten units per day of both books. The day after, I sold forty combined. By the end of the month, I had climbed up to fifty per day, and my Amazon rankings increased by the thousands.

"Now that they're selling, I can raise the price to two-ninety-nine once I get the rest of the series uploaded, which will take me from a thirty-five to a seventy percent royalty on Kindle," I said to Josh one night, my enthusiasm causing me to speak quickly. "Add that to the fifty percent royalty I'll make on the Trinket and whatever the Nook pays out. Sell two thousand copies of all titles combined per month and I'll have at least four grand coming in every month."

"Holy shit, Sun," said Josh as he smiled with delight.

"If this keeps up, I may be able to pay off my credit cards by June."

"Hell, Sun, if this keeps up, you can say good-bye to Whitford's for good."

The idea of quitting my job struck me as illogical. "Why would I want to leave Whitford's? And why would you be so supportive of my doing so?"

"Sunny, you're a fantastic stock manager—really, one of the best we've got—but come on. You're *forty years old* and you've got so much more going for you." He emphasized my age in a way that made me feel self-conscious and antiquated. Since when was forty too old to be working in a bookstore? Heck, I was a manager.

He must have seen the effect of his remark on me because he backpedaled: "At the very least, you could move down to part-time and devote more time to writing. That was the plan you had with your ex-husband, wasn't it?"

Wow. Joshua Hamilton paid attention.

I decided to brush off the remark and go with the momentum. "I think it's time to get these babies up on the Trinket and the Nook."

"Agreed," he replied. "And you really need to get your own website with its own e-mail address."

"Why?"

"Because I googled 'Sunrise M. Smith' the other day and got a ridiculous number of hits. Book blogs are reviewing your books. Kindle sites are featuring you in their trending sections. You could be news, Sun. Hell, *Newsday* or News Twelve Long Island should be interviewing you. Maybe they want to and just don't know how to reach you."

The very mention of News Twelve sent my deflector shields up. "I told you," I protested, "I don't want in on any of that."

"Who are you, Cormac McCarthy?"

"It certainly hasn't hurt *his* sales."

"Is this because of what happened with your ex-husband?"

Wow. Twice in ten minutes. The first time felt validating. The second, however, made me feel like I was under a microscope. Like he was using my greatest weakness against me.

"Not everyone wants to be in the spotlight, Josh. Not everyone needs that kind of attention. I'm a writer. I'm not an entertainer or a performer."

"There's a difference between avoiding the spotlight and being afraid of it," he said.

"In today's day and age, when everything has an indefinite virtual shelf life, I think I have every reason to be afraid of it."

He bristled at my stubbornness. Ever since the Oscars, Josh seemed more determined than ever to help make my books successful, to make *me* a success. By nature he was a proactive guy (it was what made him so good at his job), but I was starting to wonder if I was nothing more than a project for him to troubleshoot, like a store that wasn't making its numbers. Maybe that day he met me he'd only been attracted to my potential, as if to say, *"Yeah, I could work with that. I can turn her around in no time."* And perhaps that's what Georgie had taken note of, and why he objected to it. Or was I just not used to having support from someone with whom I was so intimate? Had I let Joshua Hamilton in too much too soon?

Danny Masters

S EVERAL WEEKS AFTER THE ACADEMY AWARDS,
after the barrage of congratulatory phone calls,
e-mails, five-minute interviews (during which he said
the same things: *Yes, I'm still floating on air*; *No, I don't really
wanna talk about the part of the speech that got cut off, it was
just something I tacked on at the last second*; *The next thing is to
write the next thing*) finally slowed to a trickle, Danny went
to Ken Congdon's executive office at Kingsmen Studios
for a meeting.

"Shit, man, when was the last time you slept?" said Ken
after he gave Danny the handshake-morphed-into-a-guy-hug.

"I got six hours last night. That's good for me," Danny
replied.

"Been a helluva ride for you, huh."

"Indeed." Danny took out a cigarette and put it back
again. He'd been smoking twice as much since the Academy
Awards.

"Well, congratulations. Couldn't happen to a better
guy. You deserve it."

"Thanks," said Danny. "So what's up?"

"Sit down," said Ken, pointing to one of the two upright
chairs in front of his desk.

Uh-oh. Despite Ken's friendly tone, Danny knew this couldn't be good. He sank into the leather upright and took out the cigarette again. "Something tells me I'm going to need this in a minute," he said, tapping it against the pack.

"Your show was rejected, Danny."

A storm started to whirl inside Danny's gut. He couldn't remember the last time his work had been rejected.

"What happened to the sure thing?"

"The network wasn't happy with where you were going with it. It wasn't the writing, mind you. The writing, as always, was right on the money. But they weren't ever sold on the story or the characters."

"Ken, you told me to do more of the same, so that's what I did. Now you're telling me they wanted something different?"

"I guess the tides are turning and things aren't as surefire as they once were," said Ken.

Danny fumed. "Let's pitch it to HBO. They've always had the balls to show some decent television."

"If it makes you feel better, David Kelley and Chuck Lorre just had their pilots rejected as well, and Chuck's got the two hottest shows on television right now. That is, until Charlie Sheen went batshit crazy."

Danny couldn't help but feel for the guy—he was an addict, after all; besides, he'd met Charlie's father, Martin, on several occasions and held him in high regard.

"What the fuck *did* get picked up, then?"

Ken seemed hesitant to answer. "You don't know?"

"What?"

"Seriously, you don't know?"

Danny threw his hands up in surrender.

"Grapevine says that Charlene was approached to lead a one-hour drama."

He gaped at Ken as an inner thunder began to rumble. "Say that again?"

"High-profile woman making it in a corporate world, newly divorced. Something like that. Not quite *The Good Wife*, but of that caliber."

"And network television wants it," Danny said, more like a statement than a question.

Ken nodded. "I can't believe she didn't tell you this."

Danny stood up and showed Ken his cigarette. "I need to go outside and smoke this now." He raced out the building and lit it, pacing back and forth in the shade and taking long drags—he was starting to feel a burning inside his lungs every time he did so. One moment later, Ken joined him with a cigar.

"Listen, Danny. It sucks. So you just come up with a new idea for a show and we pitch that. Or forget television and work on another screenplay. You'll have offers up the yin-yang now that you're Academy Award winner Danny Masters. Or go ahead and try HBO. Surely they'll welcome you with open arms."

"I just wanna keep writing things that people wanna watch. Oh God, this is gonna be like the *Sports Illustrated* curse, isn't it."

"Excuse me?"

"Every time an athlete makes the cover of *Sports Illustrated*, something bad happens—they get a season-ending injury, they go into a slump, they choke in the championship game, a scandal breaks out, you name it."

Ken scoffed. "Please."

"Or maybe *Exposed* was the last good thing. Maybe I've run out of ideas."

"That's even stupider than the *Sports Illustrated* thing. Look, Danny. You've had a phenomenal career. It's rare to go through an entire career without a single rejection. Don't sweat it, man. You can write your own ticket right now."

"Whatever," Danny said as he flicked the butt on the ground and headed for the door. He held it open for Ken, who bent over to pick up the butt and snuffed it out completely before putting it in the trash can.

"The building gets fined for littering," said Ken.

Danny immediately felt ashamed for his behavior. Rather than follow Ken back upstairs to his office, he said, "I've got some calls to make. Is there anything else we need to discuss?"

"That's all for now. Seriously, Danny. This is not a big deal."

He looked at Ken incredulously. "Not a big deal? God, wait until the word gets out that Danny Masters's new show flopped before it even got out of the gate. Hell, before the Oscar accumulated dust."

———

Back at his office, Danny's first call was to Jackson Dobbs, who had left several voice mails for him.

"You know what?" said Danny. "I'm gonna throw my MacBook out the window. Then I'm gonna apply for a job at a movie theater ripping tickets because that's the only other thing I'm qualified to do."

Jackson laughed, but out of frustration. "Stop being so fucking dramatic and go write something. But first, I just wanted to tell you that the script book has a release date for April first."

"What? I thought it was coming out sometime in June."

"Publisher decided to ride the wave of your Oscar win."

Danny's agent had sold the idea of a compilation of scripts to a publisher shortly before *Exposed* premiered, when the screenplay had been leaked onto the Internet, but he had forgotten about it in the wake of the premiere and everything else that had happened. His first thought was that April Fool's Day was appropriate. He was also happy the publisher changed the title from *The Danny Masters Masters* to *The Danny Masters Best*.

An idea came to mind.

"What do you think about my doing a book-signing tour?" asked Danny.

He could practically hear Jackson's wheels spinning with approval. "I like it. How many cities?"

"I was thinking just New York."

"Why just New York?"

"Because I don't have time to do a cross-country tour."

"You just said you're an unemployed writer."

"And New York is where all the action is at. I was thinking Long Island too. You know, kind of a hometown thing." He could feel his face flushing from the blatant lie he was telling, certain that Jackson was seeing right through it over the phone, albeit clueless to his motives.

"Maybe. I'll talk to a few people about it. You should at least get in the entire Northeast, maybe Chicago or St.

Louis along the way, DC… I'll check out the cities with the best film schools."

Danny shuddered at the thought of schlepping around the country, every day away from Ella one more day he would never get back. He only hoped the traveling, the wrist cramps, the posing for pictures and taking questions would be worthwhile if he could just find Sunny and make things right with her, as if she were the key to making every part of his life work in harmony, the glue that held it all together. Such thinking was crazy, he knew, but what choice did he have?

For the rest of the day Danny's thoughts festered with rejection, Charlene's new show, and an anxiety that, despite having just won an Academy Award, he could become obsolete. Any spark of energy from the book tour idea had already been extinguished by his inner skeptic, who posited that Sunny wouldn't want to be anywhere near him. There were a lot of bookstores in New York. Hell, how did he know she still worked in one of them? Maybe she quit or was laid off. Or maybe she wasn't living on Long Island anymore. And why, after all this time, did he still care?

Forget Sunny.

Charlene's question from the morning after the awards echoed in his mind: What more was there? He had to come up with something new but had no idea what that looked like. If this pilot rejection was any indication, he'd already peaked. Anything else would be jumping the shark. He'd been really passionate about *Exposed*—in fact, he'd been disappointed to type the words *THE END* when he'd finally called it finished. He'd been so eager to see that film. What did he want to see these days, on the small or big screen? What would get him excited to write again?

Later that evening, he went to Charlene's place, where she was packing to do a location shoot in Vancouver. Danny sat on the edge of the bed and watched her; she'd already done her hair and makeup in case the papa-*rat*-zi or a fan with a smartphone caught her at the airport. Something about this irked him.

"What are you working on these days?" he asked, feeling contentious and knowing all too well that he was baiting her right off the bat, inviting a fight.

"The HBO miniseries about Gloria Steinem, remember?"

"Gloria Steinem was from Canada?"

Charlene shot him a look, one that Danny could've sworn said *jackass*, before she replied, "Location outsourcing."

"Since when does HBO need to outsource?"

"I guess this crap economy has finally hit everyone."

Danny huffed. "That'll be the day," he muttered. He continued to watch her, almost with an air of suspicion. "I thought your assistant did this kind of thing for you."

"She went ahead to Vancouver without me. Geez, Danny, you're acting like you're new in town."

"My pilot got rejected. Ken told me earlier today."

Charlene stopped in mid-fold, dropped the garment on top of the open suitcase, and joined him at the edge of the bed.

"You're kidding me," she said.

"Wish I was. I think it's my first rejection since I was twenty."

"That's a helluva winning streak."

Danny's nod turned into a shrug.

"Did they say why?" she asked.

"Just didn't like it, I guess. Although here's the interesting thing," he began as he turned slightly to face her, knowing he was about to throw the match on the gasoline. "Ken said the network is picking up a new one-hour drama."

Charlene looked down and pressed her lips tight, her face turning pink.

"You know anything about a new show, Char?" His tone sounded accusatory, like he'd caught her cheating on him. "A supposed knockoff of *The Good Wife*?"

"Ken got bad intel. Nothing's set in stone. We haven't even started shooting a pilot. And it's nothing like *The Good Wife*."

"Oh, so someone's pilot script got accepted? That's good to hear."

"Danny, stop."

He played dumb. "Stop what?"

"Stop your holier-than-thou attitude." She stood up and waved her hand at him in a chopping motion. "*This.* This is why I didn't tell you. So they passed over your show for mine. It's not like you're falling into obscurity. Hell, the least you could do is be happy for me."

Danny rose from the bed as well. "You *knew* they were passing over my show, and you didn't tell me? For fuck's sake, Char, you could've just castrated me instead of stabbing me in the back. Then you could've played yourself in the Lifetime Movie: *Charlene's Got 'Em by the Balls*."

One second passed. One full second of Now.

She smacked him. Right across his face.

It sounded like the pop of a firecracker, and burned like one too.

He stood there, stunned. The entire left side of his face throbbed and stung. Charlene took a step back, her face a shade of crimson, crumpling as tears came to her.

"You have said some mean things to me, Danny Masters, but that is the *worst*. In fact, that is the most disgusting thing anyone has ever said to me. *Ever.*"

It wasn't the slap in the face that made him regret it. He knew he'd crossed the line in that one second between the remark and her reaction. If only he'd known the second *before* the words came out of his mouth.

"Where do you get off?" she asked. "Really, what makes you so goddamn superior—because you have an Oscar now? No, it can't be that, because you've always been a smug, superior asshole."

"You're right," he said. "I'm sorry about that. It was out of line and you didn't deserve it." He wanted to take her into his arms and cradle her, beg her forgiveness, but she wouldn't let him.

She went back to her suitcase and resumed packing for no other reason than to keep herself from hitting him again, he guessed. Probably not more than a few minutes of silence passed, but to Danny it felt like hours. He'd been leaning against a bureau, holding his cheek all the while. They'd had knock-down, drag-out shouting matches before. They'd exchanged nasty-isms. But never, *never* had one raised a hand to the other. He tentatively approached her, holding his arms out as if to surrender.

When he was next to her, he tried to touch her shoulder, but she jerked it away.

"Char," he said softly, practically in a whisper. He didn't want to lose her again, he realized, but not for the same reasons as the other times. No, something else was begging him to make it work this time, to stay together. Something inside him was clamoring to settle down. "I'm sorry. I really am. What I said was mean and degrading and wrong. I didn't think before I spoke. I've got to stop that."

She didn't answer him.

He tried again. "Please," he beckoned, this time rubbing her back. And then, for a second, he could feel her body giving in, and he took advantage of it. He moved in closer and took her into his arms, and she let him. "I'm sorry," he whispered repeatedly, stroking her hair. "I'm not good enough for you. I never was."

"I'm sorry I hit you," she said, her voice muffled. Her body felt tight and stiff, as if she was trying to prevent any more cracks in her exterior than she had already allowed.

"I deserved it," he said. "And worse."

She pulled away from his embrace, and he left her alone to finish packing while he waited for her outside and smoked two cigarettes. He had agreed to take her to the airport and wondered if he should call a car for her instead. Or had she called one after he left the room? Even if she had, it would never arrive in time. Poor Charlene was stuck with him.

They rode to LAX in silence until he pulled up to the terminal.

"Will I see you when you get back?" he asked. He found himself already wishing for it, genuinely afraid that he'd blown it for good.

Charlene exhaled forcefully, like an exhausted sigh, before stepping out of the car. "Sure, Danny. Whatever."

CHAPTER
TWENTY-FOUR
Sunny Smith

G EORGIE CAME INTO THE STOCKROOM. "Here," he said, and slapped the upcoming calendar of events on my workstation. "Finally, your chance to redeem yourself."

I looked at him quizzically; he gestured a nod to the calendar, as if to say, *see for yourself.* I looked at it. A date was circled in red, four weeks from today:

"SIGNING EVENT: DANNY MASTERS will sign copies of his new release, *The Danny Masters Best* script book."

My heart leaped into my throat as I gasped for breath.

"How…?" No other words would come out. I looked to Georgie for an answer to the question he already knew.

"His publicist contacted me. He's hitting every bookstore in the tri-state area, I think. I guess the publisher really wants to push it, given his Oscar win. Anyway, thought you'd like to be the first to know," he said, his voice sounding glum.

"Thanks," I managed to push out, and with that he turned and exited the stockroom.

"Holy shit," I whispered and looked around at the inventory, as if waiting for one of the books to respond. *Holy shit shit shit!*

I paced around the stockroom in a panic, butterflies fluttering frantically in my stomach as my heart pounded. Danny Masters was coming here. *Here!* To Whitford's Books & Café in Huntington Village on Long Island. He was going to sign books, which meant that he'd be here for hours. It meant that we'd be getting extra shipments of his books, and I'd have to help set up. It meant there'd be local press covering the event.

Get a grip, I silently told myself. It had been five months since our first meeting. Luc's super-cool cut and color had long grown out (I'd attempted to touch up the color myself and wound up with splotches of brown framing my forehead). If, by any chance, Danny got a glimpse of me, he'd never recognize me as the same woman from outside the theater, the bitch who'd called him a jackass. And a failure. I wouldn't be dressed to the nines this time. No, I'd just be a forty-year-old bookstore employee doing her job.

He wouldn't get a glimpse of me. He wouldn't even know I was there.

And besides, I decided, I wouldn't be there. At least not when he was.

Later that evening, Josh called from a hotel in Rhode Island. "So I heard your boyfriend is coming to the store next month—your *other* boyfriend, that is," he teased.

I hated when he teased me, especially about Danny Masters. "How'd you find out already?"

"Georgie e-mailed me the schedule today. So are you excited?"

"I have to *work* that day. You know the preparation that goes into an event like that."

"It'll be the first time you show up to work in stilettos and a cocktail dress, I'll bet!" he laughed.

That did it.

My grip on the phone tightened. "Shut up, Josh."

"Oh, come on, Sun. It's a joke."

"It's not a joke. It's you taking advantage of something I told you in a moment of vulnerability. Just leave it alone, OK? I'm done with Danny Masters. I'm gonna do my job and leave when my shift is over. Game over. Move on."

"Fine," he said, audibly annoyed. "In that case, have you checked your numbers today?"

Lately he'd been just as obsessive about my e-book rankings and hourly unit sales as I was, but I'd been so busy at work that I'd not had a chance.

"Should I?" I asked.

"Unless you don't want me to tell you that your books are listed in the top two hundred right now."

I gasped.

I couldn't help but think of the money first—my next royalty check was going to pass the thousand-dollar mark. Holy crap. My second thought was that every sales unit represented a *person* who had just purchased one or both of my books. There was no getting around it now—I had a readership, a *following.*

"That is fantastic news," I said to Josh. And then, more heartfelt, I thanked him. "None of this could've happened if you hadn't given me so much support."

"Wouldn't have been anything to support were it not for those novels of yours. It all starts with you and your talent, Sun." It sounded like more manager-cheerleader-speak, although I detected something else in his voice too. Not pride, but validation. Maybe I'd not been appreciating him all this time. Maybe I never had. It was hard for me to let any man all the way in.

"Next time I'm on the island, we're going to celebrate," he said. And then he shocked me. "I love you, Sun. You know that, don't you?"

It's not that we'd never said the words to each other before. We exchanged *I love you*s following sex or an intimate moment. Always in person. But this time they carried a fragility with them. If I didn't catch and hold them, they could shatter into a million pieces.

"I love you too," I said after I caught my breath. It was as if I'd realized it for the first time, as if I was finally seeing *him* for the first time. He was a good man, a good leader, and a good father who, despite that questionable first impression, loved his kids. I didn't have to see him with them to know that.

Maybe I had taken this relationship for granted. Maybe Josh was giving a lot more than I'd previously assumed. Maybe he wanted more.

"And I think it's high time I met your kids," I added after a beat.

This time he was taken aback, judging by the delay in his response.

"I think so too. And they want to meet you. How about next Saturday? My son has a soccer game."

"I didn't know there were spring leagues," I said.

"Rare, but yeah, they exist."

"I wouldn't miss it for the world."

"Great," he said. "I can't wait. But I intend to see you before then to celebrate your latest achievement."

I smiled in anticipation. "You'd better."

I got dressed up for my dinner date with Josh—skirt, heels, makeup; I even managed to make my hair look good. Lately I'd been trying to make an effort to use the long-abandoned New York wardrobe. It took me back to my elementary and junior high school days, when my mother distinguished "school clothes" from "play clothes." In present-day terms, my work clothes were the ratty ones, and play clothes were the nice ones, the Sunday best. And yet I still couldn't help but feel like a dress-up doll, my preferences more aligned with blue jeans and tapered long- or short-sleeved T-shirts. But the right accessories could even make those look one step above casual.

Josh looked exceptionally handsome in a tailored black suit with a crisp white shirt and no tie. He picked me up at my apartment, surprising me with a single rose, and was a gentleman through and through, escorting me and opening doors and seating me at the table. Perhaps he'd taken notes from the Cary Grant movies we watched together.

We perused our menus. "Get anything you want, Sun," said Josh. "Sky's the limit."

"Shouldn't I be treating you?" I asked. "After all, I'm the one makin' the big bucks now."

"True. Pretty soon you'll be getting into the premier restaurants without a reservation. You'll be wearing sunglasses indoors and have mineral water shipped to your beach house from overseas."

The waiter delivered our drinks, and then we ordered. Josh tasted his cabernet. "Seriously, though, Sunny. What are your plans?"

"My plans?"

"You've got two books in the top two hundred. I guarantee that they're going to go higher, and the others are going to follow fast. You're on your way."

I sipped my wine. "I don't know. It's all so surreal to me. I haven't really given it much thought."

"How could you not?"

The question made me feel self-conscious, as if there were something wrong with me. Rather than respond, I changed the subject to more mundane things: baseball and movies and other people's books. He didn't seem to be fully attentive.

It didn't take long for our food to arrive.

We took our first few bites in silence, until Josh put his fork and knife down. "Listen, I know we're not supposed to discuss work, and I so shouldn't be telling you this—"

"So don't," I cut him off; something told me that whatever was about to come out of his mouth was not good.

He ignored me. "Whitford's is in trouble. The Trinket is the only thing keeping them alive right now, but it won't be enough. We're talking store closings."

"Whoa, wait—*my* store is closing?"

"We don't know yet which stores are getting the axe. But if it's yours, it could be as soon as a year from now."

I sat and stared at him, shocked speechless. I couldn't fathom my life without Whitford's. It was like being told a friend or close family member had six months left to live, or that I was about to be evicted from my home. Where could I possibly go?

My appetite abandoned me, and I pushed my plate away. "For chrissakes, Josh, why did you just tell me that?"

"Because I think you need to start planning an escape route. Your job may not be here much longer."

"I...I don't know what to say," I stammered. "When will we know? How am I supposed to keep this a secret? And how long were they planning to keep it from us? They've been painting a very different picture in the newsletter."

"They've been placing all their bets on the Trinket."

"Still, it's not like them to be so corporate and secretive," I said, feeling somewhat betrayed.

"But they are," he argued. "They've always been a corporation, despite their mission statement. And you've got to start thinking like a corporation too. Especially since you are, in a sense. You're your own publishing company now."

"That's crazy, Josh," I said, although I wasn't sure what I was referring to—the idea that I was a corporation or that Whitford's was in trouble.

"Look, Sunny, you've got to listen to me. Whitford's is not going to take care of you. You're expendable. You've got to get out."

A tornado of anxiety was coming at me, and I covered my face with my hands as if to shield it. "Stop," I said. "Stop saying such things. I owe Whitford's everything. They've supported me, appreciated me, treated me well. I have a life because of them."

"Sunny. Come on!" I hated when he spoke to me with that condescending tone, making me feel like an awkward, naive teenager, and I glared at him as he spoke, resentment replacing anxiety in the pit of my stomach. "What life? You go to work, hidden away from the world, and you come home to me and your two friends. Plus you worship some screenwriter who insulted you. What the hell kind of life is that? If it wasn't for me—" he started, then cut himself off.

"Finish your sentence," I demanded.

He shook his head. "No."

I took the cloth napkin from my lap and dropped it on the table. "Yeah, I think you should. If it wasn't for you, what?"

"It just seems that sometimes I'm more interested in your future than you are. Do you have any idea how much effort I've made to get the word out about your novels? How do you think they got this far, osmosis?"

I looked at him suspiciously. "Just what have you done?"

He finished his wine, and I could tell he was deliberating on whether to come clean. And everything in my gut told me he'd done something that warranted a confession.

He took in a breath, then blurted it out. "I decided to use that video to your advantage."

My eyes narrowed.

"What video?" I asked, although in the back of my mind, I *knew*.

"I posted on Masterminds that Sunrise M. Smith is the same person who called Danny Masters a jackass and the same person Danny referred to at the end of his Oscar speech when he said *Sunny*."

I couldn't believe my ears. Had I been holding my wineglass, I either would've crushed it with my grip or thrown its contents into his face.

"And not just on Masterminds either. I went on Facebook, Twitter…" He began shooting off his sentences rapid-fire, as if to deflect my reaction or response. "Look, Sunny, you've been a big fish in a little bowl long enough. For God's sake, your nose is pressed up against the glass, it's so small. I'm not your regional manager here to tell you what a great job you're doing; I'm someone who loves you and is telling you that you're way bigger than Whitford's, and it's time to get the fuck out. I've been trying to tell you that all along."

He might as well have smacked me across the face.

I stood up and left him at the table. The moment I opened the door and the brisk air swept me outside, I exhaled and panted loudly, as if coming up for air after someone pushed my head underwater. I took out my phone and dialed frantically, having to start over twice because I kept pressing the wrong numbers.

Georgie picked up on the second ring. "What's up, Sunny?" he said with disinterest.

My eyes stung with tears as I sobbed. "Please, *please* pick me up, Georgie. I need you."

His voice became alert, even urgent. "Where are you? Are you hurt?"

"I'm at that French place in downtown Huntington by the water. You know, the one we took Theo to for her birthday a few years ago? I always forget the name of it."

"I know it. Can never pronounce it, but I know it."

"It's not…I'm not hurt, not physically. Just come pick me up, OK?"

"I'll be there in ten minutes."

"Thank you," I said, but he'd already hung up. I turned to find Josh approaching me.

"Get away from me," I said as softly as I could, afraid someone would think he was assaulting me. I headed out into the parking lot.

"Sunny, I know you're mad at me, but calm down and let's talk about it."

"And stop talking to me like I'm an idiot. God, I hate when you do that."

"I'm sorry, I really am," he said, and he sounded sorry too. "I know I come off that way sometimes, and I don't mean to. I just want more for you, that's all."

I kept walking away from him. A part of me knew he was being sincere, but I couldn't get past the betrayal. Then I stopped and turned to face him.

"You know how I feel about that video! You know about my ex-husband and how I don't want that kind of attention, and you went and did it anyway! And you know how I feel about Danny!"

There was enough light in the parking lot for me to see the look in his eyes and for them to tell me that last thing I said was too much.

"How *do* you feel about *Danny*?" he asked, injecting a hint of condescension into the name, as if Danny Masters and I had an actual relationship; or worse, as if I was deluded enough to think we did.

I dabbed at my eyes and cleared my throat. "Georgie's picking me up," I announced. "I think it's best you not be standing here when he does. He might mow you down."

Josh looked miffed and shook his head slightly. "Well, I'm not letting you wait in a dark parking lot by yourself."

"I could kill someone with the heel of my shoe, so don't worry about it."

"Fine." I watched him return to his car while I made my way back to the curb, near the entrance to the restaurant. He looked so handsome in his suit without a tie.

Georgie raced up in his two-door Civic (he had made it in less than ten minutes), and I burst into tears the second I stepped in and slammed the door shut. He leaned across and pulled me to him in a lopsided embrace, clenched for several minutes.

"I am so, *so* sorry, Georgie," was all I could say.

"I'm sorry too," he said softly. He was crying as well.

"I was a fool," I said.

"Me too."

"And I've missed you so much."

"Me too," he echoed.

We let go, and he wiped my wet cheeks with his thumbs, careful not to smudge what remained of my makeup, and cupped my face for just a moment. Then he leaned back a bit, as if to take a better look at me.

"Damn, Sunny—you look smokin' tonight!"

I couldn't help but laugh as I sobbed. "I do not, you idiot. My makeup's all smeared."

"But you're *wearing* makeup…and a skirt! You must really love this guy."

Another laugh quickly morphed into heartbreak. "I do. And I think we just broke up."

Georgie put the car in gear, sped out of the parking lot and up New York Avenue, then turned a corner and passed a closed Whitford's, looking dark and empty and alienated, as if its fate was already sealed.

"OK, Sunny Smith, author extraordinaire," said Georgie as we sat cross-legged opposite each other on his bed. I had changed into a pair of his sweatpants and a long-sleeved T-shirt, cuffing both at the ends; I always felt ageless when I was hanging out with my best friends. Georgie had already been dressed in pajamas when he'd picked me up. Marcus was in the living room watching TV to give us some privacy. Bless Marcus. "What did Mr. Wonderful do?"

"How clichéd am I, running off like a helpless little girl after a fight?"

"Right. It was all *your* fault. Now tell me what happened."

I started with the news about Whitford's. He didn't even change the expression on his face. Just let out a deadpan, "Well, that was predictable. What'd you think Mr. Wonderful has been up to all this time? He's been trying to assess which stores are salvageable and which ones aren't."

As this realization came into focus, I flopped sideways onto the pillow. "Ohmigod, I am *such* an idiot. Seriously. How did I not see that?"

"You've always had blinders on when it comes to Whitford's," said Georgie, before pausing to reconsider. "Maybe that's not fair of me to say. Actually, I've always envied you for that. I always wanted to adore the place the way you do, but never could. I hate the job way too much."

"Anyway, Josh went on about how I should get out. But it was the way he said it. He said I have no life, told me to get the fuck out of there—Whitford's, I mean."

Georgie fiddled with the imitation Milano cookies Marcus made, turning one with his fingers, as if to study it, before resuming eye contact with me.

"You're going to kill me for saying this, but he's right."
Then he muttered, "God, I cannot believe I'm siding with
that homophobic freak."

"He's not homophobic."

"Whatever. Did you hear me, Sunny? I said he's right.
You were always way too talented to fritter your life away
at Whitford's, and you've always known it, and you've
just been too afraid to go out into the big ol' world,
lest you get dumped again. Or succeed, for that matter. I mean, how many times have we talked about this?
Maybe I should've told you to get the fuck out too—no,
wait, I did! Many times. And you blew me off every time.
Never ran off crying, but still. What's got you so upset
this time is that it's finally sinking in now, and that's a
good thing."

"Maybe," I said as I considered this.

"That can't be all that upset you," said Georgie. "What
else happened?"

I paused for a beat, as if to prepare myself to drop
the bomb.

"Josh has been going on Masterminds and a bunch of
other sites and telling everyone that the one who called
Danny Masters a jackass, the Sunny in Danny's Oscar
speech, and Sunrise M. Smith the author are all one and
the same."

He looked at me, as if waiting for more. "And…?" he
finally asked.

"Geez, Georgie, what more do you want?"

"I wanna know what's so bad about that."

"For starters, he did it *without my permission*," I said,
my voice rising slightly.

"OK, so he gets a strike there. But I don't see where the damage was done. Your e-book sales are through the roof and you're making money. So what's the problem?"

I looked at him incredulously. How could he not see it? "The *problem*," I enunciated, "is that it's Teddy all over again."

This time Georgie looked at me in utter disbelief. "Sunny, this is *nothing* like what happened with Teddy. Not even close. Teddy demeaned and humiliated you in public. He betrayed your trust and broke your marriage vows for no good reason. All Mr. Wonderful did was confirm what was already true, and he did it to give your books some attention. And it *worked*."

I sat there, dumbfounded.

"And that's not why you're upset. I mean, that's not what made you run out of there and call me."

"Then what is?"

"You're in a *relationship* with him, Sunny. A serious one. For chrissakes, you're about to meet his kids." He read my mind before I needed to ask how he knew. "Theo told me. That's a huge step for you. And while Joshua Hamilton may be a jackass—sorry, poor choice of words—he's been good for you. He calls things as he sees 'em, and that's precisely what you've been needing. Of course, he does that after he's schmoozed the hell out of you, hence that's why he's a manipulative jerk."

"He's not a manager twenty-four seven, Georgie. There's a side of him you don't know."

"He's got some strong attributes, I'll give you that. He looks good in a suit, for one thing. And he lit a fire under you. He helped you publish your books and encouraged you to start writing again. Why do you think he did that? Because he knew what was comin' down the pike, and he didn't want to see you out in the cold. He also recognized that you have talent, and that you were letting it atrophy in that dank cavern. He was trying to *save* you, for chrissakes, just like we were. And you let him. And although I'm glad you finally did, I gotta tell you, I hate that you let him and not us."

Those last words made an incision into my chest, and remorse bled out of me. How could I have not seen it from Georgie's point of view?

"I am such a fool," I said in practically a whisper, too ashamed to look at him.

"Correction: You *were* a fool. But now you know better. Now you've finally seen the light, and you can move forward from here. And you can realize that what you're really afraid of is that the closer you get to Josh, the more the window lowers on Danny Masters."

"There was never any window on me and Danny Masters," I insisted.

Georgie shook his head and sighed, "Oh, Sunny... Sunny, Sunny, Sunny Delight. So much delusion, so little justification."

I switched my position on the bed so that I was flat on my stomach, leaning on my elbows and staring ahead at nothing, processing all of it. Georgie handed me a cookie. I accepted and inspected it just as he did, as if to observe Marcus's craftsmanship, then took a bite and looked up at him.

"Do you think Danny Masters would recognize me if I came to the signing?"

He shrugged his shoulders. "Don't know. But the fact that he might not shouldn't stop you from going."

I nodded slowly.

"I blew it, Georgie."

"You fucked up, I'm not going to lie to you. But you've always had the power to fix it. Sorry to be all Glinda the Good Witch on you, but it's true."

"What would I say to him?" I asked.

"How about, 'Sorry I called you a jackass'?"

"Then what?"

"I don't know… Then, 'Sign my fucking book and do me right now'—what, you want me to play Cyrano? Speak for yourself!"

I broke into laughter. "Yes, Georgie. That's exactly what I want. Screw it. From now on, you're my official spokesman. Hell, you can even ghostwrite my books too."

Georgie shook his head. "Won't be able to."

"Why not?"

In the blink of an eye, he stopped laughing and his eyes grew both scared and serious as he straightened his posture, took in a breath as if to speak, and then stopped and hopped off the bed. He left the room and came back with Marcus seconds later.

"What's up?" I asked, getting more nervous by the second.

"We have to tell you something," said Georgie. I moved to the edge of the bed and sat on the corner, looking up at both of them, my hands gripping the comforter. He looked at Marcus, who took his hand, and then let it out in one exhale. "Marcus and I are moving to Massachusetts to get married."

The room was still and silent; I couldn't even hear myself breathe. I tried to ask him to repeat the words, but my mouth wouldn't move.

"Sunny, did you hear me?" asked Georgie.

Still nothing. He said it again, and then Marcus took over.

"We've been planning it for a while now, Sunny. Georgie's been assisting my catering business in order to get some contacts and experience so he can be an events planner. He's already got three interviews lined up in the coming weeks: one's for a PR firm, one as a wedding planner—"

"That one was under protest," interjected Georgie. "You can just kill me if I get that gig."

"And one is at a high-end hotel in Boston," finished Marcus. "I've got an interview there as well, as an executive chef. If that doesn't work out, I'll just relocate my business."

It was taking a while for my voice to return. "But…" I started, trying to will the words. I looked at Georgie, pleading with him to read my mind instead, and he seemed to be trying to do that very thing. Finally the words spilled out. "I thought you didn't want to get married. I mean…" This time I looked at Marcus. "I knew you both were committed, but every time I brought up the subject of marriage, you totally dissed it."

"I spent so much of my life believing that it wasn't meant for guys like me that I never allowed myself to want it. And the longer Marcus and I are together, the more we realize we both want it."

"But why do you have to move? It's gonna be legal here like any minute now," I said. I knew the question was a selfish one, and thank goodness Georgie saw through it and didn't jump all over me.

"Sweet Sunrise, I've been waiting a long time to get out of my crappy job and my crappy inertia. Long Island's just not the place for me anymore. It's too little."

"It's a *long* island," I protested.

"Not for me, it isn't. It's a fishbowl."

Wow. Just hours ago, Josh had used the same metaphor. Georgie would hurl if I told him they had one more thing in common.

I sighed back a sob. "When are you leaving?"

"As soon as prom and wedding season ends," said Marcus.

The cookies I'd just consumed sat like boulders in the pit of my stomach as a single tear made its way down my cheek.

"I know I should've told you sooner, but things were so weird between us. You have no idea how much I wanted to." Now Georgie started to tear up, and Marcus turned and asked his lover—no, scratch that, his *fiancé*—to leave us alone for a moment. Georgie closed the door behind him as Marcus sat on the bed next to me while I wiped my eyes with the back of my sleeve.

"Sunny, Georgie's been a mess without you. You have no idea how much you mean to him. I told him that this whole thing between you two was stupid and that you were both stupid to drag it out, but you're both rather stubborn sometimes." He playfully clunked my head, and I couldn't help but smile; I'd liked Marcus since day one. He reminded me a little bit of Ted Allen. "Your boyfriend really demeaned him at that meeting months ago, when you first started dating. Said Georgie would be better off doing something more suitable for his *lifestyle*. And he did it all under the guise of a smile. Georgie never told you because he was humiliated. He believed everything Joshua said was true, and it took me a long time to convince him otherwise. He was even more upset because you weren't there to make it better."

The guilt was enormous enough to swallow me whole. How many times had he tried to tell me, but I wouldn't listen? Or maybe he never said a word? Or maybe he was just tired of talking.

"Why didn't he say anything?" I asked. "Or did he, and I was too clueless?"

"Georgie knew how lonely you were, how much you needed someone in your life. It was a good step for you. He just felt so personally betrayed—not by you, but by Josh. It was as if he knew what you meant to Georgie and took you away just to show that he could, that he had all the power. I'm not saying that's what happened. I'm just saying that's what it *felt* like to Georgie."

I turned to face Marcus. "Why didn't you tell me this sooner?" I asked, my guilt manifesting as anger. "I would've stopped seeing Josh that instant! I would've apologized a thousand times over! I would have—"

"No, I don't think you would," Marcus retorted. "Or at least, I *didn't* think you would. Not from the way Georgie talked, and that's all I had to go on. I probably should've come to you, gotten your side of the story. I don't know. Maybe I didn't think it was my business."

"It was totally your business," I said, yet wondering if I would've said otherwise had he actually come to me.

"By that time we had a plan, and everything became about the plan. Both Georgie and I have been working our asses off so we can save money to buy a house, have something to live on if the job thing doesn't work out right away. There's been no room for anything in life other than the plan."

We sat on the bed, side by side, and Marcus took my hand into his own. We sat in silence for a few moments, both of us staring at the floor.

"I just got him back, and now he's leaving," I cried, sounding almost like a little girl.

"It's not that far," Marcus said. "Five hours, maybe? You can take the Orient Point ferry to New London and skip all the bridge traffic out of New York."

Just then Georgie opened the door following two soft courtesy knocks, and carried a cup of ginger tea to me. I took it as he instructed me to scoot over, prodding me gently, and sandwiched me between him and Marcus. I watched as the two of them exchanged knowing glances, realizing they'd mastered the art of mind-reading between each other, and that that was the way it should be. At that moment, a wave of calm overtook me, a feeling of all being right in my world. I hadn't felt it in a long time, couldn't remember the last time I'd felt it, or if it would remain, and I knew I had to seize it in the Now.

I wiped away the last of my tears and sniffled. "So who proposed?" I asked, an attempt to regain a sense of normalcy. I diverted my eyes to Georgie in a teasing way, for I could've bet money on the answer.

"He did, of course," said Georgie, rolling his eyes and nudging toward Marcus's direction. "Like you had to ask."

"That's not true," argued Marcus. "It was a mutual decision. I just decided to make a special engagement dinner."

"So, no official proposal? No one knee? No ring?" I asked. As if on cue, the two of them made exaggerated gagging noises and gestures, and the three of us erupted into laughter.

"We're gonna need an old maid of honor, Sunny Delight. Better start planning to use all that vacation time you've been hoarding, especially before Whitford's goes belly-up."

I laughed and looked at my best friend lovingly, adoringly, and told him that I wouldn't miss it for the world.

Danny Masters

D ANNY SAT UPRIGHT ON THE COUCH IN RAJ'S
office, tired yet jittery. He'd developed raspy cough-
ing spells from all the smoking and could feel the painful
burn in his throat and chest every time he had one, like
someone was lighting his larynx on fire.

The writer's block had never been this bad, or gone
on for this long, he told Raj. Ever since the Oscar win, followed by the television show rejection, Danny was terrified
of the page. Even Ella's encouragement wasn't enough to
bolster his confidence. He knew first drafts weren't final
drafts. He promised himself that whatever he wrote could
be as crappy as it needed to be, that no one would ever
have to see it, that he could erase it from his hard drive
so that no hacker could get a look at it (he'd rather be
caught with porn than bad writing, he joked). As long as
he wrote *something*.

But nothing. Absolutely *nothing* came to him.

It was as if all the voices in his head had been silenced
when he won the Oscar, like they'd been banished, blown
out by January Miller's voice announcing his name following, *And the Oscar goes to...*

Exiled.

As if he had nothing left to say.

But he had plenty to say. All those pain bodies that had been dredged up in the last six months—his parents, his childhood house, the little girl lying in the street with the contorted dog (that ghost never stopped haunting him, despite the girl's survival), and *Sunny*... For fuck's sake, why couldn't he get Sunny out of his head? This woman he'd met once, who'd called him a jackass and a failure, who'd put him in his place and then iced him out. It was all *her* doing. She had reached into his chest, grabbed hold of his heart, and squeezed it like a stress ball day in and day out.

"It's that old adage of wanting what you can't have, right?" he said, hoping Raj would confirm. "That's why I'm obsessed with her."

"I don't think you're obsessed," answered Raj. "I think your soul is telling you that you *can* have what you want, but you're insisting otherwise."

"Bullshit," said Danny. "That's got to be bullshit."

"Why?"

"Because it's too easy. Life just doesn't work out that way. It's not all hearts and butterflies. You're buying into the very thing you sell, which is wishful thinking, only you're cloaking it under mystical language of 'the soul.'" He made quote marks with his fingers as he said the words. "Just think happy thoughts, and make it so. Life is not a vending machine. You don't put in your coins and press a button."

"The candy bar gets stuck sometimes, doesn't it?" Raj asked, ever-amused.

Why, oh why couldn't he ever win an argument, just once, against Raj? Just once, why couldn't Raj put up his hands in defeat, as if to say, "You caught me, man"?

He shook his head. "Quack," he said. Raj laughed loud and hard. Danny joined him. "Charlatan. Snake oil salesman. Fucking cult leader!" Raj's laugh only increased in volume and intensity, and he stood up with outstretched arms to hug his friend.

Danny loved Raj. And he wanted to believe him, to believe it was all that simple and spiritual and mystical. He wanted to believe there were unseen forces looking out for his best interests, intervening on his behalf in spite of his skepticism, to give him all his heart desired. But he just couldn't. To do so would be to secretly believe in fairies or fortune-tellers. He'd be too afraid his father would find out and call him a sissy or a chump, even from the grave. And it was the stuff of after-school movies, soap operas, and self-help, happy-crappy books. Not good for writing, although given where his career was going, it might be the only thing left for him to write.

Following his visit with Raj, Danny arrived at Frannie's house in the cul-de-sac just before sunset and honked the horn. She opened the front door and waved him inside. *Uh-oh*, he thought. *This can't be good.* His abdominal muscles constricted as he turned off the engine and got out of the car. She left the door open and he entered, the scents of freshly baked rolls greeting him. Thanks to the settlement, she was financially set for life, but she still worked part-time as an aesthetician at a day spa in LA. Ella had never seemed to mind the constant shuttling between both houses (sadly, so many of her friends did it that she viewed it as a normal way of life), but he sometimes wished there were a way the three of them could have continued to live under one roof, if for no other reason than convenience and stability for their daughter.

"Hey, Frannie," he said casually. Despite their painful divorce (what divorce wasn't painful?) he and Frannie had always managed to be amiable toward each other once the dust had settled. They had established the ground rule even before Ella was conceived that no matter what, their children were never going to hear one parent speak poorly of the other in their presence. And both had lived up to that rule. Frannie had forgiven him years ago, he knew, but it didn't seem to assuage the guilt he had for fucking up the marriage in the first place with his drinking. And yet he also knew that sobriety had just shed light on some of his other flaws, and that's what had kept them from reconciling.

"You been sick?" asked Frannie as she shut the door behind him.

"No. Why?"

"You look a little pale."

To tell someone in LA that he or she looked a little pale was really saying something.

"I've not been sleeping well again."

"Try melatonin. It's a natural alternative to all that Ambien crap."

"Where's El?" he asked.

"She'll be down in a minute. I wanted to talk to you about something."

"What is it?"

"I heard you're planning a book tour."

"Yeah, it'll probably be just a bicoastal thing for a week or two. Nothing long-term."

"When?"

"Next month."

"You've been away from Ella a lot lately."

"No, she's been away from *me* a lot lately," he said before his defensiveness gave way to worry. "Why, did she say something?"

"*I'm* saying it," said Frannie. "Danny, your daughter needs you."

"You think I don't know that? You think I wouldn't take her on tour with me if I had a choice?"

"What's up with you and Charlene?"

Again he felt the need to go on defense. "What does Charlene have to do with this?"

"Danny, we've talked about this before. I really don't think this on-again-off-again thing you've got going on sets a good example for Ella. You know she's still seeing that boy Richie, don't you?"

"Yeah," he said. Thoughts of his daughter with any boy made him want to reach for a baseball bat.

"They text incessantly. And when they're not texting, they're talking. I hear her sometimes," said Frannie. "And Danny, sometimes she sounds like you."

"In what way?"

"In the way you get when you think everyone has a right to their opinion until they disagree with something you say."

He looked at her, irked. "People are free to disagree with me anytime they want. And while I may try to persuade them to see my point of view, I certainly don't think less of them for it. Especially not my daughter."

"Well, I don't know if she got the message. All I can tell is that she sometimes talks to him as if her words have no consequence, and when I asked her about it, she told me to mind my own business."

"She's a teenager. So what does that have to do with Charlene's and my relationship status?"

"Well, I think that's one of the reasons she acts this way. You can say anything you want if you take for granted that the person is coming back to you in a week or month or eventually. Besides, it's not good for her to see you so noncommittal, don't you think?"

"As long as she knows I'm committed to *her*. Besides, lately she's been too busy with her band competitions and going steady with good ol' Richie to even return my phone messages, much less get together with me."

"Maybe that's because she's gotten as complacent as you have."

Danny felt that familiar feeling in his stomach, the anger that started to bubble and boil and rise up into his chest. "Tell me this doesn't have to do with your disapproving that Charlene and I are together at all and maybe I'll take seriously what you've just told me."

"You see what I mean? Right there. Just now," said Frannie, pointing sharply at him, her fingernail lacquered a blood-red. "You just completely undermined me with that condescending tone of yours and dismissed me like I'm some jealous ex who has no life of her own. I'm fine, Danny. I'm happy. In fact, I've recently started seeing someone myself."

This news startled him. Frannie wasn't a serial dater by any means, nor did she get into relationships lightly, because of their potential effect on Ella. For her to tell him about it meant it was serious, or potentially moving in that direction. Moreover, Danny felt a jealousy of his own building up inside. He knew it was completely irrational, of course. After all, it was long over with his ex-wife, and he was hungry for Charlene even as they spoke, so why in the world should it bother him that Frannie was finding love without him? Why couldn't he be happy for her like he knew he should and wanted to be?

He meant to say "That's great" to Frannie, but heard himself say "Who is he?" instead, matching her interrogative tone.

She crossed her arms and glared at him. "You wanna do a background check on him or something?"

Just then Ella bounded down the stairs and bounced over to her father, giving him a boisterous hug and kiss just like she used to when she was a little girl, jumping up to try to reach him. Danny's heart melted, comforted that she wasn't fully grown up just yet.

"Hey, El," he said. "Ready to go?"

"Sure," she answered, and kissed her mom good-bye. As he left, Frannie gave him a final warning: "Just think about what I said."

"I will," he said earnestly. He owed Frannie a lot more. He owed it to her and Ella to be a better person. "Thanks, Frannie. And I hope everything works out between you and this guy."

The minute they were in the car and Ella fastened her seat belt, Danny put the car in gear and said, "OK, kid, tell me all about your mom's new boyfriend."

Ella rolled her eyes. "Pull-eeze don't tell me you're jealous. That's like totally gross."

Danny laughed. "In my day, the word was *rank*. Then it became *grody to the max*."

"You're old, Dad."

He dropped his jaw in mock indignation. "Just wait till it happens to you. You'll be forty-five and sitting around with your friends reminiscing about how iPods were, like, so millennial, and you'll still be waiting for flying cars."

The sound of her laughter rang like sleigh bells in his ears, dissolving any trace of the negativity he'd felt at the house. Danny loved their instant connection and kinship.

"So?" he asked. "Who is he? Do you like him? Hate him? Does he go tanning? Is he a Democrat?"

"I've only met him a couple of times. He's OK, I guess. Mom really likes him. I think he really likes her too. I'm happy for her. She needs someone in her life besides me."

"What's his name?" asked Danny.

"Steve."

"Steve?"

"Yeah, Steve," said Ella. "Why?"

"I don't trust guys named Steve."

"You don't trust anybody," said Ella. The conviction in her words rendered him speechless. He stared straight ahead, lips pursed, and listened to the purr of the Mercedes's engine, occasionally disrupted by bumps from driving over cracks in the pavement. Ella took this as her cue to listen to her iPod, and she began to untangle her earbuds. Not wanting to lose her attention, he found his voice.

"So I'm just playin' around here—nothing serious—but what would you think, hypothetically speaking, if I moved back to New York? Not that I would ever leave you…"

"*Yes*," she said emphatically. "Dear God, yes, and take me with you."

Danny nearly stopped short—so not the reaction he was expecting.

"What? Why do you want to leave?"

"I *hate* LA. I mean sure, the weather is great and all that, but come on, the people here are just so *fake*! I would much rather live in New York."

"How long have you felt this way?"

"I guess our Christmas trip clinched it, but I've been thinking about it for a while," she said.

"But why?"

"I told you, I'm tired of all the phonies out here. New York is just so much more real. It's got all four seasons and it's OK to wear something bigger than a size zero and I just feel like I belong there more than I do here."

Had Ella really inherited her father's outsiderness? he wondered.

"Sure, it's got all four seasons, but that also includes *snow*," he said. "Besides, what about Richie? Wouldn't you miss him?"

"I doubt we'll make it past high school. I mean, I'd be totally heartbroken, but I'm just thinking practically, you know?"

Danny nodded his head. God, when did she start growing up? Like, *really* growing up?

"Why do *you* wanna move?" she asked. "You said back at Christmas that you had no interest."

Danny turned a corner. "I'm just doin' what ifs."

"Sure," she answered, but her voice seemed to indicate that they were both keeping the game going for the sake of humoring each other. Then she added, "I would kill to go to the School of the Arts."

"Doing what?"

"Music," she replied. "And I've been thinking of taking up painting too."

This surprised him. Up until now, her involvement in the school band had seemed to be nothing more than an extracurricular activity, something that looked good on college applications. He had no idea she was so committed to it.

"I would take you with me in a New York minute," he said, acknowledging the tacky pun with a foolish wink, "but I don't think your mother would approve."

"Yeah, you're right." And then, as if they'd been talking about nothing more than the weather, Ella casually inserted her earbuds as a preparatory measure and started scrolling through her iPod. "Is Charlene moving to New York for good?" she asked.

"This isn't about Charlene."

"Then what is it about?"

"I told you, I'm just doin' what ifs. You had asked me to think about it, and I've been thinking about it."

"Dad. Please."

"It's not about Charlene," he said more firmly.

"How come you didn't tell me you've been thinking about it?"

"Because I've had a lot of other things to think about as well."

"Are you homesick?" she asked. The question struck him as mature and reflective, and he looked at his daughter, as if finding her remarkable. He'd had this reaction so many times when it came to Ella, and loved that it felt like a unique experience every time.

"Maybe," he answered. "I'm not sure."

"Well, I'd miss you. We could Skype each other."

"Yeah, I'm not a fan of Skyping."

"Get with it, Dad." She paused for a beat. "Thing is, I'll be going off to college soon—"

"In what—four years?" he interrupted.

"It goes fast," she said.

"Don't remind me."

"So then it wouldn't matter where you live 'cause I'll be off on my own."

"So you're saying I should wait a few years?" he asked.

"I'm saying you shouldn't wait if your only criteria is being there for me."

"You don't think you're worth the wait?"

Ella looked at him adoringly. "I'm just saying I want you to be happy."

Danny stared straight ahead, pressed his lips tight, and tried to will the tears that were brimming to the surface to not escape. Ella turned on her iPod, stared out the window, and bobbed her head up and down to the beat of whatever she was listening to. He was more determined than ever to make it work with Charlene. But he wasn't sure he'd ever truly be happy. Perhaps that had died in him the night of the accident.

CHAPTER
TWENTY-SIX
Sunny Smith

I WAITED TWO DAYS BEFORE RETURNING JOSH'S calls. (Georgie, Marcus, and Theo were all in agreement to let him sweat it out, despite the consensus that I had overreacted.) He picked up on the first ring, which was uncharacteristic of him.

"Hey, Sunny." He sounded simultaneously hopeful and worried.

I took a breath. "Hi."

Already an uncomfortable pause passed between us.

"How are you?" he asked.

"OK," I replied. "Listen, I wanted to apologize for walking out on you the other night."

"You had every right," said Josh. "The fault was entirely mine. I deserved it."

More silence.

"Sooo...where are we?" I asked.

"New Jersey."

"No, I mean, where are *we*?"

"Oh. Well, I guess that's up to you."

Ugh, I was afraid he'd say that.

I sighed. "I really don't know, Josh. And it's not because of what you said in the restaurant. It's just..."

"Look, Sunny, can you give me another chance? At least enough of one so that if you still feel this way, we can break up in person and not over the phone. I really, really don't want that."

Score one for Joshua Hamilton.

"I can do that, sure."

"You said you were coming to my son's soccer game this Saturday," he said.

I looked at the calendar hanging on my fridge. "Wow, that's *this* Saturday?"

"Will you still come?"

I trembled inside. "Meeting your kids for the first time is a big deal, both for me and them. I don't think it's a good idea when things are so fragile between us. Suppose I meet them and then we break up—what kind of stability does that teach them? What happens to them, and the next woman you bring around?"

Every response so far had been preceded by a second of silence, as if he were taking the time to carefully choose his words.

"Maybe now you have an idea of how serious this is for me. I'm willing to take that risk and gamble on the fact that it won't be a one-time meeting."

"That's an awfully big risk."

"You sound like you've already made up your mind, Sun."

Perhaps he was right. And yet I didn't want it to be so. There was a part of me that loved the idea of going to Josh's son's game, of making it a ritual to sit on the sidelines and cheer him on, going out for ice cream or pizza afterward. I loved the idea of his kids excitedly telling me how many goals they scored and how well they were doing in school, competing for my attention.

Georgie and I used to make fun of women who said this: *I'm in love with the* idea *of getting married. I'm in love with the* idea *of him* (whoever "him" was). However, I'd been too short-sighted to see that I was one of them. I had been in love with the *idea* of having a family. Teddy had made it sound so simple and idyllic. And I had wanted idyllic. I wanted picture-perfect. So I did just that—I nurtured the picture without knowing how to live a life.

The picture was long gone, and I still didn't know how to create the life I wanted. Was I supposed to get a new picture, or take Gandhi's advice and *be* the change I wanted to see? I thought about something Josh had said to me on our first date: If I had really wanted to be a mother, I wouldn't have let anything stop me. I wouldn't have made any excuses, wouldn't have dumped my writing aspirations (although I'd never demonstrated much tenacity there either, had I?). I would've found a way to be everything and anything I wanted to be. I would've *paved* a way.

Meanwhile, the 40 for 40 list sat next to my bed, recently neglected.

"OK, I'll go to your son's game."

He practically let out a sigh of relief. "Thanks, Sunny. I can't wait to see you."

"Me too," I said.

———

I had been anticipating whether we were going to have sex—throughout the entire two-hour drive to New Jersey

Friday night, and at his place, right up until John Lennon's (or was it George Harrison's?) lingering guitar jangle at the end of the Beatles movie *A Hard Day's Night.* I suspected Josh had been as well. If he made a move, would my accepting be seen as shallow, especially if things didn't work out with us? Would it be an act of intimacy or getting laid? Would it further complicate my deliberation of whether to stay together? If *I* were to make the move, would I be construed as a tease, hot one minute and cold the next?

Things had felt rather forced between us at first—we said nothing about what had happened at the restaurant or about what he'd done—and made small talk until he put on the movie and we settled on the couch, huddled together under a blanket to keep warm. Josh was a good snuggler. I would miss that if we broke up.

I washed my face and brushed my teeth and changed into a T-shirt and baby-blue cotton pajama pants with clouds on them. Juvenile, I know. Sometimes it was hard for me to believe I was forty. And although Josh thought they were cute, they certainly wouldn't have been his first choice of seductive apparel. He wore a faded Led Zeppelin T-shirt and silk boxers. He didn't look juvenile at all. In fact, he looked rather sexy. Plus he smelled good, like fresh soap and mouthwash.

Damn. I wanted him.

We each stood on opposite sides of the bed, frozen, nervous, like two kids about to do it for the first time while their parents were away.

He broke the ice first and spoke slowly. "Do you want to go to bed? I mean, to sleep?"

Aw, crap. He was lobbing the ball in my court, and I didn't want it.

"Yeah, I guess so," I said, my tone unconvincing.

We each shimmied under the covers and Josh turned out the light. You'd think he lived out in the country, the room was so dark and god-awful quiet. After what seemed like hours, he called me by name.

"Yes?" I said softly.

"Are we gonna talk about this?"

I lay in blindness. "Tomorrow," I said. "After the game."

"OK," he said after a long beat.

"Good night," I said. I turned to face him, and leaned in to meet his lips for a kiss. He found mine and kissed me softly. Then he kissed me again. And again. And the next thing I knew, our bodies were intertwined and we...

You know.

Damn Josh and his magic kissing.

We'd both wanted it, I guessed. But I couldn't stop wondering if we should have. Thus, between that and adjusting to the unfamiliar bed and the darkness and listening to the rain patter against the window, I got very little sleep.

In the morning he went out to get coffee while I showered and tried to do something with my hair, hoping the clouds would finally empty themselves out by the time his son Jeremy's game started. It had been raining nonstop since four in the morning. Josh said it would be windy on the field, so I shook the can of hair spray like I was about to graffiti the mirror and formed a misty halo around my head. Ugh. Too much.

I had just finished my makeup when he returned, balancing a cardboard carrier of two tall coffees with two bagels and a side of whipped cream cheese.

"I got breakfast and—" He stopped short when he saw what I was wearing: boot-cut jeans, the Nine West boots I'd bought in the city the day of the *Exposed* premiere, and the Stella McCartney birthday sweater. "Why are you so dressed up?"

"Because I want your kids to think me a pretty suck-up."

He laughed. "But you know the field's going to be all soggy and muddy, don't you? I mean, if there was ever a day to wear one of your hoodies…"

Oh, for fuck's sake.

"Should I go change?" I asked, dreading the usual work attire I'd arrived in last night, having driven straight from Whitford's.

He nodded. "You'll thank me later. And by the way, I think you'd look pretty wearing a barrel and suspenders," he said, interrupting his setting out two plates for the bagels to kiss me on the cheek. "And no makeup," he tacked on.

"Well, there goes my New Year's Eve outfit," I replied. "And the only reason you like me without makeup is because you've seen me without it more than you have with it."

"Don't you think that's a good thing? It meant you didn't have to go out of your way to create a false impression of yourself. I liked what I saw the moment I met you, and I'm not just talking about the outside."

Something about this touched me. "You talked to me for, what—five minutes? And I talked about my stockroom.

What on earth was so stimulating about hand trucks and pallets?"

"Because you called it *your* stockroom. You called it home. That didn't just appeal to me as a manager."

And then I thought about those five minutes with Danny outside the theater. So many times since then I wondered if he would've looked at me that way if I'd not had the makeover or the new outfit. Who was I kidding? He wouldn't even have stopped me to ask for the time of day.

I picked at my bagel, too anxious to eat. Josh kept assuring me that his kids were polite and well-behaved, that they understood his father dated, and that one day he might even get remarried. He assured me that there would be no sneers, no rude comments or fights picked just because, and no scrutiny. "You're going to a soccer game, not walking down a runway," he said. "The point of the day is to have a good time."

We arrived at the field five minutes before the game was scheduled to start. I carried a fold-out chair—already soaked—and tried to warm my other hand with the hot chocolate we'd bought along the way. The rain had mixed with the hair spray (even with my hood on), and my hair wound up clumping together, looking not unlike that of an abandoned brunette Barbie doll. Both teams were on the field, in separate circles as they warmed up passing the ball to one another (only there were three soccer balls in each circle) and then giving the goalies a chance to warm up with practice penalty kicks. I asked Josh to point out Jeremy to me, and he scanned the green-jerseyed team (the opposing team wore yellow), squinting in the rain.

We set up our chairs away from the coach and the moms at the table with Gatorade and carrot sticks and trail mix snacks, closer to the cluster of grandparents and other divorced dads (and I was surprised to see how many divorced dads there were. Or, at the very least, I presumed they were divorced).

Josh's eyes registered recognition as he pointed ahead. "Number forty-two." Then he put his pointer fingers in his mouth and whistled so loud I actually jumped. "Hey, Jeremy!" he shouted and waved. The entire team (including the coach) turned their heads upon Josh's whistle, but only one among the wet-headed, rosy-cheeked boys waved back, nonchalantly, as if not wanting to be associated with Big Scary Whistler Guy.

"He plays right forward," said Josh. "That's a good position. Do you know which one it is?"

I looked at him in mock offense. "Are you kidding? I'm from Long Island, remember? As a kid you either joined a soccer league or you were sent off to day camp and forced to play dodgeball until you got embolisms on your legs."

He laughed. "I should've known better."

"I lasted for two years as a fullback. Most boring position on the team. Then I became the kid who stayed indoors and read all day. That, and occasionally I hung out with Tim and his friends, of course."

Before he could respond, a girl in a pink raincoat and matching boots ran toward us (actually, it was more like waddling). "Daddy!" she cried. It was his daughter, Mattie.

His eyes lit up as he crouched down to meet her height and extended his arms where, seconds later, she crashed into his chest as he enfolded her into a sopping hug.

Oh, yeah. Her boyfriends wouldn't stand a chance when she turned sixteen.

I watched them interact with each other with a strange kind of fascination, as if I'd never seen a father and daughter interact before and wanted to know how it worked. Of course I'd had those kinds of affectionate moments with my dad when I was Mattie's age, although I couldn't remember any of them happening in a public place.

Josh introduced me as his friend Sunny. She giggled. "That's not a good name for a day like today."

"Nope," I replied. "I guess it's not. Should I change it to Cloudy on days like today? Or Rainy?"

"How 'bout Snowy?" added Josh.

She giggled even harder, "No! That's just too much to keep up with."

"I like your name, though," I said. She shrugged a thank-you.

"You wanna sit with us or stay with your mom?" he asked.

She glanced at me not quite apprehensively and only for a nanosecond before choosing to keep her mom company.

"No problem," he said as he looked ahead and made eye contact with a woman in a blue slicker, jeans, and sneakers, her hair hidden in her hood, just like the rest of us. I couldn't help but wonder if she was feeling as self-conscious as I, wishing the day had not been so cold and crummy, preventing a better opportunity to impress her ex and his new girlfriend. I wondered if she, too, was squinting in the rain, trying to get a better look at me and secretly hoping Mattie wouldn't like me, yet not wanting to interfere with her relationship with her father.

Suddenly parenthood seemed really foreign to me, and my thoughts turned to Teddy, presumably going to his own sons' muddy, drippy soccer games—what if they had been *my* sons as well? What if we'd had kids and divorced anyway? I imagined myself as the one sitting away from the sidelines, joining the divorced dads and grandparents, the *guests*. For some reason I imagined us having joint custody, but them living with Teddy. Maybe that picture was easy to form because he had the house. If we'd had kids and gotten divorced, would I have kept the house? Would I have fought for it?

Just then, Jeremy jogged toward us. "Hey, Dad," he said as if he were a mature twelve-year-old rather than nine.

"Lookin' good, Crush," said Josh. "Don't forget to avoid the offside."

"I will," said Jeremy. Then he turned to me. "Hi."

"Hi," I said. Josh quickly apologized for his lapse in manners and introduced us. I was surprised when Jeremy wiped his hand on his uniform and extended it to shake my own.

"Nice to meet you," he said.

"You too," I said. "Good luck."

"Thanks. Talk to you later," he called out as he ran back when the referee blew his whistle to signal that the game was about to start. Mattie also took it as her cue to run back to her mom. I watched him watch them with pride, and my heart warmed.

"Told ya they're polite," he bragged. "He shakes hands with everybody."

"Crush?" I asked.

"He wanted a soccer nickname, so I came up with Crusher. I'm not really good with names, but he never complained."

"I think you have a lot to be proud of," I said.

He nodded in agreement. "I do."

On the sidelines we huddled together, shivering, in an old comforter on our canvas fold-out chairs. The rain fell on us like slick little nails. Jeremy was competitive and confident, charging the ball with ferocious intensity. *A smaller version of his dad*, I thought. And yet I found it endearing. Josh and I exchanged play by plays, referee calls, and team stats as if we were sitting in the stands of a professional game, and we both jumped out of our seats (throwing the comforter off us in the process) and cheered when Jeremy scored a goal.

I was having a wonderful time, and cuddling with Josh under the comforter was plain ol' nice. At one point I looked at him, focused on his son, yet occasionally looking over at his daughter and ex-wife, waving to Mattie or motioning for her to come over and keep us company. He caught me and met my eyes. We locked our gaze and held it, and for the first time I think we each knew what the other person was thinking.

We didn't want it to end. Not yet. Give it another chance.

I kissed him, and we simultaneously broke into a grin when we opened our eyes.

"I'm fucking freezing," I said, laughing. We scrunched our seats as close together as we could while swaddled in the damp comforter.

Jeremy's team won the game thanks to his goal, and he ran up to us afterward, straight into his dad's arms for a quick hug, lest his teammates catch an uncool glimpse of him.

"You killed it, Crusher. Awesome game. Fantastic. Keep this up and you'll make the travel team."

"Thanks."

I wasn't sure whether to say anything. Would my praising him be construed as sucking up, or would my keeping silent be construed as indifference?

"What your dad said," I blurted. Well, that was stupid. However, it seemed to suffice.

"Thanks," said Jeremy. "Team's going out for pizza with the parents. You guys coming too?"

"Sure," we said in unison. Josh gave me a look of pleasant surprise.

Jeremy smiled. "Good. I'm gonna ride with Mom." And with that he jogged back to his mother.

Josh turned to me. "You're OK with this?"

"Of course I am. Why wouldn't I be? Besides, I've never tried New Jersey pizza."

"A bunch of nine-year-olds in a pizza place? I hope you brought some Advil with you."

———

Five slices and four Advils later, we got home sometime after two thirty. You'd think we had worked a twelve-hour day during the Christmas rush in the store, we were so worn out. I peeled off my clothes and changed into Josh's sweatpants, fleece sweater, and socks. While he piled up my clothes and put them in the dryer with his own damp heap, I flopped on the couch and stretched out as if I lived there. He poked me to keep me from dozing off and beckoned me to make room for him. I groaned and hoisted myself up; he sat down, a grunt escaping from him as he did, and he pulled me to him, enveloping me in his arms. I rested my head against his shoulder and closed my eyes.

"This is nice," I said.

"Mmmmmm," he replied. I could tell his eyes were closed as well.

"I had a nice time today."

"I'm glad you came."

I took in a relaxed breath. "Me too."

A moment passed. "So what do you think of parenthood?" he asked.

It took me a moment to put my words together for an answer. What I'd experienced today was far from day-in-day-out parenthood, but I knew what he was really asking me.

"It has its moments," I said. He chuckled. "Actually," I added, "for the first time I think my life turned out OK. I mean, you were right when you first told me that I was romanticizing having kids. I can finally see that."

"I never said that."

"Well, maybe not in those words… But I really liked watching you interact with Mattie and Jeremy."

"They like you," he said.

I opened my eyes and looked at him. "How do you know?"

"I just know. And you were good with them."

There was something satisfying about being a witness to Josh being a dad. Even seeing him with his ex-wife, I found myself studying their mannerisms toward each other, the way they communicated and were so reserved yet so committed to putting their kids' welfare above all. And I was glad Teddy and I didn't need to do that and never would.

There was also something satisfying about interacting with Jeremy and Mattie like an aunt or a pal. I imagined going to more soccer games and taking them out for pizza afterward, just me and them, trading stories and making jokes and giving advice. More so, I imagined myself as a *stepmom*. And although I'd never cared for the word or its negative connotations, I believed it was something I could do or be.

I looked at Josh lovingly, and he mirrored the same.

"Are we OK?" he asked softly, a touch of worry in his voice.

"I think so," I replied, just as softly, before adding, "but there's one thing." I pulled away, sat up straight, and looked at him sternly. "You owe Georgie an apology."

"For what?"

"For being a condescending jerk to him."

He looked at me, agape. "When was I a condescending jerk to him?"

"Please, Josh." I spoke in the same tone he occasionally used on me. And I have to admit, it was empowering. "It's obvious you don't like him. I don't know why, and God help you if it has to do with his sexual orientation—"

"Sunny—" he interrupted, visibly annoyed, but I wouldn't let him continue.

"But you've got to know that I'm closer to him than I am to my own brother, and I'm not going to let you treat him like that anymore. I mean it. Any disparaging remark to or about him, any eye-rolling, any hint of sarcasm, and you and I are over."

"Did it ever occur to you that he's overreacting?"

I shot him a warning look. "I'm dead serious. Georgie gets the benefit of the doubt from now on."

He looked at me in disbelief. "You're giving me an ultimatum?"

I didn't even bat an eye. "He's family. Tell me you wouldn't give me an ultimatum if it came down to your family."

He grew cold in an instant. "Whatever, Sun."

"No, not whatever. If you and I are going to move forward, then this is going to change. I'm not saying I'm perfect, nor have I given a hundred percent to this relationship. I want to do better, and I'm willing to go all in now. But I'm bringing Georgie with me. He's as much a part of my life as my parents and Tim and Theo and Whitford's. Take it or leave it."

And just as quickly as he'd turned cold, his expression then turned to one of equal parts consternation and fascination.

"OK," he said.

"Thank you," I replied.

You'd think I'd just won a court settlement, or grew ten inches, or performed a corporate takeover. It was like finding a little piece of me. She'd been there all along, buried underneath the dark curtain of Teddy's betrayal, underneath the shelves and stacks and shipments and pallets of Whitford's Books and Café, underneath the fear that being me was unsafe. I'd nearly smothered her, buried her alive, and for what?

Elisa Lorello

At that moment, if I could've, I would've done it all over again—would've told Teddy that I could serve his balls to him with more force than Roger Federer. Would've given Danny Masters my name and number. I would've welcomed adulation. Would've welcomed the chance to be loved and the chance to love someone in return.

Perhaps Josh's arms were a start. But as I buried my face in his shirt, I realized that in my mind's eye I was embracing that lost self. She needed that hug so badly.

"So, we're really OK?" said Josh.

I smiled and let go. "We're OK."

Danny Masters

D ANNY HADN'T SEEN OR SPOKEN TO CHARLENE since he dropped her off at LAX the night he made the crack and she hit him. He'd called twice, but she'd not responded. Of course, this could have simply meant that she was on a tight shooting schedule, up until all hours of the night, but he figured otherwise.

It occurred to him that she would never call him again, and he couldn't blame her. Perhaps it was for the best, he thought.

But finally she did call him, and he picked up immediately.

"Know what I hate?" he said when he pressed Talk, pretending as if all was well.

She didn't respond. Perhaps this wasn't such a good strategy.

"I hate interleague baseball. You know, when the American League plays the National League during the season. Does that make me some kind of baseball racist?"

What the fuck was he saying?

"Maybe you should get some counseling for that," Charlene retorted.

Every muscle in his body tightened. He fired off the basics: How are you? How's the shoot going? How's the weather? Charlene gave him one-syllable responses: Fine. Good. Cool.

"Is that cool as in not warm, or cool as in *cool*?" he asked. Man, he was trying so hard.

"Take your pick."

"So, I was wondering..." He hesitated. "If you're free next weekend, how about spending it in East Hampton with me. Just the two of us. Robbie Marsh has a house." She'd wanted to get him out to the Hamptons since last summer.

The silence on Charlene's end seemed to increase in duration with each response.

"I don't know, Danny." She sounded wary.

"You can throw me into the ocean if I get out of line. It's off-season. No one will know I'm missing until my body floats ashore on Memorial Day."

He could've sworn he heard a faint chuckle. Or maybe it was just the crappy reception. God, he missed landlines.

"C'mon, how 'bout it?" he pleaded. "We'll even try to catch a play at the Bay Street Theater in Sag Harbor."

He closed his eyes and crossed his fingers.

"Sure, why not," she said.

Danny had flown to MacArthur Airport in Islip and arranged for a car to take him out to the East End on Thursday night (Robbie kept a car at the house and offered it to Danny for the weekend). Charlene showed up the next evening—Danny had offered to pick her up at the airport, but she refused and arranged for her own transportation. Never had he been so nervous while waiting for her. His mind was too cluttered to enjoy the ocean outside. When he wasn't on the lanai smoking cigarettes down to little stubs (and practically eating those too), he paced the many rooms of the house, peering out the front windows every so often (as if doing so would make her magically appear). When she finally arrived, he raced outside to greet her and help her bring in luggage. It wasn't until he saw her heading up the path that he realized just how afraid he'd been that she wouldn't show.

He kissed her on the cheek, then took her in his arms and exhaled a sigh of relief. "I'm so glad you came," he said. He was slow to release his gaze upon her—it was as if they had only recently met, spending their first weekend together. He couldn't remember the last time he'd felt this hopeful, this optimistic. He wanted to start fresh, get to know Charlene Dumont all over again. He wanted to *finally* get it right.

"I need a drink," she replied.

He was taken aback by the sharpness of her demand. She was usually more considerate around him, curbing such statements. Robbie had asked the housekeeping staff to lock the liquor cabinet out of respect for Danny. The wine cellar, however, was not locked, and Charlene retrieved a sauvignon blanc made by Pindar, one of the many Long Island vineyards. Together they went to the high-ceilinged living room, furnished with contemporary styles and bold colors and big artwork. Danny was sitting in one of the uprights, nervously watching Charlene drink on the couch and listening to Ella Fitzgerald while they talked about her goings-on in Vancouver. He could barely complete a sentence, so preoccupied with every raise of the glass to her lips, wondering whether he should stop her. Or, at the very least, ask her *why* she was doing it. When she refilled the glass a third time, he could feel a pain in his chest. And while he watched her fearfully, she eyed him seductively.

"Come here," she said.

He padded to the couch and sat beside her. She pulled him by his shirt and was about to kiss him, but withdrew and squinched her face.

"Ugh, you ssmell like an asshhtray. Full," she slurred.

He covered his mouth. "Sorry. I've been smoking more than usual lately." As if on cue, he coughed.

Charlene rose from the couch, stumbling as she did, before taking his hand and pulling him up with her. "Why don't you fressshen up. I'll go pick a bedroom an' you come find me." She grabbed the bottle of wine and took it with her, staggering away. Danny could feel that usual feeling—the rush of blood, the quickening of his heart rate, the release of adrenaline. However, this time it felt less like sexual arousal and more like a panic attack. She was drunk. She'd gotten tipsy at the post-Oscar party, but nothing like this. He went to the master bathroom, brushed and flossed his teeth before gargling with mouthwash for as long as he could stand it. He stood before the mirror and pushed his hair back with his fingers, noticing the gray hair growing out around his temples, and leaned in for a closer look: Was this how most forty-five-year-old men looked? Did they have crow's feet, circles under their eyes, a modicum of gray hair? Did they feel this weary? Did they worry about whether they'd accomplished anything, about whether it was enough? Did they get as much sex as he did? Did they get as little sleep? Did they inherit the sins of their fathers?

He stepped back. Charlene was waiting.

He practically tiptoed down the L-shaped hallways, opening doors and peeking in. Almost every room was furnished as a guest bedroom, hotel-style, picture windows offering majestic views of the Atlantic Ocean. Not a bad place to spend a night.

Halfway down the second hallway, he opened a door and found Charlene sitting upright in bed, the duvet teasingly pulled up above her bare chest. The near-empty bottle of wine sat on the nightstand beside her; she was holding the glass and taking a sip when he found her. Why did she drink so much? Should he have stopped her? Should he tell her to stop now? Was he envious? He eyed the bottle cautiously, as if it were a pit bull poised to attack. If he stared at it too long, would it turn on him?

"You found me," she said in a sing-song voice.

"I sure did," he said, his voice quavering, as if he'd just met her for the first time, strangers rendezvousing for a one-night stand. He removed his T-shirt and dropped it on the floor, followed by his sweatpants, and climbed onto the bed. Charlene took a final sip and set the glass aside before she knocked Danny to his side and pinned him, kissing him hard.

Oh God, he could taste the wine.

His heart started to race.

It had been so long since his palate had been privy to that sensation, that sweet flavor (all wine had tasted sweet to him, or so his memory said), that extra kick that sent signals to his brain, putting it on notice that he was off to the races. He could taste it on her tongue and lips and teeth as clearly as if he'd sipped it from her glass. And, God help him, he wanted to keep kissing her just to let the flavor linger.

Had she wanted him to feel it? Was this her way of getting back at him for what he'd said to her the last time they were together? If so, it seemed too cruel a revenge.

Danny forced himself away. "Char, I can't. You…" He paused to let the sudden wooziness pass. "The wine is too strong."

She slowly, deliberately turned her head to look at the bottle, feigning an innocence that seemed to say, *Are you afraid of this little thing?* before resuming eye contact with him.

"*Quel dommage.*"

He grew hot with anger.

"I'm going to go to bed someplace else," he said, and left the room.

As he lay in the master bed, he stared up at the skylight framing a not quite yet full moon. His body ached with anger, disappointment, sympathy, regret, confusion, cravings.

This was no way to live.

———

Early the next morning, Danny stood under the spray of the shower for a long time, letting any remnant of resentment wash away, to the point where he'd decided not to confront Charlene. What worried and puzzled him was *why* she'd drunk so much in the first place. He knew all too well that downing practically an entire bottle of wine on one's own was an intention rather than a happenstance. Perhaps he *should* confront her—not for the purpose of accusation, but concern. And yet he remembered how many friends and lovers had tried that approach with him, and how unsuccessful they were.

No. Charlene wasn't an alcoholic. But she sure as hell wasn't having a good time last night either.

After he shaved and dressed, he went downstairs and found her sitting at the island in the kitchen: sunglasses on, head resting on her arm, a little bottle of Excedrin in front of her. The smell of French roast coffee filled the entire room.

"Morning," he said gingerly. He watched as she attempted to pick up her head, then thought better of it.

"Ugh," she replied.

"Coffee ready?"

"Arghhh," she groaned. "Not so loud."

"Sorry, Char."

"What the hell, Danny? Why'd you let me drink so much?"

"I honestly didn't know if it was my place to stop you. You never drank like that in front of me before."

"I didn't do or say anything stupid, did I? I mean, how did we end up in separate bedrooms?"

She'd forgotten everything, and he was relieved. Lord knew he wanted to forget it. Sitting there, she suddenly appeared to be so vulnerable to him, the previous night being nothing more than a failed cry for help. He was filled with remorse and compassion for her.

"You wanted to play a game of guess-which-room-I'm-in. Unfortunately, you passed out before I had a chance to find you. Either Robbie's house is too fucking big or I started looking for you at the wrong end," he joked, pleased with his lie. "I decided it would be better for you if I went back to the master bedroom."

She looked at him apologetically, a feeling of foolishness hidden behind it, he guessed.

"It's no biggie," he said. "You've been working hard lately. I figured you needed to cut loose."

Charlene's expression changed from regret to gratitude, and Danny felt good.

"So," he said, "you up for going out? It's going to be ridiculously gorgeous today, and I think we could both use some fresh air."

She willed herself off the stool and on her feet, gripping the edge of the island counter to steady herself. "Give me two hours," she said. "I'll be as good as new."

Danny took his iPad out to the lanai, checking e-mails and other sites, and trying hard to refrain from smoking another cigarette. The coughs were coming more frequently, the burning even more pronounced. He decided to go to Masterminds, not having been there since posting a message of appreciation two days after his Oscar win. He scrolled back to the day of his post and found himself touched by his fans' stories about their Oscar parties, about rooting for him the way they rooted for their sports teams, about shedding tears as if their brother or best friend had won. He was touched that they actually *cared*, were willing to overlook his flaws. Yet it was their overlooking his flaws that made him equally distrustful of their intentions. Maybe that's why Sunny was different—she had called him on his flaw, not as some fan pissed off because she didn't think she got her money's worth or because she thought Danny Masters owed her something. No, Sunny had seen him in action, and it had nothing to do with Danny the writer. She had called him out for the jackass he was.

He wanted to be a better person. Not for Sunny, or Charlene, or even Ella, he realized.

He continued to skim the discussion threads as he scrolled, until his eyes stopped on one that made him sit up and take the iPad in his hands:

Remember Sunnyside? Well, she currently has a novel for a dollar on Kindle. I read it and it's really good. Don't let the price fool you.

Wasn't Sunnyside the one who gave Danny a hard time about his apology?

Yes, she did. Sunnyside was also the one who called Danny a jackass and a failure. I know her personally. She confirmed.

No shit! I can't help but notice she's not here anymore.

And I hope she never comes back either. She disrespected DM and drove him from the boards.

Excuse me, but DM never came here before. If you recall, he came here to apologize, not to make friends with all of us. Sunnyside was always a breath of fresh air in here. There are plenty of us who miss her. And she had good reason to give DM a piece of her mind. He called his fans wannabes, issued a disingenuous apology, and probably didn't lose a wink of sleep from it. His movie grossed tens of millions of dollars and he went on to win the Oscar. Sunnyside, on the other hand, was treated like some kind of pariah.

Point taken. But no one told her to leave.

No one encouraged her to stay either.

And by the way, her real name is Sunny. She's the one Danny was addressing at the end of his acceptance speech when his mic got axed.

How do you know?

Dude, I *know*.

Well, now we know that the sunny to which he referred in his Oscar speech was a Who rather than a What. Do you think DM has spoken to her since?

Maybe he was telling her to get bent and that's why he was cut off.

It's douchebags like you who give forums like this a bad name. Sunny challenged DM, but she was never mean or disrespectful to him.

Dude, you're calling me a douchebag and saying *I* give forums a bad name? And tell me how calling a critically acclaimed screenwriter a failure is not disrespectful.

What's the name of her novel?

It's called "Long Island Ducks." It's under the name Sunrise M. Smith.

Danny couldn't believe his eyes.

He had been right all along. Sunny was the woman outside the theater, the woman who had confronted him both in person and on Masterminds. *An author!* But she had told him that she'd not been published!

A lot could happen in six months, he told himself.

He immediately went to Amazon, entered *Long Island Ducks* into the search box, and downloaded the book. He then opened the book to the end, looking for an author photo, but couldn't find one. Google was next. Her Facebook profile photo was a still of Cary Grant and Audrey Hepburn from *Charade*. Seeing it made him grin profusely—it said so much about her, all of it good. Her Twitter photo was the book cover.

Danny googled her name again, this time in Images, and was bombarded with an array of stock photos of sunrises. Suddenly he felt like a stalker. He logged off and went back to the beginning of the book, reading the first line:

Betty Greenfield had never seen such a big duck.

Already he loved it.

He read more, with a clear intent—he was reading *her*, just like with her past comments on Masterminds, trying to find any keyhole or opening from which he could enter.

Her family had recently moved from a tenement in Queens to one of the new houses in Levittown, the ones that still smelled like paint and fresh-cut wood. Their lawns once blanketed acres of

potato fields, and Betty swore she could smell those too. Levittown,
in comparison to Queens, was like being on vacation. The houses
stood sparsely aligned at attention; kids passed by on bicycles or
in red wagons, and it seemed like every other day a moving truck
was depositing yet another family on Meeting Street. Her childhood
friend Dorothy (whose family had also migrated years before, to
a town farther east with an American Indian name Betty could
never pronounce) was home from college in a brand-new Chevy.
Shelter Island was their summer destination, but first they stopped
in the town of Flanders.

Charlene opened the screen door to the lanai, and
Danny looked up, startled—not just by Charlene's trans-
formation, but that the two hours had passed like two
minutes. By the time she appeared, Sunny's novel had
teleported him back in time to a general store in the
mid-fifties, its owner mysteriously missing.

"Wha—" Danny said, baffled. "Who are you, and what
have you done with Hungover Charlene?"

Her hair and makeup were done and her outfit of
jeans, a long-sleeved, fitted tee, and flats made her look
perky. "My nutritionist in LA gave me an herbal remedy
that kicks the crap out of hangovers. I keep it in my bag
along with my Excedrin. It. Is. The. Bomb. It doesn't work
unless you have a full stomach, though."

Danny forced Sunny out of his mind, stood up, and
embraced Charlene. "I'm glad you're feeling better. You
look terrific."

The weather was postcard-perfect, a rare preview to
spring, traces of snow all but melted away. Despite the season,
the entire town of East Hampton was taking advantage of the
sunshine and warmth, its inhabitants and visitors strolling

leisurely, walking in and out of shops and boutiques with doors open to let in the fresh air, and opting for face-to-face conversations over electronic ones. Danny and Charlene both seemed to be on their best behavior, he observed, laughing and teasing each other in that new-relationship sort of way, even showing public displays of affection, papa-*rat*-zi be damned. Perhaps she felt guilty about having drunk so much the night before, he speculated. And perhaps he felt guilty about reading Sunny's novel, wanting to be closer to her.

While window-shopping along Main Street, Danny picked up a realty book and started perusing it.

"You finally thinking of buying another house?" asked Charlene. Danny figured she'd lost count of how many times she'd made the suggestion to him, that he was the only Hollywood guy she knew who owned only one house, not counting the apartment he kept at the Plaza Hotel in New York City. "It's a little weird," she'd said when they first started dating. "What have you got against real estate?" Danny had answered in the way his father would've rationalized: that no man needed more than one piece of property, that despite everybody saying what a great investment it was, it was nothing more than a headache, that the working world rented and that was fine with him. "Commitment-phobe," Charlene had called him.

"Besides," he had added, "the Hamptons are passé. It's cliché. Banal. Snooty. It's for people who want to be seen."

"Hypocrite," had been Charlene's next retort.

How had Charlene never figured out that it was Long Island he'd wanted to keep his distance from? he wondered. But now it seemed to be beckoning him like the foghorns beckon the sailboats across the sound.

"Ella expressed some interest," he said in the present moment.

"Ah," said Charlene. "Anything for Ella." Danny couldn't tell if she was stating a fact or being passive-aggressive. He opted for the former in order to resist the old pessimism. Fresh start, remember?

———

Later that evening, as they sat on the lanai overlooking the ocean, Danny turned to Charlene. "Mind if I take a walk on the beach by myself?"

"It's almost dark out."

"It's a full moon."

"What, have you got a rendezvous with a lover or something?" Her words came out in a sing-songy voice undercut by a sharp edge. *More passive-aggressiveness*, he heard an inner voice say before he shushed it yet again. No. She had a point. Why was he suddenly withdrawing from her after they'd spent such a lovely day together?

"I just want some time alone, that's all. No big deal." He tried to sound casual rather than demanding.

She gestured toward the beach, as if to state the obvious—*there it is*—and give her permission. He put his phone in his pocket, grabbed his cigarettes and lighter, and started down the path that led directly to the beach. As he padded along the sand barefoot, biting cold for April (the temperature had dropped considerably since the afternoon), he shoved his hands in the front pocket of his sweatshirt and pulled the hood over his head to shield him from the wind that was equally biting. The only thing louder than the wind was the ocean, its waves cresting and threatening to claw at his toes, maybe snag one and carry it off. He practically had the entire beach to himself, lit by the full moon and houses in the distance. He found a place to sit and smoothed out the sand before parking himself on it, pulled out a cigarette, and lit it.

Halfway through, Danny started to feel sick. He then snuffed the cig in the sand, making sure it was fully extinguished before burying it. But he unearthed it just as quickly and put it in his pocket, sat, and stared at the ocean. Then he closed his eyes and lost himself in the rhythm of the surf, in harmony with the seagulls and accompanied by the wind.

And then he saw her face. Clear as day. Like a sunrise, she just rose from the horizon and filled his mind's eye. He could almost feel the warmth of her handshake, see the smile behind her bashful, smoky eyes.

Sunrise. That was her name.

He coughed and couldn't stop, wheezing and holding his chest. Finally he regained his breath, but his heart was racing. *Holy shit*, he thought.

This has got to stop. Now.

It was over with Charlene. Really, truly over.

He was about to toss his pack of cigarettes into the ocean when he remembered the butt in his pocket and begrudgingly carried them on the walk back to the house. Charlene was no longer on the lanai. He entered through the sliding glass doors and went to the bathroom, where he flushed the cigarettes down the toilet and threw away the package. He then ambled through the cavernous rooms one by one, some decorated sparsely in nautical colors, others ready for their magazine spread, until he arrived at the master bedroom, where Charlene was sprawled on the bed, scantily dressed and watching a basketball game.

"Char, we've gotta talk."

She looked up at him lackadaisically before reaching for the remote next to her and turning off the television. It was as if she'd been waiting for him, as if she already knew this conversation was going to take place. She'd probably rehearsed it in her mind, he thought, prepared her lines, her listening, her reactions, her cues.

"Why'd you drink so much last night?" he asked.

She paused, as if in deep contemplation, before answering, "I needed to let loose."

It was a lie. He knew it. She knew it. And she knew that he knew.

Danny paced to the other side of the bed. "We've got to end this now, once and for all."

"Really?" she said as if he'd mentioned some piece of inane trivia.

"I mean it. I know we've cried wolf more than either of us can count—hell, I think we lasted longer this stretch than any other, but it's just not working. I want more. I want a deeper relationship. I want commitment. I wanna stop being hungry all the time, dammit."

She glared at him, taking her time to speak. "Is *she* the one you want this deeper commitment with?"

He met her eyes, yet couldn't hold his focus. "There's no one, Char. Not yet. But I want there to be." He paced back to the other side of the room. "You and I have said and done a lot of things to each other, but I have never cheated on you. I've never cheated on any woman." He said this with so much conviction, thinking of Artie Gold, whom Danny was sure had cheated on his mother many times over, yet he had never been able to prove it. Could Charlene at least acknowledge him for that, hell, thank him?

"But you have, Danny. You cheated on me emotionally. You think I didn't know there was someone else you were thinking about night and day? You think I couldn't see the look on your face that said you were begging to get the hell out of there and wherever she was?"

Was she right? Had he been emotionally unfaithful all this time? Was it possible to be emotionally involved with someone with whom you'd only had five minutes of interaction?

"If that's what you think, then why didn't you say anything?" he asked.

"And be the jealous, clingy, controlling girlfriend? No thanks. Half the time you're looking at me like I'm a bitch on wheels. I don't need the fight on top of it."

"I don't think you're a bitch."

"On wheels," she added.

"Charlene, stop. That's horrible. You know I don't think that of you."

"Well, you sure as hell were resenting me for something."

Danny stood there, his mouth open. He suddenly felt as if he'd just stepped outside of his own body and saw his life in reverse, watching himself sleepwalk through the last six months—the holidays, the Oscars, even his trip to New York with Ella—and had awakened, being thrust back into his flesh and bones. He had resented her. She wasn't Sunny.

"You're right. You're right, Charlene, and I am so sorry. I never meant to negate you like that, honest to God."

She pressed her lips together, and Danny could tell she was fighting with all her might to keep from crying.

"I have to get out of here," she said with a sense of urgency, scanning the room for her belongings, mentally assessing what was where and what to grab first.

"Char, don't. It's late."

"I am *not* staying here tonight."

"Then *I'll* go," said Danny.

"No," she said, and found her empty suitcase in the closet. With two hands she picked it up and practically threw it on the bed, flinging the lid open. Next she shuttled between the chest of drawers and the bed, taking handfuls of skimpy shirts and silky lingerie and haphazardly dropping them in the suitcase. She then hurled a matching satchel to Danny and instructed him to go pack her stuff from the bathroom.

"I don't know what's yours," he said helplessly.

"I don't care if you steal the goddamned towels!" she yelled, and he jumped and ran to the bathroom as if she'd just cracked a whip at his feet. He removed bottles and jars from the sinks and showers, opened and closed cabinets and didn't recognize anything of hers, but took more bottles anyway, just in case, resolving to apologize to Robbie and reimburse him. Ten minutes later, he reemerged. Charlene had changed into yoga pants, tennis shoes, and a T-shirt with some designer's name plastered across her chest.

"Where are you going at this hour?" he asked.

"I'm having a car come pick me up and take me back to the city."

"Can't you just wait until tomorrow? This house is big enough so that we both can stay in it without one of us running into the other. Or at least let me be the one to leave."

"No. Robbie is your friend, and he loaned you his house for the weekend. And I don't want to be anywhere you are right now."

"Can we not leave things so badly for once? Please? Can we—" He cut himself off before adding *Can we not be so dramatic?* She would've gone for his throat. He put his hands up in surrender. "OK." He also thought it unwise to tell her at that moment that he hoped someday they could be friends. "I'll let you go now," he said.

"You already did," she retorted.

Danny went back out to the lanai despite it being forty degrees outside without factoring in the wind chill coming from the ocean. He was surprised to find himself craving neither a cigarette nor a drink. He sat on a cushioned lounge chair and fixed his gaze on the moon hanging low above the horizon, illuminating the ocean. He watched and listened to the tide coming in and might've fallen asleep there had it not been so damn cold. He refrained from reentering the house until he heard the slam of the limo doors. And as he slid the screen and glass doors closed behind him, he retreated to one of the guest rooms, where he took a shower and went to bed, collapsing in mental and emotional exhaustion. And, he discovered, relief.

CHAPTER

TWENTY-EIGHT

Sunny Smith

<hr />

B ECAUSE OF HIS WORK SCHEDULE, JOSH AND
I had only seen each other twice since getting back
together—or rather, since deciding not to break up. But
time away from Josh gave me more time with Georgie,
and we had a lot of catching up to do. He'd already put
in his notice at Whitford's and started packing, and every
night after work I went to his place to help. Cleaning out
the closets was an exceptional ordeal; Georgie was all
for throwing stuff away, while Marcus wanted to keep
everything, having attached some sentimental value to it.

"It's a fucking *plastic spoon!*" yelled Georgie, enunciating every word, as usual. "What, you want to save the
DNA from it?"

"It's from our Vermont trip to the Ben and Jerry's
factory. Look, it's even got the cow print! I wanna put it
in the scrapbook."

I couldn't help but laugh at their bickering, enjoy
being witness to their couplehood. I tried to remember
a time when Teddy and I were this way, in the early stages
of our own couplehood when such fights were fun and
our future stretched out before us like the Camino de
Santiago—a personal journey of discovery and miracles

just waiting to happen. I tried to imagine Josh and me like this—going through our possessions, merging our lives, happily bickering. It was a pretty picture, no doubt. So why didn't it *feel* right?

Best of all, Georgie, Theo, and I were back to our old selves; it was as if the last six months had dissolved like morning fog. We sat on the floor in the walk-in closet, facing each other (a black fedora perched on Theo's head, a feather boa wrapped around Georgie's neck, a paisley necktie wrapped around mine), drinking beers and talking as best friends do. At one point, I felt as if I'd stepped outside of myself and watched us. And it struck me that Georgie and Theo were the only two people I could spend time with and still feel like my true self.

God, I had missed him. And I was going to miss him even more once he and Marcus left.

"So," Theo said. "I have news."

"Oh no," said Georgie. "Not another Lovematch-dot-com boyfriend."

Theo slapped him with a necktie.

"Spill," I said.

"I'm going to Thailand."

I nearly did a spit-take. "You *what?*"

"Well, first I'm going to Thailand. Then I'm going to go to Haiti with an organization similar to Doctors Without Borders."

"OK, I know this is going to sound rude, and I apologize in advance, but I would think that of all the medical attention Haitians need right now, a good back adjustment wouldn't be one of them," said Georgie.

"You're forgetting that I went to nursing school before I became a chiropractor, Georgie. But I'm not going officially as a chiropractor. I'm going as an assistant. My hope is that I'll get to do some AIDS education and visit children in the hospitals, that sort of thing. And yes, some of them really do need chiropractic treatment."

"What are you going to do in Thailand?" I asked.

"Fulfill a lifelong dream. Your Forty for Forty list inspired me, Sunny. And since I'm going to be forty this year as well, I thought, why not?"

"Beats the shit out of a makeover," I remarked, and we all burst into laughter.

"Don't worry," said Theo to Georgie, "I'm not leaving until after your wedding."

"How long will you be gone?" I asked.

"At least six weeks. Eight, tops."

I stared at her in admiration. Georgie raised his beer bottle and toasted her, and we clinked in unison.

"So what about you, Sunny Delight?" Georgie asked. "What are you going to do once Whitford's goes belly-up?"

"He said it *might* go belly-up," I said.

He waved his hand in dismissal of my correction. "Whatever. Regardless, don't you think it's time for you to leave the nest? If your books keep selling at this pace, you'll be set for at least a year or two. Heck, you might even be able to get an agent and sell the movie rights. And by God, if Spielberg invites you to his boat in the Hamptons and you don't invite me along, I'll leak nasty things about you to TMZ complete with Photoshopped pictures."

I ignored his threat. "I thought you were all for Shane Sands."

"Networking, baby. It's all about the networking."

"And really, you think TMZ even knows my name, much less gives a crap about me?"

He considered this. "Good point. In that case, I'll sell your entire telephone collection on eBay without telling you."

"Now that is truly evil." I turned to Theo and back-tracked the conversation. "Are you traveling alone?"

"For Thailand, yes. Unless you wanna come with me."

Considering what a big deal it was for me just to drive to New Jersey, I couldn't even fathom what it would be like to get on a plane to Thailand. Still, something about the idea, the sense of adventure, appealed to me. I was learning to consider the possibilities.

"Would be a helluva way to use up my vacation days. Although Josh and I talked about taking a trip together."

"Has Mr. Wonderful said anything else about you quitting Whitford's?" Georgie asked.

I shook my head. "He's backed off from that particular topic."

"He's in breakup anxiety mode and afraid to piss you off again. Good for you," he said. "Gives you the power."

"I don't want power," I insisted. "What the hell kind of relationship is that?"

"Are you forgetting what it was like with Teddy?" he asked. "You got married in *his* church. You moved where *he* wanted to live. You agreed to alter *your* life to have *his* babies. You gave *him* the house. Where the hell were you in that marriage?"

"And why are we still talking about it seven-plus years later?"

He held up his hands, exasperated, and then dropped them back into his lap. "Exactly! Trust me, Sunrise. Enjoy the upper hand for a while."

I didn't want the upper hand. I didn't want the lower hand either. Wasn't the sign of a good relationship all about holding hands?

I felt weary and unsettled. "Do you see Josh and me together long-term?" I asked. "Like, getting married one day?"

They looked at each other, then at me, each taking a moment to respond, and I saw sympathy in both of their eyes. "I don't know," said Theo. "But if *you* did you probably wouldn't have had to ask the question."

To my surprise, Josh had beaten me to my apartment after work, his car already sitting in the driveway when I pulled up. When I entered, I found a luxurious orchid sitting on the table in the dining area, but no sign of Josh. I called out his name, and he emerged from the bathroom.

"Hey, Sun," he said with a lilt in his voice. I had heard him use this voice at managers' meetings. You just knew a pep talk was coming. From what I could tell, it rarely worked.

"Hey," I replied. He kissed me hello, pulled me to him in an embrace, and held on a good ten seconds longer than usual, at least. I let go and looked at him, somewhat bewildered. "Everything OK?" Then I remembered Georgie's diagnosis: breakup anxiety mode.

"I'm happy to see you," he replied.

I smiled. "Me too." My attention returned to the orchid. "That from you?" I asked.

He nodded. "You haven't been keeping up with your Forty for Forty flowers item, so I decided to give it a little kick."

I walked over to the orchid and took in its beauty, thanking him as I did.

"Did you wanna go out tonight? I've been putting in overtime at Georgie's all week and had a double shipment today, so I'm kind of spent."

"We can stay in if you want," he answered. It was hard to read whether he was genuinely accepting, or disappointed and politely acquiescing. He turned on the TV and flipped to the Yankees game.

I showered and reemerged in a T-shirt and pajama bottoms. He pulled me to him on the couch and took in a whiff of my hair.

I filled him in on my latest sales numbers, progress on Georgie and Marcus's wedding plans, and Theo's news about Thailand and Haiti. "Have you given any thought about where you'd like to go on our trip?" I asked. "As exotic as Thailand might be, I was thinking about something a little lower maintenance, like Hawaii. I've never been there."

"Actually, I was thinking more along the lines of Disney World. You, me, and the kids."

I pulled back and dropped my jaw. "Wow."

"Is that wow good, or wow are you fucking nuts?"

I found myself thinking a little of both.

"Just...wow," I said. "I didn't think we were up to that step yet. I mean, I had a wonderful time with your kids at the soccer game, but an entire vacation? Is that something you've ever done before?"

"Nope. And that's not all, Sun. I'm thinking of buying a house here on Long Island. I spend most of my time here anyway, so why not?"

Some inexplicable force moved my body from its seated position to standing up and several paces back from Josh, as if escaping the reach of his grasp.

"A whole house?"

He laughed. "Why not? I've been divorced for a long time, almost as long as you. I have enough for a down payment. It's better for the kids to have a backyard to play in—"

"One that they have to take a train to get to?" I interrupted.

He ignored me. "Plus you can have a room of your own to use as an office-slash-writing space."

"Josh, slow down," I said, making a pushing away gesture with my hands and feeling woozier by the minute. "Where do you fit into the picture? I mean, what if Whitford's goes under? What happens to you?"

"Maybe I'll manage your self-publishing venture. I've really enjoyed working with you on that. And the bigger it gets, the more help you're going to need. Hell, maybe I'll start my own e-book publishing company. There's definitely a demand for it right now."

"Whoa. Wait just a minute, Josh."

"I thought we were on the same page, Sunny. You said we were OK. You said you were all in now."

"I am, but…just not so *fast*."

A thick silence suddenly filled the room. I could practically see it, like a soot-colored fog. More frightening was when I saw it fill his eyes.

"I'm sorry," he said, sounding embarrassed.

"No, I am," I said. I sat beside him again. "Can we just watch the game? Then we can talk about it afterward."

He let me snuggle up to him, but his body felt stiff, the muscles in his back and arms clenched. Derek Jeter hit a blooper midfield, one hit closer to his three thousandth, while the crowd cheered as if he had knocked it out of the park. Neither of us even flinched.

We watched two more innings in silence before Josh suddenly grabbed the remote and turned off the TV with a flick of the wrist.

"There's something more between you two, isn't there," he said.

"What are you talking about?"

"You and Danny Masters. It's not just a little celebrity crush."

"I…" My mind drew a blank. What was I supposed to say?

"What happened that day you met? Was it just the wannabe thing or did something else take place? I swear, Sun, I've pored over that YouTube clip like it was the freaking Zapruder film and there's no denying that he's *looking* at you. Like he knows you and *wants* you." He continued after a beat, as if impatient for me to respond. "And I watched you watch him on the Oscars with that *exact same look.*"

My first thought was, *He pored over the clip?* Something about this admission creeped me out a little. Yet once the superficial was out of the way, it sank in that Josh had noticed the very thing I had hoped and prayed all this time had been more than just a figment of my imagination: Danny Masters was *looking* at me. And I at him. *Something* was there. As if after all this time, there was finally confirmation. But how to explain it? How to put it into words?

"I don't know how to say this without sounding like some obsessed, idiot fangirl, but there was a connection. It couldn't have lasted more than five minutes, but it felt like in another place and another time, we were meant for each other." My voice quavered slightly as I said the words—I had never said them out loud. "And ever since that day, I've felt like I belonged there instead of here." This time I was the one who couldn't wait for a reply. "I'm sorry, I know that's crazy."

Josh's expression turned to ice. He quickly stood up and crossed the room, as if repulsed to be near me. Then he turned to face me again. "Your little *we have a connection* delusion is just that. It's an excuse to not be in this relationship and to not be in the real world. For crying out loud, Sunny, when are you going to wake up? If Danny Masters *really wanted* you, he would've combed the ends of the earth looking for you. And if you *really wanted* him, you would've done the same. It's a pipe dream, don't you get it? Just like your *Leave It to Beaver* dream with Teddy was, and that stupid list of yours."

As I watched his mouth in seeming slow motion, that thick cloud of silence had morphed into a funnel cloud of anger, whirling around the room, threatening to suck me into its center. He was bitter. Resentful. And although I couldn't blame him, I didn't need the classic Joshua Hamilton condescension that was about to follow.

"I'm putting in my two weeks at Whitford's," I blurted.

He looked as if someone had just smacked him in order to shut him up. "When did you decide this?"

"Just now."

"Holy God, and you say *I'm* moving too fast?"

"You've been wanting me to quit for how long now?"

"That's not the point, Sun. You can't just quit on a whim. You need a plan first."

"So I'll make a plan," I said, resolute.

"And will it include me? Or will it include your other boyfriend? Because I gotta tell ya, it's pretty crowded in this apartment already."

I don't think I had ever desired to hit someone the way I desired to hit Joshua Hamilton at that moment.

I grabbed my peacoat, messenger bag, and keys.

"Where are you going?" he asked.

"Theo's," I snapped.

"In your pajamas?"

"You're right, Josh. This apartment is too crowded right now."

"Forget it," he said, and gathered his own belongings. "I'll go."

"Back to Jersey? At this time of night?"

"I could use the night air," he said, and walked out without even saying good-bye.

Danny Masters

H E WOULD'VE SCRIPTED THE BREAKUP WITH
Charlene differently, Danny thought the morning
after she left.

The other breakups had been far more histrionic—
shouting matches and hurling non-life-threatening objects
at each other or the walls, insisting that this was *it*, they
were done, finito, kaput, adios, be-sure-to-let-the-door-
hit-you-in-the-ass-on-your-way-out. It had occurred to
him after the fact that Charlene probably thought that's
why he'd taken her to the Hamptons to begin with—and
hell, that would've pissed him off if he were in her shoes.
And yet Danny saw the lack of dramatic effect as a sign
that this one would stick.

He scripted the scene in his imagination as he would
have wanted it to happen, could see the camera angles
and points of view. But no matter how many times he mentally revised the dialogue, it had all the makings of a bad
Lifetime Movie. Perhaps Ken had been right all along and
romance wasn't his thing. Still, the bad Lifetime version was
better than the way the breakup had actually happened.
In his imagined breakup, he didn't care that the writing
was bad or the dialogue was forced and phony, that had it

been actually filmed, audiences would be demanding he return his Oscar. In his imagined breakup, the breakup he would've preferred, there was nothing but tranquility. It took place on a beach at sunset, for starters. The sunset was overly symbolic and cliché, of course, yet hopeful; the sun would rise in the morning. Charlene was casting stones in the ocean, symbolic of letting go, tossing out the bad with the good rather than an angry assault. Letting go of hostility, resentment. Perhaps he should join her, skipping stones. The ending was consensual, final, satisfying. Closure. Roll credits. What's on next?

He was sick of confrontation, both in reality and in his writing.

Danny stayed in the Hamptons for one more day. He spent most of it driving around town and looking at properties, walking the beach, meeting whoever else happened to be in town for lunch or dinner—anything to stay out of the house—and then flew back to LA, finishing Sunny's first book on the plane and beginning the second one. He liked her writing style, the rhythm of the words and the crafting of each sentence, so deliberate and thoughtful. The plot was fun yet unpredictable, a combination of detailed history with tongue-in-cheek humor. Characters were quirky yet likable; antagonists were cunning and slippery. Like him, she had a flair for dialogue, and he could easily see this story on a wide screen, shot on location. He was casting roles in his mind as he read, trying out different actors for different scenes.

He especially liked the Long Island depicted in the story. He would live on *that* Long Island.

After landing, he went straight from LAX to his office, where Dez greeted him with, "Oh, don't tell me. Geez, can't you two stay together for like two seconds?"

Danny peered at her over his sunglasses and nonverbally communicated, *Don't.*

"Mike Nichols wants to talk to you about a book he bought that he wants you to do the script for. Might get you out of the slump you've been in."

Danny paused to consider this as he thumbed through the mail that had been waiting patiently on his desk. "Did you set up a meeting?"

"I thought you'd want to call him yourself," she answered.

"Good thinking. OK, I'll do that. Thanks, Dez."

She closed the door behind her and Danny plopped into his chair, a strange combination of jitters and fatigue overtaking him. He hadn't had a cigarette since throwing out the pack in the Hamptons but had drunk two cups of coffee on the plane. He called Jackson first, who asked Danny if he wanted to comment on whether he and Charlene had broken up for good.

"Oh, for fuck's sake—don't even tell me it's on the Internet already. How did they get it so fast?"

"You mean they're *right*?" said Jackson. "Geezus."

"No comment," replied Danny.

Jackson proceeded to discuss the book tour. "You start in the Northeast, just like you requested. At least three stores on Long Island. One in the city. New Jersey, Connecticut…"

As Jackson spoke, Danny was on Twitter and scrolling through Sunny's last dozen or so tweets, a mix of self-promotion, responses to fellow tweeters, and factoids about Long Island. Listed with her bio was a URL for a personal website. He clicked on the link, perused the site (sparse in content with an "Under Construction" sign on it), and found another link to an e-mail account.

He took in a breath. He finally had a direct line to Sunny, an opportunity to contact her, apologize, say whatever he wanted to say.

"Are you listening to me?" said Jackson.

"No, I'm not," he confessed. "Sorry. Look, this was a dumb idea. Maybe we should forget the whole thing."

"Are you kidding?" said Jackson. "You can't just up and cancel on everyone. Besides, it'll be great. You get to talk about the Oscars, drum up DVD sales for all your work—although I imagine they've already skyrocketed thanks to your win."

Dread churned with the coffee in his stomach.

"I guess you're right. Well, thanks for everything, Jackson. And so help me, if you comment on me and Charlene, I'll kill you and eat your liver for dinner." He said good-bye and hung up the phone and went to the next call, and the next. From there he moved on to snail mail, and then back to the Internet. He opened his e-mail account and pasted in Sunny's e-mail address.

But he couldn't think of a single word. Became completely paralyzed.

"Forget it," he said out loud. *It's over.* Do the book tour and move on.

He canceled the e-mail and returned to his in-box. When he scrolled halfway down, he stiffened when the name of a sender and subject heading caught his attention.

He opened it and began to read:

Dear Danny,

I hope this e-mail finds you well. I know this comes a little late, but I wanted to congratulate you on your recent success. I saw Exposed and thought it was really good. I also watched you win the award, and I was very happy for you.

I'm getting ready to graduate from UCLA in June, and although I know there's no chance you can attend my gradu-ation (my parents would have a fit if they even knew I was writing this, much less were I to invite you to my graduation), I was wondering if we could meet somewhere, even just for coffee. I can't really explain why, but I feel like I need some kind of closure.

If it's not something you want, then I understand. I know how busy you must be, and I'm sure the last thing you want to do is dig up something from your past. But if you do, then name a date, time, and place, and I'll make sure I'm there.

I hope to hear from you soon.

Sincerely,

Teresa Flowers

He didn't even realize that he'd been holding his breath as he read until his lungs prodded him with a cough as a reminder. He wiped sweat from his brow and pushed his hair back and stood up and did two nervous laps around his office.

Holy shit.

He sat at his desk again and reread the e-mail. Then he got up and did two more laps around the office before sitting at his desk again. He picked up the phone and dialed Raj's personal number.

"Are you free? I mean, do you have clients today?"

"I'm working from home."

"Can you see me now? Please? It's an emergency."

"Of course, Daniel. Shall I come to your office?"

"No, I'll come to you. I'm leaving now." He hung up the phone, stormed out of the office without telling Dez where he was going, and sped to Raj's house, where Raj was patiently and peacefully waiting for him, his home office decorated almost exactly the same as his other office. Danny wouldn't sit down; rather, he resumed his frantic pacing.

"Please, sit and tell me what's troubling you," said Raj.

"Oh God, Raj, I need a smoke so bad. I haven't had one since—" He cut himself short.

"You quit smoking?"

"Yeah, but that's not why I'm here. She wants to see me, Raj."

"Who wants to see you?"

"Teresa! The little girl I hit the night of the accident. Only she's not a little girl anymore—she's graduating *college*! Can you believe that?"

"I think it's wonderful."

"It's not wonderful, it's terrifying! How can I face her after what I did to her and her family? And besides, I'm not supposed to face her. I mean, I was ordered to stay away from her. It was a condition of my plea bargain."

"But she contacted you, Daniel. Obviously she wants to see you."

"She said she wants closure."

"It can be closure for you too. This is an opportunity for you to finally free yourself from this chain that has bound you for the last fifteen years, the one thing that's been holding you back from living a life of true greatness. One that has nothing to do with money or power or awards."

Danny asked for a glass of water, and Raj brought it to him. He chugged it like a beer.

"I broke up with Charlene this past weekend," he said.

Raj sat still, not even a hint of reaction registering on his face. "That couldn't have been easy for you."

"I wasn't planning it—in fact, I had invited her out to the Hamptons as a way to make amends and start over. But then, I don't know—it just became clear to me that it was futile. She's not the one I want."

"Who do you want?"

He forced himself to say her name, out loud. "Sunny. I know that's crazy to want someone you only talked to for five minutes, and one who called you a failure at that. But I can't stop thinking about her, and now it turns out she has these novels, and I'm reading them and they're really good and all I want to do is *see* her again. I just want to say her name and have her respond." He was speaking so quickly, barely pausing to take a breath. "And I have her e-mail address now, Raj. I finally have that chance, and I can't bring myself to do it."

Danny finally stopped speaking and impatiently waited for Raj to respond.

"Say something," Danny commanded.

"I wanted to make sure you were finished."

"For fuck's sake, Raj…"

Raj smiled. "Daniel, don't you see? It's happening."

Danny's head was too clouded to think straight. "What's happening?"

"You can't bring a new sofa into your living room until you take the old one away. And since you're taking the old sofa out, you might as well take out the chairs and the lamps too. Especially since the lamps haven't been working for years."

"What, you're a fucking decorator now?"

Raj laughed. "Relax, my friend. Take a deep breath."

Danny did as instructed.

"You're clearing your own path," said Raj. "Or at least you've started to. The moment you made a decision to let go of Charlene, the moment you accepted that she could no longer give you what you truly want, you opened the door for the universe to bring it to you. But you need to clear everything that's been holding you back. The universe knows this, Daniel."

He looked at Raj pleadingly. "I want to believe you."

"What stops you?"

For the first time, Danny leaned back in the seat, finally stopping the barrage of anxiety swirling inside him. He stared past Raj, desperately searching for an answer. Tears rolled down his eyes.

"My fucking father."

Raj pulled his chair close enough to Danny for their knees to touch. He put his face up close to Danny's, forcing Danny to look at him.

"Daniel Gold, your father can't hurt you anymore. Do you know why?"

Danny shook his head, feeling like a child as he sobbed and tried to avert Raj's intensity.

"Because you have the power to change the way you *think*. A man can be beaten and belittled. He can be tortured and taunted. A man can have everything stripped of him *except* his power to choose his thoughts. All these years, you've *chosen* to listen to your father. You've chosen to think that all those things he said to you were true. But you've never chosen not to believe him. You've spent your whole life trying to *prove* him wrong, but you've never chosen to *believe* he was wrong. And he was, Daniel. He was one hundred percent wrong about you. As is everything you've believed about yourself since."

The fog in Danny's head began to dissolve, as if Raj's words were cutting through them like sunbeams. The concept simultaneously reeked of simplicity and magnitude.

"Raj, that day Sunny called me a failure—why do you think she said it? Of all the things to call me."

"Because she looked in your eyes and saw your deepest fear."

"So why don't I hate her the way I hate him?"

"Because you looked in her eyes and saw her deepest fear too. And here's the thing, Daniel: The things we fear most about ourselves are usually the things that make us most lovable. But we've got to love ourselves. Your father hated himself so much that there was no room for your love. Do you know what saved *you* from going down that same road?"

Again Danny shook his head.

"Ella," said Raj. "She's the one part of you that you've always believed in. But even she can't love you enough to erase all those thoughts you have about your being a failure. But that's all they are, Daniel—*thoughts*. They can be *changed*."

Raj pushed his chair away to give Danny space again.

And suddenly Danny understood. Ella had saved him the night of the accident, when he had planned to kill himself if Teresa didn't live. And when Ella was born, he knew; he *knew* he was going to give her the best of him. And in order for him to do that, he had to find it within himself every day. And somehow, he always did.

That meant he had to believe it was there to begin with.

As long as he had Ella, there was no way he could be a failure. Not in *that* way.

He had failed the day of the premiere. He had failed to be who he really was. He was so busy being Danny Masters for the crowd—for Sunny, even—that he had ignored Daniel Gold, who had just met this wonderful woman and wanted to know who she was.

Maybe that was who he was trying to find when he drove back to his neighborhood, drunk, fifteen years ago. Maybe that was why Charlene never could be the one for him. She loved Danny Masters, not Daniel Gold. And although he had tried to be Daniel Gold for Frannie, by then it was too late—he'd already lost too much of himself. Sold it to pay for Danny Masters's adulation.

He stood up and embraced his friend, his face streaked with salty tears. And when he let go and looked into Raj's eyes, he noticed for the first time why he loved his friend so much.

Raj saw the real him. And loved him for it.

Danny couldn't help but break into a smile. He took a deep breath.

"You're still a quack," he said.

Raj returned the smile. "And you are my favorite writer."

Two hours later, Danny called Dez as he left Raj's office, apologized for leaving so abruptly, and told her he was going home. Back at the house, he opened his MacBook and logged in to his e-mail account again. His fingers shook as he typed, and he knew it had nothing to do with his not having had a cigarette. Having already checked his schedule with Dez, he then suggested a date and place for him and Teresa to meet.

Five minutes later, she responded, confirming the date. *Looking forward to finally meeting you face to face*, he read.

CHAPTER

THIRTY

Sunny Smith

S ATURDAY MORNING, I CALLED GEORGIE AND
Theo and met them for lunch at the Town House
diner. During our college days, Town House was the final
destination following a night of dancing and drinking,
the place we went for our buzzes to come down.

My milkshake sat untouched as I stirred it with a straw,
filling in my friends on the previous night's events.

"You told him you're *quitting* Whitford's?" said Georgie,
unable to hide his delight.

I nodded slowly, still astounded.

"When did you decide to quit?" asked Theo.

"I swear it just came out of nowhere."

"Nonsense," said Georgie. "It came from that place
in you that knows it's time to move on. That is, if you're
really ready. I mean, are you really going to quit?"

"That's the most shocking part of all: I think I am."
They both quietly squealed with excitement. "And
here's the other thing," I said to Georgie. "What do you
think of my taking over the lease on your and Marcus's
apartment?"

"Why would you want our place?"

"For starters, it's bigger than mine. It has an extra room for an office, which I clearly need now, and your landlord allows pets."

Georgie sat up straight in the booth. "Whoa. I never even thought of that. We already gave the landlord notice, so for all I know he's promised it to someone else, but I'll talk to him about it."

"Ohmigod, Sunny, this is *so* exciting," said Theo. "But where does that leave Mr. Wonderful? Not to take his side, but he had a point. You did tell him you were all in. Although there is also Danny Masters. Anyone who knows you well enough can see it in your eyes every time someone mentions his name. You can't expect Josh to live with that, and neither can you anymore."

"Let's make a list," suggested Georgie.

I groaned. "Another list? What are we calling this one?"

He grabbed a clean napkin as Theo searched her bag for a pen. He drew a vertical line down the middle, crossed by a horizontal line up top, and wrote *DM* on the left side and *JH* on the right.

"OK, we'll start with Mr. Wonderful," said Georgie.

"You know, I know you both call him that sarcastically, but he really is a wonderful guy," I said.

"Go on," said Georgie. "Make his case. Seriously, Sunny, now's the time."

"Well, he is good-looking," said Theo. "And he's been really supportive of Sunny."

"He smells good too," said Georgie. We both gave him a surprised look. "Well, it's not like I dream of the guy at night, but it's something I noticed, OK? Shoot me."

"He can be really thoughtful, like buying me the orchid," I added. "Plus he's great with his kids. He's very attentive with them and doesn't try too hard to compensate for being divorced; he never says a bad word about his ex-wife in front of me or them, and even to her…" I paused while Georgie scribbled everything we said in stunted, bullet-pointed, block caps. "He's funny, intelligent, good at his job, and…" I paused again.

Georgie stopped writing and looked up. "And?"

My voice caught in my throat. "And he loves me."

Georgie wrote *LOVES SUNNY* and underlined it twice. "OK. On to Mr. Masters."

"Well," I started, searching for something. "He thinks I think he's a failure."

"And he lives in LA with Charlene Dumont," said Theo.

"I don't think they live together," I corrected.

"Plus I heard they broke up. Again," said Georgie. "But he did mention you at the Oscars, so he can't hate you that much."

"How do we know his mic didn't cut out because he told me to go fuck myself or something?" I offered.

"Because he's Danny Masters, not Kid Rock," said Georgie. "C'mon, what else? There has to be something else we can put in his column."

"I can't think of anything else," said Theo. They both looked at me, and I shrugged my shoulders.

Georgie straightened his posture again to announce the results. "Well, clearly Joshua Hamilton is the better man on paper."

I stared at my milkshake and stirred it slowly. Teddy was great on paper too, I remembered. I could recite scores of platitudes for him. And look how that turned out. And then it dawned on me: I could no longer take stock of what the facts told me. History was all a matter of interpretations of the bits and pieces of information we put together to tell the story of what happened. But they weren't always accurate. Sometimes we told the stories we wanted to hear. Teddy had been one of them. And there in that diner booth, we were trying to do it again with Josh.

I piped up. "There's that five minutes outside the theater."

My friends looked at each other, then back at me. "What about them?" asked Theo.

"You asked if there's anything else to add to the Danny Masters side of the list. Add that."

And as Georgie scribbled the words *FIVE MINUTES* onto the napkin, I suddenly knew exactly what I wanted. Or, more specifically, what I didn't want.

Danny Masters

D ANNY COULD BARELY SIT STILL AS HE WAITED
in his office, and the bagel and coffee Dez bought
for him sat untouched on his desk. Writing was futile; he
couldn't even comprehend a two-sentence e-mail from
Paul Wolf.

Dez opened the door and poked her head in. "She's
here."

His mouth went dry and the blood drained from his
face and he felt woozy as he stood up. "OK, thanks," he
said, his voice cracking.

"You OK?" she asked, fully entering the office and
closing the door behind her, leaving it open only a sliver.
He gripped the side of the desk.

"You know who she is?" he said.

Dez nodded. "I took a guess." She went up to Danny
and hugged him. The gesture of affection took him by
surprise for only a second, until he realized how much
he needed it.

He looked in her eyes. "Thank you," he said. Then
he smiled and said, both earnestly and lovingly, "You're
a great assistant."

A look came over her, like a teenage girl who just got a compliment from her big brother. She tossed her arms around his neck and hugged him again, less tender and more playful. She then let go and opened the door fully, standing aside to let him through.

He tried to clear his throat and coughed. Then he took a deep breath and stepped out of his office.

Teresa looked nothing like he'd imagined—at twenty-four years old, she was almost as tall as he was, with long, cascading black hair and a petite frame. Her eyes were brown and round, lined in thick black mascara and liquid eyeliner and a bronzer for foundation. Her lips were glossed in an apricot color. She wore a plain cotton floral-print dress with periwinkle flats. Every casting director's dream for a girl-next-door role. Perhaps he'd been expecting to see the little girl in corduroys and a baby blue windbreaker (he remembered like it was yesterday) with a pageboy haircut with bangs that had been cut too high.

She stood there, looking as apprehensive as he felt.

"Teresa?" he asked in an uncertain voice, as if needing confirmation.

"Hi," she said shyly in what still sounded like a teenager's voice as she extended her hand to shake his own. "It's nice to finally meet you in person," she said.

Danny took her hand carefully, as if doing that alone could break it. "Same here," he said. "Did you make it OK?"

"Yeah, it was fine. Thanks for the limo. Definitely attracted a lot of attention at school." She quickly added, "Don't worry, I didn't tell anyone I was coming here. Except for my very best friend in the world, and she goes to school at Michigan State."

"That's OK," he said. He was trying hard not to stare at her, to look for traces of permanent damage. "If you don't mind my asking, I'm curious as to what you *did* tell people."

"That I had a job interview with Google. Which, by the way, if you had any connections, I would *totally* be up for that for real."

He shook his head, feeling disappointed. "Sorry, I don't."

He led her into his office, where she took in its surroundings.

"I expected something bigger, more elaborate," she said. Then she caught herself. "Not to be rude…"

"It's OK," he replied. "Most people think the same thing." He accidentally banged into the coffee table in an effort to move out of her way and gripped the armrest of the couch to steady himself. *Be cool, be cool, be cool…*

She spotted his Oscar on the shelf near his desk, set apart from his Emmys and other awards, and her eyes grew wide with excitement. "Is that…" She pointed to it.

He grinned. "Sure is." He picked it up and offered it to her. "Go on, hold it."

She was visibly starstruck by the statue as she tentatively held out her hand. She wrapped her fingers around its torso and marveled at the weight of it as her arm sagged. "Whoa," she said. "You can really work out your triceps with this thing." Seeing her holding the Oscar made him look at it with more awe than ever before, for it had suddenly become tangible evidence of how hard he had worked to redeem himself for her.

He laughed, trying to sound casual. "It's the latest Hollywood workout."

"You must, like, look at this thing every day. I'm surprised you don't sleep with it beside your bed."

"I did for the first week after I won it. I can't help but picture my Jewish grandmother lecturing me about worshiping false idols, though."

"Is she alive?" asked Teresa.

Danny shook his head again. "No, and neither are my parents. She would've been very proud of this, though. Would've bragged to all the ladies on the block and in her knitting club about it. I've never been religious anyway."

He felt as inept as a guy bombing out on a blind date.

She handed the Oscar back to him and moved on to the Emmys next, touching each one. She then turned around, and she and Danny faced each other, encountering their first lapse of awkward silence.

Danny broke it with a question. "Ever been on a studio lot before?"

She shook her head, still silent and seemingly starstruck.

"Would you like to?"

This time she nodded vigorously. "But—" She stopped him just as he picked up the phone to call over to the lot. "Can we go somewhere and talk first?"

"Sure." Danny hung up the phone, hoping she couldn't see how badly he was shaking. At least he could blame it on quitting smoking, although he knew that wasn't the reason. "There's a café downstairs."

He escorted her to the first floor of the building, doing his best to avoid any more awkward silences, even in the elevator. He asked her the standard questions of how she liked UCLA and why she'd chosen it and what she majored in and what were her plans after graduation and who was this year's commencement speaker and did she know that he'd been asked to do it one year? Teresa dutifully answered all his questions, no doubt bored to tears from having to recite them for every aunt, uncle, cousin, and potential employer. He could relate, having been asked the same five questions by virtually everyone when doing the press for any premiere, not to mention the how-does-it-feel-to-be-an-Academy-Award-winner, which he'd sworn on the ghosts of Thespis and Aristotle that he'd never complain about if he actually won. But he was terrified of the silence, babbling in his effort to fill it.

"Most kids graduate when they're twenty-two," he said. "Did you go to work first?"

"Oh, no, I was a year behind my classmates because of the accident. Then I did the five-year plan, ha ha ha."

How did she talk about such a thing so casually? he wondered. She was *left behind* for *a year* because of *his recklessness*. That's how he would've said it.

"I'm sorry," he said, the words a gross understatement.

"Turned out to be a good thing, though," she quickly added. "I learned twice as much as my classmates in my regular grade. And I made honors at UCLA."

In the café Danny ordered another coffee, this time with a Danish, knowing he still couldn't eat. He instructed Teresa to put her wallet away when she extracted it. "You're going to need to save every penny after graduation, trust me," he said. She smiled bashfully and thanked him.

He scanned the café for the most remote table and led her to it. Teresa dumped a packet of sugar in her cup and stirred it with the stick she'd picked up at the self-service bar, and she tore the blueberry muffin's top away from its bottom, occasionally picking off little morsels from each at a time.

Danny picked up his coffee to take a sip, then changed his mind and put it down again.

"So..." he started, and trailed off.

"So..." she repeated.

"Am I the only one who thinks this is weird?"

"No," she answered, "it's *totally* weird."

"How so?" he asked.

"Well, you know, you're, like, *famous.* And hello—you're an *Oscar winner!*"

Had any random stranger or fan said these things to him, he would've smiled graciously, secretly appreciative for the validation. In front of Teresa, however, this person who'd almost lost her life thanks to his stupid, negligent, abhorrent recklessness, the descriptions sounded shallow, as if he'd wasted his life on frivolous things.

"I'm nothing special," he heard himself say. "Just a writer who got lucky early on."

"I'm no writer—I mean, God, I barely passed English with a B-minus..."

A B-minus was barely passing?

"...but even I know you're an exceptional writer. Everything you've ever done has been a success. That's not just luck. That's talent. And believe it or not, you've inspired me to be very good at what I love. For me, that's computers. I know—rare to find a girl who's so geeked out on computers. But, oh my God, I *love* them. Given a choice between a pair of Manolos and a fully loaded

MacBook Pro, I would take the MacBook Pro without even thinking about it!" She laughed.

Danny laughed as well. "That's good. That's a great way to be. I tell my daughter that: to find what you love and then get very good at it, even if that means missing a bunch of parties—which you won't remember anyway—or football games or whatever it is you think you absolutely can't miss."

"I know—I saw a speech you gave at a film school in New York on YouTube, and you said the same thing. I was googling you one day, looking for old articles about the accident, and that was one of the things I found. It was really good."

Danny was both flattered and horrified. "Why were you looking for things related to the accident?"

She ate another morsel of muffin and sipped her tea. "I don't remember anything about that accident," she said. "All I remember is taking my dog out for a walk and waking up in the hospital. I don't remember you, the car...I don't remember the legal stuff either, mostly because my parents and their lawyers took care of all that. It took me a long time to recover. Funny, I can barely even remember what *that* was like anymore."

A part of him wished the little girl was sitting in front of him rather than this grown-up who mildly resembled her yet felt equally familiar and unfamiliar to him. Again he was filled with agonizing shame, guilt, and remorse that no amount of money, praise, or acceptance could dissolve, all pushing themselves to the brink of his tear ducts.

"I don't mean for this to be as selfish as it's going to sound," he started, "but I actually envy your memory loss.

You have no idea how that accident haunts me. Every waking day, and night too."

"I guess that's why I wanted to talk to you, because I have always gotten that feeling about you. It's not just because you've sent me so much money over the years—"

"And please don't think I've been trying to buy your forgiveness or anything like that," he interjected.

"I don't think that at all—my parents do, but I don't. If anything, I think you've been trying to buy *your* forgiveness."

The revelation hit him like a bucket of ice water.

"I'd say you got a good education at UCLA," said Danny, "but I'll bet you were already wise beyond your years."

"That's just the thing," said Teresa. "Ever since the accident, I've always kind of *known* certain things. It's really hard to explain. It's almost like having X-ray vision into people's hearts or something." She blushed slightly. "That probably sounds stupid."

"It doesn't," he assured her, realizing that Raj probably had this same gift; he just knew how to capitalize on it. "It *isn't*." He fidgeted with the plate in front of him, turning it left and right. "I'm still not sure why you wanted to meet with me, though."

She looked pensive for a moment. "I'm not sure. I think about what happened from time to time, and I wonder about you. Something like this had to be eating you alive. You can kind of see it in interviews and stuff. Or maybe I'm just projecting that."

He swallowed hard. "And here I thought I'd been hiding it all this time."

"I just really wanted to meet you. I wanted to see you for myself, and put us both at ease. I thought, *He needs to see with his own two eyes that I'm OK.* Danny..." It was the first time she'd called him by name. "Look at me—I'm about to graduate from UCLA with a bachelor's degree, with honors; I've got a boyfriend who's amazing and who I'm going to marry once we're both done with grad school. As far as we know, the accident didn't screw me up too much—just some memory loss and muscular pain and an occasional nightmare and things like that."

Every part of him cringed—she spoke about such dysfunction as if it were something she was born with, something that hadn't been inflicted, something she'd adapted to as easily as the weather or a new school.

"You're incredible, Teresa," he said, in awe of her. "I'm not worthy to be in your presence."

"But that's just the thing—you *are.* You're worthy to be in my presence and anyone else's. You're no better or worse than anyone else. Look, I'm not condoning what you did. Of all people, I know the trouble it caused. And I did hate you for a time, during my teens especially. But then one day we were watching *Gandhi* in my social studies class—have you ever seen that movie?"

"A long time ago," he said.

"There's this scene where this Muslim man has just killed a Christian man who killed the Muslim man's son, or maybe I've got them mixed up... Anyway, Gandhi is on a hunger strike, and the man, who is so full of hate and rage and grief, asks Gandhi what it'll take for him to eat. So Gandhi tells him—and this part makes me tear up every time—Gandhi tells him to adopt the boy whose father he just killed, but to raise him in the religion the boy was born into." She dabbed at her eyes with a napkin. "Isn't that the most powerful scene ever?"

Danny's eyes were glassy. "Yes," he barely managed to choke out. "It is."

She composed herself and continued. "I totally burst into tears when I saw that scene. Right in the middle of class. That day I went home and wrote in my diary that I'd rather spend the rest of my life being a good person than wasting a lot of time hating you."

He was afraid to speak. Afraid he'd lose it right there in the café, the way she had just described.

"I don't know what to say." The words came out in a whisper.

"That day I also vowed to not make what happened something I built my life around or identified myself by. I'm not 'the girl who got hit by the drunk driver and almost died.'" She gestured quote marks, saying it as if it were the title or label bestowed on her. "That's the way my parents have treated me my whole life, and it drives me crazy. I'm more than that. I made the track team in high school, won the district spelling bee, even acted in a couple of plays in school."

Danny perked up at this last mention. "Really?"

"I never made it beyond the chorus," she laughed, "but it was fun. And I love ice cream and peanut butter, and bike riding, and just being outdoors. I've never let anything get in the way of my living, least of all any stupid resentment toward you or anyone else."

"You're a better person than I am," he said.

"Oh, I have my meltdown moments. I'm terribly impatient. Every time we had to do a team project for a class, my teammates all hated me because I was so bossy and nagging." She laughed again, and he smiled as he found himself wishing he could introduce her to Ella.

"And sometimes I have a short fuse," she said. "A shrink told me a long time ago that that's probably how I deal with the accident. I try to channel it more positively, like going for a bike ride—and just so you know, I almost killed myself on a bike ride once too. Totally stupid, my fault. So you see? You're not the only one." She laughed again.

"My God," said Danny. "I never apologized to you for killing your dog."

For the first time, he saw a flicker of a flashback in her eyes—in an instant, he saw the little girl she'd been in their reflection, and they looked down for a moment. "Yeah, that was sad," she said in a child's voice. "He was my best friend back then."

Almost involuntarily, he reached across the table and rested his hand upon hers. She seemed startled by the gesture, but only for a moment.

"I'm so very sorry," he said, practically choking on the inadequacy of the words.

"I forgive you, Danny. I forgave you a long time ago. Anyone that drunk had to be someone who was in a lot of pain. You can't have any compassion for anyone if you can't see past their insanity."

He took his hand from hers and pinched the bridge of his nose between his eyes to keep the tears at bay. She seemed to wait for him to resume eye contact with her before speaking again.

"I heard this really funny line about resentment: 'Resentment is when you drink the poison and expect the other person to die.'"

Danny couldn't help but laugh. "That's fucking brilliant," he said, wondering if she took offense to profanity.

"I just wanted you to know, I never drank the poison."

Of course not. *He* had been drinking it. By the gallon.

Danny saw Teresa as if a spotlight shone on her, like they do in those supernatural love stories to show who's the angel and who's the mortal. At that moment, every muscle in his body had let go, become suddenly weightless. But it was more than physical well-being—all was right in the world, in his world. All was right with *him*. He couldn't help but grin, and had a mirror been nearby to show his reflection, he would bet that his expression would match that of Raj's amused contentment.

He sat with that grin for what seemed like a long time, but was probably no more than a few seconds, before speaking again.

"Your name is very pretty, by the way."

"Teresa was my great-aunt's name."

"You certainly did her proud. I like your last name too."

"Thanks," she said, beaming. "I read that your last name isn't really Masters."

"No," he said, "it's Gold."

"Why'd you change it?"

"My agent thought it was catchier. At this point I've been Danny Masters longer than I was Danny Gold."

"Have you ever thought about changing it back?"

"I have," he said. "Just now."

She seemed as pleased to hear this as he was.

"Shall we take that studio tour?" he asked.

Teresa straightened in her seat and clapped her hands together. "Ooh, yes! How exciting!"

On the Kingsmen Studio lots, Danny drove Teresa around in a golf cart, pointing out classic sets for famous shows, including the *Winters in Hyannis* family compound, modeled after the actual Kennedy compound. She took it all in like a child at Disney World, wide-eyed and open-mouthed and speechless, save the occasional *Oh. My. God.* Occasionally someone would look up and wave to Danny, shouting a hello or something inaudible to him. He was delighted to find Robbie Marsh on a break, dressed in a baseball uniform for a new movie, and he motioned him over to introduce her ("a friend of my assistant," he said) and request an autograph on her behalf. Robbie signed the back of her café receipt before posing for a photo that Danny took with her smartphone.

"Allow me," said Robbie, who then took her phone and snapped a photo of her and Danny. Another surreal moment overtook him, yet she didn't seem to feel it. Perhaps she was too enamored with having just met *the* Robbie Marsh.

"We should get back," said Danny, and they returned to his office. "What are you going to tell your friends?" he asked her along the way.

"I'm not sure. Hard to keep this from them. But I swear, I won't tell a soul, except for Kelly, my best friend in the world. We've known each other since we were kids, even before the accident. You can trust her. And I promise you'll not see any pictures on Facebook or anything like that. Especially the one of the two of us together."

"You can show and tell anyone anything you want," he said. "And you'll send me a copy of that photo, right?"

"Of course."

The car was already waiting for Teresa when they pulled up to Danny's office.

"Listen, there's one more thing," she said before departing. "All that money you gave me over the years? I hope you don't mind, but I donated it—well, most of it." She didn't wait for his reaction. "I know you wanted me to have it, and I really, really appreciate your giving me so much. But it just never felt *right* to take it—and I never thought you were bribing me or anything like that," she added quickly. "It's just...you never *needed* to. You quit drinking. And you paid all my medical expenses and made it possible for me to go to the college of my dreams. That's atonement enough."

Danny trembled all over. *That* was atonement enough? Nothing could atone enough.

Then he heard a voice, something Raj had said many months ago: *The little girl lived, Daniel.*

She was standing there, right in front of him, and she was OK. She had been OK all along.

Finally the dam broke, and the remorse, regret, guilt, and shame rushed out, trickling down his cheeks and coursing through his bloodstream and pounding in his temples.

"I'm sorry," he cried. "I am *so* sorry." He said it repeatedly, and whether he took her into his embrace or she took him into hers, he couldn't be sure.

She had succumbed to emotion as well. "It's OK," she said, "I know you are."

"Thank you," he said. "Thank you for your forgiveness."

They held each other for a long time. He didn't want to let her go. And yet he knew that if he did, he'd be OK.

But he couldn't bring himself to look at her when he finally did. At least not immediately. He wiped his eyes, which had started to sting, and pushed his hair back with both his hands and tried to take a couple of slow, deep breaths. He wanted to erupt into a wail, could feel it bubbling, but willed it back.

"Thank you for contacting me," he said. "That took a lot of guts."

"I never hated you," she said "I mean, I thought I did. I hated the person my parents told me to hate. I don't know why, and maybe I should, but I don't hate *you* and I never will."

"I have. Enough for both of us," he said. He'd never admitted that to anyone other than Raj.

"But you don't have to anymore," she said. "There's no point to it. I mean, you're sorry—anyone with eyes and a brain can see it. You made a huge, big-ass mistake fifteen years ago—I'll give you that. It was cruel and thoughtless and beyond stupid. But it was a mistake. It's not who you are."

"Who am I?" he heard himself ask, uncertain of where the words came from.

"You're free, if you let yourself be."

She said it with such authority, and it stunned him. Suddenly the meaning had become clear as day. He'd given up the alcohol, but he'd never given up the guilt and the shame and the punishment. Those things had consumed him, become him. *But it's not who you are.*

He wasn't his father, nor was he the worthless boy he'd always felt in his father's presence. He wasn't his mother either. He had a voice, and he'd been using it.

He also wasn't Danny Masters. He was not a man to be revered, praised, bestowed with awards and accolades and adulation. Neither was he to be belittled, demeaned, or abused.

He was in recovery. He finally knew what the word meant. Finally understood it. He finally felt as if the word applied to him.

He was a writer. Or perhaps he just wrote for a living, and wrote well.

He was a father. And that was the one thing he never questioned, the one part of him that never felt fraudulent.

Teresa smiled and waved good-bye from the open window as the car drove off and left him standing there, lightheaded. Danny went up to his office (he'd given Dez the rest of the day off) and closed the door. Then he sagged into his sofa and his body let go. He wept again—let forty-five years of emotion out, and when he was finished, he closed his eyes.

He slept there all night. When he woke up, Dez was hovering over him with a wet towel on his forehead.

"My God, you scared the shit out of me," she said, her voice shaky. "Another ten seconds and I was gonna dial nine-one-one."

He felt disoriented as well as an inexplicable lightness, the cliché of an anvil having been removed from one's body, only on the inside. If he didn't know any better, he would've believed he could fly out the window and to his car.

"What time is it?" he asked.

"It's a little after eight in the morning. You were here all night. I thought you fainted."

Danny laughed. Like a giddy, crazy person.

"What's so funny about that? Geez, what if you really had fainted and got a concussion?" she asked, more as if she were talking to herself.

"I'm fine," he said, and he hugged her. "Wow," he exclaimed, noticing for the first time, "you smell good!"

"That does it," said Dez. "I'm taking you to the ER."

Danny laughed even harder.

Wait until he told Raj!

CHAPTER
THIRTY-TWO
Sunny Smith

I ANNOUNCED MY RESIGNATION TO ANGELA IN the conference room, with Phil on speakerphone, my voice shaking on every word. Georgie was with me, holding my hand. As expected, they were shocked, yet supportive.

"I don't have to tell you how much we're going to miss you," said Phil, "but given your recent success, it's time."

"Thanks," I said, squeezing Georgie's hand and trying to keep my composure.

Angela was crying. "First Georgie, now you."

"I'm assuming Josh knows," said Phil.

"Actually, he doesn't. I'm telling him tonight, so please, don't say anything." Gossip circulated the company like blood through arteries—it wouldn't have surprised me if Josh had somehow found out before Phil even picked up the phone.

I texted Josh immediately afterward and spent the next hour trying to work off the anxiety of waiting for him to call me, plunging my box cutter into the shipment like a knife into a pumpkin. I nearly jumped out of my skin when the stockroom phone rang.

"What's up, Sun," said Josh in his manager's voice. We'd not spoken since he'd angrily left my apartment the other night.

"I was wondering if I could come out to Jersey tonight and meet you."

"Everything OK?" he asked.

"I just really want to see you." I knew my attempt at a casual, loving-girlfriend tone was betraying me, that he could see right through it.

"I'm in Connecticut today. Why don't I take the Port Jeff ferry and meet you at your place."

Already the guilt was needling me. "No, I think it's best if I come to see you," I said.

"OK," he said. "If that's what you want."

He was dressed casually in Dockers and a button-down shirt when I arrived and sporting a slight five o'clock shadow. He looked handsome, yet tired. He drove us to a café in town, where he bought me a latte and a slice of peanut butter cheesecake for us to split, although I couldn't even swallow one bite. We sat opposite each other, and he could read the fear on my face.

"Before you say anything, I want to apologize for the other night," he said. "You're right, I was moving too fast."

I took in a deep breath.

"I officially put in my two weeks at Whitford's today," I said.

The muscles in his face relaxed as he broke into a grin. "Sunny, that's fantastic. I had a feeling something was up when I spoke to Phil today." He reached for my hand, and I let him take it. "I know what a big step this was. It must be scary for you. And I know I wasn't supportive of you the other night—you blindsided me, that's all. But I just know it's going to work out for you. And I'm sure you checked your rankings today. I think you're going to be in the top one hundred by the end of the month. You're at least set for the rest of this year, financially speaking."

Please, please stop being so wonderful and supportive right now. Be a jackass, will ya?

"Josh," I started. "There's more."

"What?"

I took in another breath. "I..." God, this was hard. Even worse than resigning. "I don't think we should see each other anymore."

A tear slipped down my cheek as I watched his demeanor turn to one in which he'd just been sucker punched.

"Say that again?"

I was about to open my mouth when he put up his hand to stop me. "Never mind. I heard you the first time." He looked flabbergasted. "Look, I admit I was rushing things, but *this*?"

"That's just it, Josh; looking back on it, I don't think you were rushing things. But it scared me, and I think the reason why was because I realized this is not what I want."

"Why?"

He had been in cheerleader mode as he listened to me. Then he was human Josh, real Josh—vulnerable and visibly heartbroken—and it pained me not to be able to reach out and touch him and love him the way he'd wanted me to, the way I wanted to at that moment.

"I wish I knew. On paper, we're the perfect match. We can talk to each other, and you're funny and supportive—I can't tell you how grateful I am to you for all you did to help me get published and make my books a success. I couldn't have done it without you."

I stopped to search for words while he waited for the next stab wound.

"But I don't want to make the same mistake with you that I made with Teddy—and I'm not comparing you to Teddy," I said quickly. But he took offense anyway.

"And what mistake is that?" he asked, a bite to his tone.

"Teddy was perfect on paper too. At least when we first met he was. But something was missing. I was in love with the idea of the package Teddy was selling me—house, kids, picket fence—you name it. But it wasn't *my* package. It wasn't my *passion*. I didn't feel for Teddy the way you should feel when you're going to spend the rest of your life with someone you love. Like you can't wait to get up every morning. I know every relationship is work, but honestly, it was manual labor with Teddy."

"And what, you think that's your fate with me? I've never made any demands on you other than for you to better yourself for *you*, not me."

"I know," I cried. "And I love you for that. I really do. You're so *not* like Teddy. That's why I really wanted to make it work. But I don't feel that passion for you that I should. You deserve that from someone."

Josh shook his head, a gesture somewhere between exasperation and an ache to comprehend. "And you don't think that can come to you if you just put off the absurd notion that you're going to end up with a screenwriter you're fixated with?"

"That's what I thought with Teddy. I thought it would come to me. Once everything was in place, then it would just happen. Kind of like the rationale that some people who are trying to lose weight or quit smoking have—they think that life will be so much better as soon as they lose the weight or are smoke-free. But all they do is put off their happiness. It never occurs to them that they can create the life they want in the meantime."

"Isn't that what you've been doing for the last seven years?" he accused.

"I did worse," I said. "I gave up completely once I realized that I'd wasted all those years waiting for something that was never going to happen. Not with Danny, but with *Teddy*." And then, at that moment, I had an epiphany. "You know, it just occurred to me: Not being able to have children might have been the greatest blessing ever. Can you imagine what would've happened if that dream came true, and I was still miserable? Can you imagine what that would've been like for my kids?"

"I can understand that," he said, no doubt thinking of his own kids, worried about the scars his unhappy marriage and divorce left on them.

The more I spoke, the clearer it came into focus. "I wouldn't want that for *your* kids either. Or you. You deserve more, Josh. So do they. I can't take that risk. It's tearing me apart to hurt you right now. But if I went even further, and my worst fear was realized... It would kill me to hurt you, Jeremy, and Mattie like that."

Josh looked utterly defeated.

"I want you to be happy," he said, his voice catching slightly on the last word.

Another tear slipped away from me. "I want the same for you."

He looked away for a moment, as if trying to come up with a Hail Mary play, a game changer, before the clock ran out. But clearly he had nothing, and he knew it. His eyes met mine.

"Guess there's nothing more to say. You've made up your mind."

"I am so sorry," I said.

"I'm sorry too."

We left the café and drove back to Josh's place in silence. When he pulled up to my Beetle, I opened the passenger door and stepped out of his car. He turned off the ignition and walked around to meet me. And we stood, facing each other, each of us desperately wishing for a way to make things different between us, less painful.

"You still going to see Danny Masters when he comes to the store?" he asked.

"Yes," I said.

"And what will you say to him?"

Good question.

"I really don't know."

Josh opened his arms for one final embrace, and we held each other tightly.

"I'm going to miss you so much," I said between sobs.

"I'm going to miss you too."

He let go of me and I wiped my eyes. He did the same. "Take good care of yourself, Sunny."

"You too."

And just like that, Joshua Hamilton and I were no more.

I cried over the George Washington and Throgs Neck bridges, the Long Island Expressway and Northern State Parkway, Route 110 and New York Avenue, right up the steps into my apartment until I flopped in my bed, my clothes on, and turned out the light.

Where would I have ended up had I done this ten years ago, before Teddy and I got married? Where was I going to end up now?

I had no idea. But it was time to stop fixating on the what ifs and the shoulda, woulda, couldas and the supposed tos. It was time to move forward. Time to make a plan.

Danny Masters

DANNY WENT HOME TO SHOWER AND CHANGE. He considered going back to the office, but realized he wanted to go for a drive. Just get in his car and cruise up the coast, stopping wherever he so desired. Or maybe he would call Raj first. Or Paul Wolf and have lunch. For once he didn't feel flummoxed by the buffet of choices, wasn't afraid to make a wrong move.

He was about to leave the house when Ella called.

"Dad, get over here *right now*," she said.

He became alarmed. "What's wrong, El?"

"Everything's fine—you just have to come over, I don't want to tell you over the phone!"

Danny hung up, grabbed his keys, and sped off to Frannie's house. Along the way his mind flipped through various scenarios, hoping it had nothing to do with Richie the drummer. He arrived at the house in record time and knocked on the door twice before entering just as Ella raced up to open it, her bangs flying in a flurry. She jumped up and threw her arms around her father's neck, almost knocking him over.

"What's up?" he asked. "I can't take the suspense."

Frannie entered the room and immediately noticed a change in him. "Did you get some good news about the new show?" she asked.

"More like I got a second wind." He sent Frannie a message with his eyes: *What's going on?* Frannie shrugged, her eyes responding, *Your guess is as good as mine.*

Ella took him by the arm and pulled him into the living room, her eyes bright and her face glowing.

"C'mon! You too, Mom."

They sat side by side on the couch, while Ella stood in front of them.

"OK," she started. "Remember when I told you that I wanted to go to the School of the Arts in New York City?"

They nodded. "I thought you said you weren't old enough," said Frannie.

"I'm not right now," said Ella. "But I will be in September, as a freshman. So I applied. And guess what: *I GOT IN!*"

Danny jumped up. "Sweetheart, that's terrific!" He picked her up and spun her around. "I am so proud of you!" When he put her down he saw Frannie was not enthused.

"I thought we discussed this," she said. "What made you go behind my back and apply?"

"Mom, what is the big deal? It's just New York."

"The big deal is that I don't want you living there."

"Oh, and LA is such a paradise," said Danny, knowing there would be hell to pay for not presenting a united front with Frannie, but he was too selfishly excited. It made his plans that much easier. Perhaps Raj was right, and the universe had been busy lining things up for him.

Frannie glowered at him before turning to Ella. "I don't want to move to New York City. I'm a Californian. I don't like New York. I never have."

"So don't move," said Ella.

"Then where will you live? And with whom?"

She pointed to Danny. "Dad."

Frannie's glower became even fiercer as he put his hands up in surrender. "Hey, this wasn't my idea."

"Sure sounds like you discussed it."

"It was a hypothetical conversation," he said, instantly regretting sharing this bit of information.

"Hypothetical," she repeated, skeptical.

"Well, it started out that way. But then I decided to go through with it—the moving part, I mean. My moving, not Ella coming with me." It seemed the more he tried to dig himself out of the hole, the deeper it got. "You know I wouldn't keep something like that from you, Frannie. Ella just beat me to the punch."

"See, Mom? It's perfect."

"Ella, I wanna talk to your dad alone."

Ella groaned. "Oh, come on, Mom. Don't kill my buzz."

"It's OK, El," said Danny. "We need to talk about this."

Ella left the room sulking, yet still maintaining a bounce in her step. Danny turned to his ex-wife. "I swear I had nothing to do with this. I assumed that if she discussed it with me, then she discussed it with you."

"And what the hell makes you think I would approve of something like that?"

"Why wouldn't you? Look, it's something she really wants."

"She's only fifteen!"

"Don't rush it—she still has a couple of months," said Danny.

"How can she know what she wants?"

"You can't be committed at fifteen? Or fourteen? Or thirteen or twelve? I can rattle off the names of people I've worked with who knew what they wanted to do with their lives when they were just children." He paused for a beat. "Or is this about you not wanting to go with her?"

Tears came to her eyes. "I don't want to lose her, Danny, but I just…I can't…"

He embraced her, that tenderness he'd always felt for her pounding in his heart.

"Look, I'll take care of her. You know I will."

"And what about when you're not there? Who'll look after her then?"

"I'll be home more often. I'm making some life changes. Paring down."

Frannie released herself from his hold and looked at him, astonished. "Since when?"

He tried to act casual. "I've been wanting to take a break for a while now."

She looked at him, her expression registering equal parts skepticism and curiosity. "This about Charlene?"

"Charlene and I are over for good," he said, his tone solid and resolute, and this seemed to surprise Frannie just as much as his desire to simplify his life. He could practically read her mind at that moment: This wasn't Danny crying wolf; he and Charlene Dumont were never going to be a couple, ever again.

"Is there someone else?"

He paused for a moment, uncertain of how to answer. "It's complicated. I met her a while ago, at the New York premiere of *Exposed*, but had a hard time tracking her down since then. Nothing's set in stone, but I—" He stopped short. What came next? Was he really about to turn his whole life around for her?

No, it wasn't for her—it was for *him*.

He wanted to move anyway, he suddenly realized, regardless of whether Sunny was there or not. And then, as if he had taken off a pair of dark glasses, everything around him brightened, became crystal clear. Yes. It wasn't for or about Sunny. It was about *going home*, and bringing his daughter with him. And he felt a moment of well-being, that no matter what the outcome with Sunny, he would be OK. He'd never had that feeling with Charlene—in the beginning, every time they broke up felt like a catastrophe. Then it felt just plain lousy. He didn't believe he'd be able to go for the rest of his life without her intoxicating scent, her sex, her seductive nature. He didn't believe he'd be able to endure seeing her on the screen or stage without feeling the pain of being apart from her for prolonged periods of time. He remembered having those same worries about giving up alcohol until the night of the accident, and how those worries turned out to be illusions that vanished the moment he found out that Teresa was going to survive. He'd always have his temptations to drink, and those tricksters would try to deceive him, but one thought of Ella or Teresa was enough for him.

"Look, Frannie," he said. "If the shoe was on the other foot and it was me staying here instead of you, I know it would kill me to live so far away from Ella. But this is a once-in-a-lifetime opportunity for her, and she's a good kid. She'll do well in New York. It suits her."

"She gets it from you," Frannie retorted.

Ella returned to the room, and he guessed she hadn't gone very far in the first place. "Can I say something, please?" she asked. They turned to her. Ella directed her attention to her mother. "Mom. You know I love you. You've been like the best mother in the world. Half my friends wish you were their mom. You've had me more or less to yourself for the better part of my life. But I think…" She gestured toward Danny. "I think Dad deserves just as much time with me, especially before I go off to college. And I want to live with him."

A tidal wave of emotion in Danny's chest barreled toward his tear ducts. He pressed his lips together tightly and dabbed his eyes before a single salty drop could escape.

Frannie asked him, "What about your agents? Ken Congdon? Your office? You've got so much tied up here."

"I need to get out of here, Frannie."

She looked defeated and looked at Ella helplessly. "What about Richie?"

Danny grimaced; leave it to Frannie to play the boyfriend card.

"Weren't you the one telling me to slow down with Richie, like, a month ago?" said Ella.

Bless you, he thought.

As if waving a flag of surrender, Frannie raised her hands and dropped them, shaking her head twice. "I guess your mind's made up," she said, and she took her daughter into her arms and held her close.

"Thank you, Mom," said Ella in a muffled voice.

After a few minutes, Frannie released her daughter and gave Danny a threatening look. "If I find out you're gallivanting all over the place and leaving her home alone at night..."

Danny took a step back and raised his right hand. "I swear to you on my Oscar, I'm gonna take care of her."

And upon hearing that, Frannie gave her blessing. Ella let out a piercing scream and hugged them one at a time before rushing away to text her friends. He waited for the ringing in his ears to cease before saying to Frannie, "I don't know, do you think she's happy?" and then raised his eyebrows in Groucho Marx fashion. Frannie was not charmed. He put his arm around her one final time. "Don't worry, hon." He hadn't called her that since they were married. "She's awesome, and she's going to be OK. Better than OK. She's going to be great. She's a lot less like me than you think."

"Being you isn't such a bad thing, Danny."

For the first time ever in his life, he agreed.

Sunny Smith

M Y APARTMENT WAS BEGINNING TO RESEM-
ble the Whitford's stockroom—shipping boxes
occupied every room, each set coded by different-colored
Sharpie pens, filled with the artifacts of my life: vinyl
records, DVD sets of *Winters in Hyannis* and my Cary
Grant and John Hughes collections, winter clothes and
snow boots, and shoeboxes full of letters and keepsakes
and ticket stubs from just about every concert I'd ever
attended. For every two boxes I'd packed, I filled one
with stuff to give away—namely all but two of my hoodies, assorted pairs of shoes and tops that had gotten no
more than two wears in their lifetimes, housewares that
had been wedding gifts for Teddy and me that I'd never
used, and dinosaur computer parts.

Forty years compacted between slabs of cardboard and
bubble wrap. And I'd barely even made a dent.

Georgie and Marcus weren't leaving until June, but
they were thrilled that their apartment was coming into
my hands, as was I. It was definitely a step up for me; the
last writing space I'd had was in the house I shared with
Teddy, and he had always made it clear that it would be
given up in no time if we had more than two kids—no

sharing rooms for his offspring, which I had thought was ridiculous. Nevertheless, I was already decorating my new space in my mind's eye, collecting paint swatches and dusting off my writing desk.

My plan was to move into the new apartment, live off my royalties for at least six months, then evaluate whether it was feasible to go another six months. I'd already put together a strict budget, making sure to put money aside both for a house and a retirement fund. Phil assured me that there would always be a place for me at Whitford's should I need to return.

"But what if there is no more Whitford's?" I asked. I bit my tongue a second later when I realized I might have gotten Josh in trouble for revealing to me information about the company's status, but Phil didn't indicate such.

"One way or another, we'll always look out for you," he said.

I was glad to have the safety net. And yet I knew that I would never return to Whitford's. At least not as an employee. It was like moving out of your parents' house for good. And starting over wasn't going to be easy by any means, but at least it was finally on my own terms.

I had a new mystery novel idea and couldn't wait to get going on it, already making character sketches and lists of names, and jotting down what ifs. But when *The Danny Masters Best* script books arrived and I put one aside for myself and thumbed through it, I found myself thinking that the novel idea could work better as a movie. Although I'd never written a script before, I'd toyed with the idea of taking a screenwriting course back when I'd first become obsessed with *Winters in Hyannis*. However, screenwriting had always seemed to be a different beast from novel writing. More daunting, in a way. But after reading the opening scene of *Exposed* during my lunch break, it occurred to me that I had a good teacher sitting right in front of me.

Everything was in place. Well, almost everything.

At least I finally knew what I was going to say to Danny Masters when I met him.

Danny Masters

D ESPITE HAVING BROKEN UP WITH CHARLENE
and being on the road and away from Ella yet again,
Danny couldn't remember the last time he had felt this
giddy. Ever since his meeting with Teresa, he'd felt as
if he had a new lease on life, a second chance. For the
first time ever, the Incident was behind him—in fact, it
was no longer "the Incident" with a capital *I*, but simply
"the accident." He'd always refused to refer to it as such
because accidents were typically something beyond one's
control, unintentional. Certainly he had never intended
to hurt anyone, but it had been preventable. He didn't
have to get in the car that night.

Better yet, he was writing again. When he'd spoken
to Mike Nichols about the adaptation project, Danny had
proposed to obtain the rights to *Long Island Ducks* and
adapt that as well, and Nichols agreed to consider it. Not
only was he writing, but he also couldn't keep up with
the deluge of words. He scrawled things down on scraps
of paper when he didn't have an electronic implement
handy. He talked into the voice recorder on his iPhone
while jogging or driving. He rushed out of the shower,
dripping wet, to jot down a snippet of dialogue. Sunny's

book was coming alive, and he wished he could show it to her. The writing hadn't been this fluid since his first draft of *Exposed*. Even most *Winters in Hyannis* scripts had been arduous labor, and that was with a writing staff to assist him. Moreover, he didn't find himself second-guessing every scene, every transition, every exchange between protagonist and antagonist. He wasn't worrying about whether it was good, whether *he* was good. He was simply immersed in the process, feeling something akin to a runner's high, where the destination wasn't nearly as much fun as the running itself.

And yet he still went frigid every time he tried to compose a letter to Sunny.

The book tour had been going well so far. He'd been to six bookstores in as many days, in New Jersey and Manhattan, and although there was no sign of Sunny, he found himself eager to meet each person and sign every book with the hope that she would appear and he would recognize her. In all the googling he'd done, nothing revealed where she worked, whether she was still a book-store employee, or living in New York. But he'd scripted every scenario possible, ranging from Sunny going postal and opening fire in the middle of someone asking him if there was going to be a *Winters in Hyannis* movie for the umpteenth time (although Danny had imagined doing it himself in response to that question) to Sunny showing up and introducing Danny to the goon that had interrupted them outside the theater (*We're planning a June wedding...*) to Danny breaking into a cheesy courtroom confession: *Yes, I'm guilty. I'm guilty of being a jackass in the first degree.* This temptation was especially strong when, in some stores, fans actually called him *jackass* as an affectionate moniker, part of a cheer. One day he'd look back on it and embrace it tongue-in-cheek, he thought, the way much of the Brat Pack did twenty-five years after first being labeled the Brat Pack. But for now, the word conjured the visual equivalent of a fork scratching a plate.

Nevertheless, he politely laughed it off and let the fans pose with him for photos and thanked them all for coming.

After two more signings in Connecticut and a fear that carpal tunnel syndrome was setting in from writing his name and shaking hands so many times (Purell was the crack of hand sanitizers, he'd decided), Danny was starting to lose hope that Sunny would show.

He could still e-mail her, he reminded himself. Or send a tweet. But what could he say, especially in a medium designed to be so casual, even though so many times it was anything but? He didn't know how to go beyond mere conventional apologies or make amends without sounding like the recovering alcoholic he was. He didn't know how to articulate what he felt because he couldn't identify the feeling.

He didn't know what story to tell.

Even if he did meet her in person, he still wouldn't know what to say. But at least then he wouldn't be clamoring for the perfection. No, this time he'd opt for being human.

Long Island was next. He was going to visit three stores: Book Hampton on Main Street in Sag Harbor, Barnes & Noble in Lake Grove, and Whitford's Books & Café in Huntington Village. While on the island Danny hoped to do some additional house-hunting as well as visit some of the locations Sunny referred to in her novel. She had obviously done a lot of research; and although her novels were set in the 1950s, '60s, and '70s, respectively, he thought it would be fun to visit the towns and see what stood where, perhaps even take some snapshots. He liked the idea of getting to know his home all over again, to see it in a way he'd never seen it before. It simultaneously felt both new and familiar.

The Book Hampton gig brought out the East End crowd, including Alan Alda and Jules Feiffer. The Barnes & Noble signing lasted until well past midnight, there were so many people.

But still no Sunny.

He had a day off between the Barnes & Noble and the Whitford's Books & Café gigs and spent it in the city, writing. He'd decided to use his apartment at the Plaza as the hub for the tour, and although it sometimes resulted in exhaustive travel, having the same place to come back to each night without the need to check in and check out made life much easier. Dez had flown out for a couple of days at Danny's request; most of the tasks could've been done long distance, but Danny sensed she already knew that the real reason he'd summoned her to the East Coast was because he was lonely—once he'd signed every book, smiled for every photo, answered every question, he went back to a well-decorated emptiness that Charlene was no longer around to fill. Ella was too busy with school for him to call or for her to stay with him. And although many of his fans, male and female alike, offered to accompany him back to wherever he was staying for the night, he always left alone.

Dusk had set in, causing the room to dim, but Danny was oblivious to it. For the last twenty minutes he had been circling the bedroom, repeatedly reciting scenes out loud in order to capture the right timing and rhythm, when something in the mirror on the opposite wall caught his attention. Perhaps it had just been the reflection from something outside the window, a sliver of light bouncing off a building. He moved closer to the mirror, his pupils trying to focus. He'd noticed lately that his eyesight was weakening and he was going to need glasses. He hadn't realized how dark the room had become. The closer he came to the mirror, the more puzzled he was by what he was seeing, to the point that he thought perhaps there was something on the glass itself.

And then, just as he was about to lean in, he tripped over a pair of sneakers he'd left on the floor and banged into the mirror. He fell back, tripping on the sneakers a second time, and covering his nose with his hands and yelping.

Dez rushed in from the other room the moment she heard the crash.

"What the hell happened?" she asked.

He had fallen on his ass and was rocking from side to side like an injured football player, his hands over his face while his nose throbbed. "My nose!" he exclaimed in a muffled voice and couldn't help but conjure an image of Marcia Brady. "Son of a bitch!"

"What'd you do?"

"I hit the mirror with my face," said Danny.

"What were you doing so close to the mirror?"

"Reciting dialogue." Danny took his hand away from his face momentarily and went queasy when he saw blood.

"You what?" asked Dez, startled.

"I was reciting dialogue when I saw something in the mirror and wanted to see what it was, and then I tripped."

"You tripped?"

"It was dark in the room."

"Why didn't you turn on the light?"

"Because I was practicing dialogue," said Danny, as if the answer was obvious.

"I don't understand—you're writing shows about wrestling now?"

"I think it's broken," he said.

"The mirror?"

"No, my nose!"

She pulled his hand away and inspected his face. "It's not broken, but it's going to swell up big time. You should probably cancel tomorrow."

"I don't wanna cancel tomorrow." He felt a shooting pain across his lower back just as he said the words, and winced. "Oh, geezus."

"Suit yourself," said Dez. "But you're going to do a signing looking like a raccoon with bad rhinoplasty."

Danny moaned. "Call a doctor, please." He would decide about whether to cancel after he got a couple of painkillers in him.

She called the Plaza concierge, who sent up an on-call physician. The doctor inspected him, made sure he hadn't gotten a concussion and assured him that his nose wasn't broken and, once the swelling went down, would be good as new. "No Owen Wilson for you," he said and laughed as if he'd been the first to think of such a joke.

The next morning Danny awakened to a splitting headache and a nose the size of a basketball. At least that was how it looked and felt to him. It had swollen and bruised in purplish-greenish hues and had spread to under his eyes, just as Dez had predicted. Everyone told him to cancel his appearance at Whitford's Books & Café—Dez, the doctor, even Ella. He'd taken a photo of himself with his cell phone and sent it to her, to receive a text message in return with the word "gross" in block caps and excessive exclamation points, followed by an actual phone call. He sent the same photo to Jackson, who practically screamed at him over the phone. "Cancel! Cancel, you asshole! You've already done the biggest store there. You'll probably get the exact same crowd tonight from the other two stores. For God's sake, we don't want this to be a Grateful Dead tour."

Danny shrugged as he inspected his face in the mirror, careful not to get too close this time. "You're probably right," he said, sounding doubtful.

"Incidentally, how'd you do it?" asked Jackson.

"I was reciting dialogue," said Danny.

After an extended pause, Jackson replied, "Yeeeahhh, how 'bout we say you got into a bar fight instead."

"Right. Because a recovering alcoholic would get into a bar fight."

"Punched out one of the paparazzi?" suggested Jackson.

"With my nose?"

"Really? *Reciting dialogue* is the story you wanna go with?"

"It's the sad truth, man," said Danny.

"Hell, it'd be more plausible to say you got it during sex. Or that Charlene punched you out after you broke up with her—are you still broken up with her?"

He rubbed his pounding temples. "Yes, Jackson. I'm still broken up with her." He didn't blame Jackson for asking the question, given how his and Charlene's relationship status moved like the weather patterns. "But that's going to be the rumor, isn't it—that she punched me out."

"Just go with it, man."

"Great."

"Anyway, cancel the gig."

"I'll think about it," he said. He hung up the phone and said out loud to no one, "Yeah, I'm not canceling this gig." Then he popped a painkiller and napped for two hours.

Of course, he couldn't tell anyone why he didn't want to cancel the signing: that he was holding out hope that perhaps this would be his last chance to see Sunny, to say something, to make amends and then go on with the rest of his life. And he'd made a deal with himself when he began the tour: If she didn't show up, then that was that. He would finish the tour, go back to LA, spend time with Ella, and move to New York regardless. Whenever he started a new script, Danny always needed to know two things: the beginning and the ending. He especially needed to know the ending—knowing where his characters were going to wind up somehow made it easier for him to get them there. Or maybe he just didn't like uncertainty.

He felt a dull throbbing in his nose.

———

Thanks to a tractor-trailer accident, Danny spent two hours in a Suburban stuck in traffic on the Long Island

Expressway. The pain from his black eyes and swollen nose was starting to return—he'd not taken another painkiller because he didn't want to be too zonked out—and he tried to sit back and close his eyes and avoid telling himself that he was indeed an asshole for not canceling this gig, which, at the moment, he was dreading like a summons to jury duty. Screw it all—he just wanted to go to sleep.

"How much longer to you think it'll be?" he asked the driver.

"Soon as we get around this thing, we'll fly like a rocket," answered the driver in a hybrid of British and Middle Eastern accents.

When they finally arrived at Whitford's Books and Café, the lot was packed with cars. He watched as people pointed to the Suburban, excited expressions on their faces knowing who was behind the tinted windows, and nausea settled in him.

He was over the adulation, he decided. Just like that.

The driver steered the car around to the back of the store, parked alongside a faded yellow Volkswagen Beetle, and Danny saw a door open from the building and a woman emerge. She approached as he thanked the driver, put on a pair of lightly tinted sunglasses, and exited the Suburban.

It took her less than a nanosecond to notice the flesh-colored bandage poorly concealing the bulbous mass of ugly on his face. She cringed, but quickly recovered with a smile and emphatically shook his hand. "What happened to you?"

"Funny story," said Danny, "I was reciting dialogue, when—"

Before he could continue, she asked if he was feeling all right, did he need anything, would he be OK to do the signing, did it hurt? Yes, no, I certainly hope so, and it's not so bad—all true but the last. More like I-now-know-what-it-feels-like-to-have-a-Mack-truck-drive-straight-up-your-nose.

"I'm sorry—where are my manners? Welcome! I'm Angela, the store manager." She spoke several decibels louder than was necessary, or at least that's how it sounded to him.

She held the heavy door open for him, yet as soon as he entered he followed a few steps behind her as she took him through the stockroom, a well-organized maze of shipping boxes and metal shelving and clipboards and a workstation that Danny noticed had been decorated with, among other things, a Volkswagen Beetle shaped from yellow Play-Doh with number-two pencils sticking out of it, like some sort of automotive voodoo doll; a *Winters in Hyannis* cast poster (very rare—he had never seen one outside of his own office); and an old touch-tone telephone plugged into a jack. It looked a little like the Bat Phone from the campy sixties *Batman* TV series.

"Our stock manager is a huge fan of yours," said the manager, whose name he'd already forgotten. He looked around for signs of life, but didn't see anyone else.

"Where is he?" he asked, curious.

The woman turned her head, "Oh, he's not a—"

Before she could finish her sentence, another door swung open and another employee (also female) entered, firing off something about additional books needing to go out and where were they? She then noticed Danny, smiled, and waved casually, unfazed by his celebrity. "Oh, hi," she said at the same time the manager replied something about Kenny knowing where they were. And yet, strangely, the employee asked, "Where is she?"

"I don't know," said the manager, who then led Danny away from the door that opened to the store, down a short, claustrophobic corridor and into a conference room barely big enough to hold an oval table that seated no more than eight. "You can wait here, and I'll call you when we're all set up and we're ready to introduce you."

"Thanks," said Danny.

She peered at him. "Are you sure you're OK?"

He nodded. "Just a little wonky from the meds, but I'll be fine. I'm really sorry I'm not at my best tonight, but I didn't want to cancel and disappoint anyone."

"Well, we certainly appreciate that. You just sit tight, and someone will come for you in a few minutes. We've got plenty of bottled water on hand at your signing table and plenty of snacks."

It occurred to Danny at that moment that he hadn't eaten in several hours, and his stomach rumbled as if to corroborate.

"Thank you…I'm sorry, tell me your name again?"

"Angela."

"Thank you, Angela."

She left him alone, and the place fell silent. He contemplated putting his head down on the table, but thought better of it. What felt like hours but couldn't have been more than five minutes later, he looked at the picture window opposite him and watched an effeminate man enter through a different door than the one the manager led him through. For a moment he thought the man might be Kenny the stock manager (for some reason he'd put the two together), but decided he was too well dressed to work in a stockroom.

"Hello, Danny. I'm Georgie Spencer." Danny shook his hand firmly. "It's a pleasure to finally meet you in person. I'm the outreach coordinator here—not that that means anything to you. I'm in charge of planning events such as these."

He smiled. "Nice to meet you." He sensed they'd met before, but after so many signings and so many events, it wasn't surprising to have that feeling. Perhaps it was the way he greeted Danny so informally.

"Heard about your schnoz from Angela. Looks painful. You OK?"

"I'm fine, thanks."

"Ready to go?"

He nodded. Georgie held the door open the same way the manager had, and once again he lagged behind slightly.

"It's a full house," said Georgie, turning back to look Danny in the eye when he spoke. "That's good for us, of course, but it looks like you'll be here all night. We've got ice packs for your hand if it cramps up after all the signing."

"Thanks." Of all the stores he'd been to, this was the first to be so thoughtful, and he said so.

"Today's my last day at Whitford's, actually," said Georgie.

"Really? How come?"

"I'm getting married. Hey, congrats on the Oscar. Nice speech too."

"Thank you. Did you see the film?"

Georgie nodded. "Premiere night. Was quite a show," he said. Danny wasn't sure what he meant by this.

"Well, I'm glad you liked it. And hey, good luck to you."

"Thanks," said Georgie.

Angela had just finished the introduction. "Ladies and gentlemen, Danny Masters."

All heads turned in his direction, and they erupted into applause and cheers and whistles. Once again he became nauseated, just like when the Suburban pulled up to the store, and he attributed the visceral reaction to painkillers on an empty stomach. He walked alongside the crowd down an aisle cleared for him, the applause sounding like popping balloons rather than the usual sweet melody. He approached the podium, took a swig of water, and discreetly asked Angela for a candy bar. She then leaned in to Georgie and relayed his request.

Danny had been speaking briefly at these events. There wasn't much to say, really. He praised bookstores, their employees, and patrons, which usually drew a smattering of applause. He would then explain that although he often recited the dialogue aloud while writing his scripts, he didn't like to *read* it aloud to an audience, for he couldn't do the words justice. Without the actors, directors, locations, lighting, scenery, props, and music, they were just lifeless words on a page. And yet, that said, he believed and hoped that anyone who bought the book could bring them to life in his or her own way, perhaps with the intention of learning to write scripts by reading along while watching the films or episodes. He was proud of each and every one of these scripts and every single person who helped get them to the screen, and he was grateful to everyone who bought a copy and supported him throughout his career. This would draw more applause and cheers.

He practically had it memorized word for word.

He would then do about ten minutes of Q&A and finally sign books and pose for pictures.

He gripped the sides of the podium as if to keep from falling over, scanned the panorama of the crowd, and swallowed hard. He suddenly felt like an actor with stage fright.

"What happened to your face?" someone in the front row asked.

Thank God for his fucked-up nose. "Oh, that. Funny little story." He went on to explain what happened the night before, and the crowd laughed not in solidarity but with skepticism, as if he were making it up. "No, really," he coaxed, but that only made them laugh harder. Jackson was right—a bar fight or Charlene decking him would've been much more plausible. He decided to play up to the crowd as if he knew that they knew that he was pulling one over on them, and at least it was enough to get him back on track. Georgie had returned and handed him a Hershey bar as inconspicuously as possible.

"Anyway, it's great to be here," he started, and then went into his speech.

More applause.

Georgie dispensed a wireless microphone to the patrons for questions that ranged from why did his new show get rejected to would he work with Shane Sands again.

After a couple of questions, Danny noticed that a look of utter delight came across Georgie's face as he practically ran to hand the mic to someone in the back. But Danny couldn't see the recipient. Lots of people were standing behind the full rows of chairs, and the sunglasses he wore to cover up his black eyes restricted his long-range vision.

"Mr. Masters, I've been a writer for a really long time. Your words have inspired me to be an even better writer. More than that, they've brought joy to my life, as have you. And so I just wanted to say thank you."

It was the way she said "Mr. Masters" that registered first. He took off his sunglasses and squinted to get a better look at her, trying to match the face before him to the seven-month-old memory he'd been trying so desperately to retain. And yet, he *knew*.

And there, as if manifesting on the spot, she stood before him. She looked different from that day outside the theater. Longer hair. Less makeup. Jeans and sneakers and a sweatshirt with the sleeves scrunched up. But he knew who she was. He'd known all along.

And for a split second, the dull throbbing of his nose and the pounding in his head and the nausea and hunger all disappeared.

"Thank you, Sunny," he said.

At that moment, he had a realization that was equal parts epiphany and matter-of-fact. And he finally knew what that amused look of Raj's was all about.

PART THREE

Sunny Smith

WE FACED EACH OTHER, THE REST OF THE store silent. He looked so different from the frazzled yet handsome guy he'd been outside the theater that day, and not just because he was wearing Bono-like sunglasses to cover up the bruises that peeked out from under the bandage covering his swollen nose. His hair was even longer than it had been at the Oscars, more gray showing through, and he looked pale. He didn't look like an Oscar-winning screenwriter. More to the point, he didn't look like Danny Masters. He didn't look charismatic or charming or like someone Charlene Dumont would be seen with.

Ohmigod: He called me *Sunny*—he knew who I was!

"Holy shit," I blurted. The audience laughed, and suddenly I could feel all eyes on me as I stood there, once again right in the spotlight I hadn't sought.

I turned on my heel and practically ran back to the stockroom.

"Wait!" Danny called out. He followed me and caught the door just before it could close and lock him out.

I stopped at the workstation and turned to him, and he looked at me for a second, catching his breath. It was just the two of us now. No Manhattan traffic, no fans, no press or lurkers waiting to steal the moment on their smartphones.

Just Danny and me.

"Sunrise," he said and smiled, as if he were trying on my name like a shirt, liking the way it fit. "You work here?"

I nodded.

"In here?" he clarified, looking around the stockroom.

I nodded again, at a loss for words. They were so much easier to come by on paper or a laptop. He then zoomed in on my workstation, took in its knickknacks and my *Winters in Hyannis* poster. "I thought you were some guy named Kenny," he said.

I looked at him with utter confusion, desperate to find my voice. How often did a person get this kind of second chance? How often did lightning strike twice? And what were the odds of my blowing it yet again?

No. I wasn't going to let that happen.

"I'm sorry I called you a failure," I said softly. "You are so not a failure."

It felt so good to release those words, and the emotion that came with them followed as tears came to my eyes.

"But I was a jackass," said Danny.

I shook my head and was about to refute it when he put his fingers to my lips and then wiped a stray tear from my cheek with a single, feather-soft caress.

"I'm sorry too," he said just as softly.

And then, before I even knew what was happening, he cupped my face in his hands and kissed me.

His mouth lingered over mine for a moment, and then he let go as abruptly as he took hold.

I opened my eyes and reconnected to his.

That kiss—oh, that *kiss*! The way my face seemed to fit so comfortably in his warm hands, like a chalice; the feel of his lips, both firm and smooth, his breath smelling of chocolate. The *electricity* I felt; actual current zapped through my body, charging my fingers and toes to the point that I thought they'd glow. Joshua Hamilton was a fantastic kisser. I'd felt sparks with Josh, perhaps even with Teddy at one time. But *this*. This was better than sparks. This was enough to start a car and keep it running.

I wanted it again. Slower this time.

So I took hold and pulled him into another firm, urgent kiss, this time running my fingers through his hair—his thick, silky hair—and he moved into me, pinning me to my workstation as his arms wrapped around me, his hands stopping at the small of my back, resting comfortably there, as if they found a place to live.

Our second kiss ended, reluctantly, and I opened my eyes slowly, feeling the cement floor underneath my feet, as if I'd just come back down to earth.

I caught my breath. "Wow," I said on the exhale.

"I've been wanting to do that ever since I saw you outside the theater," he practically whispered.

We were about to move in for a third when—

"Um, excuse me, but…"

Danny and I both jerked our heads to find Angela standing in front of us, goggle-eyed. How long had she been there?

"I'm very sorry…" Danny trailed off.

"Angela," I whispered to him.

"Angela. I apologize for leaving everyone out there. Please tell them I'll be back in ten minutes."

"OK," she said, trying to retain a voice of authority, although I could tell she was freaking the fuck out. "Ten minutes."

Danny returned his attention to me. "I've gotta go back out there and sign books before they start throwing chairs through the windows and looting the joint," he said, pointing with his thumb behind him.

I broke out of my trance and into a laugh.

"But here's the thing," he said. "As soon as this book tour is over, I'm moving to New York. I'm getting a place in the city as well as here on the Island. Sag Harbor, to be exact—it's a bit more low-key than the Hamptons, don't you think?" He didn't wait for me to respond, which was probably wise because I was caught in a whirlpool of emotions. "Anyway, I know this might sound crazy, but I read your books, Sunrise, and—"

My mind raced: *He read my books?*

I was about to interject, but he put two fingers to my lips again (and how I didn't melt on the spot both times, I don't know) and continued, trying to squeeze everything in under his allotted ten minutes.

"—and I think *Long Island Ducks* would make a terrific movie. I want to buy the film rights for an adaptation, and I want you to co-write the screenplay with me."

My brain could somehow only process strings of nouns and verbs without any conjunctions or adjectives to support them: Screenplay. Co-write. City. Live.

I attempted a coherent question. "You want to move to New York to write with me?"

"I want to move to New York *and* write with you," he clarified. He looked as if he were delighted by my bemusement. "In the past I've been too much of a control freak to work with anyone else, but I have a feeling that won't be the case this time. And right now I want to do something a little different from the kinds of things I've written before. I might even be able to persuade Mike Nichols to direct it."

More words: Freak. Mike Nichols. Direct.

"And…" He hesitated. "I thought we could give *us* a try as well."

This was fast. Like jumping off a cliff, frightening, not unlike when Josh had painted a future of me with him. But with Josh, I'd felt more like I was being pulled. This was different. There was something comforting about knowing that I wasn't jumping alone. Danny was jumping too. And he was inviting me to share his parachute.

"What about your daughter?" I asked.

His grin intensified. "I love that you just asked me that. She'll be enrolling at the School of the Arts and living with me."

I felt as if I were caught in a tailspin. Yet the assurance in his tone steadied me.

"I don't know what to say."

"Look, I know it must sound and feel really crazy to you, and I *have* to get back out there. But I want you to meet me in the city tomorrow. Please?"

"Tomorrow's Friday. I have to work," I said.

"Take the day off," he coaxed.

"I can't. Tomorrow's my last day, and—"

Shut up, shut up, shut up, Sunny! What is wrong with you?

"After work? I have an apartment at the Plaza. Look, I understand if this is all too abrupt for you or if you've already got someone else in your life or something. But can you at least think about it? Sleep on it tonight, and then come see me tomorrow."

He grabbed a Post-it pad from the workstation and wrote down the Plaza Hotel address and his cell phone number. *His personal cell phone number.* "You don't have to check in or anything like that. But just in case, I'll give them your name and let them know I'm expecting you. Tell them you want to see Daniel Gold. Or hell, even if you just want to call me, you can."

He handed me the Post-it and I studied the numbers, repeating the name in my mind like a mantra: *Daniel Gold.* I had known that was his real name, but never thought of him as such. Daniel Gold was someone I could go out with. And it occurred to me that maybe Daniel Gold was the one I'd been in love with all along. And maybe that was the feeling. Just plain ol' vanilla in love.

He kissed me one last time, slowly, gingerly, on my lips. We opened our eyes and locked our gaze yet again, and he finally let go of me.

He grinned. Not the charismatic Danny Masters grin, but one that was so much more intimate. "See you later, Sunrise." And with that he took a few steps back, as if to take a snapshot of my face, before finally turning and heading back out to the floor.

I leaned against my workstation to steady myself and took a deep breath, exhaling forcefully. He kissed me. Holy shit, *Danny Masters kissed me in my stockroom!* I wanted to shout it out from the roof of Whitford's, put it in sky-writing, post it on Facebook and YouTube and let *that* go viral instead.

No—not Danny Masters. *Daniel Gold* kissed me.

When I heard the stockroom door open a moment later, my heart went into a drum roll until Georgie materialized, with Theo behind him.

"Tell us *everything!*" said Theo, drunk with glee, as she ran up to me.

I looked at Theo, who hadn't set foot in the stockroom since she was a Whitford's employee back in college, and became disoriented for a second.

Georgie read my expression. "Yes, I snuck her back here. What are they gonna do, fire us? But never mind that. *Dish*, Sunny."

"Oh, my God," I said.

"You're *glowing*. So help me, if you tell me you and Danny Masters just had sex back here…"

Upon hearing the word "sex," it was as if Georgie snapped his fingers and everything clicked back into working order for me. I turned away and pretended to straighten up my workstation, watching their reaction out of the corner of my eye and trying to conceal the goofy grin that appeared at the mere thought of that kiss, of every word between Danny and me.

"We talked."

"You talked," he said, wary of my casualness.

"Sure," I said. "I apologized. He apologized. Finally. It was nice."

"That's *it?*" said Theo.

"*Oh. My GOD!*" shouted Georgie. He looked around the stockroom maniacally. "I have to hit you. I have to hit you with something."

"Now you've done it," said Theo. "You put Georgie over the edge."

"Oh, and he *kissed* me," I said, feigning nonchalance.

Georgie and Theo both squealed and started bouncing like teenagers.

I whistled a tune obnoxiously, teasing them even further. "And he invited me to the Plaza Hotel."

They then came at me from both sides and sandwiched me into a hug.

"The *Plaza?*" said Georgie. "What is he, slumming it? He can't afford the Four Seasons?"

I admonished him. "The *Plaza,* for chrissakes—it's the setting for Neil Simon stories and Henry Mancini songs. It's perfect!"

"For you, maybe." I wasn't buying into his disapproval for a second, and he knew it. But then he threatened, "If you tell me you said no, I'll pummel you with everything that's not nailed down to the floor in here."

"Ohmigod, Sunny!" Theo exclaimed. "It's your dream come true! So what did you say? Are you going?"

I wanted to give them an answer, but something stopped me. Maybe I was afraid it was still a dream. Worse still, what if it didn't work out? Then I wouldn't even have the dream anymore.

But if the last six months had taught me anything, it was that dreams didn't keep you going; living your life does. Rather, you keep life going. More of my dreams had come true in the last six months than they had in my lifetime, because I made it so. And now, if I wanted to, I could make a life with Danny—not because he was my dream, but because he was the man I loved and had always loved.

The rest was between Danny and me.

"What are you going to do?" Theo prodded me.

I turned to my best friends and, having never felt more confident or resolute, grinned that Daniel Gold grin. "Sleep on it."

CHAPTER

THIRTY-SEVEN

Danny Masters

D ANNY SIGNED EVERY BOOK, POSED FOR EVERY
picture, talked with every fan for "just a minute
more," and barely felt the time pass. Every so often he
looked up and past the fan standing before him, looking for Sunrise, but she was nowhere to be found, and
he guessed she'd slipped out hours ago. It wasn't hard
to pose for pictures with fans—the very thought of her
conjured up a smile within nanoseconds.

He slept soundly in the car all the way back to the
city. The driver had to shake him awake just to go into
the Plaza.

He awoke late the next morning, but with a bounce
in his step. First thing he did was check his phone messages. (Dez had flown back to LA yesterday afternoon.)
He returned some calls and fixed himself a bagel. He was
experiencing a myriad of emotions—nervous, excited,
hopeful—he could name each one, and it struck him
that he felt so *alive*.

He wasn't an apparition after all. Rather, he wasn't
Danny Masters after all. He never was.

He did a little bit of writing, his iPhone right beside
him, although his eyes always wound up fixed on the

window overlooking the city. He'd get a new place for himself and Ella, he decided. A brownstone, perhaps.

Time passed.

No call. No visitor.

He paced around the apartment.

He contemplated going for a walk, but didn't want to risk Sunrise showing up while he was gone.

Whereas hours had passed like minutes the night before, the reverse was true today. And with each passing minute that he didn't hear a ring of the phone or a knock at the door, his hope and self-assurance faded.

And he found himself wanting a cigarette. Needing it. Desperate for it.

He could run down to the corner and buy a pack, he rationalized. Just buy it and smoke it and get right back on the wagon.

Sure. That's what he used to say in the early days of his drinking. How easy it was to believe it, especially at a time like this. How easy it would be to hold a bottle of beer in his hands, smoke a few cigarettes, call Charlene up for a quickie, even just phone sex, all to appease the anxiety that he was the failure he'd always believed himself to be.

But no. He didn't have to believe that this time. He was *so not a failure*. He didn't need to numb himself out, make himself forget, punish himself another minute. And he knew he'd be OK, regardless of whether she called or showed up. He'd be OK because he wasn't really alone anymore. He never was in the first place.

And so he opted to finally get out of the apartment for a long walk. Taking his phone, he slung a jacket on; then he opened the door.

And there she stood, her fist in midair, poised for door-knocking.

She was dressed in a navy blue peacoat, jeans, and hiking boots. A messenger bag hung casually over her shoulder. She wore a little bit of makeup, and her hair just about touched her shoulders.

Perfect.

Her face softened into a warm smile, and before he could say a word, she took in a breath, speaking on the exhale.

"Let's get to work, Daniel Gold."

And with that, Sunny crossed the threshold.

ACKNOWLEDGMENTS

F OR MANY WRITERS, THE PHYSICAL ACT OF writing is a solitary one, but we need our community to help us tell the story. I'd like to thank the following people for helping me tell Danny's and Sunny's stories:

Terry Goodman, Jacque Ben-Zekry (a.k.a. "Mayor of Awesometown"), Jessica Poore, and everyone at Amazon Publishing, as well as my fellow Amazon Publishing authors, who make me proud and excited to be a part of this team every day.

Tiffany Yates Martin, development editor extraordinaire, who talked about the manuscript as enthusiastically as I did and helped me turn it into a tight, cohesive novel. I couldn't have done it without her, and especially appreciated our phone conversations.

Kate Hagopian Berry, whose detailed, insightful, and extensive feedback paved the way for revision and my work with Tiffany, proving once again that she is "Cool Kate."

Stephen Molton and Will Chandler, who taught me that good screenwriting begins with good stories and good characters. They also taught me how to develop both. I very much enjoyed working with them at the Southampton

Screenwriters Conference in 2011, and applied so much of their instruction to my novel writing as well.

Elspeth Antonelli, Jan Militello, Alexis Spencer-Byers, and Jill Weinberger, all of whom are exceptionally talented screenwriters and dear friends. They helped me make Danny's drafts—and my novel—the best they could be.

Maureen Bensa, who cheered me on from day one, read the manuscript in its earlier incarnation and initiated the "Save Part Three" campaign.

The Undeletables, who, without a doubt, are avid *Winters in Hyannis* fans as well as my good friends. So many times I envisioned them reading this novel in its finished form while I wrote.

Glenn Volkema, who read and responded to every chapter as it unfolded, sometimes in raw form. I am also eternally grateful for the virtual cups of vanilla chai and encouragement he sent me throughout the process.

Sarah Girrell, who sat with me in a hotel room in Manhattan in May 2011 and conversed for hours about Danny, Sunny, writing, and cookies. She's the first person I go to when I need to bounce off an idea, work out a scene, get through a bout of writer's block, and/or share a much-needed laugh. Even when we are not officially collaborating, she is still, and will always be, my writing partner-in-crime.

Emilio Estevez, who reminded me that I am a storyteller.

Aaron Sorkin, whose writing never ceases to inspire me.

The late Nora Ephron, who will be so dearly missed. How I wish I met her and became her friend.

My parents (Eda and Michael), siblings (Mike, Bobby, Ritchie, Steve, Mary, and Paul), siblings-in-law, nieces and nephews, cousins, aunts, and uncles, all of whom have given me their love and support throughout my entire life. My grandmother, Mary Mottola, one hundred years old at the time of this writing, is in my heart always.

Kim Lewis, who is the Wonder Woman of baking (also of friends), and Paul Lorello, who is the Spider-Man of twin brothers.

Kelly Sutphin, who is my oldest and dearest friend.

And to all of my friends, colleagues, readers, and students, please know how grateful I am for all your love and support.

ABOUT THE AUTHOR

 BORN AND RAISED ON NEW York's Long Island, Elisa Lorello received both her bachelor's and master's degrees from the University of Massachusetts-Dartmouth. She is the bestselling author of *Faking It* and *Ordinary World* and the coauthor of *Why I Love Singlehood*. When Elisa isn't writing, she can be found hanging out in coffeeshops, listening to eighties music, or tweeting incessantly about pop tarts. After enjoying six years in North Carolina, she returned to the northeast in late 2012 to live closer to her family and the ocean.

Follow her on Twitter @elisalorello, or Like her on Facebook at Elisa Lorello, Author.